We were not always freaks.

Sure, most of us occasionally exhibited freakish behavior. But that's not the same thing.

This is the story of how we became freaks.

It's how a group of *I*s became a *we*.

DEAD MERCY

NOELLE HOLTEN

One More Chapter
a division of HarperCollins*Publishers*
1 London Bridge Street
London SE1 9GF
www.harpercollins.co.uk

HarperCollins*Publishers*
1st Floor, Watermarque Building, Ringsend Road
Dublin 4, Ireland

This paperback edition 2022
1
First published in Great Britain in ebook format
by HarperCollins*Publishers* 2021

A catalogue record of this book is available from the British Library

ISBN: 978-0-00-838370-1

Printed and bound in the UK using 100% Renewable Electricity
by CPI Group (UK) Ltd

For Josianne - my niece. You brightened our lives after we lost our dad. Finding out you were a fellow bookworm, I knew we'd be kindred spirits. I can't wait to meet you.

Chapter One

Eighteen months ago he had come face to face with his abuser, and his skin crawled as he watched him smiling, playing with children in the park. Pushing a young boy on a swing while his clueless wife looked on as she set the food out on the picnic table. It seemed he had stumbled upon a party and the sight froze him on the spot. He felt his jaw tighten and then something inside him just snapped. That's when he knew what he had to do, and today it would start.

It hadn't been hard to find out where the monster lived. He had spent any spare time he had watching him from the shadows. His abuser had moved on, left his old self in the past, and while he had thought he too had moved on, bettered himself, buried his past – it all unravelled at that very moment eighteen months ago.

There was nothing subtle about his abuser. He pretty much told the world his whereabouts on his social media accounts – showing off, attention-seeking.

What a twat.

For someone who had once worked in a secure facility, the guy's poor sense of security was a testament to his belief that he was untouchable. Today he would find out otherwise.

From his Facebook account, he learned that his abuser would be at an insurance office in town – and then he even posted a stupid meme about taking out life insurance on his wife before he poisoned her. This was the level of intelligence he had to deal with.

He stayed two cars behind the white van and tracked the man to Hardy & Associates Insurers in the centre of Stafford. He waited in the car he had acquired, taking deep breaths as he contemplated whether he was doing the right thing. But when he pulled up his sleeve and saw the scarring on his arm, he realised it was now or never.

He made his way to the back entrance and jimmied the lock. It was a converted house that had been split into two office areas over two floors. One of the office spaces had been vacant; he had spotted a sign in a window with OFFICE FOR RENT written in bold.

He couldn't fail.

He wouldn't fail.

He crept up the stairs, listening for any unexpected voices, and once at the top, he took a moment and stood outside the office entrance.

When he was confident there was no one else in the office, he reached down and gently turned the handle. It was unlocked and, with a careful movement, he pulled it towards him, his ears on high alert. All he could hear was the bastard whistling. A smirk formed on his face. *Whistle while you work…*

He peeked into the office and spotted his target immediately. He'd recognise that body shape anywhere; it haunted his dreams. He spotted the headphones immediately and smiled – that would make things so much easier. He entered the room, locking the door once he was inside to ensure he wouldn't be disturbed, and crouched down behind an empty desk, popping his head up to scan the room. There were only three other desks, and then a smaller room off to the right, but its door was closed. Keeping his eyes on the bastard, he crawled towards the closed door and held his ear against it. Nothing but silence. He reached up, twisted the handle, but it was locked.

Adrenaline coursed through his veins.

He removed the small baton from his back pocket and crept up behind the unsuspecting man. The *thwack* as the wood hit his victim's skull sent a bolt of excitement through him.

The prick dropped like a sack of potatoes.

It was happening, it was finally happening.

He didn't know how much time he had but he wouldn't waste it. He could enjoy the moment later as he replayed it in his mind. He placed the backpack he had been carrying down onto the floor and set to work.

He pulled a chair out from the desk to his left, and as the monster from his nightmares lay face down on the floor, he bound his hands and feet with twist ties before turning him over and stuffing a rolled-up sock he had purchased at Poundland into the bastard's mouth.

He kicked the motionless lump in his side and waited.

'Wake up, arsehole.' He bent down and shook the man's shoulder. The man started to come around and he had to calm himself – he'd never imagined how excited he would feel when the moment finally came. Even more so when he saw the terror in the man's eyes. 'Recognise me?'

The man shook his head and tried to get up.

'Stay where you are, fucker, I'm the one in control here.' He grabbed the man from under his arms and heaved him up, pushing the chair behind him in his direction. 'Sit down.'

The man stood on the spot.

No time to be stubborn – you arrogant prick.

'I said sit the fuck down. Don't make me do it for you.'

The man sat, eyes pleading, but he ignored him.

'I'm going to remove the gag in your mouth, but if you make any noise, you are going to be so fucking sorry. Do you understand?'

The monster nodded and the gag was removed.

'W-w-w-what do you w-w-w-ant from me? My wallet is in my back pocket. I just got paid, so you can have whatever is in there. You can even take my bank card… I'll give you my pin number.'

He shook his head. Did this guy actually think he could pay his way out of the situation?

'Shut the fuck up.' He removed the pliers from his bag. 'Now open your mouth.'

'What are you going to do with those?' His eyes glistened.

Ooh, this was just too much! 'Did I say you could ask me questions?' He smacked the bastard across the jaw with the back of his hand. 'I said, open your mouth!'

The man slowly opened his mouth and his lower lip trembled, realisation about what might happen setting in.

He placed the pliers on the right incisor tooth and leaned close. 'Remember this?' He yanked hard and the bastard screamed. He did the same to the left incisor before shoving the gag back in the bloodied mouth. The once white sock was now blood red. Tears rolled down the man's face.

He reached into his backpack and pulled out a plastic sports bottle filled with petrol. The man's eyes grew wide.

He had an overwhelming urge to laugh – a deep, satisfying belly laugh, but he controlled himself.

'You'll choke on your own spit if you keep that up. I'd hate for that to happen – we've only just got started.' He squirted the petrol all over the man's jeans and shirt, and splashed the dregs that were left over the bastard's face and hair. He placed the plastic bottle in between the man's legs – it could burn with the fucker. The less he had to leave with, the better.

He stood back, creating a distance, lit a match and threw it on the carpet, watching as the fluid lit. The flames were hypnotic. Shadows danced on the wall behind while the man struggled in the chair. He pulled out another match, striking it against the side of the box and throwing it onto the man's jeans. They caught fire quickly and he stood back as the flames crackled and rose.

Muffled screams could be heard, but not loud enough that the sound carried. He watched, transfixed by the clothing that was burning away, exposing the skin. There was a crackle and pop as the skin bubbled with the extreme heat.

'You should be thanking me, at least you'll know what Hell feels like before you get there.'

He had once heard that the smell of burning flesh was acrid, but as he inhaled the air around him, other thoughts came to mind. He wafted his hand in the air, bringing the scent deep into his nostrils. There was an aroma of beef… you know, like when you fry those thin burgers in a pan. He raised his head slightly and sniffed the air again. Another scent caught his attention... a subtle whiff of... hmmm... fatty pork, perhaps? He inhaled again – with a hint of copper and even a musky, sweet perfume. The smell was so thick and rich, he almost tasted it. He licked his lips. The sirens in the distance warned him it was time to go. He shook the two teeth he had extracted earlier in both his hands like dice, and for a moment recalled the power he had felt as the bastard screamed in agony.

And so it began...

Chapter Two

The Major and Organised Crime Department based at Stafford Police Station were still shaken after the events that happened only weeks before. Burying a colleague was never a nice scenario, but when they had been murdered – it made the memories harder to forget.

DC Maggie Jamieson sat in the coffee shop and stared into space, tapping the plastic lid of her coffee cup on the table as she waited for Dr Kate Moloney to arrive. A fire engine in the distance caught her attention for a brief moment. She hoped it wasn't anything serious.

The team had begun calling Kate 'the Doc' as it caused less confusion when DC Kat Everett was in the room. Kate had just returned to the UK after taking time off in Ireland with her family. The few times Maggie had spoken to her since her return, she could see small tells – rubbing her hands, a slight twitch in her eye – and knew Kate was still spooked from her stalker experience. The Doc tried to hide it behind that veiled smile of hers, but Maggie noticed.

The bell above the door to the café jingled and Maggie smiled when she looked up and saw Kate walk in.

'I still can't get used to the new haircut. Your hair was so long before and jet black. Anyway, it looks great – what are you having?' Maggie waved over the waitress and wished she had the nerve to do something different to her own hair. The short bob and purple highlights Kate was sporting weren't Maggie's style, but a new colour might be. Something she'd consider as part of her focus on herself this year.

'I'm desperate for an Americano. No milk or sugar, please.' Kate took off her jacket and placed it on an empty chair along with the satchel she was carrying.

The waitress took note before asking Maggie if she would have another.

'I'm fine, thanks.' Maggie waited for Kate to sit. 'Is your new flat sorted out then?'

There was a gleam in Kate's eye as she spoke. 'Yes. Everything's signed and the movers are delivering my furniture later today. I was hoping I could come round and pick up Salem this evening, unless you have plans?'

'No plans. That should be fine. Andy and I have already given him a fuss and said our goodbyes. I think even Scrappy might be sad to see him go.' They had all become accustomed to having the black moggy plodding around the house.

'Ah, bless. You're more than welcome to visit him any time. I'd just like to get back to some normality, if I'm honest. Moving to Stafford town centre will make it easier to juggle my work with the MOCD and the work I'll continue to do in Tamworth with the Integrated Offender Management unit.' Kate blew on her coffee before taking a sip.

Maggie had heard rumours that the Domestic Abuse and

Homicide Unit (DAHU) were disbanding and merging with the IOM because their work was quite similar – targeting the most prolific and priority offenders in the surrounding area. From what Kate had just said, the change had already happened.

'You'll definitely be kept busy! When's the flat-warming party? I'm dying to check out your new place.' Maggie had once considered buying a flat in the town centre but thought they were too small. She also hated moving, so opted for a house, and with her brother, Andy, doing all the redecorating and saving her a fortune, she might never need to move.

'Not sure I'm ready for a party of any sort, but once I'm settled and Salem is used to the place, I'll definitely invite a few of ye's around.' Kate smiled but Maggie noted the dip in her voice.

'You sure you're OK?' Maggie's eyebrows drew together.

'I'm grand, I promise. There's just a lot to do before I officially start back at work next week. Anyway, what's been happening since I've been gone?' Kate rubbed her forehead. 'I'm sorry, that was a stupid question. How has the team been?'

Maggie put her mind at ease.

'I knew what you meant. Thinking about the last case still sends shivers down my spine, if I'm honest. I'm sure you'll hear enough about it next week. You'll be happy to hear that DI Rutherford is still singing your praises for all your help, even though you were supposed to be off.' Maggie's voice trailed off and she wondered whether she should tell Kate about Julie Noble. Nothing more had happened between the pair, but she had been spending more time with the journalist… as friends.

'What are you keeping from me, detective?' A slow smile formed on Kate's face.

'Ha! I'll never be able to keep a secret from you, will I?' Maggie laughed. 'OK. So, you know that investigative journalist – Julie Noble?'

'The one who makes you cringe and curse every time she walks in a room, but also puts that sparkle in your eye that is blinding me right now? Yeah, I know her. Spill!' Kate tipped the mug of coffee against her lips and sipped.

Maggie was still trying to understand the complexities of her status with the journalist and shifted in her seat as she thought about how much to tell Kate. Before she had a moment to think too long about it, she blurted out, 'I actually went out on a date with her.' She didn't have long to wait for Kate's reaction.

Kate spat the coffee from her mouth, forcing Maggie to push her own chair back to avoid the spray. 'What? Now, I wasn't expecting that answer. Tell me more!' Kate squealed as she used the napkins on the table to clear up the coffee and wipe her face.

Before she could get into it, Maggie's phone buzzed. She looked at the screen and held a finger up to Kate. 'Hold that thought. I have a feeling this isn't going to be good news.' She swiped to accept the call. 'Hey, boss, what's up?'

'*I hope you haven't eaten yet…*' Nathan's tone was serious and Maggie's nerves tingled.

'Nope. Pleeeeease don't tell me we have another case already.' Maggie moved the phone to her other ear.

'*I'm standing outside of Hardy & Associates Insurance, not far from the station, in fact. I just finished speaking to the Fire*

Investigator and he's advised that a body was found inside the premises.'

'Oh Christ. How awful! But what has that got to do with us?' Maggie crossed her fingers, hoping that a new case wasn't about to ruin her plans with Kate.

'The Fire Investigator suggested the victim may have been covered in an accelerant and the fire was set intentionally. It's not a pretty sight, I'm told. I'm texting the address to you now – I'll see you soon.'

Maggie stood, picked up her bag and threw her jacket over her arm. 'Sorry, Kate, gotta go – looks like we have a new case – don't be surprised if you get a call from Rutherford to see if you can start before next week.' She headed towards the door.

'Call me later!' Kate shouted after her.

Maggie waved and strode towards Nelson Avenue. She remembered a time when she'd been told that it was easier to recognise the smell of a burning corpse than to describe it and now she'd find out if that were true.

Chapter Three

M aggie jogged the last five minutes to the crime scene. The area had already been secured. It was actually just on the outskirts of the town centre, but if you walked a few steps, you'd find yourself in the town in a matter of minutes. She looked at the two-storey house that had been converted to office spaces, and her eyes were drawn to a plume of black smoke that was blowing from an open window. Maggie looked around and when she saw Nathan, she waved and headed over to him.

'I don't know why, but I was expecting the place to be burned down. I guess the fire was contained inside the building?'

'Yeah. The Guv is talking to Nigel Bates, he's the lead Fire Investigator. She hopes to find out when we'll be able to go in. Apparently, a wallet and some other personal items were found inside so an officer went over to the owner's house...' He opened his notebook. 'The name was familiar – Sarah Hardy. Recognise it?' He looked up at Maggie.

Maggie's mouth fell open momentarily. 'If it is the person I'm thinking of, we've worked with her – she's based at Markston Probation. Shit... who was the victim?' Since Nathan had become a DS, most of the operational work was left to the team while he occupied himself with strategies and resources. She wasn't surprised that he had forgotten who Sarah was, as they worked with so many agencies and people.

'We'll have to wait for a formal ID, but based on what was found inside, it could be Justin Hardy – her husband. He rents the office space, and it doesn't look like there were any other employees, so they've gone around to Sarah's for more information.' Nathan paused for a moment and looked over Maggie's shoulder. 'Stand by, the Guv has just given me the thumbs up. Get suited and meet me inside.'

Maggie hoped that they had it wrong in terms of the victim. It was still too early to confirm, but given everything Nathan had just relayed, it was likely that the post-mortem would confirm this. Maggie walked over to the Forensics van and put on the required gear, gloves and mask, tucking her hair in the hood before she headed back towards the building. She was stopped by DI Rutherford just outside the front door.

'I'm on my way to a Priority Crime meeting at Stafford County Council and wondered if you could do me a favour once you've finished up here. I need someone to call Kat – she's off today. I meant to tell Nathan but it slipped my mind. Let her know to be in early tomorrow.' Rutherford pulled the collar of her jacket towards her nose and sniffed. 'Ugh. No time to change.' She reached into her bag and pulled out a small bottle of spray perfume, nearly choking Maggie as she squirted the spray on herself. 'Right, I'll catch up later.'

'Sure thing, Guv.' Maggie walked into the building and

headed up the stairwell. When she reached the top, the stench hit her instantly. There was a charcoal-like smell mixed with an almost sulphurous odour. Forensic pathologist Dr Fiona Blake and a colleague were talking in the corner beside the body. Although the victim was severely burned, there were still pieces of clothing and pink skin visible. The victim's hair had been burned off, bar a few patches, and more than half his face was unrecognisable. Maggie looked around the rest of the office area. The fire had been contained in just that one corner space. Although there was clearly smoke damage, there didn't seem to be any other burn patches or marks present. Maggie walked as close to the body as she could get and greeted Dr Blake, with Nathan close behind.

'Hi both. I'm afraid this one's not pretty, as you can see, but other than the wallet, wedding ring and mobile phone we found in the lockbox on the desk here, confirming the ID of this poor fellow may take a little time. I believe some of your colleagues have gone out to speak to someone who may be connected to him.' Dr Blake's eyes narrowed, pulling her brows down in concentration.

'The items belong to the husband of a Probation Officer we've worked with in the past.' Maggie stared at the charred corpse and shook her head.

'Oh, I'm sorry to hear that.' Dr Blake offered an understanding nod. 'It's always more difficult when we come across someone we might know. We're jumping ahead of ourselves, though. The tools over there –' she pointed to the back of the room '– might mean he had someone else in the building – but I suppose his wife could confirm that? I can't really tell you much more than that for now.'

Maggie and Nathan thanked Dr Blake and headed to the back wall, behind the victim.

'Is that fresh paint on the wall?' Maggie leaned in close and tapped it. It was sticky. 'Definitely feels like a new coat of paint.'

'I can't smell anything other than him at the moment. Dr Blake is right though, could be a handyman…'

'I'd like to pop round to Sarah's if that's OK. Not much else we can do here until Forensics have finished up.' Maggie checked her watch.

'Sure. Just make sure that you don't lead her to believe anything until we have the full facts.' Nathan held her gaze.

'Will do – I'll stick to what we know. I just want to reassure her that we'll be doing everything we can to find out what happened.'

'I'm going to hang back here. I'll see you tomorrow.'

Maggie left the scene and headed back to Stafford Police Station to grab her car. Her brother was working nights so she took the opportunity to use the car during the days when she could. With the colder mornings, it was much more comfortable to drive in than wait on the breezy train platform. After trying Sarah's work mobile and getting no response, she contacted Probation to see if they had a home number for Sarah. The receptionist advised that due to GDPR they couldn't give out those details. Instead of arguing with the woman, who was only doing her job, Maggie hung up. She'd just have to show up unannounced.

Maggie spotted the police car in the drive as she pulled up next to Sarah's house. She grabbed her bag from the passenger side and caught a pungent whiff of herself. DI Rutherford's perfume trick would have to do and she dug around in her bag before finding what she was looking for. She stifled a cough as the fragrance hit the back of her throat, but it made no difference. She could still smell the stench from the crime scene, only now she smelled like a Dior-covered corpse.

Maggie approached the front door and rang the bell. The police officer answered and Maggie showed her warrant card.

'She's in there.' He pointed to a door on the left. 'I'll just be in the kitchen; can I get you a cup of tea or coffee?'

'No thanks.' Maggie knocked gently on the door, going over what she would say when she saw Sarah. When she had no reply from the other side, she opened the door and stared at Sarah's puffy eyes and shaking shoulders.

'Hi. How are you holding up?' Maggie noticed Sarah had some shopping bags at her feet.

'Oh Maggie! Is it him? Is it really Justin?' She burst out crying and Maggie rushed over, sat down and put a reassuring arm around Sarah's shoulders.

'We don't know anything definite yet, hun. What've you been told?'

'They found his wallet. Did you see him? Is it bad?' Sarah's eyes blinked rapidly and Maggie guessed she was trying to process everything she had heard so far.

'I've been to the crime scene, but...' The mobile phone on the table in front of them rang. Maggie looked at Sarah. 'Do you want me to get that?'

Sarah nodded.

Maggie picked up the phone. 'Hello. This is Sarah Hardy's phone; can I help you?' Maggie nearly dropped the phone as she listened to the voice on the other end. Handing the phone to Sarah, Maggie smiled. 'I think you'll want to take this. It's your husband.'

Chapter Four

Maggie handed the phone to an open-mouthed Sarah. She'd give her some privacy and walked to the large window that overlooked the front garden.

What the hell was going on?

Her own phone vibrated in her pocket and she didn't even have to look at the screen to guess who it would be.

'*You're never going to believe what happened,*' Nathan's voiced chirped down the line.

'My psychic abilities are telling me that Justin Hardy is alive.' She held in a laugh and waited for Nathan's reaction.

'*What the hell? How did you know that? Never mind. Justin told us he was having the office redecorated.*'

'Do we know who it was in the building?' Maggie kept her voice low, so she didn't disturb Sarah.

'*He said it must be Daniel Firth. A FLO has been sent around to the Firth family home. What a day! Look, it's getting late and there's nothing more we can do this evening, so why don't you head home when you're finished there. Just be in by 8 a.m. tomorrow, OK?*'

'Sure. Do you want me to send the FLO home or is someone else on it?'

'That was my next call, so if you could do that, I'd appreciate it.'

Maggie could hear someone call out Nathan's name in the background.

'I have to go now.' The line went dead.

Maggie pocketed her mobile and turned towards Sarah. She was wiping her nose. 'I'm just going to tell the officer he can go home. Do you want anything from the kitchen while I'm in there?' Just as Maggie was about to head into the kitchen, the officer came through the door with a tray of hot drinks and a half-eaten packet of biscuits. 'That worked out well. Can I have a word?' Maggie flicked her head in the direction of the hallway.

'I just got off the phone with my boss and he advised that you could head off home now.'

'But…' The officer frowned.

'Sarah's husband is not deceased. In fact, he should be here shortly. I'll stay with her until he arrives. I'd like to speak to him anyway, see if I can gather any further information.'

The officer popped his head back into the living room and said goodbye to Sarah. Maggie walked him to the front door and returned to the living room. 'Are you OK? That's quite a shock to have to deal with in a matter of a few hours.'

Sarah wiped her eyes. 'I can't get my head around it. Was Justin the target? Why did he leave all his things at his office? Where the hell was he?' Sarah was pacing the room, the confusion written all over her face.

'Didn't he say when you spoke?' Maggie poured a cup of tea for Sarah and pushed it towards her, pointing to the chair.

'Why don't you sit, have a cuppa and let it all sink in.' She then poured one for herself.

'Thanks.' Sarah took a sip of the warm tea and wrapped her hands around the mug before she spoke again. 'No – he didn't really say much, as he had to finish speaking to your lot. I think he said he was at Stafford Police Station. He just wanted to let me know it wasn't him, as someone told him the police were here.'

'Has Justin been threatened recently or behaving oddly?' Maggie took out her notebook.

'I… I don't think there's been any threats, but…' Sarah took another sip of her tea and shook her head.

'What is it?' Maggie leaned forward.

'Well, money is missing from our savings account. I mean, *a lot* of money, and I could never get a straight answer out of him when I asked about it. He said he was putting it back into the business and we would get it all back once he could secure more clients, but… that didn't make sense to me.'

Maggie wrote the information down and agreed with Sarah's assessment, although she didn't vocalise that. When you worked in the criminal justice system you processed things a different way and questioned everything. Sarah could be on to something. It might be that Justin was being blackmailed or had got himself involved in something that was way over his head. Maggie didn't want to cause Sarah any more distress, so kept that thought to herself.

'I'm a mess right now. One minute I think my husband is dead and I'm wondering what I should do. Now I'm furious. Has he done something that puts us at risk? I'm a Probation Officer. Anything he does that brings attention from the law reflects badly on me. I'll kill him myself if it turns out he's involved in something dodgy.' When Sarah realised what she'd said, she quickly explained. 'You know I'm not serious, right? Sorry – I forgot I was speaking to you as a police officer.' A nervous laugh escaped her lips.

'I totally get it. I'll keep that bit out of my notes.' Maggie winked while she continued to question Sarah, but it was clear she had no clue what was going on.

She'd need to speak to Justin to find out more. A noise from outside had them both turn and face the window. Headlights lit up the room as a car pulled up in the driveway. Sarah rushed to the door. Justin Hardy was home and Maggie had no doubt that once she left, Sarah would have her own questions for her husband.

Maggie waited in the living room so the pair had some privacy. She placed the cups on the tray and was about to take it into the kitchen when a meek-looking man followed his wife into the living room. He put out his hand. 'I'm Justin. Thanks for staying with my wife.'

'You're welcome. Would you mind if I asked you a few questions before I leave?' The tray could wait.

'I'm pretty exhausted, if I'm honest. Can we do this tomorrow morning?' Maggie saw the look Sarah gave her husband, and he sat, inviting Maggie to sit opposite. Sarah cleared the table and left Maggie to ask her questions.

'I'm sure this is all a huge shock, but I promise not to keep you long. Just a few preliminary questions – you'll probably be asked more of the same questions over the coming days.' She waited for him to settle and once he nodded his understanding, she continued. 'Why did you leave your phone, wallet and wedding ring in your office, and where were you at the time of the fire?'

'I explained all this to the other officers, can't you just check with them?' His shoulders slumped.

'I could. But I prefer to hear things first-hand.' Maggie could often tell if a person was being truthful by observing their body language.

'I had asked Danny to come by and start the DIY work in my office. He arrived about 11 a.m. or so, we chatted for a bit about what I wanted. I had used him before for odds and ends around here, and he seemed trustworthy. I was going to the gym just around the corner and wasn't going to be gone long, so I left my things at the office. I don't trust the lockers at the gym. I left just before noon.' He rubbed the back of his neck. 'My business is suffering, and I need an associate, so I thought if the office was more inviting, I might be able to poach someone from another agency.'

Justin sat forward then and played with a pen on the table as he jumped back and forth with his version of events. 'I fell asleep in the spa room. They have these awesome beds... Sorry, you probably don't need to know about that. Erm... where was I? Oh yeah, when I woke up and saw the time, I headed back – late afternoon. That's when I saw the police and fire engine outside my office. Long story short, they said my personal items were bagged up and would be at Stafford Police Station, so I called Sarah when I got to the station, answered their questions, and here I am now.' He shrugged his shoulders, but not like it was no big deal, more like he couldn't understand what had happened or why.

'Have you had any trouble recently? Could you have been the actual target?'

'What? Why are you asking that? I've no problems at all. In fact, everything was on the up. I think I was just lucky I wasn't there, as I could have been killed too.' Maggie clocked that he averted his eyes every time she looked at him, and his defensive tone concerned her.

She found it curious that Justin didn't mention anything about financial problems.

'Thanks for your time. I'll be going now.' Maggie was putting her notebook away, when Sarah returned to the room.

'Are you off now?' Sarah's eyes were red; she must have been crying again in the kitchen.

'I am. Someone will be in touch over the coming days. I'm sure you both have a lot to talk about. I'll see myself out.'

Maggie left the house and couldn't help but wonder if there was something more going on. Justin Hardy was hiding something. His body language had spoken volumes.

Chapter Five

What a rush! He didn't think of himself as a killer, but he had to admit that his first kill left him with a bit of a buzz. He had hung around a bit before leaving the scene at Hardy & Associates, then dumped the car and set it alight. When it was found, there would be no trace of him.

He hadn't stolen or burned out a car since his early teens, but it wasn't as hard as he thought it would be. Fire was good for a lot of things – it was easy to trace someone from their DNA, hair or skin cells, based on everything he had learned over the years. He ran his fingers through his hair and removed the hairnet, laughing as he threw it in the burning car. They wouldn't catch him. At least not until he was ready for them to.

He walked for a few miles, through the fields and backroads, until he reached his shithole of a flat. He hated this place. He hated the people – scum – druggies trying to block out chunks of their lives with whatever substance they could get their hands on, only to find the memories returned once the gear had worn off. Not him, though. His pain was his power. This place was temporary and a necessity if he wanted to avoid scrutiny. He left his previous home and became one of them – the invisible ones – and thus became the person his abusers thought he would.

After the buzz of watching the emergency services arrive at the office in the town centre, and even being asked by one of the attending officers if he had noticed anything suspicious, returning to his mould-ridden flat with cracked paint and musty carpets really put a downer on things. He felt low. He wondered if this is how his neighbours felt as they came down from their highs. On some level, he understood why they continued to chase the dragon. The only difference was, he had a choice, and they didn't.

He was smart enough to know that when everything came to light, he'd have to pay for what he was doing. It didn't faze him though, as his abusers would get what they deserved first, and he'd feel vindicated after having to live with the pain for so long. Justice comes in many forms.

He had had to build up to the idea of taking a life – it wasn't something that came naturally, not to someone like him. Of course he had thought about it, dreamt about the day he could stop the nightmares, but never thought he could do it – until he saw Danny at that park.

He did his homework, and afterwards he realised that everything he had read about the 'first kill' appeared to be true. He laughed, and a strange feeling came over him. Like he had answered his calling – courage raced through his veins. He had to be careful though. One down, four to go. Nothing could go wrong between now and the last murder.

His mind flashed back to the scene. Other than being

caught out by the one officer, he'd been careful not to be seen by using the back entrance, because he knew there was only one CCTV camera and it faced the opposite direction.

When he had broken into Daniel's house a few weeks ago and looked through the diary that sat on the living-room table, he saw the address and details which allowed him enough time to put his plan in place. He had worked so hard at changing his life, but old tricks came back easily and it wasn't hard to slip back into those habits. Needs must.

He had scoped out the office of Hardy & Associates during his lunch breaks and after work. His day job made dressing up like a professional easy, and this assisted in his plan to go inside the premises and pretend that he was interested in taking out some insurance. The man, however, quickly brushed him off and told him to leave. Fucking prick. If he'd been any other way, he'd go back and teach him a lesson too. But that just wasn't in his nature.

When he tried hard enough, his looks generally made sure of two things: people kept their distance, and he could easily hide in plain sight. He pushed his hand into his pocket and pulled out the teeth. He held them up to the light, and flashes of the hours before circled in his head. He smiled when he recalled the bastard wetting himself. No mercy. They never showed him or the others any, and he'd make sure they never got any in their last moments either.

He walked the few paces into the kitchen and turned on the tap, rinsing the teeth under the water. His reflection from the small mirror that perched against the mug on the window-sill stared back at him. His eyes looked dark, circled with blackness. His longish hair added to the look of menace, along with his pocked cheeks – the aftermath of teenage acne. He couldn't bear to smile – so he hid it behind the beard he had grown over the years.

He dried the teeth, turning around sharply to look for his jar of treasures. He rolled the incisor between his fingers as he recalled every blow, muffled scream, and the smell of sulphur as Danny-boy – the bastard – burned.

He was so excited, he almost got a semi. But this wasn't about sexual pleasure. He turned his focus back to his task and opened the cupboard, moving the chipped and stained mugs around until – *Ah, there it was* – he found the mason jar.

He pulled it out, twisted the lid and dropped the teeth in, shaking it around to let the teeth mix with the others. He returned the jar to the back of the cupboard and when he closed it, his hand remained on the door for a moment – they were back where they belonged, safe in the darkness.

He felt a connection now to Daniel Firth – only this time, he was the one in control, and he was the one they would all fear.

A few steps and he was in his living room, sparsely furnished with a bed-cum-settee, a small table, and a rickety chair, all of which he found thrown out on the roadside. One man's trash is another man's treasure. He sat at the table and picked up his laptop. The fuckers in the building had better not be using his Wi-Fi again. He punched in his password and waited as the computer booted up. He opened the notes folder he had encrypted and saw the list. He had another list which he kept in a book on the shelf behind him – but the paper was thin and the writing faint after all these years. He looked at the screen and put a cross beside Daniel's name.

Who would be next?

Eeny meeny miny mo.

It's your turn now.

You've got to go…

He smiled when he saw where his finger had landed. She'd been one of the instigators – barking orders and waiting for her sheep to do what they were told. The woman with two faces. The reason the abusers were never brought to justice.

To the outside world she was quiet, caring – a true angel on earth.

To him and the other young boys, she was mean, cruel – the devil in disguise.

He sat back and smiled. This one would need more careful planning. After suffering a stroke, a few years back, mobility issues had her in a wheelchair now and again. She could walk, he had seen her, but some days she had to use a cane or her high-end wheelchair. At least that was one thing he didn't need to worry about. There was no way she would be able to run away.

Chapter Six

On the drive home from Sarah's, Maggie rang her brother Andy, using the car's hands-free unit, to see if he wanted a take-away. She had to decipher his responses because she had woken him up, but he said he fancied fish and chips – at least that was what she thought he'd said. She stopped at the chippy and arrived home just before 7 p.m.

There was a vacant spot to park her car just outside her home. It was unusual at this time of night, but she wasn't going to worry about that right now – never look a gift horse in the mouth, as her mother would say. Once inside, she dropped her work bag against the wall and kicked off her shoes, stretching her toes. She looked up when she heard a creak and waved as she saw her brother stumbling down the stairs to greet her.

Andy took the take-away bag from her and brought it into the kitchen. 'Mmm. Thanks for this. I'll plate up – you grab the drinks.'

'Water OK with you?' Her brother nodded. She grabbed the

ice tray from the freezer, put some ice in a jug and sliced up some lemon. It had seen better days, but Maggie hated chucking anything away if it could be helped. Something else her mother had taught her. Placing the jug under the tap, she filled it and then put it on the table.

Maggie had been tempted to have a glass of wine but when she had a case, she did her best to keep her alcohol intake down. She never knew when she could be called back into work. The smell of vinegar was strong and she smiled as her brother placed her fish and chips in front of her. 'They always give you more than you can eat. I should have just got one, but I'm starving – so I might just finish this.' She tucked into her meal, taking a chunk of fish and dipping it into the tartar sauce at the side of her plate. She was glad her brother was conscientious about the fact that she liked things separate on her plate. He used to joke that it was because she wanted to be in control, but the more she thought about it, the more it seemed he was probably right. She wouldn't let him know that though – he'd be unbearable to live with then.

'I'm sure the cats will gobble up anything that's left over. How was work?'

Maggie's nose wrinkled as she watched her brother shovel fish, chips and mushy peas into his gob. 'How are we related? I can't stand the sight of mushy peas or the smell, for that matter – and putting them all together. Ugh.' She looked away. 'Speaking of cats, where are they?'

'Salem was fast asleep on my bed when I got up, and Scrappy is still out, I guess. Kate's back now, isn't she? When is she coming to collect him?'

'Shit. You just reminded me, I told her I would call her when I finished work, and then the time just got away from me. I'll text her after dinner. She wanted to come this evening, but tomorrow is probably better. Have you fed them?'

'Yeah, I was up earlier, sorted them out and then dozed off for a bit again. You still haven't answered my question.' He raised a brow. 'Work OK?'

'Sorry – I'm a bit distracted. Work was fine. New case, you'll probably see it on the news at some point.' Maggie heard her mobile ringing in the hallway. Scooping the last piece of fish into her mouth, she scraped the remaining chips onto Andy's plate, popped her dish into the kitchen sink and went to answer her phone.

'Hello?'

'*Hey, Mags. What you up to?*'

Maggie bit her lip and refrained from snapping back at the journalist. She hated the nickname that Julie Noble had recently assigned to her. 'What took you so long? It's been a few hours since the incident. That's what you're calling about, right?'

'*I was being courteous – figured you'd had your hands full today. Are you doing anything? Fancy a drink?*'

Maggie couldn't deny that the offer was tempting, but she had an early start and didn't want any distractions. She would need a clear head to be able to focus on the new case. 'Going to have to give you a raincheck. I'm shattered. Why don't you just spit it out and ask what you really want to know? Then I can tell you that I have no info to share, you'll have a dramatic strop and I'll see you at the press conference...'

'*Oooooh, touché, Mags. Can't blame a gal for trying though. How's Sarah Hardy?*'

'She's f— Oh, you nearly had me there. Look, I really am knackered, so can we carry this on another day?' Maggie didn't have the energy for any of Julie's banter and wanted to avoid falling into any trap set by the savvy investigative journalist when she was tired. DI Rutherford wouldn't be happy, that's for sure. 'How about we have a catch-up, non-work-related, later this week? I'll text you when I'm free and you can let me know.'

Maggie had made a promise to herself, after the last case really wiped her out, that she would try to focus on activities that had nothing to do with her work. She'd recently signed up for some yoga classes – they had numerous slots available throughout the day, especially catering for people with busy lifestyles. 'I registered at the gym, like you suggested. Maybe we could do a yoga session and grab a coffee after?'

'If it means seeing you in a leotard, I'm there!'

Maggie cringed but couldn't help the slow smile that formed on her face. She was about to say something when Julie interrupted:

'Your silence speaks volumes. It was a joke, Jamieson. Lighten up. Look, I'll catch you later.' The call ended.

Maggie looked at the screen and was slightly surprised by the abrupt ending. She still didn't understand Julie – she thought they'd both agreed that the timing for anything other than friendship was wrong. Her thoughts were disrupted by Scrappy rubbing against her leg. 'Thanks for the reminder, buddy.' Maggie sent a quick text to Kate to apologise and let her know she'd make sure that Salem was back home tomorrow. As she grabbed her charger from her bag, Kate responded with a snooze followed by a thumbs-up emoji. At least that was one thing off her mind.

Maggie called out to her brother, 'Leave the dishes, I'll do them in the morning. Think I'm going to crash. Can you lock the cat flap before you go? Keys to the car are in the bowl by the door. Salem is staying one more night, by the way.'

'No probs. G'nite.'

Maggie headed upstairs and jumped in the shower after realising she still probably smelled like death. Her brother's sense of smell must be crap, as he'd never mentioned it, but the pungent odour had danced in her nostrils at the top of the stairwell.

After the shower she changed into her PJs, set the alarm on her phone, plugged it in and lay back in her bed. Although she was physically exhausted, her mind was still churning. The last thing she thought of before drifting off to sleep was the question that had been niggling her all day: *Is this just the start of something bigger?*

Chapter Seven

Maggie yawned and pushed her notebook around on the table as she waited for the rest of the team to assemble in the incident room. She'd arrived early at the office, hoping to go through the information from the case while it was still quiet, but nothing stuck out and it frustrated her.

Nathan was at the front of the room talking to DI Rutherford. She tried to make out what they were saying but no matter how hard she focused on their lips, she could only make out the odd word, and none of them made sense.

There were so many unanswered questions.

'What a fucking surprise that was, eh?' DC Kat Everett plonked herself down in the seat beside Maggie, the smell of cigarette smoke clinging to her clothes.

'You mean Justin Hardy turning up alive? I know. I was with Sarah when he called.'

'Holy shitballs! That must have been something. Though on the positive side, it made identifying the body easier. The fella was a workman or something, right?' Kat was rifling through her notebook.

'Yeah. From what I could gather, Justin hired him to do some DIY around his office in the hopes that it would entice more business. Obviously, we have to wait for Dr Blake's report before it is officially confirmed, but when I checked the database this morning, the wife had confirmed that he hadn't been home and she had last seen him about ten that morning. The FLO is still there, she's inconsolable.'

Kat straightened and Maggie looked around the room. It was near full capacity as the field team joined the briefing. A new whiteboard with three panels faced them all, details of the current case plastered across the top. They would be filled as the case progressed. Nathan took a seat at the front, in close proximity to DI Rutherford.

The DI cleared her throat and the room quietened. 'First, I know that some of you are still shook up over the unexpected and tragic passing of...' Her voice cracked and she shook her head. 'It's difficult to jump back into a case when something like that happens to a team. I know this has already been said, but I'll just say it again. If you're struggling, please let me know and we'll make the appropriate arrangements.' She paused and looked around the room. Maggie was grateful the Guv had addressed the elephant in the room. The team could now focus their energy on catching a killer.

No one said a word and Rutherford continued. 'The scorched remains of a male, who we believe to be Daniel Firth, were found just on the outskirts of town at Hardy & Associates Insurance. Some of you may recognise the name from your work with Probation – it's Sarah Hardy's husband who owns the office. Mr Hardy attended the police station yesterday to go over some questions we had, and the gym confirmed his alibi, but we're not going to sit on our hands. At the moment, he's helping us with our enquiries. We're waiting for the forensic results and a report from the Fire Investigators, but for those of you who weren't in attendance, I can tell you that the victim had been bound to a chair and set alight by an accelerant. Most of his body was burned on the front, however the back of him was only partially burned. A search of the property found his wallet in his tool bag – hence we believe it is Daniel Firth.' The Guv took a deep intake of breath and looked to the floor as she breathed out. 'Right now, I'd love to hear some of your theories based on what you found from your door-to-door enquiries. The floor is yours.' Rutherford stumbled and caught herself on the table before sitting down. Maggie looked her in the eye and tilted her head but the Guv looked away.

Odd.

'I spoke to some of the neighbouring offices around the crime scene, but no one had a bad word to say about Justin Hardy – and they didn't see anything they classed as suspicious in recent days.' Kat kicked things off and flipped through her notebook as she relayed what she had discovered. 'In fact, they said that Justin was friendly and seemed to run a respectable business, even though he didn't appear to have too many clients. One person confirmed that they had seen the victim entering the premises a few days before, but she didn't notice anything unusual about that.'

DI Rutherford turned to PC Bethany Lambert. 'I'd like you to check out Justin Hardy's financials. Did he owe anyone money? Does he have any links to organised crime? I know he's the husband of a Probation colleague and we may be going out on a limb here, but if one of Sarah's offenders knew him, perhaps he was being blackmailed and someone was sending him a message?'

Maggie had wondered the same thing, and as callous as it may sound to those in the public realm, it would make it much more of an open-and-shut case if Justin was involved in something that pissed off the wrong people. Maggie was shaken out of her thoughts when Bethany began to speak.

'Will do, Guv. Do we still have Hardy's phone? I can check those records too.' Bethany was writing everything down as she spoke.

'Yes, we still have his phone, wallet and wedding ring. Once they've been checked over for trace, and if nothing is found, they will be released back to him, so let's strike while the iron is hot. Hardy's been informed of this – though he wasn't too happy. In fact, he was more agitated by the fact that we were keeping his phone than his wedding ring. Trouble in paradise perhaps?'

Maggie concurred. 'He did seem a little on edge when I spoke to him last night, and Sarah mentioned that he had wiped out their savings but never offered her an explanation when she confronted him – other than he was investing it back in the business. He never mentioned any of this when I asked him – I even gave him an opening. It could all be innocent, of course, but I didn't like how fidgety he got when I questioned him, and as soon as Sarah came back into the room, he clammed up.'

'OK – so that's one angle to look at, get it on the board. Another is that the actual target was our victim.' She got up and went to the whiteboard, circling Daniel Firth's name. 'We need to find out as much about him as we can. Maggie, I'd like you and Kat to go and interview his wife – find out if there was any trouble recently. Dig into his background. Bethany can add PNC checks on him to the list she's scribbling down. Nathan is putting together a press release so the vultures will ease off, until we know more.'

'If I may, Guv?' Maggie stood and headed to the front, making a beeline for the crime scene photos that were stuck to the board. 'Something struck me at the scene yesterday. It was organised – there was no fight from the victim that we can tell, nothing appeared out of place. Why didn't the victim hear the killer when he entered? There's a bell on the front door which is connected to the main office area.' Maggie pointed to the area by the door. 'No one other than Justin was captured on the CCTV at the front of the office.' She tapped the photo she was referencing. 'There's the back entrance which leads to both office areas. I noted the field officer's recorded that the cleaners use this entrance and although the door was secure, it looked like it may have been tampered with. It's a service entrance that leads onto the back alley. There's some limited parking spaces and large rubbish bins, but nothing else. Let's hope our CCTV whiz,' she nodded at Bethany, 'will find more. How would the killer have known this? Let's trawl through a few weeks of CCTV – maybe our suspect followed Justin or Daniel? It doesn't feel like an opportunistic crime. The killer must have come prepared for what followed.' No one disagreed.

'Carry on. Talk us through your initial thoughts at the scene.' Rutherford returned to her seat.

'Honestly? I was confused by it all. It couldn't have been a random burglary or robbery, as Daniel's tools were found in the corner and some of them looked expensive – surely worth a few bob at a pawn shop. Plus, you say he still had his wallet on him, and Justin's valuables in the lockbox were openly available to take. Was this a warning from someone? But who were they warning and why at the insurance office? Were Daniel and Justin involved in something?' She looked back at the crime scene photos. 'I just don't know...' Maggie sat back down.

'That's good insight. Let's focus on the things we *do* know. Get talking to the right people. They might be able to answer some of those questions. Dr Blake will be joining us to go over her findings when they're available, and Dr Moloney is starting back tomorrow – a little earlier than expected, but she advised she'd have a preliminary profile to work from. The sooner we solve this, the better, as far as I'm concerned...' Rutherford dismissed the team.

Understatement of the year...

Chapter Eight

With the briefing over, Maggie headed back to the open-plan office, collected her things and waved to get Kat's attention. 'You ready?'

Kat popped the phone handset back and picked up her jacket. 'We'll have to take my car, as all the pool cars are signed out.' They made their way down to the back parking lot. Normally Maggie wouldn't be fazed by using someone else's car, but Kat's driving often had her biting her nails. She looked at her hands.

Kat unlocked the doors and smiled. 'Don't think I don't see you checking those nails of yours. Don't look so worried, I promise to take it easy.'

'I hope so – I've been avoiding a manicure since we started working together.' Maggie laughed and held up her hands. She chucked her bag in the passenger footwell, sat down and buckled up. She tugged the strap for extra reassurance.

'Fucksake – are you serious? My driving isn't that bad.' Kat slipped the car into gear and once out of the car park, they drove towards Daniel Firth's residence.

Kat had kept her promise and they arrived safely, with all nails intact, at their destination. Kat pulled up in front of the Firths' house and Maggie took in the surroundings. From what she could see, their victim was reasonably well off. A two-storey detached home with a well-groomed garden made her wonder how someone who owned a small DIY business could afford something that seemed out of her own price bracket.

'Nice area...' Kat pulled up the hand brake and they exited the vehicle. As they were walking up the path, the front door opened and the FLO greeted them. 'Come through. Mrs Firth is waiting for you in the kitchen.'

They followed the FLO down the hall and Maggie glanced at the framed photos which covered the walls. 'Hang on a sec.' Maggie grabbed Kat's arm. 'Look at this.' It was an old picture – dull in colour but clear enough so that faces were recognisable. Some sort of a group home with a handful of kids – all boys – and seven adults standing behind them.

Maggie pulled out her phone and took a picture. She couldn't explain why she felt the pictures might be significant but as soon as she saw the children's home, her stomach clenched. The fact that none of the boys were smiling irked her. Many of the offenders she'd arrested over the years had been former occupants of homes like these. 'May be nothing, but no harm checking it out.' She pocketed her phone and carried on into the kitchen.

Mrs Firth looked broken, with puffy red eyes and a chapped nose. She probably hadn't slept a wink since hearing the news yesterday. 'We're sorry to bother you during such a difficult time, Mrs Firth. I'm DC Jamieson and this is my colleague, DC Everett. We'll try and make this as quick as possible.'

The woman glanced up and pointed at the chairs opposite her. 'Please sit, and call me Joan. Who would do this to my Danny? WHO? He was such a good soul…' She pulled a tissue from the near-empty box beside her and blew her nose.

'We wondered if Daniel had mentioned anything odd or concerning in the last few weeks.' Maggie opened her notebook.

'Uh… I don't… Well… I guess he did seem a bit on edge. I just thought it was because he was stressed about work – he'd been waiting for some people to pay for jobs done. I didn't understand what the big deal was, though, as we're not stretched for money. Do you think someone had been threatening him?' Joan's eyes darted between Maggie and Kat.

'We'll be going through his phone, laptop and anything else of relevance, so maybe that will give us something more. What do you know about his previous employment? I noticed a framed photo in the hallway. Did he work at a care home in the past?'

'We've been married a long time, DC Jamieson – I know everything about my husband. He did work at a boys' home but left that job…' She looked up at the ceiling. 'Hmmm… Must be about ten years ago. It was incredibly stressful – he'd had a heart attack just before he resigned. It was a sign – time to move on. Working with troubled children can be very emotionally draining. I'm a teacher, and boy, that can be trying at times – but the kids that Danny had worked with... they were... damaged.' Joan's voice had lowered to a whisper when she said the last word, and a memory of Maggie's mother popped into her head. Her mother always whispered words she was uncomfortable with.

'He left that job voluntarily?' Maggie cocked her head. She sensed something was off when Joan's body stiffened.

'Of course he did. What are you implying?' She glared at Maggie.

'I'm not implying anything, I'm just trying to piece things together. Can you tell us when your husband started his painting and decorating business?' Maggie was curious about how defensive Joan had become when she asked about the care home and made a mental note to speak with Claire Knight, her contact in Social Care.

'Didn't I just answer that? Once he recovered from his heart attack, he needed to keep busy, so he started on small jobs and then worked his way up – all by himself, I might add. Our home was his first project. If you're not going to pay attention, why should I bother answering any more of your questions?' Joan looked away as she shifted in her seat.

Maggie glanced at Kat. She had better start wrapping things up before Mrs Firth threw them out. The woman's eyes were drooping. She was tired now but Maggie wasn't quite done yet. 'Do you know if Daniel had any arguments with his clients – for instance, Mr Hardy – any fall-outs over money?'

'Daniel? Stop calling him that, only his mother called him that,' Joan croaked. 'My husband is... was a good man. He volunteered in a lot of charities, was well liked at church and in our community here… He's an honest businessman. You're making him sound like this is all his fault, and I won't stand for it in my house!'

Kat raised a brow at Maggie and flicked her head towards the exit. Maggie had crossed one too many lines. 'I apologise if my questions came across that way, Mrs Firth. I had no intention of upsetting you, but…' The temperature in the room seemed to have dropped.

'But nothing, DC Jamieson. You *have* upset me, when really, it's the last thing I need. Have you forgotten? My husband is the victim here… *I'm* the victim…' She thumped her chest. 'I think it's time you both left. I'm done answering your nonsense. You should be out there,' she pointed towards the door, 'finding the monster that murdered my Danny.' Joan turned her head and stared out the window. They had been dismissed.

Maggie removed a card from her front pocket. 'I'll just leave this with you in case you think of anything else. We're sorry for your loss – you can rest assured that we will do our utmost to find out who did this to your husband.' Maggie and Kat followed the FLO out.

When they were out of earshot of Joan Firth, the FLO whispered to them, 'Don't take it personally, she's been snapping at everyone today. She even slammed the phone down on her sister-in-law before you arrived.'

That titbit piqued Maggie's interest. 'Thanks. Please call us if she shares anything else with you.' Maggie doubted Mrs Firth would be very forthcoming with the FLO after what had just happened, but after she had slept a few hours, she might be in a different mind-set.

'Will do.' He shut the door behind them. They got into Kat's car and left the property.

'Well, that was awkward…' Maggie played with the strap of her bag. Speaking to victims' families was not one of Maggie's strong points. It was her least favourite part of the job but also an important one.

Kat scratched her leg. 'You sure rubbed her up the wrong way. Like poking a bear – I knew to keep these lips zipped! I dread the day I have to take the lead in situations like this. Hard to get the balance right, eh?'

Maggie looked over at Kat. 'I wasn't being too hard on her, was I? Joan put those barriers up so fast, I don't think anything I could've said would've changed her mind. I got the impression she didn't want to co-operate with us.'

'You're not wrong. Maybe Firth isn't as squeaky clean as she made out to us. There was definitely something off with her.'

'I think we should contact the sister-in-law. We could pay her a visit. You up for that?' Maggie checked her watch; they still had time if the sister-in-law was close by.

'Sure – get the deets from Bethany. I'm going to pull in here, fill up and use the loo. Bloody busting for a piss, and didn't feel right asking Joan before we left. I think she would've enjoyed watching me suffer rather than let me use her toilet. You want anything from the shop?' Kat pulled into the service station.

'Bottled water for me – sparkling, if they have it. Thanks.'

While Kat used the restroom, Maggie radioed Bethany at Stafford Police Station and got the details for Daniel Firth's sister. Bethany confirmed that she would let Nathan know where they were at.

From everything they had learned so far, Maggie had the feeling that there was more to their victim than met the eye. Two questions niggled at the edge of her thoughts: How did Justin Hardy fit in? And did Sarah know more than she was letting on?

Chapter Nine

Maggie had just spoken to Firth's sister and watched through the windscreen as Kat sauntered back to the car. Her partner opened the door and chucked the bottled water in Maggie's direction before she sat down. 'Don't worry – it's *still* water. I'm not that cruel. Are we good to go to the sister-in-law's?' Kat started up the car.

Maggie opened the water and took a mouthful. 'Yeah. Just punching the coordinates into the Sat Nav.' Maggie studied the numbers on her phone. 'I spoke to the sister briefly while you were in the shop, and she's free now for about two hours. She lives towards Markston. If there's time, we might be able to pop into the police station afterwards… as long as nothing else comes up.' Maggie wouldn't mind catching up with some of her old colleagues – it had been a while. She hadn't spoken to them since the last case and wondered if PC Mark Fielding was back at work.

'Fuck yeah. I heard Pete's wife is preggers, it'd be great to congratulate him in person.'

PC Pete Reynolds had been new to the DAHU when Maggie had been seconded there two years ago. 'Sounds like a plan.' Maggie looked at her watch. 'We should be there in forty-five minutes – oh wait – scratch that – make it thirty minutes, with your driving.' A sly smiled formed on Maggie's face.

'Is that a challenge? It sure sounded like one to me.' Kat raised a brow, hunched forward and revved the engine.

'Don't you bloody dare! If you wind me up any more, I might just have to think of a way to pay you back when you least expect it... Oh, that might be fun.' Maggie rubbed her hands together. She looked down and noticed Kat's knuckles whiten. Her hand gripped the gear stick tightly before they returned to their pinkish hue and she reluctantly conceded by driving more slowly.

The journey towards Little Coombes village was filled with small talk. Despite having worked with Kat off and on for the last two years or so, Maggie was still getting to know her, but it was mainly work-related.

'Have you ever thought about having kids?'

Maggie's eyes widened. She wasn't prepared for such a personal question, but given they had just been talking about PC Pete Reynolds' news, it sort of made sense.

Maggie coughed. 'Um. I guess it has crossed my mind now and again. Why? You're not going to tell me you're pregnant, are you?'

'Hell no! I can't see me settling down just yet – now that my career is just really starting to take off, let alone having a few little shits to look after. I know I don't need to be married or even have a steady partner, but I also don't want to be a single mum – that's bloody hard work. Fuck – some days it's hard enough looking after myself.'

'Don't take this the wrong way, but I never had you down for someone who would be worried about any of those things.' When Kat tilted her head, Maggie realised she would have to explain further. 'What I mean is, I figured you for someone who would just go after what she wants and then figure it all out – no matter how it happens.'

'Huh? You lost me…' Kat glanced at Maggie before concentrating back on the road.

'Shit, I'm making this sound bad, aren't I?' Nathan had always told Maggie to try and think about what she said first, before speaking.

Kat laughed. 'Yeah, you are, but I kinda get what you mean. Maybe I'm a little more traditional than I let on. I mean, I don't judge people for their choices, I have a lot of friends who have raised kids on their own, and it's hard, and with a job like ours… well, I'd prefer not to have to do it on my own. What about you?'

Maggie wished Kat would change the subject. Although she wasn't a closed door, she also didn't initiate conversations about her personal life, because it was an area she liked to keep separate from work. She'd thought about having children one day, and where they might fit into her life, but for purely selfish reasons she didn't see them in her immediate future. 'I can just about manage my cat now.' She glanced out the window. 'Ah, sadly we'll have to come back to this conversation, as it looks like we're here…'

Thank fuck for small mercies… Maggie breathed a sigh of relief. There were other reasons why children weren't something she spoke of often – and it was complicated to talk about now.

Back when she was in the College of Policing, she had been diagnosed with endometriosis after having a miscarriage. A one-night stand had changed her life, and although now she could see that she wasn't ready for a child back then, her fear of the answer as to whether she could conceive again was stopping her from finding out any more. No one knew this – not her brother, not Nathan – and for now, she wanted to keep it that way.

Maggie felt a tap on her arm.

'You OK? You were miles away. I hope I didn't put my foot in it.'

Maggie shook the thoughts out of her head. 'Yeah, I'm fine,' she lied. 'Just trying to piece things together for when we get in there.' She pointed at the house.

They exited the vehicle and headed up the newly paved drive towards the front door. Maggie knocked and smiled when it was opened by a woman who looked about sixty. Both Maggie and Kat held up their warrant cards and the woman stepped aside so they could enter the property.

'You have a lovely home.' Maggie admired the marble flooring and bright white walls.

The woman ignored the compliment. 'Not sure why you want to speak with me. I haven't spoken to my brother in years. It's *him* you're here about, isn't it?' The woman pointed to a doorway. 'Have a seat in there. I was just making a cuppa when you knocked. Would either of you like one?'

Both Kat and Maggie shook their heads. They wiped their feet on the rug before stepping onto the tiled floor towards the living-room area. There were two large antique cabinets, packed with trinkets and figurines. A few pictures adorned the walls, including a yellowed photo of a young couple dressed in vintage clothing. Maggie guessed they were the Firths' parents. Kat took a seat while Maggie nosed around the room. Another photo had a wooden frame with the word GRANDMA carved into it, and two young kids smiled at the camera.

Kat cleared her throat and when Maggie turned, she saw that the woman had joined them. She took a seat beside Kat and ignored the stern look on the woman's face. This would not be a pleasant conversation.

'Thanks for agreeing to meet with us at such short notice. We're deeply sorry for your loss.'

'Humph.' The woman took a sip of her tea and didn't offer any more than a grunt.

'You mentioned that you haven't spoken to your brother in years. Was there a particular reason for that?' Maggie was getting a bad vibe from the woman and suspected if they didn't get straight to the point, they would be leaving before long without learning anything new.

'What's so unusual about that? We just didn't speak, OK? It does happen in families, you know – you grow up, start your own families, drift apart…' The woman looked in the direction of one of the pictures Maggie had clocked a few minutes before. 'My grandkids. So sweet and innocent. My daughter and her husband don't live far from here…'

Maggie didn't want to go off topic and interrupted the woman before she gave them a rundown of the family tree.

'They're gorgeous girls. You're obviously immensely proud. Did Daniel have much contact with your daughter and her kids?'

'Absolutely not! Why would he?' The woman's leg began

to shake. 'What are you saying? Have you spoken to my daughter?'

Maggie was taken aback by the woman's reaction – she was on the verge of becoming hysterical. 'What should we know?' It was an opportune time to get some background on Daniel Firth. Maggie had known from the beginning that something was off – there was something that no one was talking about and Maggie wanted to get to the bottom of it. It might be nothing... or it might explain why Firth had been chosen as a target.

The woman took a deep breath and composed herself. 'I'm afraid I am not going to be much help to you – I don't know anything about my brother's life that would be important to your investigation.'

Maggie wasn't convinced. 'We've reason to believe that you and Joan spoke on the phone earlier today. Can you tell us what that was about?'

The woman stood and Maggie noted a vein pulsing at the side of her now reddened neck. 'I've no idea who's been feeding you those lies. Honest to goodness, do the police normally come around and harass people? I'm afraid I've nothing more to say to either of you.'

Maggie and Kat looked at each other, a little taken aback by the change in the atmosphere.

Kat shrugged. 'Look, we can see that you're upset by everything that has happened. We can come back another time. Before we go, could you provide us with your parents' details or any other relatives that we may be able to speak to?'

'Not a chance in... Look, my mother passed away about twenty years ago and my father is in a care home – he has dementia, and the prognosis is not looking good – he doesn't have much time left.' The woman's eyes glistened. 'My own father doesn't even know who I am and would have no idea who Danny is. I won't have you upsetting him. It's time you went – sorry I couldn't help you the way you thought I might.'

Without another word, the woman led them to the front door and looked at the floor as Maggie and Kat left. The door was slammed shut behind them and Maggie jumped.

They returned to the car and sat for a moment.

'What the hell was that all about?' Kat shifted the gear stick and started the vehicle.

'You're guess is as good as mine. Would you be OK if we skipped Markston and headed back to the station? I'd like to do a bit more digging before we clock off for the day.'

Kat's face dropped but she would understand. Today they had rattled a few cages and Maggie was keen to find out what secrets the family was hiding.

Chapter Ten

M aggie's computer hummed and she booted it up. Movement in her peripheral vision caught her attention and she turned to see Nathan walking towards her.

'Any luck with the sister or wife?' He pulled a seat up beside her.

'Nothing. But Kat will back me up when I say both are hiding something. The sister denied having any contact with Joan Firth, but we can confirm whether that's true by looking at their telephone records. They both shut down any conversation, especially when we asked about Firth's work at a children's home. Something happened in that family but no one's willing to talk. It may be the motivation we're looking for – why Daniel was targeted in the first place. I'm going to look deeper into his background, see what I can find out.'

'Can I make a suggestion? You can start looking into Daniel Firth's past tomorrow. It's been a long day and tomorrow is going to be even longer. Dr Blake and Dr Moloney will be joining us, so it's going to be a lot of information.' He turned in the chair and stood. 'Oh – and bring a shovel…'

Maggie tilted her head and frowned.

'You may learn something more to help with your digging.' Nathan chuckled.

'You really need to work on that comedy routine of yours, boss.'

Maggie could feel Nathan's eyes burning into the back of her head, but before she logged out, she glanced briefly at the records, and something caught her eye. One of the field officers had made a note about 325 Lansdowne Road, a secure unit for boys which was closed in 2010. Maggie wrote down the details on a sticky note and placed it under her pen holder. It wasn't the same name as the boys' home pictured in Mrs Firth's house. She'd follow up in the morning.

'Catch you tomorrow.' Kat tapped Maggie's desk as she headed out. Bethany followed her shortly after, though Nathan remained in his office. Maggie knew if she didn't leave soon, he'd be out, giving her the evil eye.

She tapped his doorframe as she left. 'Heading out now. If you're sure you don't need me to stay for anything else, I'll see you in the morning.'

He grunted and gave her a wave.

Maggie wasn't ready to go home just yet and decided to make use of the yoga lessons she had signed up for. She took out her mobile phone and scrolled her contacts. Swiping call, she waited as the phone on the other end rang.

'Hey, Mags, to what do I owe this surprise call?'

'Fancy a yoga session and then coffee?' Maggie needed to unwind, or she'd be up all night thinking about the case.

'I'll meet you there.'

Maggie hung up the phone and wondered if she had made a mistake.

Chapter Eleven

The evenings were getting colder. Maggie zipped up her jacket as she walked to the gym in the town centre. The police station had a small gym set-up but it didn't offer space for yoga – only three treadmills and a punching bag.

At the gym, Maggie got changed into her T-shirt and cropped leggings. She'd only just entered the work-out area when something assaulted her eyes. 'What the actual fuck?' Maggie didn't know whether to burst out laughing or pretend she hadn't noticed Julie Noble, but the decision was taken out of her hands when she heard her name being called and Julie waved her over.

'I got us a spot over here.' Julie patted the floor beside her.

Maggie quickened her pace so that the journalist wouldn't draw any more attention to them. Maggie waited as Julie began to unroll her yoga mat. The instructor walked past them while Maggie unrolled her own mat and placed it on the floor.

'Are you auditioning for an Olivia Newton John video or

something? What the hell is with that outfit?' Maggie leaned across and whispered.

Julie wrinkled her brow. 'Olivia who? I just wanted to see if I could crack a smile on that glass face of yours, and what do you know – it worked... sort of. I promise to wear my normal gear next time.' Julie stood and did a twirl. 'Come on. The shiny spandex matches my sweatbands perfectly, don't you think?'

'Would you just sit down?' Maggie tugged at Julie's arm. 'We'll be kicked out of the class if you carry on, and there won't be a next time.'

'Loosen up, Mags. It's a yoga class, after all.' Julie burst out laughing at her own play on words until a loud cough at the front of the class reminded them they were not alone.

'OK! It's great to see so many new faces this evening... Let's get started with the corpse pose.'

'That's fitting, isn't it?' Julie lay on her back and turned her head towards Maggie.

Maggie ignored her, tuning out everything but the calming music and the instructor's voice.

———

An hour later and after a few downward-facing dogs, Maggie didn't know whether she felt better or worse. Her mind was cleared but her body ached. She changed quickly and called out to Julie, 'I'll see you out front.' She didn't wait for Julie's response before leaving the building and finding a bench just opposite the gym. She took out her mobile phone and scrolled through her emails while she waited, and prayed that Julie had brought a change of clothes with her.

'Hey, dirty bird! No shower? I would've kept my eyes to myself, you know.' Julie stood in front of Maggie with her hands on her hips.

'I'll have a hot bath later. I hate public restrooms and showers.' Maggie stood. 'Should we just go to Starbucks?'

Julie nodded and as they walked side by side, Julie's hand brushed up against Maggie's. It felt nice but she chastised herself for enjoying the moment. It was she who had set the boundaries in the first place. She placed her hands in her pockets.

'You grab a seat and I'll get the orders in – cappuccino, I take it?' Julie took out her wallet and handed her bag to Maggie.

Maggie scanned the room and found two seats that looked out onto the town centre. People were still milling about – either leaving work, rushing to the railway station, or strolling casually as they window-shopped. Maggie stared at the nameless faces, wondering if any one of them could be the killer they were looking for.

Julie placed the cardboard cup in front of her. 'Thought I'd get it in a take-away cup in case you needed to make a quick exit.'

'Thanks.' Maggie held the cup in her hands and took a sip – she did love her cappuccinos. 'Hmmm. This is good.'

'How's that Probation Officer? Sarah, right? It must have been a huge shock for her to find out that her hubby wasn't in that fire after all.'

Un-fucking-believable. Maggie raised her brow.

'What? It's a genuine question – no ulterior motive. All off the record, if it makes you feel any better.' Julie crossed her heart and Maggie couldn't suss whether she was being sly or was genuinely interested in Sarah's well-being. She knew what she suspected, though.

'She's fine – I guess.' Maggie wasn't going to say any more or give Julie any way of using snippets from their conversation in one of her stories.

'I tried to get an interview with her hubby, but he has some slimy lawyer acting as his PR. Bit unusual for someone who is apparently a victim, don't you think?'

That *was* odd, but Maggie maintained a straight face and shrugged her shoulders. 'I don't know, maybe he knew he was going to be badgered by journalists and decided that he'd rather have someone else deal with them. They can be pretty annoying in their persistence, you know.' A sly smile crept on Maggie's face. She wondered whether Julie would bite back. Then another thought hit her. Sarah had said they were having financial difficulties, so how could they afford a savvy lawyer?

'Oooh. What are you thinking? Your face has gone all funny.'

'What do you mean?' Maggie shifted in her seat and looked at her reflection in the window.

'Your brows crease, your nose scrunches and you bite your bottom lip. Not to mention your fingers tapping on the table, which is pretty annoying, by the way.'

Maggie stopped mid-tap and instead ran her fingers through her hair. 'Can we just talk about something else? No work shit. Don't make me think that you only agreed to meet so you could pick my brains for a story. I wouldn't have bothered, if that was the case.' Maggie picked up her coffee and stood, ready to leave, when she felt a hand on hers.

'OK, calm down – there's no need to get your frilly knickers in a twist. Cards on the table – I got hold of some video footage which I thought might interest you, but I didn't want to hassle you at work in case it was nothing. Plus, I wanted to see you – sue me. If you'd rather wait until I break the story on the news – be my guest...'

'Fucksake. Why does everything have to be a game with you?' Maggie looked at her watch. 'It's getting late and I need to get home. This is work-related, so why don't you drop by the station tomorrow and we can look at what you have – by *we*, I mean the team I work with. If you have something important on that footage, we all need to see it.' Maggie left the shop and could feel Julie's eyes on her as she passed the large window. The journalist was always pushing the boundaries, but there was no way she'd let Julie Noble manipulate this case.

Chapter Twelve

A crash on the dual carriageway on the way into work had people rubbernecking and Maggie had to try to keep her temper under control. The last thing she wanted was to be moody and snap at her colleagues – Nathan had already had words with her about that in one of their supervision sessions, and she knew that if she didn't keep it under check, it wouldn't be long before he had to give her a verbal warning, or someone would complain.

She arrived at the office with minutes to spare before the briefing, and wasted no time. Most of the seats in the incident room had been filled but Maggie smiled when Kat waved her over and pointed at the vacant seat she had saved for her.

'Thanks – bloody traffic this morning was a nightmare.' She slowed her breathing and placed her notes in front of her.

'Looks like it's about to start.' Kat turned.

Dr Blake cast her eyes on her audience. After a brief introduction from DI Rutherford, the pathologist began to share her findings.

'I'll try not to bore you all with technicalities, but a little backstory as to what we needed to do might put some things in context for you all.' Dr Blake clicked on the slide show and Maggie leaned forward to observe the crime scene photos. 'When it comes to fatal fire scenes, remains are typically difficult to detect, recover and handle. We have to be very careful, as the fire has already modified the appearance and we don't want to miss, disturb or alter the scene or any evidence we could've collected.' Dr Blake clicked to the next slide, showing the burned remains of Daniel Firth – Maggie heard a collective gasp from some of her colleagues who hadn't witnessed the crime scene first hand.

'Human remains in this form make the task of an autopsy and laboratory analysis more problematic – but not impossible.' The next slide appeared with the body in an awkward position on the cold, metal slab in the lab at Stafford Police HQ. Dr Blake had specially commissioned the lab for her work with the police in the area. 'What my team needed to distinguish were perimortem trauma – at or near the time our victim died – and post-mortem trauma. It was a daunting task, but we did it.'

Maggie noted Dr Blake's top-lip curl. The pride in her team was evident.

Dr Blake waved a stack of papers and began passing them around the room. 'I have the Fire Investigators' findings, and these are most helpful, as they tell you the cause and origin of the fire. It also assisted me in collating evidence relating to the cause and manner of death.'

Dr Blake carried on – complicated details that had Maggie zoning out momentarily.

'I'm sure Dr Moloney will agree with me when I say that

assessments of cause and manner of death are significantly more difficult if the scene and the victim are subjected to fire. We can surmise that perpetrators often use fire in order to totally destroy the body – destroy features to delay victim identification, or destroy evidence related to the circumstances surrounding the death.'

Maggie noticed that Dr Moloney pursed her lips and nodded her agreement.

'Fortunately for me, there was enough soft tissue on the body, as the fire had burned but not completely destroyed the remains. Otherwise I would have had to hand them over to one of my forensic anthropologist colleagues.'

Maggie glanced briefly at Kat's notepad and had to stifle a laugh when saw the big *WTF?* circled on the page.

'Now that I've laid the foundations, let's jump ahead to my findings. Interrupt if you have any questions.' Dr Blake skipped a few gruesome slides before she stopped on a picture showing a close-up of the semi-charred remains.

'I can tell you that the victim was alive… barely… when he was set alight. The presence of soot in the airways, mixed with mucus in the distal airway, confirmed this to be true. When I examined his body further, I found lacerations on his wrist, and further analysis of the carpet surrounding the victim found trace amounts of blood in those fibres that had not been completely burned away. I must confess that I nearly missed this, as his arms were the most severely burned part of the body and displayed heat-induced splitting of the skin – in short, your killer sliced the inside of each arm in a vertical position and the victim, who I can confirm from DNA testing as Daniel Firth, bled out. The official cause of death is cardiac arrest.'

'Whoa! What a way to go. Though I suppose he suffered less? How long would something like that take to kill him?' Maggie wondered if there was something significant in saving the victim the pain of burning to death. Or did that show inexperience?

'Precision in wounds such as these...' Dr Blake forwarded her slide to a picture showing what looked to be a large incision on the arm, 'is key to whether they would be fatal. Your killer used some sort of straight blade, like those used by barbers. It's likely that Mr Firth fell unconscious not long after, and death would have occurred anywhere from two to ten minutes following this.'

'Do we think that was deliberate? He must have set the fire, then, to destroy evidence...' Maggie only realised she said that aloud when all eyes in the room were on her. 'Sorry, thinking out loud.'

'Dr Moloney may be better suited to offer insight on that front, because as I said earlier, the fire must have been started within seconds of the blade wounds being inflicted. I work with the body, she works on the mind. The fact that I found soot particles and other thermal injuries in the airway indicates that Daniel Firth was breathing in fire, albeit for a short time. Having said that, soot particles may, under certain circumstances, occur in the respiratory tract also if the burning was exclusively after death, but this generally happens during the autopsy, and I can assure you that I considered this and had another colleague confirm that the small amount present in the trachea was not because of anything I did.'

With everything Dr Blake had just presented, it seemed this could be just a one-off murder – revenge being the motive.

'I'm still waiting for a few results back from the lab as well as the forensic odontologist. Once I get those back, my full report will be available. You have a murder on your hands, of that I can be sure. The victim's wrists were bound to the chair with plastic ties. Unfortunately, we weren't able to recover enough of the material to give you anything more specific than that. If there are no more questions, I'll say my goodbyes and hand you over to Dr Moloney...' She looked around the room and when no one else spoke up, Dr Moloney stood and suggested that they should take a break, grab a coffee and come back in thirty minutes, ready to discuss her current profile.

Maggie welcomed the break. There was a lot to take in and she needed some time to think things through. With homicide confirmed, she hoped the Doc's profile would help piece more of the puzzle together.

Chapter Thirteen

K ate sat in the incident room, re-reading her profile. Her return to work had brought a whole new level of anxiety which she had become an expert at masking, but she needed this.

She'd spent more hours than she'd expected working on the finer details, but after earlier discussions with Dr Blake she felt confident she was on the right track. Refreshed-looking faces began to fill the room and Kate smiled at Maggie, who had given her a thumbs-up.

Her heart began to race and she took a moment to shake the tension from her arms, like her therapist had suggested. She'd just have to dive right in, like ripping off a plaster – it was her first time presenting in person to a roomful of people since the Living Doll case, and she felt slightly self-conscious. All these people knew what had happened to her.

Deep breaths, Kate. It's like riding a bike.

'I think we'll all agree that Dr Blake's presentation was a lot to digest, but it's also a great window into what we are dealing with.' Kate handed out a sheet of paper printed on one side with some points for the team to refer to. 'I can only talk about what we know so far and I'll say from the outset, I don't believe this is a one-off. This murder was all about power and control, or more specifically, in my opinion, taking that back.'

'Like a vigilante or revenge killing?'

'Precisely that, Maggie. You're all probably wondering how and why I came to this conclusion, and I'll talk you through this as we go along. My first observation was that this is a very organised killer, and taking in the details from the crime scene itself, it screams premeditation.' Kate walked over to the blank whiteboard and began writing as she spoke. 'Your killer thought about *who* the victim would be, *what* he needed to do to ensure his plan would go through without a hitch, *when* he could grasp the opportunity – he may even have been following his victim.' She stopped writing and turned to face the room. 'You may find that the person you are looking for broke into Firth's home or workplace, so if you haven't already done so, I would advise you check whether Firth or his wife called in a burglary, or ask the wife if he had mentioned any concerns. Finally – the *how* would have been meticulously thought out. The killer had no intention of failing.' When Kate turned to face the room, Maggie caught her attention.

'Do you think the killer knew the victim?'

'Based on what we know so far, Maggie – there is a good chance that Daniel Firth was known to his killer. But I'd like to hold off on confirming that for definite at this moment, as it is still too early to tell. Organised offenders are often antisocial and although they know right from wrong, they often show no remorse for their actions. Whether Firth was chosen based on specific attributes, or he had a personal connection to the killer, is not clear.' Kate watched as Maggie noted the information down.

'Patterns relating to these types of individuals also show that they are likely to be of above average intelligence. He may be married or in a relationship, employed, very cunning and controlled. He may present as very friendly, charming even – and probably the last person you would suspect, so bear that in mind when interviewing persons of interest.' Kate flipped through her notes and then looked out into the room. 'I feel like I am talking at you. Please feel free to interject. I want this profile to be a joint effort, including your assessment skills as experts in capturing killers.'

Kate bit her bottom lip. 'Actually, there is one thing that is typical of organised killers but doesn't seem to fit, and if I talk you through it, maybe you all could add some insight?' Kate returned to the whiteboard and noted down some points. 'Right, so with organised offenders, there are typically three separate crime scenes: *where* the victim was approached, *where* the victim was killed, and *where* the victim's body was disposed of. This is what makes them very difficult to apprehend, because they go to inordinate lengths to cover their tracks and often are forensically savvy. They will have thought through *your* moves and therefore do their best to make sure you are thrown off track.'

'That's certainly interesting. A little off track here, but are there ever combinations of profiles? Everything you've said makes sense in terms of the opportunity, but maybe he did this on purpose – to confuse us? We have no idea when the victim was initially chosen or why, but he's combined all your *wheres*: approached, killed and disposed of in the same place. Plus he set fire to the body, which fits with trying to destroy evidence, right?'

'It does, Maggie, but I'm not convinced that was the reason behind the fire. The one thing about profiles is that with new information, they can be improved and should only be used as guidance – so it is possible that other traits fit better. The fire was focused on the victim rather than the whole room or building, maybe part of a ritual for the killer. What does everyone else think?'

'Would he be following the news? Should we be sharing bits of information with the media, to try and draw him out?'

'Excellent question, Kat. My instinct tells me yes. This individual is likely to follow media reports and he may even correspond with the press. Ted Bundy is a prime example of a typical organised killer. This murder seems more personal to me, though. The way the body was staged. The killer would have total control, standing over his victim, torturing and taunting Daniel Firth, leaving him feeling totally helpless.'

Kate spotted Maggie leaning forward in her chair and waited for her to say what was on her mind. The room was silent as the team absorbed the information. 'I think our victim and killer knew each other. I got the impression that this wasn't a random attack, from the way the crime scene was set up, to all the things that were left behind. We've already ruled out burglary because Firth's and Justin Hardy's wallets and other valuables were left behind. So why did he burn Firth? Was it an integral part of the kill – pleasure seeking? Or was it because he was trying to cover his tracks? I know you said you didn't feel the latter was the case, but maybe he made a mistake, worried that his DNA was transferred? Noticed something that could lead to him being discovered on the body?' Kate watched as Maggie closed her eyes as she spoke. No doubt using that uncanny sense she had of visualising the scene again, looking for some small clue that may not have been obvious at the time.

'At this moment in time, it could be either, but I am leaning towards it being a combination of both. It served a purpose of making sure no trace evidence could be found on the body, but it also added a level of torture – showing the victim who was in control. As Dr Blake noted – the victim was alive... albeit barely, but still alive when he was set alight, so our killer wanted him to suffer. To me, this feels like payback or revenge.' Kate noticed that some of the officers were losing focus. A few yawns and shuffling of papers made her realise she had been talking for some time now. She glanced at the clock on the back wall and decided it would be a good time to pause and allow all the information to be absorbed. Her profile was a work in progress, and she'd need more from the officers before anything final would be available. She signalled DI Rutherford and got a nod back in response.

'I think you've enough to start with. Sorry to have taken up so much of your time, but hopefully this preliminary profile will help you identify some persons of interest – think back to who you have already spoken to and if they don't fit, who might? All this information will be uploaded to the system so that you can compare anyone you think may be involved to the profile.' Kate stepped aside as DI Rutherford joined her at the front.

'Thank you, Dr Moloney, you've certainly given us a lot of food for thought. OK, people – now is the time to take everything you've heard here today and use it against what we've collected so far – who do you need to go back and question? Does anything you've heard today raise any red flags? Focus on the facts...' DI Rutherford wrapped up the briefing, and Kate hoped she had given them enough to identify a suspect – otherwise, she feared they hadn't heard the last of this killer.

Chapter Fourteen

M aggie walked back to the main office with Kate. 'Have you decided where you'll be setting up base? We have a few desks free, and if you're looking for somewhere quiet where you can concentrate, I'd recommended the far corner by that window there.'

'It's like you read my mind. I'm having some things sent over from the DAHU – sorry, IOM – it's going to take me a while to get used to another new acronym. Do you know if there are any free cabinets? Just one, mind, but it needs to be lockable.'

'You'll probably have to ask Nathan or DI Rutherford for anything specific like that. There is a small cabinet under each of the desks with two drawers where you can lock away confidential bits, if that would help in the short term?'

'That's grand. How did I do in there?' Kate bit her lip.

Maggie had wondered if the Doc was still anxious about returning to work after her ordeal with the Living Doll Killer, and her question confirmed Maggie's suspicions.

'You were succinct, informative and, well… fabulous, as ever. What you've given us is focus – now we just need someone to direct that profile to. This is the part I really hate about an investigation – when everything is up in the air and the clues are limited. Hopefully after we speak to a few more people, we'll at least get some sort of idea of a list of people who meet those criteria.'

'I'm sure you will. I'd better let you get back to it and settle myself in. Catch you later.'

Maggie stood in front of her own desk and looked out the window, but a whistle from the opposite corner of the room brought her back to reality. 'Was that you trying to get my attention, Bethany?' Maggie walked over to her.

'Yeah, sorry. I didn't realise I did that out loud. Look at this.' Bethany turned her screen slightly so Maggie could get a better look at the grainy images.

'What am I looking at?' Maggie could see a street with a few cars parked on one side and a blurred figure with their head down.

'That's the street view from the alley behind the buildings and that person might be someone we want to speak with. Unfortunately, the camera angle is pretty shit but I think they may have come out of the crime scene or a building very close to it. If we follow the footage, you'll see he gets into that white vehicle. We can only see part of the licence plate, but I can run that, along with the make of the vehicle, through the DVLA and ANPR to see if we can get a hit.'

'You're a bloody genius.' A surge of excitement hit Maggie. This could be the break they needed.

'Uh.' Bethany held up her hand. 'Let's see if I get something first. I wouldn't want to get you too excited and then have it turn out to be nothing.'

Maggie noticed Bethany blush. 'It's one step closer and more than we have now, so take the praise. Do you want to let Nathan know?'

Bethany shook her head. 'I'd rather stick with this and see what I find.'

'OK. I'll update him but I'll be sure to let him know that the credit is all yours.' Maggie squeezed Bethany's shoulder and headed towards Nathan's office.

'Hey boss. Bethany may have found something.'

He waved her in. 'What is it?' He pulled his eyes away from his computer monitor and gave Maggie his full attention.

'A partial plate and make of a vehicle – as far as we know, no one has spoken to this person and he hasn't come forward, so worth speaking to. Maybe you can mention it when you speak to the press? Might jog someone's memory and nudge them to come forward.'

'I'll run it by Rutherford. If it's a person of interest, it may be better to keep that bit of info under wraps.'

Maggie shrugged. Her thinking was that if the person knew the police wanted to speak with them, and didn't come forward, they'd have more leverage when they finally caught up and interviewed him. But Nathan was now her boss and she trusted he would have his own reasons, so she didn't share. When they were partners, Maggie and Nathan ran ideas by each other regularly, but with his new position as DS, she didn't want him to feel that she was questioning him or trying to undermine his decisions.

'Before I forget, I'm going to do a bit of background on the boys' home – Chatham House. Kat and I saw a picture at

Daniel Firth's house when we spoke to his wife. When we mentioned it, she clammed up completely, which I thought was odd.'

'Oh fuck. I'm not sure I like the sound of that – if this has anything to do with kids...' Nathan shook his head and looked relieved when his desk phone rang. 'Right, I best get this and let you get back to your digging.'

Maggie returned to her work-station and opened the Chrome browser. In the search box she typed Chatham House and waited as pages and pages of hits loaded on the screen. 'Holy hell, where do I start?' she mumbled to herself. According to his wife, Daniel Firth had left his job at the home at least ten years before, so she decided that would be a great place to start. Her jaw dropped as headline after headline noted fundamental failings in the home flagged up in reports by Ofsted and by the Children's Commissioner for England. Maggie's understanding of Ofsted was limited to knowing only that they use complaints to inform inspections and regulations of children's Social Care services. It couldn't be a coincidence that Firth had worked at a children's home which was brought to the attention of Ofsted. When something set off her spidey sense, she knew she needed to know more. Finding any official reports about the home that their victim worked at would be a good start, and she knew just the person who could help. Maggie picked up her phone and dialled Stafford Social Care.

'You've reached the office of Stafford Social Care Services. All our lines are busy now, but if you know the extension of the person you wish to speak to, please dial that now...'

Maggie grabbed her notebook from her in-tray and riffled through the pages until she found the information she needed.

She keyed in the extension and waited as the phone rang through.

'*Claire Knight speaking.*'

'Hi, Claire! It's DC Jamieson... Maggie – from Stafford Police. I wonder if you have any time later today to meet up. I have a case I'm investigating and you may have some of the answers I'm looking for.'

'I'm free after 4 p.m. today – sorry I can't meet up earlier, but we're short-handed, so I'm helping with some duty cover.'

'That's perfect. Thanks so much. I'll see you then.' Maggie hung up the phone and started to print off the details of the stories of interest: allegations of a technique called *pindown*, neglect, poor housing conditions, and physical abuse of children in their care... The list seemed endless and goosebumps formed on Maggie's arms. She didn't like the direction this investigation was pulling her in. Child abuse was something she and most of her team felt strongly about. She hoped that Claire would have some answers, but it would have to wait until after the press conference.

Maggie was curious how much detail would be released to the public, plus it would also inform what she could or couldn't disclose to Claire later that day. She checked her watch. There was still time before the press conference to gather more details, and a call to the police Child Exploitation and Abuse Unit, who specialised in cases involving children, might be a good place to start.

Chapter Fifteen

A dozen thoughts were going through Maggie's mind as she headed down to the press conference. Is the killer targeting paedophiles? Is this case personal? Is this a one-off? Maggie knew others on the team would be having similar thoughts. Dread wrapped its unwelcome arms around her and sent a shiver down her spine. No one liked cases where children might be involved, particularly if trusted individuals were implicated.

She entered the conference room and was surprised to see the Doc at the front of the room with Nathan, DI Rutherford and the Comms Officer. It wasn't because she believed Kate wasn't qualified or couldn't add another dimension to the media coverage, it was more what she would be saying to the press that piqued Maggie's interest. They barely had a profile to work from and still needed more information about the victimology so they could understand why Daniel Firth was chosen. What would Kate be sharing with the press?

Maggie stood at the back of the room and took in all the

faces, desperate for a story that could propel them from their mediocre positions to possible fame. She was surprised to see that Julie wasn't front and centre.

'Looking for me?' a familiar voice whispered in her ear.

'Not like you to be late.' She didn't even turn to look at the journalist.

'Had some things to wrap up first. Is that Dr Moloney I see with your colleagues? She's certainly looking more confident than the last time I saw her. Ooooh. Best find myself a seat.' Julie rubbed her hands together. 'Catch you later, Mags.'

Maggie flinched at the shortened version of her name. She had hoped that once Julie realised she wouldn't get a reaction from her, she'd stop using it, but that didn't seem to be the case. It wasn't like she hadn't been called that before, it was more about who was saying it – it had been an intimate greeting from a past relationship. Maggie had promised herself that she wouldn't let the journalist get under her skin, but the harder she fought it, the deeper it went. *Fucking feelings…*

Her attention returned to the room when she noticed DI Rutherford adjusting the tiny microphone that was pinned to her head. 'Good afternoon, everyone. Thank you all for coming at such short notice. We'll keep this short and to the point. Following details from the post-mortem, I'd like to confirm today that we have launched a murder enquiry into the death of Mr Daniel Firth. The victim's family has been informed and we'd appreciate it if you'd respect their privacy at this time. We are currently trawling CCTV of the surrounding area and we'd like the public's help. If anyone was in town or around Hardy & Associates on the day in question, please contact the hotline. I'm going to hand you over to my colleague, DS Nathan Wright, who'll give you some further information on

the investigation, before we open the floor to any questions.'
Rutherford stepped aside as Nathan took the floor.

'Thank you. As DI Rutherford has said, we're appealing to
anyone who can help us piece together Daniel Firth's
whereabouts leading up to his murder. We'd also like to speak to
anyone who knew him personally and may have information that
will help us get a better understanding of him, his relationships –
perhaps you knew him in the past… that sort of thing. Dr Kate
Moloney,' Nathan turned and pointed in Kate's direction, 'has
recently the joined the MOCD and will be consulting with us on
our investigation. We're working with her to develop a profile of
the suspect. So, any help from the public would be appreciated.'
He paused. 'OK, I'll open the floor up for questions.'

Was Kate not contributing?

Sometimes silence spoke volumes and Maggie wondered if
it was a ploy to throw the killer off guard. The less said, the
more the killer might be tempted to make contact. Returning
her gaze to the front, she wasn't surprised to see Nathan's eyes
roll when Julie Noble stood.

'Ms Noble.' The tone was not missed on others in the room
and Maggie sniggered to herself. It was Julie's own fault – her
brashness rubbed people up the wrong way. Then again,
people often said the same about her.

'What can you tell us about the condition of the body? With
the fire, was the body intact when it was found?'

Maggie winced. Trust Julie to be the first to jump in with a
question like that – no pussyfooting around, Julie went straight
in for the jugular.

'The victim suffered severe burn injuries to a portion of his
body. The fire was contained to a corner of the office where our

victim was located.' Nathan left it at that, but it seemed like Julie wasn't done with her probing.

'What about the owner of the office space... Justin Hardy? What is his involvement in this case? Do you believe he was the intended target?' Julie shifted her stance to her other foot and held her phone out to record the answers.

'We're not at liberty to discuss those specific details at this time. What I can say is that Mr Hardy is assisting us with our investigation.' Maggie admired the way Nathan was giving the journalist as little information as possible while seemingly feeding the other news organisations with enough. They were listening intently, some jotting down notes while others raised their recording devices as far above their heads as they could reach.

Now that the press had hold of Justin's name, Maggie made a mental note to contact Sarah – after this was released, she'd be bombarded by the press outside her home and possibly at the Probation office.

'Do you think this is a one-off? Or was anything else discovered that would lead you to suspect that the killer hasn't finished yet?'

Maggie waited to hear how Nathan responded to this. Kate's suggestion that the murder appeared to be a revenge kill meant that there was always a possibility of more murders if they didn't figure out who was behind killing Daniel Firth. With public protection as a primary focus, they would need to play this card carefully, as they didn't want to raise the fear of further crime, but they needed the public to be aware of the chance that this was not over.

'We're treating this as a single incident, as we have no

evidence to suggest otherwise. How about you let your colleagues ask some questions now?'

That was Maggie's cue to leave. She didn't want to be cornered and quizzed by Julie at the end of the conference, and she wanted to make sure she had the chance to read some more about the care homes before she went to see Claire.

As soon as Maggie had made the connection between Firth and children's care homes, her stomach churned. The police and others in the criminal justice system often had a sixth sense when it came to recognising patterns. It wasn't something they could easily explain and it certainly wasn't something they could use to arrest a suspect, but it was something they couldn't ignore. If Maggie's instincts were correct, Claire Knight could be the key to uncovering why their victim was targeted and who might be responsible.

Chapter Sixteen

'How was the press conference?' Kat swivelled around in her chair to face Maggie.

'It's still on. I wanted to get out of there before it finished. Nathan was just vague enough to not give away anything that could compromise the investigation, despite Julie Noble's efforts, I might add. Here's hoping we'll get some calls through to the hotline. The field team are going to be busy…'

'I've already had a few calls sent my way, but nothing significant. Need to follow up on some details, and then I'm off to speak to the field team.' Kat returned to what she had been doing and Maggie took the hint. Kat would share when there was something to share – she didn't like to waste people's time.

Maggie opened her emails and was pleased to see that Bethany had worked wonders with her ANPR and DVLA checks on the car spotted via the CCTV. They had the owner's name. The bad news was, the owner had reported the vehicle stolen two days before the murder, and now Maggie understood what Kat had meant about finding out more from the field team.

Maggie spent the remaining time before her meeting with Claire looking at old newspaper articles on the internet, trying to see if she could link their victim to any of the investigations into Staffordshire's children's care homes in the time period she suspected Daniel Firth had worked in that field, given the scant details provided by his wife and sister. Maggie's spidey sense was on red alert – why did they become so defensive when they were being interviewed? Maggie wouldn't stop looking until she found an answer.

Chapter Seventeen

After glancing up and realising the time, Maggie grabbed her bag and let her team know where she was heading. The main offices of Social Care were only a ten-minute walk away from the police station. A gust of wind caught her off guard and she regretted not bringing her jacket. Once at the building, she signed in and took a seat in the designated waiting area until Claire came and fetched her.

Ten minutes later, Claire popped her head through the door. 'Nice to see you again, DC Jamieson. Pity it's always under such awful circumstances. Come through.'

Maggie stood and stretched her legs before following Claire into an office. 'Oh, this is new? Have you redecorated?' Maggie was sure Claire's office was smaller the last time she had been there.

'I've recently been promoted.' Claire blushed.

'Great news. Congrats! Does this mean you are less hands-on with cases?' Maggie hoped not, because she valued the social worker's input.

'I do have a caseload of my own because – well, you know, government cuts.' Claire rolled her eyes. 'But I now supervise a small team of social workers – I'm not exactly sure what possessed me to accept the promotion, if I'm honest – no significant monetary gain and a lot more pressure. Plus accountability falls on my shoulders...' She shrugged. 'So how can I help you today?' Claire sat and crossed her legs.

'I was hoping you might know something about a man named Daniel Firth and Chatham House Boys' Home. You may have seen on the news that he was murdered and when I was speaking to his wife, I saw a picture of this children's home on his wall. When I googled it, quite a few old articles came up describing an investigation of the children's home... Something is telling me I need to look into this further, so here I am.'

Claire looked up at the ceiling. 'Hmmm. That was an awful matter. Allegations of the controversial pindown method...' The social worker shook her head.

'Pindown what? I saw that mentioned, but if I'm honest, I have no idea what it actually means. Any chance you can give me a quick run-down?'

'Of course.' Claire shifted in her seat. 'Pindown was a method of behaviour management used in children's homes in Staffordshire in the 80s or thereabouts. It involved isolating children, sometimes for weeks on end, and in some cases it drove children to the verge of suicide. When concerns were raised, the council ordered a public inquiry into the practice. I believe the report that came out was very damaging and called the method unethical, unprofessional and illegal; it had a major impact on children's law in the UK.'

'Jesus.' Maggie's eyes widened. 'Could you give me a bit

more context?' She took out her notebook and waited for Claire to continue.

'Sure. Not surprisingly, Staffordshire children's homes were, in the 1980s, underfunded and understaffed. They were also severely overcrowded. If you bear with me one moment...' Claire started typing something into her computer. 'Here it is. It looks like that home, Chatham House, was overcrowded with fifteen additional children. Oh, and here's something else...' Claire's voice dropped, and Maggie leaned forward. 'Again in the late 80s, a deputy director of Staffordshire County Council's social services department was called by a solicitor, who raised concerns about a group of teenaged boys who had made allegations of abuse in the children's home. Looks like it wasn't the first time such allegations had been made. The following day, the Director of Social Services at the time issued instructions that pindown must cease at the boys' home and any other children's homes. Information had been leaked to the press and once that got spread around, the council had no choice but to determine that a public inquiry must be held.'

'What the heck? Surely once the first round of allegations had been made, the matter should have been investigated?' Maggie couldn't believe what she was hearing.

'You'd think so, but apparently it was condoned, or at least a blind-eye approach was taken, and the social workers in charge were told basically to just get on with things and ignore any complaints, as long as nothing could be proven.'

'How they hell they got away with that is beyond me. So the pindown method definitely occurred at Chatham House? Could you give me more specific details on what it entailed?'

Claire nodded. 'From what I can see here,' she pointed at

her screen, 'Chatham House was one of the first places to introduce the method. Children were often required to wear pyjamas all day in order to prevent their absconding, though it didn't seem to be very successful. You should look into historical police records, as apparently there were a lot of complaints from the local police saying that they were spending too much time dealing with runaways in their PJs.'

Maggie recorded the information on her notepad and circled it. She would definitely be looking deeper into the police records and she still had to make that call to the Child Abuse Unit. Something wasn't sitting right with her and her concerns grew as Claire continued to explain.

'Says here that the children were regularly deprived of their clothing and shoes. They were locked in rooms called "pindown rooms", sometimes for periods of weeks or months, like a lockdown in prisons. It also says here that they were required to perform physical exercise outdoors in their underwear and were subjected to corporal punishment. Sometimes they were deprived of food, water or toilet paper, and not allowed to go to the toilet at all, and doused in cold water. You won't believe this bit...' Claire squinted as she read off more information from her computer. 'The staff recorded all this as *loss of privileges*.'

A knot formed in Maggie's stomach and she could feel her neck burning as the anger within her was fighting to get out.

'Looks like all agencies were criticised for this failing – the report asserted that the police, teachers, the Probation Service and the Social Services Inspectorate had all failed the children of Staffordshire. And it was at this time that the pindown method was stopped, along with quite a few other recommendations, as I'm sure you can imagine.'

'How long after that was Chatham House closed down?'

'Looks like it was officially shut in 2011.'

'So even after all that controversy, it still remained open?'

'Of course. There was nowhere to house the kids. However, it was closely monitored...'

'Closely monitored, my arse. How could anyone think that any of that was acceptable?' Maggie shook her head.

'Needs must, I'm afraid. You wouldn't believe some of the techniques I've heard used in secure units and care homes. Thankfully, most of them have stopped, but there are always a few people who take matters into their own hands. It's all about power with some of them.'

Claire looked down at the floor. Was that shame Maggie could see? She hoped not, as she believed Claire was a great advocate for Social Care and the children they worked with – previous colleagues' behaviour was no reflection on Claire, in Maggie's mind.

The last sentence Claire spoke sparked a thought in Maggie's head: *Who wanted to take that power back?*

Chapter Eighteen

The MOCD office was empty when Maggie had got back. Her phone bleeped and she read the text from Andy – he was getting a taxi and told her not to rush home with the car.

Shit. She hadn't realised the time.

Maggie shut down her system and drove home thinking about how everything she had learned from Claire could help form their victimology

She was still trying to process things some forty minutes later as she pulled up outside her house. Maggie had always known about historical cases of child abuse but hadn't realised how many cases there were in Staffordshire prior to her joining the police force.

Stepping out of the car, she took a deep breath. She was home – time to shut off for the evening.

Once inside, she went into the kitchen and flicked on the light, grabbing a tin from the cupboard. 'Scrappy! Salem! It's your favourite time of the day...' Maggie grabbed a fork and tapped the tin of tuna, a special treat for the pair. The cat flap smacked against its frame as Scrappy slid across the floor. 'Where's your partner in crime?' She reached down and rubbed his head. When Salem didn't appear after a few minutes, Maggie emptied half the tin into Scrappy's bowl and placed it on the floor. She walked to the bottom of the stairwell and called out. No thud. No patter of paws. Maybe he'd got locked in one of the rooms?

She jogged up the stairs and checked the spare bedroom where Salem had made his home. It was empty.

In fact, on closer inspection, Maggie realised the room was completely empty of all his things. Kate must have come by when Maggie was out. She returned downstairs, dug her phone out of her bag and texted Kate.

Did you come by and get Salem today? X M

A speedy response from Kate came back:

Yes. I rang the landline and Andy let me come by before he went to work. Sorry. I should have texted you to let you know. Hope you didn't panic. How was the soc care meeting today? Kate

Maggie replied:

Will catch you up tomorrow – too long to text and too tired to call. LOL. Give Salem a cuddle from me. X M

Maggie returned to the kitchen. 'So, your kingdom has been returned to you.' She bent down and scratched Scrappy behind the year. He didn't move from his food.

She chucked a frozen lasagne into the microwave and brought it into the living room when ready. She wanted the comfort of her couch rather than a hard dining-room chair. She plonked herself down on the couch, and her mind returned to her meeting with Claire, as she suspected it would.

Maybe the internet could help fill in some of the blanks. Claire had told her that she couldn't find any information specifically relating to Daniel Firth but would try and find out as much as she could. If it was there, Maggie had no doubt Claire would find it.

Maggie hadn't disclosed anything to the social worker that wasn't already in the public domain. She was careful not to share specific details with Social Care, as it was still early stages, and she didn't want to bias Claire in her search for information.

Maggie grabbed the notepad off the coffee table and started to put her thoughts together.

1. *Children's homes across Staffordshire 2008: under investigation for neglect of children in their care.*
2. *Chatham House boys' home: closes under suspicious circumstances – records sealed. 2011.*
3. *ALL were run by a board of trustees – Find out who was on this board!*

And then a final thought: *What is Daniel Firth's connection? If anything?*

Maggie rubbed her temples. Was she just trying to fit a

square peg into a round hole? She chucked the notepad back on the table and picked up the remote. Flicking through the channels, she stopped when she saw a familiar face – Julie Noble. For once it seemed the journalist was reporting on something that wouldn't piss Maggie off and was unrelated to the current investigation – she was reporting on the homeless.

Maggie's eyes were glued to the screen as she watched Julie walk the streets of Stafford town centre in the early morning hours – the camera zoomed in on the poor souls tucked in the shop doorways, using cardboard boxes as mattresses and newspapers as blankets. Maggie's eyes widened.

That coat.

Where had she seen that before? Was it on her way to Social Care? She closed her eyes and ran through everything she had come across today – she recognised that coat. Damn – nothing immediately came to mind. She looked around the room before remembering her phone was still in the hallway. She got up and retrieved it from her bag.

Maggie dialled Julie's number but for once, there was no sarky hello – instead, it went to answerphone after a few rings.

'Hey. It's Maggie. I just saw that programme on the homeless that you did. Looks like it was pre-recorded. If you're near the station tomorrow, would you be able to drop that footage in to me? I'll explain when I see you. Uh… take care. Bye.'

Maggie hated leaving messages. It felt awkward and she always rambled. Tiredness crept over her and she yawned. She cleared up, locked Scrappy's cat flap after spotting him snoozing on one of the dining-room chairs and called it a night.

Chapter Nineteen

H e awoke on the couch with a start. Memories from the past had haunted his dreams and he knew then that what he was doing was right. His face tightened. 'Fucksake...' He grabbed a tissue from the table and wiped the sticky drool from his face.

He stretched his arms above his head and yawned. A sharp pain shot down the left side of his body. Pulling his sleeve up, he rubbed the scars on his arm. They were faint now but were a stark reminder of the physical pain he endured at the hands of those who were supposed to protect him.

Over time the scars had faded – but the emotional scars remained. These days, it seemed like anything could trigger him. Therapists fed him a bunch of mumbo jumbo about PTSD.

Fuck that shit.

When he went to them, he had wanted something, drugs... to forget, to stop the memories and flashbacks, but the doctors had refused to give him anything without some form of counselling attached. Cruel bastards. How did they expect him to trust anyone after what he had experienced?

Yeah. Fuck that shit. FUCK IT.

With his next target chosen, he smiled. He had wanted to save her for later, but with the police now on the hunt, he might not get time to finish his mission – and there was no way he would let them off the hook. He hoped all the sons of bitches were shitting themselves right now. Once those bastards realised the significance of Daniel Firth's murder, and if they were clever enough, they would know.

With her though… he needed to map out where and when. He wanted time with this one. He grabbed his notebook off the table and looked over what he had written. He ran his fingers over the pages. It was his bible – a handbook he had been working on for the last eighteen months. The bastards didn't know he had been following them – detailing their most common routines. People really were stupid – they made it too easy. He glanced at his laptop – *way too easy*. It was karma.

A low chuckle escaped his lips.

He stood and stretched his legs. Sometimes walking around gave him the answers he sought – as if the heavens were directing him. A late-night stroll around the block was exactly what he needed. He put the notebook away, grabbed his coat and headed out into the crisp, fresh evening air.

He loved this time of night – it felt like the world was his for the taking. During daylight hours, he blended in – he was one of them – normal. Even so, many avoided his gaze, his smile, his wave. They were right to, as well. He had nothing but misery to offer.

Out of nowhere the rain came. Pelting down on him like bullets. He didn't run to find shelter, though. He stood and opened his arms. Each drop splashing on his face, the cleansing of his soul. At that very moment, he felt invincible.

Someone brushed by him quickly, bumping his shoulder as they passed. 'Fucking idiot...' they murmured without even looking back.

He could go after them – but he wouldn't. He wasn't crazy. The only blood he wanted on his hands was the blood of those that deserved it. That arsehole may deserve it – but someone else could pick up that cause.

A roar of thunder brought him back to his purpose and then it came to him. He knew it would. He turned back and headed home. He wanted to share his plans in the forum before he went to bed. Maybe now they would believe him.

Chapter Twenty

Maggie made sure to collect her notes from the table before she headed out to work that morning. She took the train in. As she walked through Victoria Park towards the police station, she had to avoid the puddles from the flash of thunderstorms they had last night.

The police station was just ahead, and a figure was waving in her direction. She looked over her shoulder; there was no one else around her. Maggie squinted to see who it was. 'Early bird catches the worm and all that...' Maggie cocked a brow.

'I thought you'd be delighted to see me. I bring gifts...' Julie tapped her bag.

'I hadn't expected you this early, though. Come in then, let's see what you have...'

Maggie swiped her card and the automatic doors swooshed open. 'We'll have to go into one of the interview rooms down here.'

'You ashamed to be seen with me?' Julie nudged her shoulder.

Maggie ignored the tingle that raced through her at Julie's touch. 'My computer doesn't have a USB drive that will work with a non-secure flash drive – the ones down here do... follow me.'

'Yes, ma'am.' Julie saluted.

Maggie held the door open and directed the journalist to the interview suite with the equipment they needed.

'Which do you want to see first, then? The fire or my homeless exposé?'

'Let's start with the fire.' Maggie threw her coat over the chair and booted up the desktop computer.

'Are you even going to offer me a drink?'

'I don't expect that you'll be staying long enough to drink it – but I promise that the next time we go out, the coffee is on me. Deal?'

'Deal. Now shove over...' Julie bumped Maggie out of the way, rummaging through her bag and then sticking the USB into the desktop. Maggie watched the screen as Julie opened the file aptly titled 'FIRE' and hit play.

Maggie moved closer and focused on the footage. She knew what she was looking for but for now, needed to keep its significance from Julie. At eight minutes in, she saw exactly what she hoped she would. Maggie glanced over at Julie and then wished she hadn't.

'Ooooh... what did you see?' Julie raised a brow.

'Nothing. What about the next video, can you start that up?'

'Not until you tell me what caused those wrinkles on your forehead.' Julie tugged at the USB stick.

'Don't be like that. Look, I'm not sure I saw anything... Can you send me those videos via email?'

'What's in it for me if I do?' A crooked smile caught Maggie's eye.

Maggie took a deep breath and counted down from ten in her head. 'I'm sure if anything comes from the footage, you'll get first dibs on any story that follows. But if you would rather be an arse, I can just as easily contact the newsroom and get one of your more helpful colleagues to send them over or google them – they are public record.'

Julie began typing and forwarded the videos to Maggie. 'Well, you should have just done that in the first place. If you really wanted to see me, you could have just asked… I thought you said you didn't want to play any games.' Julie pulled the USB stick from the computer and placed it back in her bag. Her tone was serious but Maggie didn't have time to explore it. Instead she just reverted to what she knew best.

'Get over yourself, Noble.' Maggie held the door open and gave a sarcastic wave as Julie left the building. Another reason why she didn't want to get more serious with the journalist – it was too hard to separate her personal feelings from the professional without coming across like a bitch. She raced up the stairs to her desk – she had to be sure of what she had seen before speaking with Nathan. They could have a person of interest if she was right.

Chapter Twenty-One

K ate Moloney looked up briefly from her computer screen and nodded in Maggie's direction. There was something about her demeanour that had Kate's curiosity piqued. She also knew she'd have to wait – once Maggie had figured out what she needed to, she'd share with the rest of the team.

'Have you had any luck on identifying the person on the CCTV footage yet, Bethany?' Kate took a break from the profile she was working on because her mind was drawn to the recording. She hadn't wanted her own assessment to be skewed by irrelevant details, but the way the unidentified male in the CCTV had deliberately tried to hide his identity couldn't be ignored. She was struggling with this one.

'No. The vehicle was found burned out in a cul-de-sac the following day, so it doesn't look like we'll get any evidence from that either.'

'Hmmm. OK.' Kate had been feeling slightly disconnected from the case, which unsettled her.

Before returning to work, she'd been speaking to a counsellor about her experience with the Living Doll Killer, and initially felt that she was moving forward, but she hadn't had any active cases at the time. She hadn't been feeling herself since she'd been back. Was she just feeling self-conscious and worried about missing something? Or did she feel she had something to prove? She couldn't work it out.

'Kate, would you mind coming over here for a minute?' Maggie called out. A perfect distraction. She pushed her chair out and made her way to Maggie's work-station.

'Oh, where did you get those?' Looking over Maggie's shoulder, Kate noticed Maggie had two videos up on the screens and was rewinding and playing them side by side. She then opened a third video and Kate leaned forward.

'Have a look at these and tell me if you notice anything significant.' Maggie pressed play and Kate's eyes shifted between the three videos.

'Hey, wait. Can you rewind and stop when I tell you?' Kate tugged her ear. 'OK…' She stared at the screens. 'Stop there…'

On one video there was a man – head down, hoody up and a large green duffel coat pulled around him. On the second video, a homeless man lay in a shopfront with a green duffel coat on top of him. 'Is that the same coat?'

'That's exactly what I was thinking! But there must be hundreds of this type of duffel coat around, so I wanted fresh eyes to check it out.' The excitement in Maggie's voice was addictive.

'Can you zoom in?' Kate had spotted something but wanted to be sure before she shared with her colleague.

'I can't – but I know a person who might be able to.' Kate waited as Maggie opened her emails and forwarded the videos. 'Bethany, I'm sending you over two videos. Do you think you and that computer of yours can zoom in on some images?'

'I'll see what I can do... OK, got it.'

Kate and Maggie joined Bethany at her desk.

'What am I looking for?' Bethany loaded the videos.

'The green duffel coat in the crime scene video and the homeless man in the second video. The left side pocket.' Kate pointed at the screen. 'There! Do you see that?' She looked at her colleagues. 'It can't be a coincidence that the left pocket on both these jackets is torn and has a black ink stain, can it?'

'No, it bloody can't.' Maggie ran back to her desk and grabbed her coat.

'Where are you going?' Kate noted the determined look on Maggie's face.

'I'm off to find a homeless man in a green duffel coat – do you fancy a field trip?'

Kate nodded; she was feeling restless and the fresh air would do her some good. She put on her jacket and placed her bag across her chest. 'Are you not taking your partner with you? I don't want to piss anyone off...'

'Once I find her, she'll be joining us. Where is she?'

'Where's who?' Kat walked into the room holding a mug of coffee.

'Maggie thinks we may have a lead. You coming?'

Chapter Twenty-Two

Once outside, Kat and the Doc listened while Maggie explained in detail to Kat what they had discovered on the videos provided by Julie Noble.

'Well, at least she's good for something.' Kat pulled out a fag and lit it. Maggie wondered if that would be Julie's epitaph one day, as it was a common reply when her name was brought up.

'Yeah, she has her uses sometimes.' Maggie looked down the road ahead. 'Right, the doorway is around the corner on the left but at this time of day, all the homeless would have been moved on. There are a few shelters in the town centre. I think we should split up and start there.' Earlier, Maggie had snapped a picture on her phone of the person of interest from the image on the video. 'I've just forwarded you the photo, Kat – why don't you and the Doc join forces. Let's see if anyone recognises the man in the picture, or maybe even confirms if the homeless man has claimed that shopfront.' Maggie knew from the various multi-agency meetings she had attended over the years that the homeless often claim their 'beds', so she hoped that their person of interest would be easy to identify if he perhaps slept there regularly.

'Here's hoping he hasn't moved on. He might have only been in the area for a short time.' Kat took a drag from her cigarette.

She was right, but Maggie didn't want to deal with that possibility now, so ignored the comment. 'Check back in an hour – or sooner if you've found something.' Maggie doled out the shelter details and after waving goodbye to her colleagues, walked briskly towards the one she had designated for herself. Never Alone Night Shelter (NANS) had only been in the town centre for the last eighteen months or so, according to their website. They had a daily drop-in centre where the homeless could get help with forms, some new clothes and a hot meal, and some bed spaces for the evenings, along with outreach services whereby individuals would drive around the town with packages to help those less fortunate. Maggie recalled hearing about them at one of the Multi Agency Public Protection Arrangements (MAPPA) meetings, when one of their offenders had been accessing their services. The Manager had been helpful at the time and Maggie hoped he would be able to offer some insight.

Maggie pressed the intercom and waited for someone to respond.

'Never Alone – how can I help?'

'Hi. My name is DC Jamieson from Stafford Police Station. I wondered if Mr Reed is available for a quick chat.'

The door buzzed and Maggie pushed it open. The hallway was darker than she had expected for the time of day – she clocked the emergency lighting strips across the ceiling which led down the hallway and she followed it to the end, where a young man sat behind a Plexiglas window. 'I've let Alex know you're here. If you'd just sign in, I'll buzz you through to the waiting area.' He passed a clipboard through the gap and Maggie signed the sheet, scanning the previous names in case she needed the details later.

The reception area was much brighter than where she had just come from – more welcoming. Maggie took a seat and looked around at all the brochures for hostels, charity shops and agencies who might be able to assist those in need. Five minutes later, she immediately recognised Alex Reed as he called her through to yet another area in the building.

'Thanks for seeing me at short notice. I don't know if you remember me, but we met at a MAPPA meeting a few months back?'

'How could I forget?' He gave a half smile. 'What can I do for the police today?'

Maggie followed him into his office and took a seat, taking in the clinical feel of the room.

'Do you get many people coming here?' Realising she needed to be more specific, she added, 'I mean, how well do you know them personally?'

'Some months are busier than others – like winter for instance, but we get a steady flow of people through our doors. Of course, I can't know everyone, but as I was once in the position they're in now, I do my best to get to know as many as I can.'

Maggie's eyebrows rose. She hadn't realised Reed had once lived on the streets.

'What? I don't look like someone who could have been homeless?'

She coughed in a poor attempt to hide her embarrassment. 'Sorry. It's just, you seem so...'

'Put together? Clean? Intelligent? Don't be embarrassed – I can understand how easy it is for people to look at me now and think there was no way I could have been living on the streets – but I did.'

Maggie warmed to Alex immediately. He was straight-talking and reminded her how easy it is to jump to the wrong conclusions, but rather than make the person feel stupid, he had a calming tone to his voice that put you at ease.

'With government cuts to agencies... particularly those that work with youths or people with mental health issues, it seems...' He shook his head. 'People become homeless for lots of different reasons. Poverty, unemployment, life events – you see, people can become homeless when they leave prison, or care... or there may be childhood trauma that they just can't cope with in their adult years...' He paused, and Maggie got the feeling the last one was significant to Alex Reed. 'It can be the trigger. Being homeless can, in turn, make many of these problems even harder to resolve.' He shifted in his seat. 'My apologies. You didn't come here for a lecture, and I said I'd help. So, what is it I can do for you today?'

Maggie pulled out her phone and showed Alex the picture on her screen. 'I know it's a long shot, but do you recognise this man?'

He reached forward, brushing Maggie's hand as he grasped the phone. 'May I?'

Maggie handed him the phone.

She watched as he enlarged the picture on the screen. Did she see something flash in his eyes? A moment of recognition?

It went as quickly as it came, and he returned the phone to Maggie.

'It's really hard to tell from that picture but he does look familiar. I recognise that shopfront. We do late-night outreach services and I've been by there many a cold night, handing out blankets and hot coffee.'

'Any names jump into your head?'

'With the face partially covered... I'm sorry – I can't think of any, but if you want to send me that picture, I can perhaps ask around, give it to my team and ask them to keep an eye out when they are doing outreach this evening?'

'That would be really helpful.'

He passed his card to Maggie and she forwarded the picture to his phone.

'I don't mean to speak out of turn, but can you tell me what all this is about? I mean, has this person done something serious?'

'No, at the moment we just want to speak with him to help us with our enquiries.'

'An investigation? Do you think he may have witnessed something? I mean, should I be warning my team to be extra vigilant?' He sat back in his chair and frowned.

Maggie didn't think the homeless community were at risk specifically, as Daniel Firth certainly wasn't homeless at any time in his life, from what they had learned so far. 'No, we don't believe there is any direct risk, but I would advise that if you do come across the person in the photo, you call me immediately or contact the police station. We don't want anyone trying to be a hero...'

Alex stood. 'OK. Well, I'll make sure to pass on the

warning, and thanks for coming by. If you need anything else, please don't hesitate to contact me.'

Alex Reed escorted Maggie to the exit but before she left, she reached into her pocket and took out a ten-pound note and placed it in the jar at the reception desk.

'Thanks so much. Truly kind of you.' He brushed her arm.

Maggie smiled but felt uneasy at his over-friendliness. Her initial assessment of the manager was shifting; the change in his demeanour made the hair on the back of her neck stand up.

Chapter Twenty-Three

I t was time. After dealing with some unexpected distractions, he was ready to put his plans into action. Her diary had indicated that she was off today. It still amazed him how easy it was to access what should be confidential information. He tapped the lid of his laptop closed and locked it away.

After wrestling with his thoughts on the best mode of transport, he decided that this one would require flexibility, so the bus and his own two legs were the best way forward. He worked out everything meticulously; he wasn't ready to be caught – there was still too much to be done. He grabbed his backpack and the two water bottles filled with petrol. Wrapping them in a towel, he placed them securely in the bag. He laid the bag down carefully and went to change – things could get messy. Returning to collect the bag, he put some spare clothing in it, along with everything else he needed.

He was ready.

Outside, he pulled a scarf up around his neck and a

baseball cap down over his eyes and walked to the bus stop. He spent the bus journey thinking of the various ways he could make her pay for what she had done to him – to all of them.

She lived in a well off area just on the outskirts of Stafford in a village called Bletchley Fields – it was a bitch to get to. The good thing, though, was that it was fairly secluded, so it was unlikely that any of the stuck-up neighbours would hear the bitch scream.

And boy, was he going to make her scream.

He got off the bus about a mile before her address because he wanted to run through everything in his head again. He'd been to the house before – checking out the neighbourhood, looking at access, doing a dry run of his travel time and escape route, and he'd even made it inside once when he posed as a gardener touting for business.

If he walked through the fields at the back, he could climb over the stone wall surrounding her property. He knew she'd be home alone after he'd overheard her at the Courts telling a colleague she was having a 'me' day. Then he'd double-checked her online diary.

A fucking me day. Stuck-up bitch.

Prosecutor Sadie Ramsey had had no time for him or the others all those years ago.

'There's not enough evidence…' Her voice was etched in his mind, on repeat like a sticking record.

He remembered how she had looked at them all – like they were just dirty little scrotes. She didn't say it out loud, that wouldn't be professional, but her eyes spoke volumes. He wasn't even convinced now that she had ever believed them and their statements to the police. Nobody wanted to listen.

She'd listen now.

At the back of the house, he scaled the stone wall, peering over the top before dropping down behind the shed. He landed awkwardly and had to stifle a cry when a pain shot up his left leg. He shook it out. Nothing was going to stop him from completing his mission.

He crept along the edge of the garden, crouching down and keeping an eye out for anything that might ruin his plans. He stopped at the side of the conservatory and reached into the small pocket on the front of his backpack, pulling out his lock-picking kit. The door was a simple lock, and he was inside within a minute or two. He stood still, cocking his head to listen out for sounds. Silence all around.

A creak from the left stopped him in his tracks.

'What? No. You'll have to wait until tomorrow – I am not dealing with anything today.'

He cringed at the sound of her voice.

She was on the phone. He edged around the couch and lay flat on the floor. Her shoes clapped slowly on the tiled floor in the kitchen as she carried on talking to whoever had called. He spotted the wheelchair in the corner. She had suffered a stroke a few years back and her mobility seemed to come and go. Seems today was a good day for her.

'I'm hanging up now. Get someone else to deal with it – it's hardly an emergency. Bye.' He heard her mumble something that sounded like 'twats' and then a deep sigh. He crept slowly along the floor towards the door that led to the hallway. With her in the kitchen, he could sneak up and surprise her easily.

From the hallway he followed the corridor, making sure not to make a sound. He peered through the archway. She stood, hanging onto the counter, staring out into her garden – luckily he had arrived when he did, or she might have spotted him. That was karma reassuring him. He knelt and crept behind the counter – she turned and was walking in stilted movements towards him now. He would wait until she reached the end of the counter unit and... He grabbed her legs and pulled her to the ground. She tried to scream but he crawled on top of her and covered her mouth with his gloved hand.

'This can go easy or it can go hard. Keep your mouth shut and do what I say.' He smiled when her eyes widened, and she nodded her head. He lifted his hand off her mouth slowly.

'OK. OK. I'll do whatever you say. The safe is upstairs and my wallet is in the living room. You can have whatever you want.' The words spluttered from her mouth.

'I don't want your money.' He pulled himself up and straddled her chest, pinning her arms down with his knees.

'Ow. You're hurting me.'

'If you think this is bad, just you wait...' He stopped himself from saying any more. 'I don't want to ruin the surprise.'

'Do... do I know you?' She stared at him closely.

The bloody cheek of her. His neck burned. 'Oh, you know me... but you probably don't remember me. I'll help you with that once we get everything sorted.'

'Please, can you get off my arms? I promise, I'll do everything you say. I can't get away from you anyway, I had a stroke – you could outrun me easily. You're really hurting me.'

'Oh, shit. I'm really sorry. Let me fix that for you.' He started to lift himself off her and when she moved to sit up, he punched her in the face. She fell back and hit her head on the tiled floor and there was no movement after that. She was knocked out cold.

That's better. He was sick of listening to her whine anyway. He removed the backpack from his shoulders and unzipped it. He pulled out the gaffer tape and cable ties and taped her mouth before securing her hands behind her back. He lifted her over his shoulder and took her towards the dining table, placing her down on one of the chairs. He had thought about using the wheelchair, but preferred wood – it burns, metal doesn't. He tied her ankles to the chair and looped another cable tie through the one on her wrists, tightening it to the back of the chair. Once she was secured, he closed the curtains. Although the surrounding houses didn't overlook her property, he couldn't be sure that someone might not be out walking their dog in the fields.

He looked forward to what would be next. She was still unconscious – but not for long. He walked into the kitchen and poured a glass of water. He heard a low groan from the other room and when he returned, he threw the water in her face.

'Wake up, bitch. Time for you to face your *justice*.' He spat the word at her. 'Think I want to have a little *me* time too.'

Chapter Twenty-Four

On her way back to Stafford Police Station from the shelter, Maggie bumped into her colleagues. They chatted and compared notes, Kat confirming that a few people recognised the homeless man but couldn't tell her a name other than 'the music man'.

'Maybe he's been cautioned or arrested for breach of the peace? Not sure how we are going to find out that information without more details, but it's worth speaking to the Neighbourhood team who do patrols in the area.'

'Great idea, Kat. If he is known in the community, it may be something we can use to reach out to the public as well. I know I wouldn't want to be woken in the early hours by a trumpet, no matter how good the player was, and I certainly wouldn't forget it if I had been.'

'I think Kat can fill you in on everything, so if you don't mind, I will leave it up to you both – if you do find anything out, let me know and I'll cross-reference any information with my profile. Would you mind if I head back now?' The Doc looked at her watch.

'Totally fine by me. Kat, are you OK if we continue to canvass the area? I wonder if some of the local shops may have some useful information. Catch you later, Doc.' Maggie waved.

'Someone around here must know where we can find him.' Kat was looking around the town square.

'Let's first head to the shop in the picture.' This & That, a pawn shop, was in the middle of the town centre. When they arrived, a young, long-haired man who looked like he could use a good wash was behind the counter. Maggie introduced herself and they both showed their warrant cards. Maggie noticed the man's eyes shift to the door on his right and her curiosity got the best of her.

'I'm not sure why you think we're here, so I'll clear it up before you make a foolish mistake and try to bolt for that door.' There was an odd smell in the air.

'I've no clue what you're talking about, officer.'

'OK – if you say so.' Maggie pulled out her phone and showed the man the picture. 'Do you recognise this person?'

He moved in closer and stared at the phone. 'Yeah – that's the geezer with the trumpet. We have to kick him out of the front door most mornings. Called the police a few times, as well, when he got a bit aggro and waved his trumpet around – like he was gonna hit me. What's he done?' Maggie noticed his shoulders loosen.

'We'd just like to speak with him. Might be a long shot, but would you happen to know where he goes once you move him on?'

'Nah, but there are a lot of homeless people in the underpass – you know, the one that leads to the prison?'

'I know where he's on about – it's about twenty minutes' walk from here.' Kat pointed towards the door.

'Thanks so much for your help. Can I get your details, in case we have any follow-up questions?'

The man shifted from foot to foot. 'Why? I told you everything I know.'

'Like I said, we may have further questions for you.' Maggie took out her notebook and glared. Reluctantly he shared his information. She handed him one of her cards and told him to ring if he saw the music man in the area. 'Just don't be a hero, OK?'

The man shrugged, placed her card in a pile with others, and the pair headed towards the underpass.

'What was his problem?' Maggie turned to Kat.

'Couldn't you smell the weed? He must have thought we were going to bust him for drugs. I'll pass the information on when we get back to the station, but he doesn't come across as one of the big players, so probably for personal use or dealing to mates. He doesn't strike me as a fucking criminal mastermind.'

'I thought I smelled something, cat piss actually. Must be a new strand.'

'Yeah, not the usual skunk weed we normally come across.' Kat tapped Maggie's shoulder and pointed. 'There's the underpass over there.'

They crossed the road and Maggie was shocked to see the number of homeless men, women and even teenagers under the bridge. 'Shall we split up? I'll take the left side.'

Kat nodded and made her way towards a group of men playing cards on the ground. Maggie scanned the area quickly to see if she could spot the jacket, but if the music man was there, he wasn't wearing the coat. Maggie walked towards two youths who were sitting against the wall talking. They didn't look up when Maggie stood in front of them.

'Do you smell bacon?' one of the boys laughed.

'If you're referring to me, have the courage to look me in the face when you insult me.' Maggie crouched down. 'I'm not here to cause any trouble, I just want to know if you or your friend here recognise this man?' She showed them her phone.

'Music Matty. What about him? He rob the off-licence again?' The boy nudged his friend. ''Member when he got so pissed, he thought his trumpet was a bottle of vodka and then went on one when he couldn't find the bottle of voddie next to him?' The pair burst out laughing.

'Hey. I get it – you don't like police, but I'd really appreciate it if you could tell me if this Music Matty is here, or if you know where we might find him.'

'Haven't seen him today. Check the park by the station. He sometimes sleeps in the bushes by the shack. Now can you bugger off – you interrupted me and my mate. I don't know nothin' else, so move on… pig.'

Maggie let the snide remark go and stood up. She spoke to a few other people who confirmed that Music Matty hadn't been there for a while.

'Any luck?' Kat was taking a cigarette out of the carton.

'A few people I spoke to said he hangs out at the park.' Maggie looked at the time on her phone. 'Let's head there now and if he's not there, we'll go back to the station and speak to the Neighbourhood Policing Team.'

Kat lit the smoke and took a long drag. 'Lead the way.'

Chapter Twenty-Five

Victoria Park was relatively quiet. Maggie observed a few older gentlemen playing bowls and Kat was easily distracted by the birds in the aviary until Maggie tapped her shoulder and reminded her why they were there.

'How about you go across the bridge and start looking there – speak to anyone you come across and I'll do the same this side. Radio me if you find anything.'

'Will do.' Kat jogged over to and across the bridge as Maggie headed down the path, eyeing up the bushes. It wasn't long before she spotted Music Matty. He was curled up under one of the larger bushes, a thick blanket wrapped around him. Maggie didn't want to startle him and approached with caution – the last thing she wanted was to get a trumpet in the head. As she got closer, her foot caught in a branch, nearly tripping her up, and she had to catch her balance. 'Fucksake.'

Music Matty was up and running before Maggie even had a chance to say anything. She radioed Kat. 'He's heading your way. I'm following, so maybe we can corner him. He's going to be going over the bridge in about two minutes.'

'*I see him.*'

Maggie pushed herself to run faster and as she was going over the bridge, she saw Kat straddling him.

'You got him…' Maggie stopped, hands on hips, and took a moment to catch her breath.

'I had to jump him because he wasn't going to stop – even after I identified myself.' Kat looked up at her.

Maggie held out her hand and pulled Kat up. She then held out her hand for Music Matty. He swiped it away and looked to be making a move to run again. 'You don't want to do that. My colleague here will cuff you…'

He stopped and turned around to face them.

'Let me introduce us properly. I'm DC Jamieson and this is DC Everett. We just want to talk to you.'

'What if I don't wanna talk to you?' His face twisted as he spoke. Maggie didn't blame him, as they had disturbed his sleep.

'You do need to come with us to the station – we could do it the easy way, or the hard way. You see, you're wearing a coat that places you at the scene of a crime.'

He looked down at his coat. 'This? I only just got it, so fuck off, copper.'

'Why don't you tell us where you found it, then, as we head back to the station?' Maggie's voice softened.

'What's it worth?' Music Matty's head tilted.

Maggie admired his cockiness and hid a smile. 'How about I make sure you get a coffee and a sandwich? We'll even throw in a new coat, as we'll have to take that one in for evidence.'

'How about you get me a bottle of whisky or vodka? I'm not fussy.' He wrapped his arms around the jacket.

'I can't do that, I'm afraid. Hot drink and a sarnie, or we'll have to call out our colleagues and have them escort you in a police car.'

'Fuckers! OK, OK. I found the coat in the dumpster behind Sainsbury's – over that way.'

'The one off Lapley Road?' Kat was writing as they walked.

'I guess. Don't pay much attention to the road names.'

'Do you remember when that was?'

'Today? Maybe yesterday? I haven't had it long, I swear. I threw my old jacket in the dumpster – you can check and maybe get it back for me, if you're taking this one. Might still be there.' He was getting agitated.

'Kat, can you do me a favour and grab a few sandwiches and stuff?' Maggie pulled some money out of her pocket and gave it to her colleague. 'We'll head back to the station.' Maggie then leaned in and whispered, 'If you could also get forensics over to the Sainsbury's, and see if Bethany can link into and check the CCTV – we'll see if Matty here is being honest with us.' Maggie looked over at the man, whose arms were flailing. 'He's getting anxious, I better go now.'

Kat eyed her. 'You sure you'll be OK with him?'

'She'll be fine. What do you think I'm going to do to her?' Music Matty growled.

'Oi – I meant no offence. I was just asking. I'll see you back at the station.' Kat turned and walked towards the café while Maggie and the music man carried on towards the station.

———

Music Matty wasn't under arrest, but Maggie took him through to the Custody Suite so they could bag his coat. She also went through the lost and found and picked out a sweater and coat to replace the one they confiscated for evidence. When Maggie handed them to him, he snatched them out of her hands. She stood back while he put them on and a crooked smile appeared for a short time, before the scowl re-emerged.

'Uh, thanks. These are even better than that tat you took from me. What do you need to know?'

Maggie led Matty to an interview room and directed him to sit down. Just as he did, Kat walked in and dropped off the sandwiches and coffee.

'Can I have these now?' He pulled the bag towards him.

Maggie nodded and then shook her head as he offered her one. 'That's all for you. Whatever you don't finish, take with you. While you're eating I'll just ask my few questions, and then you'll be free to go.' Maggie was sure that the man in front of her had nothing to do with the murder. 'You say you found the coat in the last few days? It wasn't later than that?' Maggie didn't want to be specific with the timeline, in case Matty knew more than he was letting on.

'I don't know – could have been sometime this week. Time doesn't mean much to me and most days, I'm not exactly... sober.' He shoved half the sandwich in his mouth and washed it down with a gulp of coffee. 'You sure you can't get me some whisky? Might help me remember better.'

'No can do. Just take a moment and try and recall whether you noticed anyone else at the dumpster, or nearby, as you went to the back of the store. Maybe you heard something you didn't think was important at the time?'

'Nope. It was dead quiet. I was hoping to find some decent food – you should see the stuff they throw out. What a waste. I had to dig deep, though, before I found the jacket.'

So, the killer had hidden it, probably hoping the dumpster would be emptied before anyone found it.

'OK. That's great. Do you want to stay and finish those here?' Maggie wasn't going to get much out of him but passed him one of her cards, which he flipped around before placing it in his pocket.

'Thanks for the grub.' He stood and followed Maggie out.

'Where can we find you if we have any further questions?'

'I go to Never Alone every Tuesday and Thursday. Otherwise, I sleep in whatever shop doorway I can find, or the park. I like to keep myself to myself. Just me and the music, you know?' He tapped his trumpet case.

Maggie nodded. 'OK. It was nice meeting you, Matty. Maybe one day I can hear you play.'

She thought she saw him smile.

'Whatever…'

She watched him head back towards the park and was about to head up to the office when Sarah Hardy came through the doors and into the reception area.

'Sarah? Do you have a meeting here? I can take you through.'

'Can we go outside?' Sarah's eyes darted around the reception area.

Maggie followed Sarah around the corner of the building. 'Are you working at Stafford Probation today?'

'Breach court. But that's not why I'm here.'

'OK. How can I help?'

'It's Justin. He's been acting strange. He's hiding

something. Have you guys spoken to him again?' Sarah couldn't stand still.

'First, calm down. What do you mean, he's been acting strange? And no – we haven't. He has an appointment with Kat to go through his statement – soon, I think. I don't know when, off the top of my head. What's happened, Sarah?'

Tears started rolling down her face and she pulled out a tissue. 'Sorry. I haven't stopped crying since this all happened.' She blew her nose. 'He's putting extra locks on the house. The curtains are constantly closed, and he snaps at me for anything I say. I feel like a prisoner in my own home.'

'Oh, Sarah! I'm so sorry to hear that. Do you want me to put you in touch with…?' She stopped. Sarah was a Probation Officer, so would have her own connections. 'Sorry. You probably know plenty of people to talk to. I'm still not sure what I can do.'

'I just wondered if you could probe him when he comes in again. I mean, should I be afraid? Is someone after him? He won't talk to me about any of it.'

'We'll cover all bases, but you know as well as I do that if he discloses something, I can't discuss that with you.'

'Even if I'm at risk?' Sarah pleaded with her and Maggie was torn.

'Well… of course, if there is any risk to you, we would have to speak…'

Sarah's phone rang and after looking at the screen, she looked around. 'This was a bad idea. I shouldn't have put you in this situation. Sorry. I'm probably overreacting. Ignore what I said.' And with that she turned and headed towards the courts.

'Sarah! Sarah! Come back.' But she waved her hand in the air without even turning to look at Maggie.

What the hell was that about?

Chapter Twenty-Six

The first thing she did when she got upstairs was make a beeline to Nathan's office, but he wasn't about. 'Anyone know where the boss is?'

'He was with DI Rutherford.' Bethany looked at her watch. 'Not sure if he's still there now. Didn't even realise the time.'

'Thanks.' Maggie turned on her heels and headed to Rutherford's office. The door was closed, and she peered through the window. Nathan wasn't there, but Rutherford was. She tapped on the door. Rutherford looked up and waved her in.

'What can I do for you, Maggie?'

'Sorry to disturb you, I was looking for Nathan, but maybe you can help. Sarah Hardy just approached me downstairs. She's worried about her husband and wants us to speak with him.'

'Hang on. Was this a social call – I mean, do I need to be concerned? I had some flak letting you stay on the last case…'

Maggie had heard there was some grief when she worked

the Living Doll case and was grateful that the Guv had her back, but this was definitely not the same. 'Sarah's a Probation Officer; we've often spoken to her and her colleagues about cases… It was her husband's office where the body was found.' Maggie frowned. DI Rutherford should know this.

Rutherford rubbed her temple. 'Okay. Yes – I knew that, didn't I? Not had much sleep lately. Is there a conflict here I need to be aware of?'

'I wouldn't say so, Guv. My concern is that she believes her husband is hiding something from us and has asked me to interview him again. I did explain to her that I wouldn't be able to share that with her unless there was a risk to her. I think she's more concerned about her job and how it might impact her.'

'Right. Well, that's interesting but not really our concern. Are we looking to speak with him again?'

'Yeah, I didn't tell Sarah but I think he's down to come in tomorrow – I'd have to double-check that though. I just wanted to be clear and upfront so that nothing comes back and bites us – or me – on the arse.'

'You did the right thing. OK, let's see what he has to say first before we jump to any conclusions. If we do think he is hiding something, we'll do what we always do and push him hard. No favouritism because we've worked with his wife. It's getting late, can we pick things up again tomorrow?'

'Have a good night, Guv.' Maggie went back to her desk and collected her things.

When she stepped outside, the rain spat on her face. 'Fucksake.' She wiped the drops from her eyes. She hadn't seen Kate's new place yet and wondered if she was in. She called her mobile number.

'Hey, I didn't see you before I left, how did things go?' asked Kate.

'Good, thanks. Look, I just finished work and wondered if you were home. It's starting to rain, and I haven't seen your place, so I thought I could stop by and wait for the weather to change before jumping on the train. If you're busy – no worries.'

'That's great. I'll text the address – it's not far from the station. See you soon.'

Her phone beeped and when she saw the address, she realised it was only about a fifteen-minute walk.

Kate's flat was above an electronics shop at the opposite end of town. Maggie buzzed and smiled when Kate opened the door.

'Head on up.' Kate moved aside.

Maggie walked up the steep stairway and listened as Kate dead-bolted the door behind her.

'Did you install the extra locks?' Maggie waited at the top.

'Actually, they were already there. Probably because the owner of the shop below used to live here. Extra security measure, I guess. It's one of the reasons I chose this place – that and the fact that the police station is literally around the corner. The commute to Tamworth isn't too bad either. Come through.'

Maggie followed Kate into the flat. It was spacious and she spotted paint cans and boxes in the corner.

'Excuse the mess. I still have a few things to do before I feel like it's my place. But I've plenty of time – and who knows how long I'll stay here?'

Maggie turned to Kate. 'Why's that? I thought you liked your job.'

'Oh, I do. I just meant I'd like to buy something – rather than renting. That way I could really do what I want. You'll notice the paint – not a colour I would choose, but the landlord agreed I could paint over that awful blue as long as it wasn't too… outrageous. Her actual words.' Kate laughed. 'Can I get you a drink or anything – or maybe a quick tour?'

'I can't stay too long but a tour would be great. Where's Salem?'

'In my room. Come… I'll show you.'

Maggie saw a small corridor as she passed through the open-plan kitchen, and a door on the right which she assumed was the bathroom. Kate's room was a good size. Salem was curled up on a chair in the far corner under the window. 'Aww… I won't disturb him. Glad to see he settled back quickly.' Something caught her eye over the small desk against the back wall.

'What do you have there?' Maggie pointed to the whiteboard.

'Just some ideas about the case – it's a mess, but I like to note things down as thoughts come into my head. Have a look if you'd like… and if you can read it – I obviously don't want to breach any confidentiality, so I anonymised things.'

Maggie walked over to the board. Red circles with black writing in them and lines of various colours joining things together. 'What does it all mean?'

'Well, you see our vic's name there.' Kate pointed. 'I looked at all the notes we have so far and wanted to highlight the connections – which are the yellow lines – so care homes, and of course trying to figure out where or if Justin Hardy fits in.

Then the blue lines indicate previous jobs, and the empty circle is waiting to be filled with more specifics. We know Firth's latest job was as a self-employed painter and decorator, but also that he worked in a few care homes – the only one we know for sure is Chatham House, but I suspect there are others. Where did he train, for instance? Where did he go to school? What other history about him do we know?'

'So, all this will form your victimology? And how do *you* think Hardy fits with all this?' Maggie waved her arms around the board.

'Maybe nothing – but he did know him and when I read his initial statement and the police observations at the time, something just didn't sit right with me. He was very closed off.'

'Hmmm... I got that feeling too.' Maggie looked out the window. 'Looks like the rain has stopped, I better get going. Great place you have here.' Kate walked Maggie out and as she made her way to the station, she wondered what had triggered Kate to put Justin Hardy in the victimology details.

She had been about to tell her about the visit from Sarah, but then thought better of it. Her fear was that any additional information might affect the Doc's profile at this stage and until she knew more herself, she didn't want to jeopardise that. It would all be raised in the briefing anyway.

On the train journey home she decided she would check out Hardy & Associates before making her way into the office the next morning. She didn't like loose ends and it was time to tie this one up.

Chapter Twenty-Seven

He was so glad her husband was away; it meant he'd have more time with her – and she deserved his attention. Time was getting on though, and he had some things to get off his chest.

'Bet you never expected to see me again, did you?' The terror in her eyes excited him. He hoped that she was feeling a fraction of what he and the others had felt when she turned her back on them. 'How could you let them all get away with it? We were just kids, for fucksake...' He shook his head, not expecting an answer, but at least an acknowledgement of what she was responsible for. 'Still playing dumb, eh? Got nothing to say for yourself?' He ripped the tape from her mouth. 'If you scream, you'll be sorry.'

Her eyes darted around the room.

'What are you looking for? Someone to come in and save you? I know that feeling too – but just like then, it ain't happening for you either. How can you sleep at night?'

'I'm s-s-s-orry. I don't know w-what's happened to you, but if it was m-my fault, I am sorry. Let m-me help you now…'

He lunged forward and she flinched. 'Now is a little too late, don't you think? I thought Crown Prosecutors were supposed to be clever. Don't you know the damage that's caused to a child who suffers trauma in their early years? What kind of fucking person doesn't know that? It doesn't take a genius. You can't change that now – no matter how much therapy is offered…' He raised his hand but then thought better of it. Instead, he opened his bag and pulled out the pliers.

Her eyes widened. 'What are you going to d-do with those?'

'Exactly what was done to me and countless others, bitch. Now this can be easy, or it can be hard. That will all depend on you. You see, the more you moan, flinch or squirm, the longer this will take and the more you'll be in pain. Well,' he twirled the pliers in his hand, 'you're gonna feel a little pain because I won't be using any anaesthetic…'

Her mouth started to move, a grimace formed, and he knew she was about to scream.

'Don't you dare say a fucking word.' His jaw clenched. He pulled out another tool he needed from the bag. 'See this – I got it online. It will make my job a lot easier. Now open your mouth.'

She shook her head and held her mouth closed. So tight he could see her wince with pain as her lips pressed against her teeth.

'I didn't want to do this, but you leave me no choice.' He whacked her in the jaw and waited as her head slumped forward.

He tugged her head back by her hair and prised open her mouth. He reached into his bag and removed a small woodblock, placing it in between the top and bottom teeth to hold her mouth open. He pushed the gums with the periosteal elevator, to loosen the gum tissue from the tooth itself. Her tooth was firmly rooted, and it took him a while to release it from the jaw bone. She was starting to come around. He placed the pliers on the tooth and yanked as hard as he could. The tooth fell to the floor as she screamed.

He covered her mouth with his gloved hand and with the other, reached into his bag and pulled out a sock. He jammed it into her mouth as she spluttered.

'Careful or you'll choke – and I want you to be alive for the next bit.'

He picked the tooth up off the floor and went to the kitchen sink where he rinsed it under the tap, drying it before placing it in his pocket.

He heard a movement from the other room and when he turned, she was rocking back and forth on the chair. He laughed out loud. 'Do you think that is going to help you escape? Go on, fall over. What are you going to do then? Makes no difference to me whether you are sitting up or lying on your side for this next part.' He stood and watched her. She was determined and he had to smile at her focus.

The chair fell over and she lay on her side, struggling with the bindings that held her hands and feet to the furniture. 'It's actually your fault that you have such sturdy pieces. Any other wooden chair probably would have broken.' He clapped his hands. 'A for effort though.' He returned to the room and took the bottle of petrol out of his bag. She turned and looked in his eyes and then at the bottle in his hands. A muffled scream caused her to go into a fit of coughing.

but are relevant to the investigation. You were pretty shaken up when we first spoke. It's nothing to be concerned about.'

Unless of course, Justin was hiding something. That would explain his behaviour.

Before they left the office, Maggie had one more question. 'That's a lovely painting.' She headed towards the picture on the wall, but Justin stepped in front of her.

'Yeah. My father gave it me. Uh, I'm ready to go – I could use a coffee, actually.' He tried to lead Maggie away, but she stepped around him and moved the picture – it wasn't flat against the wall.

She had to use some force to hoist the picture down, and this revealed an inbuilt wall safe. 'What's this then?' It would have been easy to assume that the picture was just secured to the wall, though if it turned out to be something important, someone would have to answer why it was missed.

'Can you open this, please?' Maggie moved aside and watched as he punched in the safe code. Justin's shoulders slumped as he pulled open the door and revealed what was inside.

And then he gasped. It was empty.

'You seem surprised.' Maggie stood with her arms folded.

'Uh… no. I told you it was nothing. It was here when I started renting the office. But as business has been shit, there was nothing really to store in there.'

Maggie wasn't convinced by his explanation but it would be something they could pursue when Justin came into the station, as it was clear he wasn't going to say anything more on the subject here.

'Let's go get that coffee then…'

Chapter Twenty-Nine

The call came just as Maggie and Justin had started walking towards the café. 'Excuse me, Mr Hardy – I need to get this.' She waited as he walked a short distance ahead, giving her privacy to take the call.

'Hey, what's up?'

'A fire, that's what. Started in a property located in Hyde Sea – body found. Forensics are at the scene and we're heading there now. Where are you?' Nathan sounded breathless.

'Literally around the corner from the station. Hang tight and I'll be there in five.' Maggie ended the call and shouted over to Justin, 'I'm sorry – we're going to have to do this another time. Someone will be in touch.' She didn't wait for an answer before she turned and ran back towards Stafford Police Station. As she approached the front doors, a horn beeped and Kat called out through the passenger window, 'Get in.'

Maggie ran to the car and jumped in. 'Has Nathan left then? I was just on the phone with him.' She gulped in air as she caught her breath. Yoga wasn't doing much for her fitness yet.

Kat put the car into gear and pulled away from the kerb. 'Yeah. He left with Rutherford. Sounds like it could be the same killer – why else would we be called out to a fire?'

'Without knowing what happened, I wouldn't want to presume you're right... It's likely there is cause to believe it's connected to our case. Do you know anything else about it?'

'A neighbour called it in after smelling something when she was out back in her garden. She headed towards the bottom of her garden and saw smoke, so called the fire brigade. She'd spoken to the female occupant earlier that morning and believed she was inside.'

'We know who the victim is?'

'Well, not officially, but a family lived there – uh, Sadie Ramsey... she worked for the CPS – do you know her?'

Maggie gasped. 'Yes. It's her house?'

'That's what we've been told. Lives there with her husband. One grown daughter, but I don't know if she resided at the premises. You're frowning, what's up?'

'I don't know yet.' Maggie bit her lip. Her mind was racing and a knot formed in her stomach. She knew Sadie prosecuted a lot of cases involving children and wondered if there was some connection between Daniel Firth's murder and what they were about to see.

When they arrived at the crime scene, they signed themselves in, and Maggie put on the appropriate gear before separating from Kat, who had been instructed to do some door-to-door enquires. Once inside, she was careful to follow the common approach path and she looked around for Nathan. She didn't have to look far, as he was the tallest in a group of people standing around Dr Blake, who was bent over, examining the victim.

'Any ID yet?' Maggie sidled up to Nathan.

'Nothing formal, but from what we can gather, we believe it's Sadie Ramsey. Dr Blake has confirmed the victim is female...'

Dr Fiona Blake turned at the mention of her name and eyed Maggie up and down before returning to the task before her.

Maggie ignored the snub but was surprised that the pathologist still seemed to hold a grudge following the Living Doll case. One of her forensic team had been questioned regarding some unusual behaviour and the pathologist couldn't seem to let go of that. Maggie wondered if she should confront her, as it was getting ridiculous – the hot-and-cold treatment was becoming tiresome. Today was not the time or place, though.

'What a way to go.' Maggie took in the scene. The chair the victim had been secured to had been toppled on its side. Did the killer do this or did the victim make an attempt to escape, sealing her fate in the process?

'Rutherford is outside talking to the Fire Investigators. They were the first to arrive on the scene. Notice the similarities to the Firth murder?' Nathan stepped back from the crowd.

'Yes... Wonder if they knew each other? Could lead us to a viable person of interest if we can find someone connected to both victims.'

'Do you think it could be more than one person? Although similar to the last scene, there are some significant differences.

The toppled chair, the open window, the home as the primary crime scene.' Nathan looked over at her as she walked around the body.

'Maybe. Do we know how they gained access to the property?'

'Via the door through the conservatory – it was unlocked when the fire brigade arrived. There were no markings or evidence of a break-in. Front door was locked when we arrived.' Maggie followed Nathan into the conservatory and looked out the back.

'Do you think he scaled the wall? There are fields behind there. Dog walkers, hikers and the like often use it. I knew someone who used to follow the walking trails back there.' She looked at the hills beyond. 'It wouldn't be difficult to do this,' she pointed to the body, '… and then make an escape out the back there.'

'I was thinking that too. They've called the dogs in to search the wider area.' Nathan wandered back into the dining area with Maggie close behind.

'I've done all that I can here. Charlie's going to finish up and bag the body. I'll be in touch.' Dr Blake stood.

'Anything more before you go?' Nathan rubbed his chin.

'Without the benefit of the post-mortem, I'd hazard a guess to say that she died in the same way as that last fellow – she probably passed out before the fire completely consumed her, so at least that's a blessing. I can't see any obvious wounds, but that's not to say there aren't any.' The pathologist pointed to the body. 'The skin is burned badly, no telling what I'll find underneath. Oh – I did find some sort of material jammed into her mouth. I'll have something more solid to share with you soon. The quicker I leave, the quicker you'll get your info.' And with that the pathologist turned and left.

'I don't like the sound of this.' Maggie covered her nose as the smell was creeping up her nostrils. 'It can't be a coincidence that we have two burned bodies, the fires confined to the body itself, not so far apart in timing.'

'I agree. Dr Moloney's profile immediately came to mind when I arrived. Feels personal – someone getting revenge for something – we just need to figure out what… and why now?'

'Kat's speaking with the neighbours. Maybe they saw something that might help us with our enquiries. I just hope Julie Noble doesn't start putting her spin on things.'

'I meant to ask you what was happening with her.' He nudged her arm.

'Not really the place, is it?' She smiled and presumed Nathan was just trying to take his mind briefly off the horror in front of them. 'At the moment, we're just friends…'

'Maybe you can use that friendship to influence her to keep a lid on things for the time being…'

Maggie raised a brow. 'You can't be serious. You know what she's like. Anyway, I wouldn't want her to try and influence *me* in any way, so I can't expect to use our friendship for that purpose.' Nathan meant well, but Maggie had made it clear in her own mind that lines would not be crossed. It would complicate things.

'What's our next move, boss?'

Chapter Thirty

He lowered himself as close to the ground as he could get and removed a travel-sized pair of binoculars from his bag before shoving it behind the small bushes that surrounded him.

Then he watched.

He could see the officers walking around the back garden, poking the bushes, bending down and examining the ground, hoping he had dropped something... anything. They were moving so fast, but he wasn't too concerned. He owned generic boots. *Good luck finding something distinctive*, he sniggered to himself.

He saw her standing in the conservatory. Detective Constable Maggie Jamieson... She was looking right at him now. She was good at her job and there she was – watching him watching her looking for him. But only he knew that; she was none the wiser.

A loud bark echoed in the distance coming from the direction of the house.

'Fuck.'

He crawled back and dragged his bag to his feet. As soon as he couldn't see the house, he stood and waded through the creek that divided the fields from the village across the way. He looked around and when he confirmed the coast was clear, he removed his hoodie and replaced it with a yellow windbreaker he had stored in his rucksack. He placed his wet boots in a plastic bag and put on the spare trainers from his bag. He'd dispose of the boots in a bin along the way.

He put his earphones in his ears, but didn't switch on any music. He still needed to be aware of what was going on around him. Then he began to jog away, towards the village where he would blend in. Just another runner in the fields... He picked up the pace, looked over his shoulder and smiled. He was glad he had booked the day off work now – he was tired. He grabbed a coffee before he jumped on the bus and headed home.

Chapter Thirty-One

Maggie stood in the doorway of the conservatory before stepping outside and breathing in the fresh air. Officers were looking around the grounds, in the grass and bushes that lined the property.

'Every contact leaves its trace…' she mumbled to herself.

'Huh? What did you say?' Nathan approached from behind.

'Locard's theory about trace – just popped into my head as I watched them.' She pointed to the officers.

'You can be such a geek sometimes.' He laughed and she punched his arm.

'And what? My geekiness comes in handy at times. You never complained when we were partners. I mean, think about it – unless we have a super-intelligent offender, chances are they will have left something of themselves behind. It's unlikely they tried to conceal their footwear – even if they were clever enough to wear gloves or cover their face…'

Nathan nodded and his brows furrowed. He walked over to one of the officers as Maggie looked on.

'Can we make sure that we don't overlook any footwear impressions – even if they look old – our killer may have scoped out the property beforehand.' Nathan glanced up to the sky. 'Looks like it might rain, so best get someone on that ASAP.'

Maggie looked away when the officer tried to catch her eye – his face said it all – he wasn't impressed.

'On it, sir.' He turned his back to Nathan and Maggie hid a smile.

'Well, I think you may have pissed him off, *sir*.' Maggie rubbed her hands together. There was a chill in the air.

'Probably – but we can't risk having evidence dismissed, or it's my arse on the line. Two murders. We don't want a third…'

A bark made Maggie jump. 'Holy fuck. Guess the K9 unit has arrived…' She waited for her heart to stop racing. She wasn't a big fan of dogs. Cats were her animal of choice.

She knew that the dog unit plays an important role in policing – more and more. They can detect smells which persist in an area long after the source – in this case, the killer – has fled a scene. Tracking dogs might also help with the gathering of evidence, as they would track the scent of the path the offender would have taken through the garden. She wasn't a big fan of the beasts, but she admired their skills.

'See if Kat's finished and then head back to the station. We can fill in the rest of the team and plan our next steps.'

Maggie mock saluted Nathan but stood where she was for a little while longer. She watched the large German Shepherd lead the officers along the right-hand side of the garden, across the back wall and behind the shed – then he was gone.

'They're coming to get you,' she whispered before she headed to the front of the property in search of Kat.

Chapter Thirty-Two

'Fucking hell! Do we have a serial now?' Kat stubbed her cigarette out before jumping in the car.

'Hmmm? Sorry – can I just have a bit of time to process everything while we head back?' Maggie buckled her seatbelt and rubbed her temple. To others she would come across as abrupt, but Kat knew her methods and would understand why she needed the head space.

'Suit yourself.' Kat jerked the car into gear and rubbed her nose. 'By the way, you stink.' A sly smile crept across her face and Maggie sniffed her jacket. Kat wasn't wrong – the stench of death clung to her.

Back at the station, the main office was empty and Maggie thought she heard voices from down the hall in the incident room. Kat followed her lead as they headed down and joined their colleagues. Nathan and Rutherford were at the front of the room while everyone took a seat. Maggie nabbed a free seat near the front, leaving Kat to find her own.

'I know it's been a long day – but it's important that we talk through this while it's still fresh in our minds. Forensics will no doubt have a large area to cover, so it might be a while before we hear anything back – Nathan's briefed me so let me hear what your thoughts are.' Rutherford noted the date on the whiteboard while she waited for the team to feedback.

Maggie took the opportunity to reveal what she had been processing on the drive back. 'I started to wonder what sort of connection our vic might have with Daniel Firth. If Sadie Ramsey is the victim, we should look at how she and Firth may have known each other – was it socially? Could he have done some DIY for her or her husband? Was it on a professional basis? Did Sadie prosecute someone known to them both? Both crimes scream premeditation to me. The killer would have had to put a lot of planning in action rather than it being purely opportunistic. Although Firth was self-employed, he previously worked in children's care homes/secure units. And Ramsey, if it is indeed her, was a prosecutor with the CPS here in Stafford. Could we be looking at an historical child abuse case?'

Maggie watched Rutherford's face drop.

'I had the same thoughts myself, but was hoping… *am* hoping that this is not the case. Good points, though – we need to follow all lines of enquiry – even the uncomfortable ones.' Rutherford noted 'historical abuse?' on the whiteboard.

'Claire Knight is looking into Social Care records on Firth for us. Maybe we need to start cross-referencing any complaints that involve the CPS, in particular Sadie Ramsey?'

Rutherford nodded. 'Bethany and that other fellow…' She

snapped her fingers, trying to recall the name of the analyst who assisted Bethany. 'Whatever his name is – sorry – I'm usually better with names, but as we're a DCI down, trying to compartmentalise all the jobs, let alone names, is using my brain space. Anyway – they can crack on with that. Thanks, Maggie. Anyone else have anything to add?'

'I spoke to a few of the neighbours,' Kat offered. 'No major bombshells dropped. Apparently the vic lived with her husband and daughter. The daughter is at Uni most of the time – live-in – but comes home on the weekends. She's in Manchester, I believe.'

'So she was close to her parents, then. I mean, to come home every weekend – Christ, I stayed away as much as possible,' Rutherford mumbled.

'One of the neighbours did mention an incident that happened about a month ago. A guy was seen skulking – his words – around the side of the Ramsey property. When the neighbour called out, he scarpered – his words again. The neighbour said he couldn't really remember anything about what the person looked like, but did say that when he informed Mrs Ramsey, she didn't seem overly concerned, so he dropped it.' Kat shrugged.

'Has anyone spoken to the husband yet?' Rutherford looked around the room.

A field officer opened his notes. 'He's out of town, Guv, but heading back now. He'll be staying with a friend when he arrives. Said he'll let us know when he's back and we can arrange for someone to speak with him. He was pretty upset...'

'OK. Give the FLO a heads-up.' Rutherford looked at Nathan. 'Hopefully we'll have more news tomorrow. Get all this logged and then go home. We now have two murders, so any annual leave is cancelled.' There were a few groans around the room. 'I know, I know – but the sooner we solve these, the sooner you can all get that leave back.' Rutherford left the room.

'You heard the Guv. Maggie, can I have a word with you before you go?' Nathan motioned for her to join him at the front. She waited as her colleagues shuffled out and then met Nathan by the whiteboard.

'Has Dr Moloney given you any more insight on what she's come up with so far?'

'I haven't actually spoken to her about it – does she know about this new one, even? Think she's been at Markston all day.'

'I'll contact DI Calleja. Might be worth seeing if we can squeeze an additional day out of the DAHU/IOM and have her here.'

'Good luck with that. I don't think Calleja was too pleased, letting us have the three days already negotiated.' Maggie turned to leave.

'He may not be keen, but given the fact we potentially have a serial killer on the loose, I think if we have to take this above his head, we'll come out on top. I'd rather not have to do that.'

'My thoughts exactly – about the serial bit, not your office politics. Everything on that board there tells me these two murders are connected, and we need to figure it out before our killer chooses his next victim.'

Chapter Thirty-Three

K ate flinched when DI Calleja knocked on her office door. She could've kicked herself for getting rattled at the slightest thing and had debated whether she should speak to her colleagues about it, but she didn't want them to worry. It was a natural feeling, the psychologist in her reasoned. It's not every day that you end up being kidnapped by a psychopath, is it?

'Hello, Joseph. What can I do for you?' Kate noticed the DI's obvious discomfort at her using his name rather than his rank, but as a civilian she wasn't obliged to and felt it was less impersonal. She had to admit, she did get a bit of a kick out of his discomfort, and the more he insisted on using ranks, the more determined she was to refer to people by their given names. He was carrying a small pile of files and Kate expected that her workload was about to increase.

'Just had DS Wright on the phone.'

Kate raised a brow. 'And what did Nathan want? Has something happened?'

'If I'm honest, I'm surprised your pal, DC Jamieson, hasn't been in touch already, but yes, there's been another murder. They want you to work an additional day with them until the killer is caught.' He paused. Kate mused again about his persistence in calling officers by their rank. He should know by now, he wouldn't change her ways.

But another murder… That got Kate's attention and she straightened herself in her seat. 'Oh, right. Can I ask what your decision was?'

'You've a lot of work to catch up on here, but as most of it is computer-based at the moment…' He placed the files on her desk and pushed them towards her. 'I said I'm willing to be flexible – as long as you don't fall behind on the work here. You've only just returned and no one would hold it against you if you felt it was too much…'

Kate didn't know whether he was trying to be kind or if it was his way of saying that he believed she'd be taking on too much if she tried to split her time even more. 'I appreciate your concern, but I think I'll be able to manage just fine… I'm grand.' Kate hoped her curt tone made it clear that she wished people would stop walking on eggshells around her. 'Anyway, as you said, most of this is computer-based, so it really doesn't matter where I'm located.' She opened the top file and saw a risk assessment and pre-sentence report completed by Lucy Sherwood. Kate glanced briefly through the pages of the reports. Lucy was an excellent Probation Officer and although she was working with Probation via an agency, she would have completed a detailed and focused assessment, unlike some others that had come across Kate's desk.

'OK, I'll leave it to you to decide what day you will base yourself here, but I'd like you to make yourself available for the Operational meetings – as the nominals will be discussed and your input is needed. Do you have any questions?'

Kate shook her head. Nominals for the IOM were offenders chosen for the scheme based on their history of offending, the risk of serious harm they posed overall and their risk of reoffending – usually prolific in nature and based partially on a score calculated by the Offender Assessment System (or OASys, as it is more commonly known within Probation). With DI Calleja out of sight, Kate did a little fist pump in the air, as she was pleased to have the opportunity to make her mark with the MOCD. Although she had a part-time consultant role with the police now, she had heard through the grapevine that permanent, full-time opportunities would be opening in the future, and wanted to make sure she made a good impression.

Kate picked up the handset and held it between her chin and shoulder as she dialled.

'DC Jamieson speaking.'

'Hey, it's Kate. Can you talk?'

'I was actually going to call you tonight. Just packing up to leave now. What's up?'

'Ah, sorry. Joseph was just in here and told me I'd be working with you lot an extra day a week. Did you have any part in this?'

'Wow. That was quick. It may have been suggested at our briefing earlier, and Rutherford had said she would see if it was possible, but since I know DI Calleja, I wasn't holding out much hope. At least not this week, anyway. When are you starting?'

'I'll come up tomorrow. I still have to do my profiles for the nominals here, but it would be great to spend more time with the MOCD and get a first-hand feel of things. I think it adds value to my assessments – you know, chatting through things rather than just reading reams of paperwork and drawing conclusions on that basis. Do you think I'd be able to visit the crime scenes?'

'That'll be up to Rutherford. I guess if you convince her that it will be beneficial to your profiles, then I'm sure she'd be up for it. At the moment she is straddling between her role as a DI and trying to cover some aspects of DCI Hastings' job.'

A silence followed.

'I understand. Right, I won't keep you any longer, but just one more thing. If you could email me over anything about the developments from today, and any connections to the first murder – if that's the case – that would be grand.'

'Already on it. It's as if you don't know me at all...' Maggie laughed down the line.

Kate heard a ping and smiled. 'Best let you go.' Kate ended the call and opened the email from Maggie. After scanning the notes, she concluded that her original thoughts had been confirmed. The pattern in her mind was similar to a revenge killer, and she didn't think he was anywhere near finished yet.

Chapter Thirty-Four

M aggie wiped the gunk out of the corner of her eye. Despite everything going on, she had managed to have a decent night's sleep, ready to face whatever was thrown her way at work this morning.

First thing she did on arrival at the office was join the team in updating Kate on the investigation so far. As she watched Kate take notes, she heard her desk phone ring and excused herself. It was the enquiry desk wanting to patch through a call from social worker Claire Knight.

'Hey Claire, how are you?'

Claire spoke in a hushed tone. *'Hi. Sorry to bother you so early, but I've been looking into what we had spoken about and I came across something that might be of interest. I need to tell you, though, that my supervisor is not keen on me sharing this information without a formal request from the police...'*

'Why's that? Surely you're obliged to share information if it means someone's at risk?'

'It's because it's a sealed case – or partially sealed anyway – you'd

need a warrant to see the whole document. Remember when we were talking about the pindown scandal?'

'Yeah.'

'Well, I looked a little further back and there were quite a few allegations made about staff members at Chatham House. There's a Dan there, but the last name is different.'

Maggie tried to hide her excitement. 'When can we meet? I'd like to bring Dr Moloney with me, if you don't mind. She's doing a profile on the killer and I think she'd be interested in what you have to say.'

'I'm free now, but not for long.'

'We're on our way.' Maggie dropped the receiver back into its place and grabbed her jacket off the back of her chair. 'Hey, Doc, fancy coming to Social Care with me?'

'Count me in!'

'Kat, you coming?' Maggie looked at her partner.

'Nah. I can't. Nathan's asked me to go and meet with the FLO – we're going to speak to Ramsey's husband.'

'OK, I'll catch you up on things when we're back.' Maggie ran down the stairs and out the building with Kate following close behind.

'What has Claire found?' Kate pulled out a tube of clear lip-gloss and dabbed it on her lips. 'Want some?' She held out the tube towards Maggie.

'No thanks. Claire's come across some interesting allegations. I don't know any more than that, though. Claire will explain more in a minute.'

Maggie signed Kate and herself in and as they sat waiting for Claire, Maggie's leg shook from excitement.

If they could get an idea of how many allegations were made and who they were against, they might have a potential victim list to work from.

Claire opened the door and ushered them through.

'Quick. In here…' She closed the door behind them. On the table were thick files, the papers yellow with age and some torn at the edges. 'As these were historical cases, they haven't yet been scanned into the system. I had to request them from archives and they must have been flagged, because as soon as they arrived, my supervisor asked to speak with me.'

All three sat around the table.

'What's the big deal though? You must have hundreds of cases like this.' Maggie took the top file and began to browse through the contents. Inside were newspaper clippings. Court reports. Social Care records. Pictures of young children with bruised bodies. She closed the file, a knot forming in her stomach.

'We do, but prominent figures were also named in some of the allegations. An inquiry was held – and you can see the files there.' She pointed at the piles. 'Twenty children came forward and claimed they were exposed to physical abuse, in some cases amounting to torture,.by foster and residential care staff, for years.'

Kate gasped. 'I was afraid this would be something that came up, though I was hoping I was wrong.' She looked over at Maggie. 'It does fit the profile I'm working on.'

Claire's head tilted. 'In what way?'

'Well…' Kate sat back in her seat and looked at the ceiling.

Maggie could almost see the cogs turning as Kate picked the relevant bits of her profile out to share with them.

'I believe we're looking at a mission-oriented killer. Someone murdering in order to right a wrong… Seeking revenge. In some ways, they may feel that they are doing society a favour by ridding it of certain people. To put it into some context, you may recall cases where the perpetrator is murdering young women, prostitutes, drug dealers or homosexuals. People that *they* feel society could do without. These killers are generally not psychotic. Some see themselves as trying to change society. They always have a controlled crime scene, hence they fall into the category of an organised killer. Since they almost always go after specific victims, this makes them much easier to track down.'

'Or not...' Maggie sighed. 'If these are, as you've described them, mission-oriented murders, there has to be some sort of personal element to it for our guy. I mean, this killer seems to be targeting certain individuals rather than a certain sector of society, like those you've just highlighted.'

'Yes – so it could overlap slightly with serial killers, who are out for power and control. Those who enjoy their victim's terror, suffering and screaming.' Kate paused for a moment. 'These killers usually have a history of childhood abuse, which left them feeling powerless and inadequate as adults. Many of these killers also sexually abuse their victims, but they are not motivated by feelings of lust. To them, rape is simply another form of dominating the victim. Fortunately, we don't seem to have come across that... not yet – unless Dr Blake finds something in the most recent murder.'

'Wait. Did you say there's been *another* murder?' Claire's eyes widened and Maggie looked at Kate.

'Between us, yes, there has been,' answered Maggie. 'I don't think I'm talking out of turn by confirming this, as it will be reported in the news at some point today. We're still waiting for forensics to confirm the ID of the victim, but the MO was similar to Firth's, so we think they may be connected.'

'Who was the victim? Can you tell me? I promise, it won't leave these four walls.'

Maggie hesitated momentarily, as if any information was leaked, it would be her arse on the line, but she'd worked a few cases with Claire and knew that discretion was a strong part of who she was. 'We're still waiting for the formal ID, but all signs point to it being Sadie Ramsey from the CPS.'

'Oh my god.' Claire grabbed one of the files and riffled through the pages. She pulled out a newspaper article and passed it to Maggie. 'You mean her?'

Maggie looked at the picture and headline: 'CPS refuses to take allegations of physical abuse to trial.'

Fuck…

Chapter Thirty-Five

'What the hell is going on in here?' The trio jumped and looked in the doorway. Maggie guessed from the look on Claire's face that the man before them was her supervisor.

'This is DC Jamieson and Dr Moloney – the ones I told you about.' Claire turned to face them. 'And this is my supervisor – Hugh O'Donnell.' Maggie watched as Claire sank back into her chair, probably hoping it would swallow her up.

'You can call me Hugh.' He held his hand out and both Maggie and Kate shook it while they waited for him to continue. His hands were greasy, as if he had just lathered them in cream. Shea butter perhaps? She couldn't place the scent that wafted from the supervisor – but it was strong enough to make her sneeze.

'Bless you.' He moved away from her as if she had a bug he could catch.

Maggie pulled a tissue from her pocket and wiped her nose. 'Thanks.' She spotted him eyeing up the files and hoped he would offer assistance rather than shut them down, just as they were getting close to finding something.

'I'm sorry that Claire has wasted your time, but she was specifically told that this information could not be shared until everything went through the proper channels.' He glared at the social worker.

Maggie stood. 'We totally understand that and, to be fair to Claire, all the information that she has shared so far is a matter of public record. It would be great if you could join us and add your expert opinion, perhaps?' Was she overegging the situation? She hoped not. Sometimes a little flattery got the right results. She soon realised this would not be the case here when Hugh collected the files and held the door open for them.

'Claire, would you please escort these ladies out and then join me in my office.' He stomped off in the opposite direction.

'Really sorry about that – I thought he was out today, but someone must have let him know you guys were here.'

'Shit – sorry. I hope you don't get too much of a bollocking for it. It was really useful talking with you and we appreciate it. I'll go back and explain to DS Wright what happened. Perhaps he can smooth things over.'

'Thanks, but I'm sick of all the secrecy in situations like this. If people are at risk, we should all be working together. I hope what you did manage to see helps.' Claire let them out and they left the building as quickly as they could.

'Well, that was certainly interesting.' Kate ran a finger through her hair.

'I don't know about you, but I tried to take note of anything I could. I think our next move should be to speak to Nathan, and he might be able to help us get access to the full records. I mean, for fucksake, this is a murder investigation.'

'You know as well as I do about protocol, though, so you can't really blame him – remember, he'll have someone to answer to if the shit hits the fan.'

Maggie hated that Kate inserted logic into the conversation, even though she knew Kate was right. Didn't mean she liked hearing it. They walked at a swift pace back to the station and as they were about to walk through the front doors, Kate's phone rang.

'I'll see you up there, I need to take this.' Kate walked off and Maggie made her way up to the office.

'Bethany, do you have a minute?'

'That's just about all I have. What's up?'

'I wonder if you could look up anything we may have in relation to Chatham House and Daniel Firth, and include Sadie Ramsey. The Doc and I have just come back from Social Care and it looks like both our vics may have been involved in a nasty case that was never pursued through the courts.' Maggie knew it was a long shot.

'We've already done a surface look at links, but I can definitely use some keywords to try and get something more specific.'

'I can tell you that it definitely was in the papers, if that helps.' Maggie gave as much information about the article as she could remember. 'I really appreciate this. It might be hidden under other headlines or cases if no charges were laid.' She looked around the office. 'Is Kat not back yet?'

'Nope. She's still with Mr Ramsey and the FLO, I guess. She hasn't been in contact.'

'I'm just going to catch Nathan up on what we've learned. When the Doc comes back in, can you ask her to join us?'

Bethany nodded and picked up her phone. 'I'll get some help from the other analysts on this – they can start cross-referencing the information. Otherwise, I'll be here all night, and I'm shattered.'

Maggie squeezed Bethany's shoulder. The analyst worked harder than most and they often they had to force her to leave for the day. When this was all over, Maggie would push Nathan to instruct Bethany to have some time off. If it didn't look like she had a choice, she might well do it.

'Thanks.' She headed to Nathan's office and tapped on his door.

'What can I do for you? Or maybe I should be asking – what have you done now?'

This was becoming Nathan's catchphrase and Maggie wasn't sure if she liked it or not. The smile on his face said he was teasing, but it felt as if there was something more behind it.

'Depends on what you've heard.' Maggie wasn't going to offer any information until she knew what she was dealing with, and joking it off would confirm whether she needed to be worried, depending on her boss's response. A serious look came over Nathan's face, and her concern grew.

'Just got off the phone with a Mr Hugh O'Donnell. That name ring a bell?'

Maggie took a seat. 'OK – hear what I have to say first, before you have a go at me.'

He rested his chin in his hand and tapped his lip. 'I'm waiting…'

'Claire Knight said she may have found something that

could help us, so of course I went over. When we got to Social Care, she had files waiting for us and yes,' Maggie held up her hands, 'she did advise us that she probably shouldn't be sharing the details, but if it meant the possibility of saving a life, we couldn't actually ignore that, could we?'

'Nice spin on things.' He clapped his hands sarcastically. 'Did you learn that from Julie Noble? You know there are procedures that have to be followed, and had you actually come to me and explained, before charging off to see Mrs Knight, I might have been able to liaise with Mr O'Donnell so that we could avoid having to wade through the red tape to get that information. You need to think before you act sometimes, Maggie. We've had this conversation before.'

Maggie would have preferred a bollocking to the look of utter disappointment that faced her now from Nathan.

'I'm sorry. Is there anything I can do to fix this?'

'I think you've done enough. Next time, see me first – in fact, when it comes to anything to do with other agencies – I want you to talk to me first.'

'But...'

'No buts – I'm tired of having to repeat myself on this front. Now get back to what you were doing and leave me to clear up this mess.'

Maggie left his office and dropped her bag by her desk. Kate walked in as Maggie was trying to think of a way to make it up to Nathan without pissing him off further.

'Have you spoken to Nathan yet?' Kate headed to her own desk.

'He's not happy. Seems Mr O'Donnell was quick to call him the moment we left.'

'Ah, OK. Sorry to hear that, but you can jump the gun

sometimes. I'm going to review what I have so far and update my profile. Shout if you need me.' Kate inserted her earphones and that was the end of their conversation.

Kate was right. She could act before thinking things through, and it seemed to be wearing thin on Nathan too. Maggie was determined to find the link between the Social Care information and their murder investigation – it was another piece of the puzzle that would lead them one step closer to the killer and iron things out between her and Nathan.

Chapter Thirty-Six

The idea that the team could be looking at a connection to historical child abuse cases made every muscle in Maggie tense. Although not a parent herself, she found that cases of this type were never easy to deal with or to let go of, even though they were part and parcel of her job. She had known some of the strongest officers to break when they worked cases like this, the gruesome details laid out with photos to show just how horrific the crimes were. Those were images she didn't want stuck in her head.

'Mr Ramsey is definitely out of the picture as a person of interest.' Kat brushed by Maggie on her way to her desk and plonked herself down in her chair, her body like a rag doll, arms and legs splayed out and exhaustion evident on her face.

Maggie waited for more of an explanation.

'It was so awkward speaking with him. Least favourite part of this job, for sure. I mean, he was fucking devastated, but get this. All of a sudden his demeanour changed and he confessed to having an affair for years. So the *business trips* he was allegedly on were in fact meetings with his girlfriend.' Kat rolled her eyes. 'We had to stop him from going into specific details – the man wanted to give us a *Fifty Shades* version, but I pulled the plug on that.' Kat stuck her finger in her mouth and made a gagging sound. 'He gave us her number and when I spoke to her, she sounded like a weight had been lifted off her shoulders. Guess it means she won't have to be his mistress anymore.'

'I didn't think he'd be involved. He had no connection to Firth. Hiding the affair would have meant we'd be running around like idiots when it would all come out in the end anyway. Good job, Kat! Did his wife know about the affair?' Maggie wondered if the Ramseys had had an open relationship. She'd read about these in magazines, although it wasn't something she'd be keen to explore. They could at least cross this off any future questions they might have for her husband, if they had to speak with him again.

'He didn't actually say, but I got the impression that she didn't. His mate, the one he's staying with, definitely didn't, as when we spoke to him, he stuttered all the way through, saying he thought that the Ramseys had the best marriage… everyone was so envious of them… et cetera.'

'Just goes to show, you never know what goes on behind closed doors—'

Maggie was cut short when DI Rutherford barged into the office.

'Dr Blake's been in touch. She has some preliminary findings from the PM she'd like to run by us, so be ready in fifteen.' Without leaving room for any questions, the Guv left as quickly as she came.

Nathan popped his head out of his office door. 'Have

everything ready to discuss. Bouncing theories off Dr Blake to see if the evidence matches will save some time in any lines of enquiry.' He then went down the hall, no doubt to catch up with DI Rutherford and probably have a word with Dr Blake before the briefing. Seeing how Nathan was pulled in every direction, Maggie was reminded of how grateful she was about not putting herself forward for the DS position, despite passing her sergeant's exam. No matter how difficult a case was, being on the operational side would always appeal to her more.

'I'm loving the idea of Dr Blake involved in your briefings. I've always believed you get a better feel of things when you speak to a person directly rather than through reports – written words can easily be misinterpreted.' The Doc gathered her notes together. 'I'm going to grab a coffee, so if anyone wants one, shout up now.'

Bethany raised her hand while both Maggie and Kat shook their heads.

'See you in the conference room,' the Doc called out.

Maggie jotted down some thoughts that had been rattling around her head, before she too headed to the briefing. She wanted to avoid sitting with the field officers. As much as she and the team appreciated their help, she'd overheard a few grumbles about them doing all the leg work while the MOCD claimed all the glory. To avoid getting herself riled up and saying something that could land her in more bother with Nathan, she avoided sitting near the ones who she knew were disgruntled. She picked her battles carefully... most times.

'Head of the class then, Maggie?'

Maggie looked up as the pathologist walked into the room with Nathan and DI Rutherford in tow. 'Always…' She directed a slight smile towards them all, as even though the pathologist seemed in a good mood today, it was sometimes hard to read her. 'I'm keen to hear what you have to say.' And Maggie meant that, though realised that it sounded a bit on the sarky side when the frown formed on Dr Blake's face.

'I'm looking forward to hearing what everyone has so far. This case has had my mind racing since Firth ended up on my slab. Right, I best get set up.'

Maggie's curiosity was piqued. When everyone was seated, DI Rutherford kicked off the briefing by running through what they had collated so far.

'I know you're all busy, so we're just going to get right to it. Forensics have now confirmed that Sadie Ramsey is indeed the deceased found at the latest crime scene. Her husband advised that he will share the news with their daughter, but a FLO will be available to them to assist. We're hoping to inform the press tomorrow. Over to you now…' DI Rutherford sat next to Kate, and the first image put on the screen by the pathologist drew a gasp from everyone in the room.

Chapter Thirty-Seven

'Now that I have everyone's attention...' Maggie was sure Dr Blake enjoyed a bit of showboating, as a sly smile appeared on her face. She turned to face the image of the burned body. 'I'll give you all a little bit of background.' She pressed her clicker and a close-up image of Sadie Ramsey's burned body stared back at them.

'Currently, post-mortem computed tomography – or PMCT, as I know we all love a good acronym – allows us, in the case of burn victims, to differentiate the normal post-mortem changes from those that are heat-related changes.' She paused and looked around the room. Catching her eye-line, Maggie noted some of her colleagues losing focus. 'You all still with me?'

Nods and grunts followed.

'Excellent. For the purposes of today, I needed to know whether there was any other obvious cause of death, and what burn-related injuries should be examined further when I did the autopsy.'

Maggie loved this aspect of her job. Work often overtook her personal life, but having an understanding of what others did when it came to solving crime made her a better detective, in her view.

'The forensic team started by collecting relevant information during the removal of the corpse, such as the position of the body in the fire debris, its temperature and its carbonisation degree. The position we found Mrs Ramsey in suggests that she toppled the chair over – however, with her hands and feet secured, there was little chance she would have been able to escape the fire. The killer used wire bindings this time, no doubt to perfect his MO as the last victim's plastic ties burned away. Unfortunately he died before he could use this to his advantage.' She clicked to another image.

'I'll skip over all the technical details. Sadie Ramsey was alive when she was set fire to.'

'Was anything found in her system?' Maggie was curious about all the pill bottles that had been found in the bathroom cabinets. When interviews were done, the team learned from the prosecutor's colleagues that there were rumours that Sadie wasn't coping with the job after her stroke.

'Trace amounts of anti-depressants and diazepam were found, and according to her GP, she'd not been given a new prescription for some time, so she may have been weaning herself off them. The GP was concerned that her anti-depressants were interacting negatively with the diazepam.'

Dr Blake flicked through more images. 'So now we get down to the nuts and bolts of things. I mentioned earlier that the victim was alive was she was set alight, so I needed to determine what the actual cause of death was.'

A few more images flickered across the screen, and noting

her colleagues drifting, Maggie wanted the pathologist to get to the details the team were waiting for, so made the bold move of interrupting Dr Blake mid flow. 'I wondered if you could tell us—'

Before she had the chance to finish, Dr Blake held her hand up and shot a look in her direction. Maggie could feel another pair of eyes on her and avoided looking in DI Rutherford's direction. Even though she was keen to have the pathologist at briefings, this was a case where the technical could obscure what they actually needed to know, and right now they just needed the facts that would connect Firth and Ramsey.

'Had you let me finish, DC Jamieson, I was about to tell you all that Sadie Ramsey was missing a tooth…'

They had their connection at last.

Chapter Thirty-Eight

He threw his bag down on the floor and stomped into his living room. 'Where's the fucking remote?' Living alone, he directed his anger at the walls. His eyes darted around the room, and before his rage took over, he spotted it peeking out from under the pillow on his couch. He snatched it up and turned on the news.

His pulse slammed in his neck.

He had to make a brief stop at work and was worried he'd missed something, but there was nothing about her on the news, despite her body being found not long after he had left. He'd underestimated the nosiness of the fucking neighbours, and expected the find to be splattered all over the television. He smacked the remote on his leg repeatedly.

There was nothing. Not-a-fucking-thing.

Had the police already made the connection? They could be trying to cover it up... again. No one wanted to know anything when he and the others had come forward all those years ago, detailing the horrific abuse they had suffered at these people's hands. Sadie Ramsey may not have been responsible for the abuse but her decision to not take any action meant he and the others had to endure hell for a few more years. For that, she was culpable.

He fell onto the couch then. Exhausted. Thinking about it only angered him more. But he needed that anger – without it, he couldn't complete his mission. To hold them to account.

He closed his eyes. To focus, he had to go back to the time when he was the one tied to a chair. His mouth held open by one of them as another extracted a tooth – no – tore the tooth from his mouth as punishment for talking back.

His blood boiled. He'd found what he needed. He shook the memories out of his head and stood.

Who's next?

He walked over to the table, picked up the piece of paper and looked at the remaining people on his list. Closing his eyes and running his finger over the aged sheet, he whispered, 'Eeny meeny miny mo, who's the next one that's going to go?'

When he opened his eyes, he was pleased to see where his finger had landed – Father Boyle – nothing holy or *fatherly* about him. For a man of God, he took a lot of pleasure out of beating young boys. In fact, the priest had an erection on more than one occasion. Sick fucking bastard.

With the decision made, his stomach grumbled. He made a sandwich and sat back down on the couch. His body relaxed, as it always did when he knew what he had to do.

He flicked through the TV channels. Maybe he was just impatient. They could be waiting for the post-mortem to formally ID her – then the world would know. Would it be worth contacting the newspapers himself? Give them a nudge

in the right direction. It could also lead to him getting caught –
and he needed to finish before that happened.

He looked around the room. Prison wouldn't be so bad
compared to this shithole. He shouldn't really complain; he
had chosen it. He could've afforded something nicer but used
the money to buy everything else he needed – the computer,
the software, his kit…

No, he wasn't afraid of prison at all. Once he was done, if
they didn't figure it out, he'd hand himself in. He'd have the
last laugh.

His mind returned to Father Boyle. The priest was old as
fuck now so shouldn't be too difficult to deal with. And if the
fucker got an erection, he'd make sure it was the last time he
ever got pleasure out of pain. He wanted to try something new
with the priest – make him a sacrifice – and he knew exactly
what he needed to do.

The priest was easy to find. He was living in Fracton Hall, two
miles north of Stafford. It was a home for retired and
convalescent priests and contained bed-sitting rooms for eight
priests. The Hall had a large garden, spacious grounds and a
field with a few abandoned buildings; altogether about fifteen
acres.

*Bloody cheek of them. Who the fuck paid for this? They were
living off his wages, and that just wasn't fair.*

To get his bearings, he had visited the place once through
his work, after he had suggested it could benefit the
unfortunates they worked with. He and his colleagues were
given a tour and he made note of what he needed to know –

the house had two storeys with attics. The 'pinwheel' plan revolved around a central open-well staircase hall, which led at ground-floor level to three reception rooms. The hall's fireplace had a richly moulded surround.

Extravagant bastards.

He planned his next visit and opened his laptop to share on the forum. He just needed a few more things and then Father Boyle would finally meet his maker.

Chapter Thirty-Nine

W*hy was he stealing their teeth?*
        This would be the question on everyone's mind.

'He's definitely exerting some sort of power and control over them – I think that's why he's taking the teeth.' Kate tugged her ear.

'Are you reading my mind now? OK, power and control, but why the teeth? Surely tying them up and setting them alight achieves this – why are the teeth significant to him?'

'You might find out in those reports from Social Care.' Kate leaned back in her chair.

'Dr Blake, was there anything else of significance in the PMs? Drugs to immobilise the victims? Other injuries to suggest a weapon was used to beat or torture them?'

'Some injuries – abrasions on the arms, but with the skin burned off, it was difficult to tell the significance of this. Formal cause of death was a heart attack, and although there was also smoke inhalation, the pain endured from the fire could have also caused the cardiac arrest.' Dr Blake stopped for a moment and looked at the back of the room. Maggie turned and noticed she was eyeing the clock. 'Time is running away from me and I've another appointment, so if you don't mind, I'll leave you to it.'

DI Rutherford thanked Dr Blake on behalf of the team and took over from the pathologist. 'This should keep you lot busy enough, and although it may seem mundane, it is important. Bethany and Kat, I'd like you to delve deeper into the reports from Social Care once they come in. Speak to Dr Moloney about anyone you come across who fits the correct age range, and anything else she feels would be relevant to narrowing down that list of POIs. Maggie – have you followed up with Justin Hardy yet – or has anyone? He's still on the board with a question mark – and if we can eliminate him, let's do that. Also, what about that homeless man?' Rutherford looked at the board. 'Music Matty? Don't we have his real name yet? Come on people, why are we slacking here? Given the seriousness, we should be further ahead than we are now. Nathan, can you take over here – I need to get the press release sorted. People, get your head in the game!' Rutherford stomped out of the room.

Nathan had a few papers in his hand and he shuffled through them, before finding what he'd been looking for. 'Just a few more things to go through. We've had some information back about the foot impressions. I'm afraid it's not good news. A generic brand of boot, sold all across the UK, with no distinguishing marks.'

'Dammit!' Maggie said, louder than she meant. 'What about fingerprints or hair – is this guy a ghost or something?'

'He'll make a mistake,' Kate said. 'He's just committed two murders, and depending on how long his list is, he's likely to now try and get through it as soon as possible. He's escalating.'

Maggie's phone buzzed and she sneaked a look at her screen. Julie Noble's name flashed with each buzz. She terminated the call. 'What will you be telling the press and when?'

'Now that we have confirmed the ID of the latest victim,' Nathan replied, 'we'll be releasing the details to the press over the coming days – the Guv is on the case. We'll be asking members of the public to come forward, so be prepared for a lot of hoax calls.' The last comment was directed to the field officers who would be monitoring the majority of those calls and forwarding any useful information to the MOCD.

'Who remains invisible? How are they able to go unnoticed?' Kat stared at the crime scene photos.

'I think we're safe to assume we are looking for a male suspect, if we're working on the premise that most of the children's homes connected to the complaints were inhabited by boys,' Kate reminded the team.

Maggie's gut tightened. She felt that they were on the right track and that their suspect had to be someone connected to the historical child abuse cases. With so many allegations, narrowing down that list was going to take some time – and right now, time was not on their side.

Chapter Forty

While the rest of the team shuffled out of the conference room, Kat, Maggie and the Doc stayed behind. Kate wanted to talk about her current profile in more detail before sharing it with Nathan and DI Rutherford. Earlier, she'd hinted that the murders had a psychological element to them, and believed it was possible that their killer had left clues at each scene – ones that were only obvious to the killer himself.

'Let's assume that the specific victim type is linked to the killer's background. They would have been fantasising about these murders for a long time before taking any action – so a lot of *who* they are, their personality, will be left at the scene.'

Maggie looked at Kat and shrugged. Not fully understanding what the Doc was getting at, she waited for her to explain.

'The teeth being removed...' The Doc eyed them both. 'Let me explain a little further. The MO – the personal mark or imprint of the offender... It's safe to say that while every crime has an MO, not all crimes have a signature. The MO is what the offender must do to commit the crime. For example, the killer must have a means to control his victims at the crime scene, such as tying them up. Significantly, the MO is a learned behaviour that is subject to change. A serial killer will alter and refine his MO to accommodate new circumstances or to incorporate new skills and information. So instead of using rope to tie up a victim, the offender may learn that it is easier and more effective to bring handcuffs to the crime scene.' The Doc paused and took a sip of water.

'The signature, on the other hand, is not required to commit the crime. Rather, it serves the emotional or psychological needs of the offender. The signature comes from within the psyche of the offender, reflecting a deep fantasy need that the killer has about his victims. The essential core of the signature, when present, is that it is always the same, because it emerges out of an offender's fantasies that evolved long before killing his first victim. The signature may involve mutilation or dismemberment of the victim's body.'

'Is it wrong that I love this shit?'

The Doc laughed at Kat's outburst.

'Oh – probably not the right context – but you know what I mean. Can I just ask something along these lines?' Kat bit her lip.

'Of course. I need your input – remember, these are my initial thoughts and are always subject to change. Profiling is like your assessment of risk, or a particular offender and their offending history – the more you find out about their criminal behaviour, the more information you have to assess how likely it is that person will go on to reoffend in a similar manner. So, ask away – please.'

'Mr Firth was tied to the chair and set alight, tooth

removed, et cetera – but it felt like the killer was putting on a show. You know, for the shock factor – they knew someone would walk in and find the body that way, and it was a gruesome sight. What the fuck is that all about?'

'Good question, Kat. Crime scene set-ups only serve the fantasy needs of the offender. They are considered part of the signature and referred to as "posing". Sometimes, a victim's body is posed to send a message to the police or public. When I saw the crime scene pictures, I immediately felt like this was an offering of sorts. The killer is not done. Although I've nothing other than my intuition to base this on, I get the feeling that these murders are not finished yet. I think our killer fantasised and something triggered him to move from those fantasies to actual murder...'

'I was hoping you weren't going to say that. Everything was meticulously done. Why start now?' Maggie shifted in her chair.

'I'm afraid I don't know the answer to that yet... Dr Blake and I are meeting up to discuss the post-mortem in more detail. I think there are more answers to be found in how the body was displayed, so I'll need to go over the crime scene photos in more detail as well as speak with those of you who were first on the scene. Sorry, I know that wasn't the answer you were looking for – but at the moment, it's all I have.'

'What can we do to help, then?' As fascinating as the conversation was, Maggie remembered that the Doc had asked them to stay back for a reason.

'Yes, sorry. I digressed there for a moment. I need you to tell me about the scenes, since all I have are photographs and they only tell me whatever the camera lenses happened to be aimed at. Think about smells, things that may have looked out of place at the time – walk me through it all. I want to know what evidence was left at the scene. It could help us narrow down the motive and identify a suspect, or at least another person of interest.' Kate took out her notebook and waited.

'But you already know what we know – it's in the case files... and the photos are pretty detailed.' Kat's hand waved towards the wall.

Maggie walked over to the evidence boards and cast her eyes over the photos. 'Nothing is jumping out at me either...' She closed her eyes to visualise the crime scene in her mind and shook her head. 'Nope, other than what's in the pictures, I'm not picking up anything new.'

'If I think hard enough, I can definitely smell the burned body from when you got in my car – in fact, I probably should valet it, as I wondered what the smell was. It just hangs around like... well, a bad smell.' Kat sat on the edge of the table.

Maggie rolled her eyes. Jokes were not Kat's strong point, that's for sure.

'Are you willing to try something that might seem a bit out of your comfort zone?' Kate pulled out a chair and gestured for Maggie to sit down.

'Erm... I guess.' Maggie rolled her shoulders, wondering what the Doc had up her sleeve.

'While I was away, I attended some courses on hypnosis...'

When Maggie heard 'hypnosis', a funny feeling went through her. She tried to stand, but Kate gently placed her hands on Maggie's shoulder and held her in the seat.

'Hear me out first, before you try and bolt, OK?'

'Fine.' Maggie sighed and stuck out her tongue at Kat when she noticed her colleague laughing.

'Right. It's a visualisation technique. I want you to relax –
deep breath in, hold it and then release when I say, OK?'

Maggie nodded. 'Doesn't sound too difficult…'

'As you breathe in, I want you to clear your mind of the
day-to-day tasks that inhabit your head. As you breathe out,
let everything other than the crime scene go from your mind.'
Kate demonstrated the breathing technique and Maggie
replicated it before closing her eyes and going with the
moment.

'Deep breath in…' said Kate, and Maggie inhaled. Kate's
tone softened and Maggie had to admit that she felt quite
relaxed as her muscles began to loosen, and soon all she saw in
her head was the crime scene.

'You're at Sadie Ramsey's house. You've just joined your
colleagues but as you breathe in, they will slowly fall away
until it will be just you and the scene.'

Maggie followed Kate's instructions. The smell of burning
flesh hit her nostrils and she flinched. 'OK. I'm alone.' Maggie
described her surroundings – a toppled chair, Sadie's burned
body, a pool of blood on the floor… Her sense of smell seemed
heightened. 'There's a metallic smell – the blood, maybe?'
Maggie sniffed the air. 'Flowers… I smell flowers.' She looked
around the scene in her mind and spotted a bunch of flowers
in the living room. She couldn't even remember seeing them
when she was actually at the scene. She thought, *Kate may be on
to something with this hypnosis.* 'There's something else…' She
tilted her head back and sniffed again. Deeper this time.
'There's something else, hanging overhead… it's…' She
inhaled and then it hit her. 'Coconut – I think I smell coconut.'
Her body flopped. She felt spent. 'That's all I can get – it's all
mixing together now. I feel a bit sick.'

'You did well. I'm going to count backwards from ten. When I reach one, you can open your eyes and you'll feel refreshed. The smells will be gone.' Kate began the countdown.

When Maggie came round the nauseous feeling had gone. 'Wow. That felt… strange. I always thought of hypnosis as being asleep and not being aware when you come around, but I remember it all… just not as vivid.'

'There are a variety of techniques – but I'm pleased you were so open to it. The coconut smell is new – and something we can compare with what we already know.'

Kat waved. 'Little freaked out over here. That mystic mojo shit is unnerving…'

Maggie laughed.

'I wonder if the coconut is something unique to the killer.' Kate was taking notes.

Maggie's phone alarm went off. She had a reminder to ring the shelter for information on Music Matty. 'Sorry, I'm going to have to go now but I'll think about what you've said and see if I can come up with anything else. I can't recall the same smell at the Firth crime scene, but then I wasn't looking for it either.'

Maggie stretched and left the pair of them to go through the notes.

Chapter Forty-One

Maggie dug around her desk looking for the card she'd been given by the manager of the homeless shelter she'd been to. It had been buried under a pile of Post-it notes she had shoved in a rolodex that she wasn't using properly.

'Never Alone. Jess speaking, how can I help?'

'Hi. This is DC Maggie Jamieson from Stafford Police MOCD. Is Mr Reed there?'

'MOC-what?' The young receptionist's voice rose as she asked the question.

'Sorry. Major and Organised Crime Department.'

'Oh – sounds serious… Can you tell me what this is about?'

'I'm not at liberty to discuss that. Is Mr Reed there?' Maggie wanted to steer the conversation back to what she had requested, instead of engaging the woman's interest in crime.

'I think he's here. Hang on.'

Maggie tapped her pen on the desk to the beat of the music that played while she was on hold. Two minutes later and she'd almost forgotten who she had called.

'*DC Jamieson, so nice to hear from you again. Why didn't you use my personal number?*'

Maggie flipped the card over and saw his mobile number. 'I hadn't noticed it. Thanks for talking to me. I just have a few questions about Music Matty and wondered if you had any details on him? Full name, date of birth, or maybe previous addresses?'

'*That's quite the ask. Could you tell me why you need them?*'

Maggie wasn't in the mood for games. He'd been flirtatious with her when she attended the shelter and she thought she'd made her position clear. 'We'd like to do some background checks and can't seem to locate him. He's not in his usual hang-outs and no one seems to know where he's disappeared to. It's important that we find him.' Maggie hoped that he got the message.

'*You've spoken to him, so you know that he doesn't trust those in authority. Especially the police. Don't you have a database you can check for this stuff – I mean with GDPR? I can't just go and give out information willy nilly. He's been done for shoplifting in the town centre, if that helps? I'm afraid I don't actually have any personal details to share – another shelter might. He moves about, and although it's no longer needed, sometimes they'd use the shelter they attended most frequently as an address for benefits. There used to be a scheme for this...*'

'That's great. Thanks for your help.' It was clear she wouldn't get the information she needed and didn't want to waste any more time speaking with Alex Reed. He had a bit of a condescending tone that she had only just picked up on.

'*I wish it could be more...*'

Maggie ended the call before he started up again. She wasn't in the mood and couldn't be bothered listening anymore to Mr Reed and his vague words. Only a few people really understood Maggie's personality and she wasn't bothered if he wasn't one of them.

The field team might be able to help with the music man's pre-cons. Maggie was on her way down to their offices, when Kat caught up with her.

'We have to go…' Kat was out of breath.

Chapter Forty-Two

They arrived at the crime scene, located on the property of Fracton Hall Estate and its various buildings, and waited as one fire was extinguished while another, in an outbuilding, raged.

'Fucking hell.' Maggie took in the sight before her. She could almost feel the heat against her face as the flames danced up towards the sky.

'Can't we get any closer? The main crime scene fire is out, we could start there and search the surrounding buildings.' Kat began to walk towards the main hall.

Maggie grabbed her arm. 'I think we should stay here. Even if there's a risk that evidence might be destroyed by the hoses or compromised – we can't interfere. We could be putting more lives at risk. Let the paramedics and fire brigade do what they need to. Trust me, I hate waiting around too.'

While they waited, Maggie assessed the situation for when the chaos died down a bit. The limited area they were allowed to access showed that the main hall was unaffected.

Whoever the victim was must have been led away from the main building and into the outer building, which was a safe enough distance away so as not to arouse immediate suspicion. A second building was set alight, and Maggie assumed this was to confuse the police. The killer must have been here before.

'If you really want something to do, how about...' Maggie noticed Kat was distracted.

'Uh-huh.' Kat's ear was glued to the radio that rested on her shoulder. 'We've been cleared to enter the building – and they've got a body.'

———————

With the structure being deemed safe, Maggie and Kat sprinted towards the building. A hub had been set up in the inner perimeter and the pair suited up. A group of priests stood in the distance and Maggie pointed at them. 'Might be worth having a word to see what they know – maybe get hold of the visitors' log?'

Kat nodded before heading in the direction of the priests. They had spotted her and started to head back towards the main hall. Maggie stayed put. The smell of burned flesh hung in the air, mixed with smoke as the burning ashes flickered in the sky. Maggie pulled the mask up over her mouth but the stench seeped through, reminding her that despite the beautiful surroundings, they were at a murder scene. As if she could forget.

Maggie spotted Nathan, and once she was behind him, she tapped him on the shoulder. 'No Rutherford?'

'She sent me instead, I'm afraid – she had a fire of her own to deal with after the Superintendent got wind of this latest situation. You on your own?' He looked over her shoulder.

'Kat's around, she went off to speak with the priests. We figured that the killer may have visited here, so she's going to see if she can get hold of any records.'

'Good thinking. This could be totally separate from our investigation – a random act – so it's best we don't jump to any conclusions at this stage. I sent some officers to go and talk to anyone hanging about – the arsonist may be blending in with the crowd.' Maggie heard the words, but even Nathan didn't sound too convinced by what he had said.

'Hmmm. You've actually just given me a thought.' Maggie turned and spoke into her radio. 'Kat. Can you find out if the Hall or any of the residents have any links to the boys' homes we've been looking into?'

The radio crackled and Maggie moved her ear away.

'Will do.'

'What makes you think the body in there belongs to someone who worked at the homes? Do you think we have another revenge killing on our hands?' Nathan rubbed his chin.

'I remember seeing a lot of priests and nuns named in the reports I've looked at. It wouldn't surprise me. It's not uncommon for them to be involved in children's homes.'

'Just be careful where you take this – we've no idea who the vic is. The last thing we need is a religious angle to take over where one doesn't exist.'

'What do you mean by that?' Maggie had never known Nathan to shy away from anything controversial, but that was when he was her partner. Being a DS, he'd have to tread carefully, and after a previous scandal involving the Catholic

Church a few years back, Maggie could understand his hesitation. It had been a mess – senior officers in another police station had been linked to corruption, and it left a bad taste in many of her colleagues' mouths, and her own.

'Nothing. Ignore me.' Nathan looked past Maggie and nodded. 'Right, let's go.'

Chapter Forty-Three

Maggie followed Nathan into the outbuilding. The roof had been destroyed, leaving the cement walls as a barrier to any prying eyes. Maggie stepped into the room and looked around. It looked like it was used for some type of storage. She hoped that any relevant information had not been left in here, as they'd have no chance of finding out what they required if that was the case.

Crime scene integrity would be paramount at this time and they were now standing in the target scene area. A pathway was being cleared, and Maggie held back as evidence markers were being laid. The forensics team were collecting the perishable evidence – the type of evidence that could be stepped on or kicked, moving the evidence from its original location.

'What do we have?' Dr Blake didn't beat around the bush with small talk.

'I've no idea yet. This is as far as I've got.' The pathologist was still blowing hot and cold with Maggie, so she kept her tone neutral.

'Follow me. Let's have a look at this body.' Dr Blake ploughed her way through. Patience wasn't in her vocabulary but she'd be as meticulous as required once she got there.

Maggie didn't need to be asked twice. There was a secondary room to the left and they followed the pathway lit by the large police-issued torch Maggie had picked up outside.

'Ah jeez. That smell.' Maggie covered her nose again.

'Well, there's definitely at least one burned body.' The pathologist didn't seem one bit fazed.

When Maggie walked through the doorway she gasped. 'Fucksake.' A few feet ahead of her a partially burned body stared back. Eyes wide and the mouth in a macabre grimace. The victim was in a chair. Nails were protruding from what was left of the person's hands. Wire held the wrists in place. Nails also were through the ankles with more wire wrapped crudely, so it had sunk into the burned skin.

'Are you just going to stand there?' Dr Blake motioned her over. 'Looks like our vic is a male.' The pathologist circled the chair. 'I can smell petroleum distillate – probably sprayed over him, but he's not as burned as the others.' She looked at Maggie. 'Same killer as the last two? I realise that the set-up is a little different, but I think the similarities far outweigh the differences.'

'What are you seeing that I'm not?' Maggie stepped a little closer and looked at the victim's face. 'Ah. Good spot. Missing teeth. This would have taken a bit of time. Victim may have been important to the killer. There's a viciousness to this one – more personal in a way.'

'I'd agree. There doesn't seem to be any… Hang on.' Dr Blake leaned in closer and with her gloved hand, touched the back of the man's head. 'There's something here but with the burned skin, it's hard to say for sure. I think he may have been hit on the back of the head with some force. I'll know more, though, when I get him on my table.' She stood up. 'Do you have any other questions?'

Maggie shook her head.

'I'll be in touch.' She walked over to one of her team, said a few words and left.

Maggie looked around the room. There was a table behind the victim but other than the chair, no other furniture was present. And then she spotted something.

Chapter Forty-Four

Maggie looked down at the markings on the floor. It was hard to make out what they were, even with her torch. 'Do you have something that might help illuminate this area?' she called out.

The forensic officer pulled out a brighter light which revealed scratches on the floor and some brownish stains.

'Do you think that's blood?' She squinted but her eyes were betraying her. With the bright lights contrasting the darkness of the room, she was struggling to get a clear look.

'Only one way to tell.' He opened his kit bag and sprayed a liquid on the floor. Luminal. The shadows of the building disappeared as the blue light made the floor glow. 'I'd say that would be a yes.' He began spraying in other areas around their initial finding and although not much was present, there seemed to be blood spatters on the floor leading up to the lower part and mid-section of the wall behind.

'I'll take some samples.' He bent over and began to work.

The body was a few feet away and in her mind, she began to visualise what could've taken place. The killer and victim perhaps struggled here – maybe even fought. The killer initiated the blow to the back of the head that Dr Blake had mentioned. *How long had they both been in this building?*

Once he was ID'd, they could find out how long their vic had been missing from the Hall. This would help establish a timeline. He may have arranged a meeting with the killer, not knowing what the outcome would be. If that were true, Maggie's suspicions that the killer and the victims were known to each other would be confirmed.

Being careful not to disturb the area or the forensic officer who was meticulously working away, she knelt down and shone her torch directly on the floor. Around the droplets there were streaks scratched in the floor. Maggie made a mental note to ask Dr Blake if anything was found under the body's fingernails – of course, that would depend on how severe the burns to the hands were. They needed a break in this case, and if the vic had fought, they may just get some DNA.

The forensic team were bagging up the body, but Maggie wasn't quite ready to leave yet. She began to walk the perimeter of the room to see if she could discover anything else that could be a clue.

A tap on the shoulder made her jump. 'Jesus, Kat. Way to sneak up on a person! You almost gave me a heart attack.'

'Sorry. You looked like you were concentrating and I didn't want to disturb you. I missed the body.' She nodded in the direction of the forensics team. 'Same MO as the others?'

'I'd say so, but there's something different about this one.' Maggie looked around the room again.

Kat followed her gaze. 'What are you looking at?'

'There was blood and scratches over by that wall. This room is clear – empty compared to the others – and you see all those dirt patches…' Maggie pointed to different areas on the floor. 'I think the perp may have holed himself up in here before our vic was lured to his death.'

'You see all that? I mean, I see the scruffy floor, but how do you know that's not from one of us?'

'Because we're all following the pathway. Those patches are outside of the plates.' Maggie was tired and unsure whether she was seeing things to fit her theory. 'C'mon. Let's get out of here and let forensics finish up. What did you find out?'

While Kat followed behind her she relayed her discussions with the residents of Fracton Hall, and Maggie was curious about one thing she said.

'Two residents are unaccounted for?'

'When the fire broke out and they raised the alarm, two people were missing from the common meeting place.' Kat pulled out her notebook. 'Father Francis Boyle and the maintenance man, Stuart Comley… Neither have returned since.'

'Did anyone try and call them?'

'Father Boyle didn't have a mobile on him – it was found in his room. Not unusual, as apparently he liked to go for evening walks in the grounds. None of his belongings appeared to have been taken either, so he wasn't planning a trip away. They've taken his phone and laptop in.'

'And the maintenance guy?'

'He lived on the premises… over there, in fact.' Kat pointed to a small house a few yards away from the main building. 'Do you want to have a look around before we head back?'

Maggie nodded. The more they had to work with, the

better, and she didn't want to leave it to crime scene photos. Her main strength in solving cases came from seeing things first hand.

Chapter Forty-Five

The small building looked to be purpose-built to house one person or a couple, by the size of it. Maggie figured it was probably built to accommodate whoever managed the maintenance of Fracton Hall. They stepped over the threshold, and found themselves standing in a small living room, with an even smaller kitchen attached.

'Looks a bit of a mess.' Kat stepped carefully around the room.

'Uh-huh. I wonder if this is how it always is, or did Mr Comley struggle with someone?'

'There's a pool of blood behind the settee, so I'm guessing the latter,' one of the forensic officers called out.

Maggie nodded and walked towards the couch. Magazines were scattered on the floor and a pillow lay close to the now smouldering fireplace. 'You might want to collect this quickly in case another fire breaks out from those embers.' She hadn't thought about what she said until the forensic officer grunted.

'I was just about to do that.' He frowned and Maggie

silently reminded herself that these were experienced officers who wouldn't take too kindly to her input.

'Sorry.' She stepped out of his way and mentally blocked Nathan's nagging voice reminding her that she should think before she spoke.

'I'm not getting a good feeling...' The net curtain twitched in the wind. 'Was this open when you guys arrived?' Goosebumps formed on Maggie's arms.

The guy whom she'd just pissed off nodded. Maggie got Kat's attention. 'Point of entry, maybe?' She walked over to the window and then returned her gaze to the room. 'There's not many places for a person to hide in here. I can't see how there would have been any element of surprise if the killer used the window to get in and hide.' Maggie bit her lip. 'If Mr Comley was home, why would someone come through the window?' The more she thought about it, the less sense it all made.

'What are you thinking? The killer was here or the maintenance man was involved?'

Maggie paused.

'Both...'

It was time to get back to the station and fit this piece of the puzzle into the investigation.

Chapter Forty-Six

By the time they returned to the office, Maggie was exhausted. She had no time to think about that though, as Nathan shouted for her and Kate to join him in his office. He pinched the bridge of his nose and Maggie got the impression that he had something serious to discuss. Something that might put her in a mood. When she spotted Julie Noble in the room, she knew she was right.

'OK, spit it out. You've obviously got something on your mind.' Maggie leaned back in her chair and crossed her arms – she didn't like to be blindsided.

Kate sat down beside her.

'Before you jump down my throat, hear me out. What do you think about bringing Ms Noble in at this time? Get her to run a story – maybe anger the killer – force him out into the open, so to speak. How we do that is the part I'm struggling with and why I asked you both here. We don't want to place anyone else at risk, but it's a strategy that has been used successfully in the past. Any thoughts?'

'Can I just jump in here?' Julie addressed the room. 'What would my angle be?'

'Forgive me, Nathan, and Julie… I don't mean to interrupt, but you mentioned anger, and I don't think we want to pursue that angle. If we want to encourage the killer to come out, I think we need to be showing empathy. The story has to sound like we understand why this is happening…' The Doc was talking sense, in Maggie's opinion. Although she didn't particularly like the idea of having Julie involved at this time, it seemed the decision was a done deal, and for once she wouldn't kick up a fuss. At least not while everyone was in the room.

'I agree.' Maggie considered her words carefully before proceeding. 'We don't want the guy so riled up that his initial reaction is to run out and kill the next person on his list.'

'Sounds quite risky though. Not sure I like any of this.' Julie crossed her legs.

Trust Julie to throw a spanner in the works.

'How so?' Maggie looked directly at the journalist, challenging her.

'Uh, public outrage for one. I know it might please some…' the journalist shot Maggie a look, 'but I don't want my head on the chopping block any more than it already is.'

Maggie bit her tongue and held back. She'd let the Doc take the lead – after all, this was her area of expertise.

'I don't think anyone here wants that, Julie. The wording would have to be carefully chosen.'

'What do you suggest then, Doctor? How do we get the balance so we don't have the whole of Staffordshire outside my building with pitchforks and flaming torches?'

Maggie felt uneasy and noticed that Nathan wasn't adding much at this time. *What did he have up his sleeve?*

The Doc leaned forward. 'What if we get Julie to do an article on past abuse in children's care homes? Make a point of being disappointed that it seemed like investigations were brushed under the rug. A feature. We focus on the emotions of the victims who got lost in the system, ignored and suchlike, then we reach out and ask them to make contact...'

Maggie rubbed her hands on her thighs. Nathan sat up straight – Kate's suggestion had got his attention.

'Whoa.' He held his hands up. 'Hang on a minute. We'd be opening a can of worms and we don't have the resources to deal with the aftermath of that. There could be hundreds of calls.'

Although Nathan was right, it was he who had brought them all together and planted the seed – so what did he think would happen? Maggie wasn't surprised when Kate stood up.

'Yes, there could be, and what a tragedy that would be! Get a team together to actually look into that failure and take on a proper investigation. Join forces with the Child Exploitation Team and maybe a few of your experienced field team officers. Just a thought, and I appreciate that I'm only a civilian, but have any of you wondered about the fact that if you maybe pull together and investigate something that should have been taken seriously when it was first reported, none of this would be happening right now? The killer is seeking to destroy all those people who destroyed his life, his childhood, and he won't stop until that's done, or until we stop him first.' With that punch in the gut, Kate stomped out of the room.

'She's a feisty one, eh? I can see why you fancied her,' Julie blurted out.

Maggie could feel the heat rising up her neck and she shot Julie a look.

'What? Thought you said Nathan knew about it?' Julie whispered, leaning forward.

Was she doing this intentionally to get a rise out of her? Maggie bit the side of her cheek – now was not the time.

Nathan coughed. 'I do. I think Maggie is trying to tell you that there's a time and a place for comments like that, and here is neither. Can we get back to the task at hand?'

Maggie's expression softened.

'I'm up for doing a feature. I'll have to do some research but I agree with Kate. If crimes occurred in the past and weren't dealt with – this needs to be brought out in the open. No need to look at me that way either. I can assure you that no matter what I write, it will be done sensitively – I'm not about to do something that jeopardises my career, but more importantly opens wounds to those people that this affected in the past. You both have to agree that people need to be held accountable for their actions and justice needs to be served – if I can play a small part in doing that, you can definitely count me in...'

Before the day had ended, they had agreed on what the next steps would be. Nathan confirmed that Julie and Maggie could finalise the details, and they made plans to do just that. Maggie only hoped that Julie would play fair.

Chapter Forty-Seven

Maggie hadn't initially been keen on the idea of meeting Julie at her home after work, but her curiosity got the better of her. She pulled up in front of the address and sat in her car, taking in the neighbourhood. She wondered if her neighbours were annoyed by Julie or in awe that they had someone semi-famous living on their street. Maggie got out of her car and walked up the pebbled pathway, admiring the tiny garden which had been neatly planted under both windows on either side of the front. The house was almost picturesque and Maggie took out her phone to double-check she had the right address.

The front door opened and Julie stood with an apron wrapped around her waist. 'Are you going to stand there all night?' She stepped aside and Maggie brushed by her. The smell of freshly baked bread danced up her nostrils and something else. Whatever it was, it was making Maggie salivate.

'Hope you don't mind, but I made some vegetable soup

and fresh bread rolls – I figured a bit of food might get the ol' synapses working and ideas flowing. Come through.'

Who was this woman? She followed the journalist.

'Have a seat and I'll bring the food through.'

Cushions were laid on the floor in front of a large oak coffee table. The table had been set, wine ready to be poured, a single flower in the middle. Maggie left her bag by the living-room doorway, sat crossed-legged in front of the table and looked around the rest of the room while she waited for Julie to return. It was a mix of modern and antique furniture which balanced each other out. There was a warm feeling to the room but also one of secrecy – you only saw what Julie wanted you to see – much like Julie herself, it seemed. The room, and Maggie guessed the whole house, was not what you would expect.

'Here you go.' Julie placed the bowl of soup down in front of Maggie and one for herself, before leaving and returning with a basketful of hot, freshly baked, crusty bread rolls.

'Wow. I have to say, I'm impressed and absolutely surprised, if I can be frank. You're quite the mystery.' Maggie tore a piece of the roll and dipped it in her soup. It melted in her mouth – so much flavour. 'This is delicious.'

'Thanks. I like cooking and baking – it relaxes me.'

'And gardening? Your front looks magnificent.' Maggie had no qualms about dishing out compliments when they were justified – even to Julie Noble.

'Ah – I'm afraid I can't take any credit for that – I've someone to do it for me. I couldn't keep a plant alive, if I gave it mouth to mouth.' Julie shrugged.

'Well, consider me stunned. This is really great and unexpected. I figured we'd order something in, so compliments to the chef. Do you want to finish eating first and then chat about the article contents, or shall we just crack on?' Maggie hoped it was the former – she hadn't realised how hungry she was until now. She couldn't remember when she last ate.

'Eat first, then I will clear this away and we can get our notes out. I'm assuming you brought some with that bag you have there.' Julie nodded in the direction of Maggie's bulky backpack.

———————

Forty minutes later and the meal was finished. Julie cleared the table and Maggie unloaded her bag.

'I noticed something different in the information Nathan shared about the murder of the priest.' Julie grabbed a notepad and began riffling through the pages. 'Do variations suggest this could be another killer, maybe someone working towards the same end? Or would you say it's the same guy – personalising his murders as he goes on?'

Maggie wasn't surprised that Julie had picked up on the same things that the team had with regard to the latest murder. She was clever – sometimes too clever.

'At the moment, all the evidence points to one killer, and that's how we want your article to come across. Recognise and acknowledge the other victims, but direct the article towards one person.'

'This must all be very draining for you – any case involving children can really mess with a person's head. Are you looking after yourself?'

Maggie looked up from what she was reading and noticed the look of concern in Julie's eyes. She felt her cheeks heat up.

'Everyone's affected. But we just get on with things.' She stretched her arms. 'Anyway, we're hoping your article will help us narrow down the list we got in from Social Care.'

'You know, you're doing it again.' Julie leaned forward.

'Doing what?'

'Flirtatiously changing the subject?' Julie's lip curled on one side.

Maggie gave the journalist a frosty look. If Julie thought that Maggie was going to be pushed into changing her mind about moving their relationship forward, she had another think coming.

'You wish. Can we just get back to this, please? I don't have all night and I'm pretty shattered. I could use a decent night's sleep.'

'Would you stop?' Julie batted her eyelashes.

'Huh?' Maggie's annoyance was bubbling at the surface now.

'Trying to get me to bed.'

'If you're just going to fuck about, I'm going to go...' She made a move to stand up.

'OK, OK.' Julie held her hands up in defeat. 'I was just messing about. Point taken. Here... I've done a partial draft and would love to have your feedback, since you seem to have lost your sense of humour along the way...' Julie passed her over a sheet of paper and Maggie began to read it.

'Yeah, this sounds good. You'll have to run it by our comms department, and I think you'll need to be careful what details of the crimes you include, but other than that – looks like you have it all in hand.' Maggie looked at her watch. 'You know, it really is getting late. Pop by the station with this tomorrow and

we'll see if there is anything Nathan or Kate want included.'
Maggie collected her things.

At the doorway Maggie stopped and turned to face Julie.
Maybe she had been overreacting and this case was getting to
her. 'Thanks again for the soup and rolls. Um... maybe we can
do it again some time.'

'I knew you couldn't resist me...'

Maggie ignored the comment but couldn't help smiling to
herself on the drive home. Julie might be annoying, but there
was something about her that Maggie found alluring. She'd
not tell Julie that, though.

Chapter Forty-Eight

M aggie was glad that today she'd have a brief breather from the murder investigation. She had agreed to attend the Domestic Abuse Forum as the lead police contact, despite no longer working for the now disbanded DAHU. For consistency, and due to the relationships she had built with certain DA perps and victims, Nathan and DI Rutherford had agreed that passing on the task would not be beneficial at this time. She did find her work challenging as well as rewarding, but with an ongoing murder investigation, it could be stressful.

The DA Forums generally lasted two to four hours, but this one had consumed most of the day. After going through the nominal list and action plan, Maggie had offered to drop the attending Probation Officer back at the Markston Probation Office. While there, she decided she'd pop in and check on Sarah.

Sarah was at her desk when Maggie was let through into the open-plan offices – Maggie almost felt bad for disturbing her, but she was more focused on her own agenda.

'Hey! How's it going?' Maggie tapped the desk before taking a seat. She had to hide her surprise when Sarah's bloodshot eyes looked up at her.

'Well, I haven't had much sleep lately, if it wasn't obvious.' She pointed to her eyes. 'Sorry, did we have a meeting arranged?' Sarah turned the pages of her diary, looking for an appointment that Maggie knew she wouldn't find.

'No. I was dropping one of your colleagues back after the DA Forum and thought I'd see how you are. All OK at home?'

Sarah leaned in and whispered, 'Not exactly. Do you mind if we go somewhere more private?'

Maggie nodded and followed Sarah into one of the interview rooms.

'I could be making something of nothing, but when Justin and I were in town the other day, I saw him talking to this guy. I got the impression it was a pretty serious conversation and when I asked him about it, he got so angry and defensive. I... I...' Sarah burst into tears.

'Hey.' Maggie reached across and rubbed her arm. 'Take your time – what has made you so upset?'

The pair sat in silence for a few minutes while Sarah composed herself.

'When I came into work yesterday... I saw him.'

'Who?'

Sarah swallowed. 'The guy Justin was arguing with. He was here for an appointment, and when I asked his Probation Officer about him, he said he's a nasty piece of work, involved in all sorts of dodgy shit, I know I should've called your lot, but I needed time to take it all in. I'll have to speak to my manager now too. I'm a wreck, Maggie.' Sarah's head fell into her hands.

Maggie resisted her urge to shake Sarah by the shoulders and shout at her. This could be a person of interest, and Sarah just sat on it, but she also understood the implications for Sarah, should it turn out that her husband was somehow involved in all this. 'Can you tell me the name of this person and his Probation Officer?' Maggie pulled out her notepad and waited.

'His name is Alfred Headley, but he's supervised at Stafford Probation Office – he was only attending here because of a programme we run. His officer is Tony Preston.'

Maggie groaned. Tony Preston was Bill Raven's Probation Officer, and useless at his job. Maggie would be surprised if she got any information from him. 'OK. I'll check in with Tony...' She looked at her watch – it was too late now for anything. 'In the morning now, I guess. Any chance you could let him know, so that he has everything ready?'

'Sure. I better go bite the bullet and speak to my manager now.' Sarah's legs shook as she stood.

'Are you sure you're OK? I can stay if you'd like.' Maggie held her arm to steady Sarah.

'I'll be fine. Are you OK to get out?'

The doors in the main office were opened by a button release – this was so the clients could leave without having to wait for the pass card, if a situation arose. 'Yeah, not a problem. Call me if you need anything, OK?' Maggie left and headed back to her car. As she drove home she hoped that Tony Preston kept better records on Headley than he did on Raven. This could turn into another high-profile case and the last thing the police needed was scrutiny because another agency failed to monitor an offender.

Chapter Forty-Nine

The next morning, when Maggie relayed the information she had learned to Nathan, he rolled his eyes.

'Bloody hell – that Preston guy? I put in a complaint about him, you know. His records must be monitored now. Have you spoken to Probation yet?'

'Just going to do that now. I'm hoping I can pop around and maybe see if we can get some background. Bethany's pulling Headley's PNC together and Kat and I can go and pick him up for a friendly chat...'

'Let me know if I need to get on to the Senior Probation Officer or SPO, whatever you call them, over there. I'd be happy to have a go at Preston again – he was a real prick.' Nathan gripped the pen in his hand so tight, his knuckles turned white.

Maggie returned to her desk and saw the pile of papers Bethany had left. 'He's been a busy boy then.' There were about twenty pages of previous convictions and as Maggie flicked through, one in particular caught her attention. Arson with Intent – Headley had received a five-year custodial sentence when he was nineteen. He was thirty-five now – it certainly would fit the profile Kate had been working on. Maggie was keen to know the specific details and hoped Tony Preston had learned from his mistakes and upped his game.

'Kat – you ready?' Maggie picked up her bag and waited for her colleague.

'Yep. Good to go.'

Stafford Probation office was directly behind the police station, and right next to the courts. Sarah had confirmed via email that Tony Preston knew to expect them. They pressed the buzzer and walked up the stairs to the reception area. Unlike Markston Probation, Stafford still was very much closed in terms of interview rooms being separated from where Officers were based. Two POs per office, with the small admin team grouped with Probation Service Officers in a central area. It was an older building that couldn't be transformed to the new way of working that other Probation Offices had now embraced, following some changes in 2014. Though if what Maggie had heard on the grapevine was correct, Probation were going to be reunified and the new way would be scrapped. Stafford would be ahead of the game if that happened.

Once they were signed in, Tony greeted them and showed them to his office.

'Thanks for sparing us some time. We were told you're Alfred Headley's Probation Officer, and we'd like a bit of background on him.'

Tony held up his hand, palm facing the pair. 'Let me stop you right there. Could you tell me a bit more of what exactly this is all about? You can't just come in here, all guns blazing, and expect me to hand over confidential information.'

Sarah must have only given Tony the bare minimum of details.

Maggie clenched her fists. 'We've reason to believe that Mr Headley might be connected to a murder investigation – does that help?' Maggie's dislike of Tony Preston was growing stronger by the second and she was aware of the sarcastic tone in her response, but didn't care. She really had to control the urge to reach across the desk and punch him in the face. Smug bastard.

'Uh… well, I'll have to speak to my manager…' Tony Preston glared at Maggie – and she accepted the challenge.

'Let me stop *you* there, Mr Preston. We're fine if you want to speak to your manager, as obviously, if it does come to light that Mr Headley is involved, you'll have a serious further offence on your hands. But while you're doing that, if you could let us know his current address, so we can check it against our records, and when he's next due in – that would be very helpful.'

Maggie smiled inwardly as Tony's face grew pale. He looked up the address details on his computer and read them out as Kat took notes.

'He's actually due to see me in about an hour.'

'Oh, that's good timing. We'll wait, if you don't mind.' Maggie sat back in the chair.

'Well, you can't arrest him on the premises,' the Probation Officer blurted out, shuffling papers on his desk as he spoke.

Maggie was well versed in the Police/Probation policy. She always found it an odd policy but accepted that it had to do with maintaining the offender's compliance and relationship with their Officer. A person was more likely to attend if they didn't fear arrest at every appointment.

'We're not here to arrest him, we just want to speak with him at the station. He's more likely to not get lost on the way if we escort him. Are you going to have that word with your manager before he arrives?' Maggie tapped her watch.

Tony stood, glancing briefly over his shoulder before he left the room.

'Do you get the feeling he doesn't like us very much?' As much as Maggie valued the working relationship between Police and Probation, Officers like Tony weren't to be trusted.

'He needs to get that pole out of his ar—' Before Kat could finish her sentence, Tony returned.

'What information do you need, then?' Tony sat at his desk and Maggie couldn't help but feel a little bit self-satisfied.

'What can you tell us about the arson conviction?' Maggie didn't want to jump to conclusions, but this offence was relevant to their investigation, and the more they knew from the Probation perspective, the better.

'That was before my time with him, I'm afraid. I only just got his case for his current offence.'

'What's he on probation for?' Kat queried.

'Criminal damage, threatening behaviour and two common assaults. He received a two-year Suspended Sentence Order.'

'Could you tell us a bit more about the assaults and threats?' The offences piqued Maggie's interest and learning more about them might help in determining whether Headley was worth pursuing.

'I'll print off his OASys risk assessment – you'll get more details off there. All I will be doing is reading it to you, and you seem quite capable of reading it yourself.' The sarky tone was back.

Kat nudged Maggie and smiled. Tony's manager must have reminded him about his negligence on the Raven case and the importance of inter-agency sharing of information.

'Thanks. We appreciate it.' Maggie had a hard time not gritting her teeth when replying.

Tony's desk phone rang. Looking at the time, Maggie realised it could be Headley, here for his appointment.

'OK. Yep. Tell him I'll be with him in five – he's a little early anyway, so if he kicks off, point that out to him.' Tony hung up the phone. 'That's him. How are you going to do this?'

'I thought maybe you could introduce me and I'll have a bit of a chat with him at the start of his supervision. Kat can wait downstairs and I'll join her once I have had a word. Then if you bring him down when you're finished, we'll take him round to the station.'

Tony shrugged. 'Fine by me.'

'Kat, if you wait here a few minutes before heading downstairs…' Kat gave her a thumbs-up and Maggie followed Tony out to the reception area.

Before he opened the door, Tony turned to Maggie. 'I'd appreciate it if you followed my lead. I don't want him making a scene in reception.'

'Whatever you feel is best.' Tony clearly wanted to show that he was the one in control of the situation, and Maggie would give him that, since she was on his territory. She wasn't sure why Tony felt Alfred Headley would cause trouble. If he wasn't involved in anything dodgy he had nothing to fear from Maggie or the police, but she prepared herself, as you just never knew what could set someone off.

Chapter Fifty

'Who the fuck is she?' Headley spat.

Maggie waited for Tony to remind his client of where he was and how to behave appropriately, but nothing was forthcoming. Headley stood his ground and wasn't going to move. Either Tony was thick as shit and wasn't picking up on the cues, or he was deliberately letting Headley get irate. Maggie wanted to calm the situation before others arrived into reception, and if Tony wasn't going to take the lead, she would.

She held out her hand. 'My name is DC Jamieson. Call me Maggie. I'm here to have a quick chat with you before your supervision session. Mr Preston is going to take us through to the interview room.' She glared at the Probation Officer and he finally made a move.

'What the hell, Tony. You stitching me up?'

Tony held his hands up while Maggie observed the dynamics between the two. *Who was running the show here?*

'No one is stitching you up.' He opened the door and led them to the interview room. 'If we could all just take a seat.'

Maggie brushed by him and sat at the first available seat nearest the door. As tempting as it was to embarrass Tony in front of his client, she held her tongue.

Alfred Headley sat opposite the pair and tapped his fingers on the desk. 'So speak.' He changed positions and crossed his arms.

Maggie forced a smile, surprised again that Tony wasn't challenging Headley. She'd attended a few probation appointments and this was not the norm.

'I was going to wait until we were all settled in here before making the introductions, but it seems DC Jamieson couldn't wait.'

Heat burned Maggie's cheeks, but she maintained a professional approach, even though it was getting harder by the minute.

'The police want to speak with you about a serious offence they are investigating – it's just a voluntary discussion. Isn't that right, DC Jamieson?'

Maggie clenched her teeth and didn't care if it was obvious to those present in the room. *Was this guy being deliberately obstructive?* 'I think what Mr Preston is trying to say is that we'd appreciate your co-operation in a matter. My colleague and I will be waiting downstairs; we'd like you to come around to the police station and answer a few questions after your appointment.'

'I've done jack shit. What's this about?' Headley smacked the table.

Tony Preston started to speak but Maggie jumped in first and cut him off. 'That may well be the case – I don't think I said you were involved. There are just a few matters we'd like some clarification on – we won't take up much of your time.

I'll see you downstairs when you're done here.' Maggie stood. 'Mr Preston, can I have a moment of your time?' Maggie left the room and waited in the hall for Tony to join her.

A few minutes passed before he decided to grace her with his presence.

'Yes?'

'I wish you hadn't said that to him. We don't know what the outcome of the interview will be, and making false promises won't help the matter at all.'

'Thanks for your opinion, DC Jamieson – how about I do my job and you do yours. Is that all?' Tony placed his hand on the doorknob.

'Just one more thing… I want to stress that we'd appreciate it if you didn't give Headley any details about what we discussed in your office earlier. We don't want him to prepare his responses…'

'Hmmmph. I'll do my best.' A sly smile crept across his face before he returned to his supervision session.

Maggie turned on her heels and stomped down the stairs. Kat was standing outside the door having a fag, and Maggie joined her.

'You look like you could use one of these.' Kat held up her cigarette. 'What happened in there?'

'Tony Preston is an arrogant arse. That's what happened. Arrgghh. He infuriates me! I spoke to Headley and explained we'd be out here when he finishes. I just hope that Tony doesn't spoonfeed him everything we discussed and wind him up even more. He was pretty pissed off. Be prepared to call for some back-up if he gets difficult.' Maggie paced up and down the pathway outside the Probation Office.

Twenty minutes later, Maggie was surprised to see Tony Preston come out of the building on his own.

'Where's Headley?' Maggie looked over his shoulder and frowned. No one was in the lobby area.

'I let him out the back entrance, as he was extremely agitated after you left. I advised him to go for a walk and calm down before going around to see you in half an hour...'

'You what?' Maggie turned away from Tony and called out to Kat, 'Come on, if we run we may be able to catch up with him.' She turned back to Tony. 'I'll be speaking to your manager about this.'

She didn't wait for a response.

Kat and Maggie ran around the back of the building and ahead in the distance, they saw Headley walking with his phone up to his ear.

'Mr Headley. Alfred! Hang on!' Maggie waved as he turned around. When he saw them, he ran.

'Aww fuck.' Maggie turned to Kat. 'I hope those shoes are comfortable. Let's go get this arsehole!'

Chapter Fifty-One

Alfred Headley ran ahead and Maggie signalled to Kat to go down the alley to their left to cut him off while she followed from behind.

She picked up the pace and was gaining on him when she caught the eye of an old man on a bench with a cane by his side. She didn't need to say a word, the old man saw what was happening and within seconds, his cane shot out and tripped Headley. He went down like a tree that had been felled. Maggie caught up and stood over him, trying to catch her breath. She bent over.

'Stay down on the ground,' Maggie instructed while she waited for Kat to appear.

'Why the fuck were you chasing me?'

'Why'd you run? You knew we wanted to speak with you, and this behaviour is making us think you do have something to hide.'

'I don't even know what you want to speak to me about, so what the fuck could I be hiding? I was on my way to my solicitor. Can I get up now?'

Maggie nodded, stepped aside and held out her hand to pull him up. Kat arrived shortly after, gasping for air.

'I'm not going to go into details here. Your actions make me think you do know why we're interested in speaking with you – so are you going to walk back with us or do we have to arrest you?' Maggie hoped he went for the former, as they really had nothing they could charge him with. 'Once at the station, you'll be free to call your solicitor, but as I explained to you earlier, at this stage, it's just a voluntary chat.'

'Doesn't feel voluntary, but fine… I'll come.' He fixed his shirt and walked quietly back to the station in between Maggie and Kat.

At the station, they signed Headley in and Maggie stayed back while Kat led him to an interview room. She rang upstairs to Nathan.

'*DS Wright.*'

'Hey. I'm downstairs with Alfred Headley. Kat and I are going to speak with him now.'

'What took so long?'

'I'll fill you in later, but be prepared for a rant about Preston. No way am I letting him get away with how he behaved – I'll definitely be filing a complaint against Tony Preston. That guy is a total twat.'

'No need to say any more. We'll chat when you're finished.'

Maggie entered the interview room and sat down next to Kat. She waited as her colleague explained the purpose of the interview and cautioned him. She then asked Headley if he wanted a solicitor present.

'I don't know yet. I'll see what you have to say first,' he huffed.

'We'd like to ask you about your connection to a man named Daniel Firth, and Justin Hardy.'

The room was silent as Headley's face went blank. Minutes felt like hours and just as Maggie was about to ask the question again, Headley said the words she dreaded:

'No comment. I'd like to see my solicitor now.'

Chapter Fifty-Two

Kat and Maggie were speaking to the custody sergeant when they were informed that Alfred Headley's solicitor had arrived.

They returned to the interview room and Kat reminded Headley he was still under caution. Maggie recognised the solicitor. He worked with a lot of offenders whom Maggie had put behind bars.

'Can you tell us what this all about now, DC Jamieson?' The solicitor's brows furrowed, as if the whole experience was an inconvenience for him.

'I was in the process of doing that, but before I could finish, your client decided it was best to have you present,' she snapped back.

'Well, you should've let him come and speak to me in the first place. We probably could have cleared this up very quickly.' He adjusted the lapels of his jacket and pulled out a pen.

'Before you arrived, I asked Mr Headley how he knows Daniel Firth and Justin Hardy.' They weren't sure that Alfred Headley had any connection with either, but it was worth testing the ground.

The pair whispered between themselves and the solicitor nodded to his client.

'I don't know who you're talking about. What makes you think I know either of them?'

'We have a witness who saw you talking to Justin Hardy in the town centre the other day.' Maggie sat back and waited to hear how Headley would get out of this.

'Saw me? Well, if I was seen talking to anyone, I have no idea who they were… What else you got?'

'Justin Hardy owns Hardy & Associates Insurance – you may have seen it in the news recently… There was a fire and a body was found.'

The solicitor raised his hand. 'Are you suggesting my client is involved with any of that?'

'We're not *suggesting* anything. I'm asking questions and your client is doing everything possible to avoid answering.' Maggie was looking at Headley as she replied to the solicitor.

'I'm not hiding anything. I talk to shitloads of people – every bloody day. What would I have to do with a fire at an insurance building?'

Maggie tried another tactic. 'Did you know Daniel Firth?'

Headley's face grew red. 'I dunno. Name sounds familiar, but probably because I saw something on the news, like you said.'

Maggie looked at Kat… She was convinced he was lying.

'Mr Headley, I'm afraid I don't believe you're being

truthful. You need to work on your poker face a bit. I think you did know both men, but what I don't know is how you're connected to the case we're investigating. So why don't we give you five minutes to chat with your solicitor, and we can clear this all up.' Maggie stood and motioned for Kat to follow.

Out in the hall Kat's brow furrowed. 'What are you thinking?'

'Did you see the look on his face when I mentioned Firth? My gut is telling me he knows something and his vague responses are setting off red flags. I'm hoping his solicitor will talk some sense into him and get him to tell us what he does know.'

The door opened and the solicitor motioned them in. Maggie didn't want to risk any issues, should they charge Headley in the future, so she held back while Kat reiterated the formalities.

'My client has nothing further to say on this matter. He denies all knowledge of the men you are asking him about. Sounds to me like you're on a fishing expedition. So…' He closed up his folder and tucked his pen back into his pocket. 'We thank you for your company, but we'll be leaving now. If you have any more questions, backed with some evidence, here's my card.'

The pair rose and Kat showed them out before returning. Maggie hadn't moved. Her brain was trying to process what had just happened, but her gut knew there was a connection and Headley's solicitor's face spoke volumes.

'What a waste of time.' Kat picked up her notebook.

'I don't think so at all. We need to speak to Hardy again, so get him in before Headley has a chance to speak with him.

He'll be easier to crack. Then we'll have the opportunity to re-interview that twat and rub the smug look off both their faces.' Maggie stood. 'If you call Justin and give him an appointment to come in, I'll update Nathan. We can pick things up again tomorrow.'

Chapter Fifty-Three

Maggie laid her bag down just inside the doorway and threw her coat over the stair rail when she got in the door. She was shattered, and just wanted to relax. She kicked her shoes off and went into the living room where she stretched out on the couch.

Wine. She definitely needed wine. One glass wouldn't do any harm.

Ignoring the voice in her head that was trying to remind her about her decision to be healthier, she headed to the kitchen, but before she could reach the fridge, the landline rang. Only two people called her on that – Kate and her parents. She crossed her fingers, hoping it was Kate, as she'd been avoiding her parents ever since she had to cancel their last visit.

She dragged her feet over to the phone, picked up the receiver and took a breath. 'Hello?'

'Nice to see you are still alive… You've not called in weeks,' Maggie's mother huffed down the line.

'Hi, Mum. How are you? How's Dad?' Maggie walked with the handset to the kitchen and poured herself that glass of wine. Screw the voice in her head.

'Well, lucky for you, I'm fine – but what if something had happened to us? You care more about those criminals than you do your own family.'

'That's not fair, Mum. And it's not true at all. You know how busy my job is, but you're right – I should have called. Sorry.'

'Hmmph. Fine. So what's happening in Staffordshire then? What's keeping you so busy?'

It didn't sound like this was going to be a quick call. Maggie sank into the chair and put her feet up, the wine glass placed within easy reach on the side table. 'I'm in the middle of another murder investigation. I won't bore you with that. Tell me about you and Dad. Have you been on any travels?'

'Your father had a bit of a spell. He has a scan booked in for next week. Nothing to worry about, though. You know what he's like. Wants to help everyone; he was down at the neighbours' farm helping them build a fence. I reckon he forgets that he's retired... and old...'

'What? Are you sure he's OK?' Maggie was concerned. Her father was like an ox – nothing fazed him. If he had to go to the doctor's, it must be more serious than her mother was letting on and was probably the reason she called.

'Ah, he's fine. Really – no need to fret now. Do you want to have a word? He's here beside me.'

Before Maggie could answer, she heard a grunt down the line.

'Don't listen to your mother. There's nothing wrong with me.' He sounded out of breath.

'Hi, Dad. Why aren't you enjoying your retirement? You

shouldn't be grafting so hard at this stage in your life. You know we worry about you when we hear you're ill.'

'Aye, lass. Nothing to worry about, and who's "we"? Do ye have yourself a man now? Will I finally get to see a wee bairn running around the house when we visit next? I'm not getting any younger and neither are you.'

Maggie shifted in her seat. 'Sorry to disappoint again. No man on the horizon and definitely no kids. I meant me… and Andy. He'd want to know if you weren't well.'

The line grew silent.

'Why have ye brought him up? That thieving little…' Maggie's father started to cough and her mother came back on the phone.

'What have you said to your father? He's stomped off now.'

'I only mentioned Andy…'

'Why would you do that? Your father needs to be stress-free, and you have to go and upset him. Are you in touch with Andy?'

Maggie didn't want to lie to her mother, but she wasn't sure she was up for this conversation just now. Her plan had been to relax this evening, but she couldn't really avoid it any longer. 'Andy has been living with me for a while now, Mum.'

'What? And you didn't think to tell us all the times we spoke before? I hope you lock your valuables away.' Although her mother's words were sharp, Maggie also heard relief. Maggie knew that her mother might not have liked Andy a lot of the time when he was gambling, but he was still her son.

'It was complicated. He doesn't gamble anymore. In fact, he attends Gamblers Anon, has a really good job and is close to starting his own business. He's in the process of looking for his own place now. He's really landed on his feet, Mum.'

'A leopard never changes his spots. Don't be fooled, he's said that

all before, you know – right before he wiped out our savings. That boy will be the death of us. I'm disappointed in you for keeping this from us.'

'I didn't make the decision lightly.' Maggie wasn't about to tell her how she'd bailed Andy out, as that would only add fuel to the fire. 'He had to prove himself and he did. He knows how much he hurt you, hurt all of us, but I think he deserves a chance.'

'Well, I won't be telling your father, as he'd be livid and I don't want to burden him any more before he has his tests. I hope you know what you're doing.' She sighed and quickly changed the subject. *'Did I hear that you have a man? When will we get to meet him?'*

Maggie rolled her eyes. She struggled with whether now was the opportune time to finally speak about her bisexuality. Her parents were already mad at her, but her mother might understand more than her father, so she bit the bullet and went for it. 'Mum. There's no man in my life right now. But I have met someone, and although we're just friends at the moment, who knows what the future holds?'

'That doesn't make sense. You've a friend but not dating? Is he a police officer too?'

Maggie bit her lip. 'No... *she* is a journalist.'

She waited for the penny to drop.

'She? Are you telling me that you are a lesbian?' The last word was whispered like it was a dirty secret.

'No – I'm bisexual, Mum.' Maggie's shoulders slumped. She felt relieved even though she knew it would open up another can of worms.

'Are you just experimenting or something? Young people these days are always trying out new things. You've always had boyfriends. I'm really sorry, darling, but I'm confused.'

How does she think I feel?

'Yes, I've had relationships with men but I'm attracted to women too.' The line went silent. 'Hello? Mum... are you still there?'

'Uh... yes. Um... I think I hear your father calling me, sweetheart. I best go and see what he wants. Don't be a stranger...' Her mother ended the call.

Maggie placed the handset on the table and took a big sip of her wine. She couldn't believe she'd finally told her mother and wondered whether or not her mum would tell her dad. Maggie shook her head. Given her mum's reaction, it was unlikely. It was a conversation she would have preferred to have face to face, but she didn't know when she would next see her parents, with her busy work schedule.

Maggie was startled out of her thoughts when she heard the door slam.

'Fuck. What a day.' Andy popped his head through the door. 'You OK?'

'I don't know...' Maggie felt slightly light-headed.

Andy walked over to her. 'Why? What's happened?'

'I just got off the phone with Mum and Dad. Dad has a test at the hospital next week. He had a dizzy spell, but they both swear he's fine.'

Andy sat down. 'Shit. Do you think he really is OK?'

'I... think so. Let's wait to hear the test results. That's if they call me back to tell me.'

Andy cocked his head to the right. 'Why wouldn't they?'

'I kinda told them that you're living with me and...'

'Lemme guess – Dad ranted and Mum cried. Fuck. Sorry Maggie, I didn't want to put you in this position... I should probably get my own flat sorted sooner than planned.'

'Would you calm down? I think what I told them afterwards made that news seem like a walk in the park.'

'What the hell did you tell them?'

'I told Mum I'm bisexual… and then she hung up on me…' She took another sip of wine as she waited for her brother's reaction.

'I'm actually speechless… Are you OK?' He squeezed her shoulder.

'Well, there's a first time for everything, I guess.' Maggie laughed. 'I feel like a huge weight has been lifted off my shoulders. I mean, I knew they wouldn't like it – though Mum's reaction surprised me. She *actually* hung up on me…' She scratched her nose.

'She probably didn't know what to say – you know what they're like when they hear things that catch them off guard. But why did you tell them? I thought you wanted to wait until you could see them.'

'I did, but after I told her about you, and they were asking about grandkids, well… it just came out.'

'Grandkids? Shit, you're not…?'

'Bite your tongue! No, I'm not pregnant. Christ, I can just about look after myself – could you imagine?' They both laughed at the thought of Maggie as a mother.

'Well, I have some news too…' Andy handed her the keys to the car.

'Why are you giving me these back?'

'I got myself a little white van. It's used, mind you, so who knows how long it will last, but it was cheap enough and it's a start – so thank you. I wouldn't have been able to do this without you.' He reached across and smacked her knee.

Maggie was pleased for her brother but curious why he

was pushing himself so hard to get a flat and a vehicle. She didn't want to be paranoid but couldn't help but wonder where he was getting all the spare cash from.

'You know you don't have to rush with all this. Are you sure you can afford it?'

'Don't worry. With you letting me live here, I've managed to put aside a little each month. I told you I didn't want to be in your debt for ever and wanted to prove to you that I was serious about getting back on my feet...' Maggie noticed he wouldn't look her in the eye.

'Look at me, Andy. Are you sure there is nothing going on?'

Andy stood up. 'Fucksake. I'm not one of your offenders, you know! I'm a grown man and quite capable of looking after myself. I thought you'd be happy...' He stomped out of the room and Maggie jumped at the slam of the door.

She really wanted to believe him. He'd worked so hard, but even if he had been saving, it wouldn't have been enough to buy a van. The way he'd just reacted made her stomach flip with worry. The last thing she needed was to be fretting about her brother too.

Chapter Fifty-Four

M aggie had to drag herself into work that morning. Andy hadn't returned until the early hours and she was still coming to terms with the conversation she'd had with her parents. Most of the night was spent tossing and turning. At least the murder investigation would stop her from dwelling on her personal life for a few hours.

'OK, Justin Hardy is on his way in. He sounded nervous on the phone when I called yesterday and asked whether he needed a solicitor,' Kat called over to Maggie.

'Interesting. When I updated Nathan before I left yesterday, he said we should push Hardy. If anyone is the weak link, it will be him. The sooner we clear up Headley's connection to Justin and Firth, the better. Sarah wouldn't have told me about what she saw if she didn't think it was important.'

Maggie's mobile rang. She hoped it was Andy wanting to smooth things over, as his behaviour last night rang alarm bells. She didn't really need any of it now. It wasn't Andy though. Markston Probation flashed up on the screen. 'DC Jamieson.'

'What the hell is going on, Maggie?' Sarah shouted down the line.

'I guess Justin told you? You knew we'd be talking to him – why else would you tell us about what happened?'

'I... I... Well, yes... He's called me in a right state. I'm just about to meet him and we're heading there now. What's happened that you need to speak to him so urgently?'

'You know I can't discuss that with you, and you won't be able to come into the interview with Justin.' Maggie really felt for Sarah, but she had a job to do.

'Why not? I thought your colleague said it was a voluntary chat? Following up on his statement.'

'That's not how it works. If Justin wants a solicitor present, that's fine – we have a few loose ends we need to clear up.'

'That's the last time I help you...' The line went dead. That was the second time in a matter of hours that someone had slammed the phone down on Maggie. Sarah was angry but would calm down once she had time to think about things objectively.

Kat signalled her. 'Oh, if you bite any harder on your lip, it's going to bleed. I take it that was Sarah, and she wasn't pleased?'

Maggie released her lip and rubbed her chin. 'She's furious. Slammed the phone down on me. I can understand – it's her husband, but deep down she'll want the answers too. This has got to be a real shock for her, and I suppose she'll be worrying about how it might impact her job.' Maggie surmised if Sarah disclosed all the information to her manager, things would be put in place to ensure she wouldn't have access to certain individuals or information. That would be for her protection as well as for those involved. 'I'm just going to go through the Headley information before Justin arrives. Might be something in there we can use to catch him out.'

An hour later, Kat and Maggie were called downstairs by the enquiry desk – Justin Hardy, his solicitor and Sarah had arrived. Despite Maggie's advice, Sarah had decided to come anyway.

Maggie grabbed her notes and they headed downstairs.

'I'll bring them through, if you want to go straight to the interview room.' Kat headed to the reception area.

Maggie settled herself in Interview Room One. She felt a little uncomfortable, given Justin was Sarah's husband. Although they weren't close friends outside of work, she and some of her colleagues knew Sarah professionally. Having said that, Sarah was probably mortified. Maggie was reminded of Lucy Sherwood and the situation she had found herself in, having to hide that she was living with a high-risk domestic abuser.

The door opened and Maggie was shaken out of her thoughts as Justin, Kat and the solicitor entered. Maggie acknowledged them and waited for them all to sit down. Kat did the formalities, cautioning Justin and giving a brief explanation as to why they had called him in, before she handed the floor over to Maggie.

'Thank you for coming in at such short notice. As my colleague DC Everett has explained, we've recently been given some information that concerned us and we'd like to clear it up. I'm not going to beat around the bush. Can you tell us what your relationship with Alfred Headley is?'

Justin's face paled. 'I... uh... I've never heard of him... Who told you I did?' His eyes dropped to the floor.

Maggie looked at Kat. 'Really? So if I told you that you were actually seen having a heated conversation with Mr Headley in Stafford town centre, are you saying that wouldn't be true?'

Justin's eyes flitted between his solicitor and Maggie as he shifted in his seat. He seemed to be waiting for his solicitor to jump in, but the guy seemed more interested in the wall than in Justin's silent cry for help.

He leaned across and whispered in his solicitor's ear. The man nodded and whispered something back. He looked annoyed at being interrupted from his daydream.

'I don't know who Alfred Headley is. I did see a client in the town centre the other day, but his name is Al Smith. He was asking about his policy after the fire in my offices.' The name triggered something in Maggie's memory and she shuffled through her notes. Maggie showed Kat the PNC record.

Kat smiled. 'Al Smith is an alias used by Mr Headley. How would the fire have any impact on his policy, Mr Hardy? Did he also know Daniel Firth?'

'What? Wait – why would he use an alias? I dunno how it would affect his policy, that's why we were arguing. He wanted to pull out of our business transaction and get his money back, but I told him that was impossible. He may have seen Danny at my office – I have no clue whether he knew him or not. Why don't you ask him?'

'Officers, this whole conversation seems pointless and

frankly, I think we all have better things to do with our time. Are you charging my client with anything?' The solicitor yawned.

'We're sorry to have pulled you away from whatever more pressing business you think you have, but we're investigating a murder here, and whether he wants to admit it to you or not, Mr Hardy has not been forthcoming with us.' Maggie stared Justin in the eyes. 'What are you hiding?'

Justin became quite agitated. His leg was going a mile a minute under the table and Maggie sensed she had hit a nerve.

'Why are you hassling me? I told you everything I know! You know my wife is a Probation Officer, right? Do you really think I would get mixed up with dodgy people, knowing it could affect her job?'

'That's the thing, Justin. You *are* mixed up with some undesirables and so far, you've not given us a reasonable explanation. For instance, can you explain your financial records?'

'What the hell? Why have you been digging into my accounts?' Justin looked again at his solicitor for some help.

'Officers – can we just put all the cards on the table? It will make it much easier for my client to answer questions if you're not pulling things out of a hat every time you don't get an answer you like.' He sat back and crossed his arms.

'We've every right to delve into your financial records, and we've noticed large amounts being deposited and withdrawn. Care to explain?' Maggie picked up her pen and twiddled it between her fingers. The silence didn't faze her. Her training had taught her that people can be uncomfortable with silence, feeling the need to fill in the space. She wasn't wrong.

'OK, OK. I'll tell you but you can't tell Sarah. Promise me!' He twisted the ring on his finger.

'You know we can't make any promises. We're police officers, Justin – not your BFFs. What I can tell you is that Sarah will not be privy to anything you disclose in here unless you tell her. That doesn't mean she won't ever find out. But it won't come from us, unless we need to question her because she is involved. However, if you disclose that you've committed an offence, you will be charged. It will be a little difficult to keep *that* from your wife.' Maggie felt a tinge of sympathy for the guy. He was in over his head; his eyes betrayed him. She was surprised that Sarah hadn't picked up on his lies, but sometimes when you are too close to a situation, you turn a blind eye to the truth.

'Can I speak to my solicitor alone, please?'

Maggie nodded and she and Kat left the room.

'He's going to crack now, isn't he?'

'Justin isn't a criminal mastermind. I think he's got himself into something and is in so deep, he's now drowning. It might be a relief to get it off his chest.' Maggie looked at the exit door. 'I'm not sure how Sarah will take any of the news.' Something caught her eye and she looked through the window to see Justin's solicitor waving for them to come back into the room.

'Here we go!' They entered the room and waited for Justin to speak.

'My solicitor advised me not to speak with you...'

Maggie looked over; the solicitor crossed his arms and looked away.

'I can't do this anymore.' Justin's shoulders shook and Maggie gave him the time he needed. 'I've been receiving large amounts of money from people who I thought were investors –

I deposited it into my company's account in denominations of £5,000 at a time. I would then transfer that into our personal joint account before withdrawing it and returning it to the investor.'

'You've been laundering money?' Maggie wasn't expecting that. 'We'll need the names of everyone who has "invested" in this scheme. Can you tell us why?'

'Hardy & Associates was failing. I was talking about it in a pub one night when this group of lads approached me, saying they wanted to invest in the business. I needed the money… only…'

'Only you weren't actually making any money, and by the time you realised it was too late…?'

Justin nodded. 'They used me…'

'Did these people threaten you?' Kat leaned forward, raking her fingers through her hair.

'Yes – they said they would hurt Sarah and get her fired. They knew everything about us.'

'Did Sarah know anything about this?' Maggie didn't believe she did, but she had been surprised before.

'Absolutely not – she'd have killed me if she knew. God, what have I done?'

'You've got yourself in a real bad position, Justin. My colleague here is going to charge and arrest you now for money laundering under the Proceeds of Crime Act, and the case will be passed over to the team that deals with financial crimes. You'll likely be bailed and given details on when next to report.'

'What? You're not going to keep me here? They'll beat the shit out of me once they've learned I talked to you – and what about Sarah? Oh my god, what have I done?' Justin shot out of his chair and began pacing the room.

'Look, Justin. We'll speak to the team and let them know your concerns. Sarah will have to inform her manager of your arrest and charge, and I'm sure if she relays how concerned you are for her safety, arrangements will be made – we've had it before. Once you're finished here, have a word with Sarah and maybe you both can stay elsewhere for a while – you'll just need to let us know. Do you want me to go and have a word with her now? I won't give her the specifics – that's up to you, I'm afraid – but I can explain some things.'

Justin sat back down. 'Yes, I'd appreciate that.' He couldn't even look at Maggie.

'OK.' Maggie turned to Kat. 'Can you take it from here and I'll go speak to Sarah and the fraud team.' Maggie wasn't looking forward to the conversation but also felt sorry for Justin. If Headley and his associates didn't do him some damage, Sarah just might.

Chapter Fifty-Five

Maggie opened the door to the reception area and called Sarah through. She decided to take her to a separate interview room for some privacy. It would also mean that Sarah would avoid seeing Justin when Kat led him to the custody suite to be charged.

'What's happening? Why are you speaking to me in here?' Sarah stared at Maggie, her eyes filled with uncertainty and fear.

'I wanted to speak to you in private, as your husband asked me to. I can't tell you all the specific details but you'll want to be speaking to your manager after this, so I will tell you as much as I can.'

Sarah's hands shook. 'Oh Christ! What has he done?' Her eyes glistened.

'He's being charged at the moment with money laundering offences. He'll likely be bailed, but he did express some concerns about the people he was working with, so we've suggested that you both might want to stay away from your home address until the police can look into matters further.'

'Wait – you mean you won't be investigating this?'

'I'm afraid not. It will be passed over to a specific team that deals with these kinds of offences.'

'So that's what he was doing... all that money... disappearing from our account. I-I... can't believe he put me in this position. I'm not sure I even want to speak with him at the moment, if I'm honest. I'm fuming!'

'I can understand that. Is there anyone you want me to call?' Sarah would be in shock and it might be best if she had a friend with her while she processed everything.

'I have to go back into work to deliver a programme this evening. How am I going to face them? You know I had nothing to do with any of this, right?' Sarah floundered in embarrassment.

'Justin told us. Should you really be going into work? I'm sure they'd understand, given the circumstances.'

'I'm covering for someone else, so I have to go in. We're short-staffed as it is. I'll be fine. How long do you think he's going to be?' Sarah was jumping from thought to thought and Maggie wished she could do more to help her.

'No telling, though if I pop you back out into reception, I should be able to find out.'

Sarah nodded and followed Maggie out. Maggie walked down to the custody suite and noted that Justin was being processed, so wouldn't be much longer. She returned to Sarah.

'Looks like he might be finishing up shortly, so maybe ten or fifteen minutes. Can I get you anything while you wait?'

'A new life would be nice...' Sarah's strained smile pulled

at Maggie. She'd have a lot to think about in the coming months.

'Do you want me to wait with you?'

'No – thanks for everything, Maggie. I am going to go outside and make a few calls. I'll see you soon, no doubt.'

Maggie waved as Sarah left, and then returned upstairs. She knocked on Nathan's door. 'Do you have a minute?'

'Sure. What's up?'

'Sarah Hardy's husband has just been charged with money laundering. There's no evidence to suggest he's involved with the murder investigation, so I think it's safe to wipe him off the board at the next briefing. Kat's dealing with it now. He broke down after we asked him about Headley. I'm not sure we can clear Headley though, but other than his involvement in money laundering, I don't think we have enough evidence to get a warrant to search his house.'

'What *do* we have?'

'He lied about knowing and speaking to Justin. Obviously that could be because of the money laundering, but I got the feeling there was more to it. When Kat gets back, I'll see what she thinks.'

'Let me know if there is anything I can do. I'll see you in the incident room shortly. We have Julie Noble's TV report to watch, and Dr Moloney will be going through the victimology afterwards. Rutherford will want as much info as we can give her, because it looks like there may be some people in high places that had previous involvement with the care homes in question.'

'Great. Just what we need. We're not looking at another Savile situation, are we?'

'I hope not – but we want to contain it now so that we are

not caught out at a later time. Bethany is just gathering some more details on those complaints, and we'll take it from there.'

Maggie's heart felt heavy. She didn't have a good feeling about any of this, and the sooner they could wrap this case up, the better.

Chapter Fifty-Six

What was going on? He'd expected a lot more fuss in the press about Father Boyle. They should be putting the pieces all together, which meant he wouldn't have much time to finish what he started.

He walked over to the bookshelf, pulled out the old Bible from his school days and flicked through until he found what he needed – the original list. Two more left – he stared at their names. One, a retired police officer now – at the time he had been responsible for investigating the complaints from the children's home. The other – well, she ran the home where the worst abuse happened. Rumours amongst the older children were that she liked to watch through two-way mirrors or have members of her staff film when something happened. The evidence of her sickening behaviour had gone missing when the home was shut – but he had a good idea that she still kept it.

His blood was boiling as he thumbed the piece of paper in his hand. Both of these people had haunted his existence.

Sometimes when he was out in the town, hood up, head down, he would see a pair of shoes and immediately flinch as he remembered being kicked repeatedly by his abusers while Joanne Mole encouraged them from a dark corner in the room. The fact that these people seemed to have so much control over his thoughts still – after all these years… His body felt hot as his shoulders tensed. He was taking back that control now.

He replaced the list in the Bible and placed it on the table. He had to calm down or he wouldn't be able to think straight – that's when mistakes were made.

He walked to the kitchen, and flicked the kettle on. Once it had boiled, he made himself a strong cup of tea – watching the drops of milk swirl as he stirred until it reached the perfect reddish brown colour.

Back into the living room, he turned on the television and flicked through until he saw Fracton Hall flash up on the screen, and then a zoomed-in shot of what remained of the outbuildings after the fire took hold. He turned up the volume and listened to the journalist as she described the scene behind her – *devastating, ruins, great loss to the residents…*

Boo-Fucking Hoo – what about his loss?

His anger simmered and he smiled as he realised the implications for men like Father Boyle once everything was out in the open. Good – although men of God, some of them did the most horrible of things and would be held accountable.

'*… the police are appealing for anyone who may have seen anything suspicious to come forward. Did you see anyone behaving unusually on the day, or in the days leading up to or after the fire? The victim, Father Francis Boyle, was a resident here at Fracton Hall and was considered a pillar of the community, for his work in children's homes up until he retired in 2015…*'

What the fuck?

He threw the mug of hot tea against the wall – not caring what his neighbours thought. Fuck them. Fuck them all. Pillar of the community? Is that what sexual sadists were known as now? It was OK to take pleasure in beating the shit out of children in his care? He clenched his fists and thumped them hard on the table top.

No! There was no fucking way that he would accept that! This was not how it was supposed to go. Haven't they figured it out yet? Incompetent bastards.

The journalist was still babbling on in the background about Father Boyle when something made him stop.

'I've been doing some research into alleged abuse which took place in some of the children's homes. Abuse that had been swept under the carpet. Father Boyle appears to have worked at two of these homes, and what I found even more concerning was that recently murdered Daniel Firth also worked at the homes. My question is: If the police aren't looking into a connection – why not? Something happened to the perpetrator of these horrific murders, and now it seems his tormentors must pay. The Staffordshire Scorcher is taking the teeth of his victims, and we should be looking into why his victims received no mercy...'

Staffordshire Scorcher? He laughed at the ridiculous name he had been given by the press. There would be no mercy to his actions. He steadied his breathing and sat back down.

'If you know anything about these allegations, or maybe you were a victim of abuse, grew up in a boys' home – I want to hear from you. Contact me at the Stafford Gazette *– the details should be on the bottom of your screen now. We can talk confidentially. I want to make sure you are heard – I will be your voice...'*

He knew his work would open people's eyes – too little too

late, though. He and the others were already damaged. He
kept tabs on them all – though if they saw him in the street,
they wouldn't recognise him. He had changed so much – no
longer the scrawny, acne-faced boy too scared to fight back.
Most of the others were or had been homeless or alcoholics or
drug addicts – one or two were in prison. Some were all of the
above. *He* was their voice, though – not *her*. A respectable
member of society – they were in for a shock. He debated
about contacting the journalist – might be a good idea to find
out what she knew and steer her in another direction if she got
too close. He didn't want her to jeopardise his work and he
had the perfect cover.

He was thirsty now. He cleaned up the tea and broken glass
before making a fresh cup. He picked up the list once more.

Eeny meeny miny mo…

He already knew who should be the next to go, but with
only two left, he would save her until the end. His grand
finale…

He was tired. He put his feet up on the couch and stretched
out. He needed to have a nap… Murder was exhausting.

Chapter Fifty-Seven

Maggie took a sip of her coffee as they all waited for Julie Noble's pre-recorded story to come on. DI Rutherford had arranged the viewing at the station so that everyone involved could watch and then work out their next move.

'Focus, people. It's starting.' The Guv quietened the room before taking a seat herself.

They watched as Julie mentioned the fire and Father Boyle. It seemed like ages before any mention of the children's homes came up, and then fifteen minutes later the whole thing drew to a close. Maggie cringed when the journalist dubbed him the Staffordshire Scorcher and was concerned that she had mentioned the teeth. If her memory served her correctly, it had been agreed that they would keep that out of the news to weed out any bogus calls.

DI Rutherford clicked off the TV and stood before them. 'There we have it. I think our journalist friend went a little off script...' A frosty glare in Julie's direction from the Guv wasn't lost on those in the room. 'But taking a critical approach, I want to hear your views on how we can use this to strategise our next steps and examine the victimology. Nathan, why don't you start?'

'With all the information now in the public domain, we'll be looking for some of the children's home victims to come forward. We need some officers involved in sifting through any calls that go into the *Gazette*. I was a little hesitant about the teeth being mentioned, but it might actually trigger those people to come forward. I hope you have the legal department on speed dial though, Guv, as our murder victims will now be labelled as abusers.' He coughed. 'I wouldn't wanna be in your shoes just now.'

Maggie looked across at Julie. The journalist was rubbing her hands together and Maggie waited for the defensive outburst... but there was none.

'Thanks, Nathan. Excellent points. Maggie – your thoughts, please.'

Maggie took a moment to go through the news report in her head before making any suggestions. 'If our killer was watching, I believe we'll have a hit a nerve. I didn't get any sense of empathy from Julie when she spoke of the abuse allegations initially, and if this is his motivation – we need that connection. I wonder if a follow-up to the wider press should be done. Giving some power back to our killer, but we'd be in control behind the scenes. I just haven't figured out how we can manipulate things to our advantage in order to reel him in.'

DI Rutherford nodded and without any comment, pointed at Kate.

Kate cleared her throat and she shifted in her seat while she finished highlighting some passages in the notebook she had in front of her. 'I watched all of your reactions as we viewed the news report. It was obvious that you had some misgivings about the direction that Julie took, but the narrative was a group effort and related to the victimology which I'm about to discuss. We had to reach a balance that wouldn't anger the public, whilst agitating our suspect just enough to perhaps incite them to inject themselves directly into the investigation. They will see flaws in Julie's assumptions, and if we are correct in our assessments – that our victims are also perpetrators of historical childhood abuse – the killer will want this in the public domain. They may also want to try and figure out what our next steps will be so that they can revise their MO. I think we will know when the killing spree has ended – there will be a finale, and we haven't seen that yet, so he hasn't finished.'

When the Doc put it that way, it made sense to Maggie, though it could be a risky strategy.

'Thanks, Dr Moloney. Bethany, Kat – do you have anything to add?'

Bethany was never very vocal in meetings, preferring to keep herself in the background. Maggie never understood that, as she was incredibly knowledgeable and often played a key role in getting that one piece of evidence that would crack a case wide open. But focusing on the more analytical side of the cases shielded her from some of the damaging scenes and victims that the rest of them faced, and in that moment, Maggie was a little envious.

'We've been directing all our efforts on the murders, which is our job of course, but I think we need to do something more with the possibility that the victims are not innocent in the way most victims are. We think this is what is fuelling the killer to carry on – so why haven't we directed more manpower in that direction or brought in the Child Abuse Unit? I don't want to talk out of turn, but it would've have been helpful to have someone from Social Care here too – they've worked with victims of child abuse and probably have more direct insight than we do...' Bethany shrugged.

'You raise some key points and ones that I can assure you we have considered. The Child Abuse Unit have been informed and will be making their own enquiries, with instructions to share with us any leads that may be relevant to our investigation. As for Social Care, I was in contact with Hugh O'Donnell, a lead manager from across the road, but he advised that no one was available to attend this meeting. He did request that they be kept in the loop and invited to any future meetings, going forward.'

Kat said, 'I can't really add anything to what has already been said. I do think that all we've now achieved is to wind this fucker up, and he'll be doing his damnedest to complete whatever messed-up mission he thinks he's on. We need those names of anyone else who may have had allegations against them in the past. Without those, we're just chasing our tail. We've no viable suspects, either. This guy is probably laughing his arse off at us.'

Maggie nodded. Even though she agreed with Kat's view on the case so far, she realised that if they took one wrong move, the whole thing could backfire on them.

'Honesty is what I asked for, so thanks for your input. OK...' DI Rutherford looked around the room. 'Julie, we don't normally involve the press in meetings like this, but with the media being one of our many partnerships, we're glad you decided to work with us. Do you have anything more to add to what has already been said?'

Maggie sat back and waited for Julie to shoot down everyone before her – all guns blazing was her style. She would unleash her words and defend her position...

'I actually agree with a lot of what was said.'

Maggie had to stop her jaw from falling to the floor.

'Let me explain, as the look on some of your faces is quite comical. I'm not always up for a fight, despite what most of you believe – I choose my battles carefully. In order for me to have been able to even air this story, I had to convince my boss that it would be worth it – and trust me, that was no easy feat. You have to remember that the *Gazette* needs to focus on the facts we know to be true, or else the paper would be risking some massive lawsuits...'

Julie paused and tucked a lock of hair behind her ear. 'As the good Doc here said, the relevant people were around the table and agreed the narrative, so this is not all on me. It was decided that once I named Father B, I should then look at tying in the abuse allegations. The man could be innocent... though I doubt it.'

The last bit was mumbled loud enough for all to hear. Maggie smiled. There she was. Julie would never hide behind a fear of repercussions if it meant that the truth would be buried.

'We couldn't name the Scorcher's victims as abusers publicly, but I think I said just enough to poke the bear. What do I think your next course of action should be? Prepare for the Firth family and the church to come forward with complaints... When I checked my phone a moment ago, the paper had already received forty calls from members of the public – so it obviously has had some impact. We need a system to deal with this, and having the police involved would be beneficial.'

Maggie noticed DI Rutherford's eyebrow rise.

'We'll make sure someone from my team is with you when you go through those calls…' Rutherford looked around the room and Maggie saw Julie smile. She probably believed that Maggie would be joining her, but if she knew the Guv, she'd have other plans.

'Kat, make arrangements to meet Julie at the paper and sort these calls – let's sift the bullshit from the leads.' Rutherford looked at her watch. 'I think this strategy session has been useful. We can review our position once things start moving forward. We're taking a measured approach with just enough detail to strike the balance of public interest against our desire to… erm… poke the bear. Right, it's time you all went home… All we can do now is wait.'

Chapter Fifty-Eight

He'd woken up drenched in sweat. Visions of Bram Watson laughing in his face. He knew what he needed to do if the opportunity struck. Watson would meet his maker like the rest of them. He picked up the phone and dialled.

'*Yeah?*' a gruff voice answered.

Still the charmer.

'Hello. Could I please speak to the woman of the house?'

A grunt. 'No. She's not here. Who's calling?'

'When would be the best time to reach her?' He controlled his breathing as his heart raced.

'She's away at the moment. Won't be back until tomorrow. I asked who's calling...'

Sounded like Bram was getting a little annoyed.

'Thanks. I'll call back, then.' He hung up the phone and went to his closet. It was a sign. He knew exactly what he needed to do.

The navy boiler suit and high-vis vest looked legit and would be easy to dispose of once he was finished. He was calm as he walked up the path and made a sharp right, following the cobblestones to the side door. Should anyone be looking out their window, all they would recall was an average-sized bloke in blue coveralls and a baseball cap. Nothing unusual about that.

He knocked on the glass pane and through the net curtain he could see the shape of an overweight man shuffling to the door. When the door opened and he was looking eye to eye at Bram Watson, he was immediately thrown back in time, a child again, and his blood ran cold.

'I'm not interested in whatever it is you're selling.' The ex-copper went to shut the door, but he jammed his foot in before it fully closed.

'What the hell do you think you're doing?' Bram stumbled backwards, his finger waving. 'I suggest you leave right now. I'm a police officer...'

'Still telling lies. You're an *ex*-police officer. I know. Put that finger away or I'll break it.' He entered, closed the door and turned the lock. 'Now, where can we go to have a little chat?'

Bram Watson pointed at a closed door just down the hall. 'My office is through there.'

'When will your lovely wife be home?'

'Please don't hurt her. She'll be back any minute now. I've got about £400 in my office. You can have it and we'll forget all this happened. I promise, I won't say a word.' Bram's voice cracked.

Lies still dripped effortlessly from Bram's lips.

He picked up a vase and threw it against the wall, missing

Bram's head by millimetres. The coward ducked out of the way.

'I don't want your fucking money. I want a confession. A full admission to everything you did.' He pushed the man into the office and dragged the chair from behind the desk. 'You need to apologise for what you've done and then you need to pay,' he spat at the ex-police officer.

'Oh my god. You... you're the man the police are looking for. You burned those p-p-p-people alive... Why me? I haven't done anything!'

'*Exactly!* And that,' he poked the copper in the chest, 'was the problem.' He pushed Bram back and the man fell into the chair. 'You did nothing. Do you know what it was like to come to the police station and finally have the courage to tell someone what was happening...?' He stopped. He didn't owe this man an explanation. 'Do you even remember who I am?'

The anger bubbled under his skin. He swiped all the papers and trinkets off the desk. Bram seemed to think that was the moment to be brave, as he jumped out of the chair and made a run for the door.

The two men struggled for a moment before he regained control of the situation. 'Sit the fuck down now.'

'I'm sorry.' Snot bubbled from the man's nostrils and tears ran down his face. 'I'll do whatever you say. Don't kill me. Please...'

He secured Bram to the chair.

THUMP THUMP THUMP on the wall.

'What the...?' He looked around the room.

'That's my neighbour.' Bram pointed at the side wall. 'They're thin. She's probably calling the police.'

'Then we best get to it, shouldn't we.'

Chapter Fifty-Nine

When Maggie woke the next day she dreaded turning on the news. She hadn't received a late-night call, so that was positive, but she had a horrible feeling in the pit of her stomach when she thought back to the meeting yesterday. Were they doing the right thing by taunting their killer?

She arrived at Stafford Police Station to a buzz of activity in the open-plan office. 'What have I missed?'

'Briefing in half an hour – I was told to wait until then to share what I've found. After yesterday's meeting I couldn't shake the feeling that there was more to the story and came back here for a few hours.' Bethany must have seen Maggie's look of concern – the woman spent way too much time in front of that screen of hers – then again, people often said the same about Maggie and her job.

'I know what you're thinking but it's my choice – I shouldn't have but I just needed to check, or I wouldn't sleep, and then I'd be useless to everyone. Anyway – there's a definite connection with all three of our victims – and Sarah

will be happy to learn that her husband is in the clear on that front.'

'I suppose – though he still may be looking at a prison sentence… Guess it's better than a murder charge or being involved in a high-profile child abuse case, right? So is that all you're going to say? Can I see what you found?'

'Sure – your contact at Social Care was a massive help.'

'Claire Knight? She sent you the information?' Maggie noted she should call Claire as the last time they spoke, Claire's manager had made it quite clear that she was to back off. Looks like Claire was a kindred spirit when it came to following the rules… or not, in this case.

'She sure did – I don't know where she found it, as I've been looking for ages, but she scanned over some articles that don't appear online anymore. My guess is, someone high up had to be involved in gagging the press. I've uploaded everything to the case files, so feel free to have a look.'

'Well, that puts an interesting twist on things.' Maggie logged into her computer and searched for the relevant documents. Headlines of appalling abuse accusations burned into her mind. She didn't know what it was, but she could work the most grisly murder cases – until children or pets were involved. Those shook her. 'Christ – why weren't any of these prosecuted?' Maggie gritted her teeth.

'It's pretty grim reading, right? If these allegations are true, Social Care, the police, the CPS – a lot of agencies – are going to have a lot to answer for.' Bethany stood and gathered a folder full of paperwork. 'You coming?'

Maggie looked at the clock and switched off her computer. 'Yeah – I'll be there in two secs.' She took out her mobile and sent a text to Claire.

Think we need to talk. Let me know the best time. Maggie Jamieson

Maggie headed to the conference room and took the nearest available seat. New pictures were up on the board – three children's care homes – and underneath them were a list of names. Just as Maggie was scanning them to see if she recognised any, DI Rutherford blocked her view.

'Good morning, all. We've had some new information come to light via one of our partnership agencies, and Bethany's determination to make sure we had it sooner rather than later.' Maggie noticed Bethany blush. 'So I am going to hand it over to her to share what she has found.'

'Thanks, Guv. OK, I spent a few hours last night looking into the care homes where abuse allegations were made but were never prosecuted. The specific cases are all on the system now, so you can all have a read when you get a moment – but be warned, it's harrowing. Three out of the five homes I came across in Staffordshire had various allegations made against them – pinning-down practice, physical and sexual abuse, as well as neglect. Three of those homes can be connected to Nathan Firth and Father Boyle, but not Sadie Ramsey. Two of those homes can be connected to all three of our victims, so that's where we need to direct our efforts. I've handed over the details of all five to the Child Abuse Unit.' Bethany returned to her seat.

'If you don't mind, I'd like to add something?' the Doc interrupted, and Rutherford nodded. 'From what I have read so far, there were numerous complaints made by the children – some were repeated allegations, as the children were moved from home to home. The paperwork suggests they were moved because they were "uncontrollable" or "displayed

violent reactions to members of staff"... I think you need to focus your efforts on children who were in these homes between 1995 and 2010. Not surprisingly, in 2010 the three homes were shut down. The other two homes remain open and, from what I can gather, with staff changes and stricter measures in place in terms of outside oversight, there have been no allegations against them since 2010.

'When I did a quick check, it seems twenty-five children – who would now be adults, mind you – fall into the category we need to focus on. Eighteen of those children made repeated allegations of some form of abuse, but no action was taken by the Crown Prosecution Service – Sadie Ramsey declined to pursue. Obviously, I can't check police records in detail, so why the police took no further action is something you'll have to consider – in which case, members of the force could be at potential risk if the killer is making his choice based on those he feels let him down. That list on the board should all be treated as persons of interest – but also be mindful that they are victims of abuse, so you would need to handle any interrogation as sensitively as possible.'

'It might be a good idea to have you involved in any interviews then, Dr Moloney,' Rutherford advised.

'As long as you clear it with DI Calleja, I'm up for that. I have some DAHU work I need to complete, so if you'll excuse me for now – I'll catch up on anything I'll be missing from the team.'

Rutherford gave a dismissive wave of her hand and waited for the Doc to leave before she continued.

'We're still waiting on the forensic details from Dr Blake on the Boyle case – so this list should keep you busy in the meantime. The names above can be found in the system – so

take it with you when you go to the *Gazette* later, Kat – it will be important to see if anyone on the list makes contact.'

'What if our killer was abused but never came forward?' Maggie pointed out what she guessed some of her colleagues might be thinking. It was an angle they had to consider. 'Claire Knight might be able to help, as there must be local authority or Social Care records that hold the details of everyone at those homes. If our killer never came forward with allegations, at least we may be able to identify them through their history and behaviour in the system.'

'I'll speak to Social Care and make sure they co-operate,' Nathan offered. 'It's a valid point. Who knows how many people the killer holds responsible? If they are not stopped soon, the case is going to escalate to…'

'Right – we've no time to waste, then. Let's get some of these names crossed off that list.' Rutherford stormed out of the room. The pressure on her must be immense, and Maggie could tell she was at breaking point, having to take on covering some of DCI Hastings' work after his untimely departure, until they found a replacement.

As the team exited the room, Maggie pulled Nathan aside. 'Is the Guv OK? She looks worse every day and I'm more than a little concerned…' Maggie had never told anyone about the time she had found DI Rutherford had been drinking during the last case. It was a one-off, but when she was under extreme pressure – like she was now – who knew what could happen?

'She's a bit stressed, but fine – why? Is there something I should know?'

Maggie hated lying to Nathan, but without any proof that Rutherford had been drinking again, she'd be stirring the pot, and that wasn't her style. She shook her head.

Nathan cocked his head. 'Not sure I believe you, but I know you'll have your reasons. If you do know something that could jeopardise the case, though – you need to come forward.'

'Of course... Right, I best start looking up addresses and getting these people interviewed. With so many, are we going to do them individually here at the station rather than going out in pairs?'

'Yes – a full memo of the minutes and actions should be sitting in your inbox by the time you get back to your desk.'

Maggie headed back to the open-plan office and began making appointments for people to come in. Kat had been instructed to highlight anyone who called the *Gazette* that matched the list, so that would help narrow down the number of people attending. Dr Moloney had called in a few favours and had two colleagues on standby to assist with the interviews, given the nature of the original allegations.

Maggie wasn't looking forward to this one bit.

Chapter Sixty

Maggie and Bethany split the task of going through the names they had come up with. Bethany took nine of the eighteen and Maggie the other nine. When they both had gone through and contacted those they could find, they learned that three of the eighteen were dead – overdose and suicide; three others were already in prison, which took them out of the frame; leaving them with twelve potential persons of interest. Maggie was waiting to hear back from two people to confirm a time for interview when her mobile rang.

'You wanted to speak to me?'

Claire had a sharp edge in her voice. 'Hello to you too.' Maggie immediately regretted her response – the case had everyone on edge, so she hoped that whatever was annoying Claire, they could move past it. 'We've a list of people we are arranging to interview, all of whom are connected to the children's care homes. By the way, how were you able to get that information to us? After your supervisor's behaviour when we were last there, I thought we'd never get anything without a warrant.'

'*I can't say how – at the moment. There's something going on here and it's leaving me with a bad taste in my mouth.*'

'Uh… OK. Well, whatever it is, we're just grateful for as much information as you can share. Why hasn't your boss got involved? Does he even know what's happening? I don't want to put you in a position where you're risking your job…'

'*Don't worry about me. He's off at the moment…*'

'Thanks for the tip. My boss wondered, once we collected the information, would you be able to share or confirm any information—'

'*Maggie, I will share what I am able to share, but with everything that's going on here, it has to be by the book – so let's not jeopardise things by cutting corners, OK?*'

She knew Claire was right, even though it frustrated her. 'Agreed. Speak soon.' She ended the call. Picking up her handset, she rang Hugh O'Donnell and was surprised to receive a cheerful greeting – until she spoke, that is.

'Hi, Mr O'Donnell. This is DC Maggie Jamieson – I don't know if you remember…'

'*I remember you. What do you want?*'

'I understand that you might be free to come in and speak with us about the matters we raised concerning allegations of abuse at children's care homes.'

'*I'll contact my solicitor and be in touch.*'

'You do that.' His response caught her off guard. Why would he need a solicitor? Before she could say anything else, the phone call had ended. He didn't even ask what specifically they wanted to know. Maggie circled his name and called down to the enquiry desk to let them know that if Hugh

O'Donnell called back and she didn't answer her desk phone, could they pop it through to her work mobile? She wanted to make sure to be available to speak with him.

She had arranged six interviews today and the first was due to arrive. She headed over to Kate's desk. 'Before the first arrives, I was thinking that maybe once I explain why he's here, you might start the interview, and I can follow your lead in terms of questioning?' Maggie had interviewed trauma survivors in the past so wasn't concerned that she would be insensitive, but because this case had the difficult angle that the victim might also be their killer, they needed to get it right.

'Grand. Just logging out, and we can head down if you want. Have a chat before he arrives?'

'You read my mind.'

Chapter Sixty-One

After informing the enquiry desk where they would be, Maggie made her way to the interview suite. Kate had already settled herself, notebook open and writing something down. Maggie took a few deep breaths, reminding herself that the interviews today could be harrowing to listen to, but might also be the key to solving these murders.

'We'll need to be sensitive and persistent. We want them to know we're on their side so they will open up. We should ask about the past allegations, their feelings then and now, and from there, move to your direct line of questioning. The first man we're about to speak to contacted the *Gazette* himself, so he's open to talking. We have to gauge where he is in terms of his mind space, as the last thing we want to do is trigger more things he may not have dealt with. Does that make sense?'

'Perfectly clear. I'm glad you're a part of this. How likely do you think it is that the killer is on this list of interviewees?'

'I honestly don't know. Tactics like this have been used by

other police forces with some success, so let's hope we're one of them.'

A knock at the door stopped the conversation. 'Ready?'

Kate nodded.

'Come in.' Maggie stretched her legs under the table. It was going to be a long day, mainly spent sitting.

A civilian from the enquiry desk escorted Scott Bradshaw into the room. Maggie waited until he was seated and comfortable, before clicking on the recorder, introducing herself and Kate, and explaining the purpose of the interview to him. 'You are free to go at any time, we're just recording now for the purpose of ensuring we have an accurate account of the information you provide. If at any time you wish to have a solicitor present, we will pause the interview and can arrange for that. If you have any questions, ask as they arise and we'll do our best to answer. Do you understand everything I just said?'

'Yes,' he mumbled.

'For the purpose of the tape, Mr Bradshaw confirmed his understanding. I'm now going to hand you over to Dr Moloney.'

'You can call me Scott.'

'Thank you, Scott. Feel free to call me Kate. You contacted the *Stafford Gazette* in response to a recent feature on the news. Can you tell us a bit about what prompted you to call?'

'I recognised Father Boyle.' He shuddered. 'The man was pure evil, and I never understood how he could hide behind that white collar of his.'

'What can you tell us about Father Boyle?'

'He got his rocks off watching others kick the shit out of little boys, and sometimes he took part...'

Maggie noticed Scott's demeanour had changed. He'd shrunk in the chair, and his hands were shaking. 'Are you OK? I can get you a glass of water.'

'I'm fine. I just haven't spoken about this for a long time. My wife doesn't know anything about what happened to me. I mean, she does now – but up until the other day, I hadn't told her. I was ashamed – you know, like it was my fault.'

'That's a natural feeling, Scott. We really do appreciate you taking the time to speak with us. How many children's care homes were you in?'

'Four. Dumped at the hospital when I was two, according to my records. No idea who my mother or father is – don't want to know. Never adopted – I was considered *troubled*.' He balled his fists. 'I mean, who wouldn't be troubled in a place where animals are treated better than kids, right?'

Neither Maggie nor Kate could argue with his statement.

'How long did the abuse go on for?' Kate clasped her hands together.

'Pretty much the whole time I was in care. As soon as I hit sixteen, I left. I was homeless for a while, but then got a flat sorted with the local authority, enrolled in college and learned a trade, met my wife and buried my past as deep as I could. I'm not going to lie to you – I was happy to see that karma finally paid back Boyle and that other arsehole – what was his name?'

Maggie waited for Scott to remember. She couldn't give him the name that was on the tip of her tongue, for fear that a crafty solicitor would say she was feeding witnesses detail, thereby jeopardising the investigation.

'Danny Firth. He changed his last name, you know. It was Crease, I think… when he was at the homes. Probably scared that one day someone would come after him – he wasn't wrong either.'

Maggie noted the name down. They hadn't been aware of this bit of information. None of the family mentioned the change when questioned, but she supposed it would be a common thing to do if there was any controversy. The records they had seen referred to him as Firth, so maybe it was the case that as he moved from home to home, he swapped between names to hide his tracks. His sister shared the name Firth, so it was probably something they all were a party to. Could well be that the family took on the mother's maiden name. She highlighted the note and would see if Bethany could find out more.

'Did you ever have any counselling to deal with the trauma? Holding onto something like that for so long must have had an effect on you.' Maggie knew this was Kate's way of probing to see how angry Scott actually was – was it enough to kill?

'Not really. I mean, I did have a few sessions, but after a few of us went to the police and nothing was done, I didn't think counselling would help. Just buried it, threw some dirt over it, and moved on. I had a bit of a drink problem when I was younger, not anymore thank goodness, but I got more out of my AA sessions than any specific counselling for abuse.'

Kate look at Maggie. 'OK, that's all really useful. When you contacted the newspaper, you mentioned you and a few others went to the police. Do you remember when that was, who you spoke to and who else was with you when you made your complaint?'

He rubbed his head. 'It was so long ago... ummm... the copper was a Scottish fellow. I remember because his accent was so strong, I could barely understand a word he said. Couldn't tell you his name, though, or when that was – like I said, I tried to block everything out.' He stroked his beard. 'It was before I left the last home, though, so it must have been around 2007, maybe? You'd think I'd remember, but I buried this shit down deep. He was nice enough but did fuck all – said the CPS weren't interested in prosecuting, and that was that. I don't even know if he believed any of us – doesn't matter now, looks like someone else is dealing with things, eh?'

'What do you mean by that?' Maggie sat up.

'Well, first Danny, then that prosecutor, and now Father Boyle. When I heard of the first murder – it wasn't far from here, was it? Well, I didn't put two and two together – thought to myself, what an unfortunate sod – what a way to go. But when I saw his picture, I nearly threw up. Still didn't think it had anything to do with what happened to me until I saw the other two – that's why you are speaking to everyone, isn't it?' A flicker in his eye caught Maggie's attention. 'You think it was me? Is that why you wanted to speak with me?' Scott Bradshaw's chest rose and fell with rapid breaths.

'No… Well, yes, we're speaking to everyone who may have known the victims, in case you have information that could help us find who is responsible for all this.' As she had been listening to Scott, the more Maggie realised he was not their killer. The anger wasn't there. As far as she could tell, he was displaying normal feelings towards a traumatic incident that played a significant part in shaping him. 'Can we just go back a bit to the original allegations? Who else was there?'

'Uh… sorry. You did ask me that and I kind of went off on a tangent. There was quite a few of us…'

Maggie noted the names down as Scott recalled them.

'We went in groups, hoping that if enough of us made similar allegations, something would be done. One of the guys – I think his name was Tommy – later retracted what he said. Someone must have got to him – we never saw him after that, actually – think he was shipped off to another home, or maybe they killed him.' He shrugged. 'Wouldn't surprise me at all.'

Maggie's eyes widened. 'Did a lot of boys go missing in the time you were in the homes?'

'I wouldn't say a lot, but enough for me and the others to notice. It's why I kept my mouth shut after Tommy disappeared and bided my time until I could leave of my own accord. That place wasn't going to get the best of me. Out of all the homes I was in, Chatham House was the worst. It was like everyone who worked there hated children.' His eyes glistened.

'You're very brave to come forward now and deal with this head on. We know it can't be easy. I'm sorry to keep harping on about this, but can we go back to your time at Chatham House? If it gets too much, let me know and I will stop.'

'Ask away. I need to get it out now – I shouldn't have kept it in. You know, I'm afraid to have kids myself. Keep putting the wife off and she never understood why, because I love kids – but I just had this little niggle in the back of my head... Sorry – tangent again. Just bringing up feelings, you know...'

'Absolutely, and please talk freely – after we're finished we can put you in touch with some brilliant agencies and get you whatever help you need. For now though, do you have any names you can recall who worked at Chatham House and were a part of the abuse inflicted on all of you?'

He reeled off some names. 'I may not be good with the exact names, but close enough – I can't forget their faces,

though. Daniel Crease… or Firth. He's who I complained about
to the police. Pretty sure one of them died – heart attack or
something. There's one name etched in my brain though, the
bitch who ran the place – Mrs Mole.'

'Why's that?'

'She was one of the worst – when they all were together,
they were evil incarnate. Vicious fuckers.'

'I don't want to push you, but what was it about her that
made her worse than the others?'

'She initiated it all. When she first introduced herself to the
children, she was all love – a mother figure. And once she had
you under her spell – *whoosh* – whole personality changed. She
would watch and direct the fuckers to pull our teeth out. You
could hear her cackling in the corner over the screams.' He
removed a plate from his upper jaw and showed four missing
teeth.

Chapter Sixty-Two

O nce they had finished speaking with Scott Bradshaw, Maggie escorted him out with some details of counsellors that the Doc recommended. She then jogged back to the interview room, as she wanted to speak with Kate before the next person arrived in ten minutes' time.

'Holy shit! Well, that explains the teeth, then – you were on the right track when you identified the act as significant in your profile. What are your thoughts on Scott?'

Kate took a few minutes before speaking. 'He was calm, forthcoming – showed what some would term the appropriate amount of anger. Either he's a great actor or he's not your guy.'

'I was thinking the same, and he gave us some names to follow up with – a list of potential victims to work from, so at least that will narrow the focus in terms of cross-referencing. Bethany will be pleased.'

A knock on the door signalled the next person had arrived early and once he was seated, Maggie did the introductions and explained why they were wanting to speak with him. Mr

Redford had raised a few red flags when Maggie had looked him up, but she'd see how forthcoming he was before making any assumptions. She turned to Kate and noticed something odd about the way she was looking at the man before them. Shrugging it off, she waited for Kate to start.

'Sorry, do I know you? Your face seems familiar.' Kate leaned forward.

'Uh… I don't think so. Can we start now?' He looked at his watch. 'I don't have much time.'

Maggie watched his movements intently. He was fidgeting and a line of sweat formed across his brow. Kate took the lead.

'Of course. As my colleague here informed you, we're speaking to people who have connections to children's homes, and your name came up. In fact, we have reason to believe that you were among a group of young lads who came forward at one time to make allegations about abuse occurring at a few of those homes.'

'Why are you bringing all that up now? No one was interested at the time. Do you have any idea what they put us through, how they made us feel? My life is finally going somewhere, and you want to drag me back to those places. You should all be ashamed.' He wagged his finger at them.

'Mr Redford, we're here because we want to help. It was absolutely appalling, what you and those boys had to endure. We won't talk about anything you aren't comfortable with – but you may have seen on the news about the recent murders in Staffordshire. Were those the people that harmed you?'

'What if it was? So what? Bloody animals, they were, and what happened to them was nothing compared to what they did to us. It was over too quick, if you ask me. Arseholes! I wish I'd been there…' The last words were mumbled and

Maggie reached across to stop Kate from asking her next question, as she could see that if they kept pushing him he would shut down. She wanted him to stay in the moment before he upped and left the interview.

'We can see how distressing this is for you. I wondered if I could just ask you one more thing, and then you'll be free to go.'

He shrugged his shoulders. 'Fine – but you can't make me tell you anything, you know.'

'Absolutely. What I'd like to know is whether or not you have any missing teeth?' Maggie had tried to see when he was speaking to Kate, but even in anger, he kept his lips tightly pursed as he spoke.

He lifted his top lip. 'Three – why?'

'How did that happen?'

'Those fuckers pulled them out – that's how. Hope they're all rotting in hell. Are we done now?' He stood up fast and the chair behind him crashed to the floor.

Maggie looked at Kate. 'Yes, thank you so much for your time.' Maggie escorted him out of the room and gave him her card. 'If you think of anything else, my number is on the back.' He grumbled as he shoved the card in his back pocket and hurried out the door.

Back in the interview room, Maggie noted Kate tugging at her ear. She left her to her thoughts, as she had clocked that whenever Kate did this, she was working things out. Finally the Doc spoke.

'I know him from somewhere, and for the life of me, I can't place where.'

'You're usually really good with faces, so I'm sure it will come back to you. What did you think about what he said?'

'Unlike our first guy, I'm not sure he is one to be crossed off the list too quickly. He was angry – really angry – a natural reaction, especially if he had never spoken to anyone about what he'd endured, but…'

'There was something off with him – I felt it too, but we had nothing solid to hold him on, and he gave me the impression that if we kept at him, he would just clam up completely. I'll ask Nathan to get surveillance on him while we look into him a bit further. We can call him back in for a formal interview if we have to. He's not named on the list of people who phoned into the *Gazette*, but there were a few anonymous calls, so we could get a voice comparison, if need be.'

A tap on the door signalled the next person had arrived.

———

The last four interviews went without incident. Angry men – and justifiably so – retelling the same story, but most displayed what Kate and Maggie felt would be expected, given the situation. Three of the men had between one and three missing teeth, and the last man five – though he said one of them was from a fight he had got into in a pub.

It was time to compare notes with Bethany and Kat once they had finished their interviews. Maggie felt drained. Listening to the men and what they had suffered reminded her why she did the job. They had been let down before and she didn't want them to feel that way again. She'd do whatever it took to find the killer, but also make sure that any remaining perpetrators of abuse upon the men were brought to justice.

Chapter Sixty-Three

When they returned to the MOCD offices, Kate didn't waste any time in updating her profile. Maggie hadn't even had a chance to put her notes on her desk, when Kat appeared, jumping from foot to foot. Maggie put her arms out. 'What's got you all excited?'

'Missing fucking teeth! The ones I spoke to had missing teeth!'

'Same here.' Bethany walked in, looking as pale as a ghost.

'You OK?' Maggie knew that interviewing potential suspects was Bethany's least favourite part of her job. She could sit for hours trawling the web, looking at horrendous scenes on CCTV, but when it came to speaking to people face-to-face, she'd shy away at the first opportunity.

'Yeah. That was pretty tough going, though. What those men suffered! Having their teeth pulled?' Bethany's body shuddered. 'They all had similar stories – someone would pin them down on the floor after knocking two bells out of them, and extract their teeth. Rip them right out of their mouths without anything to dull the pain.'

'We heard the same. At least we know we're on the right track, and it explains why our killer is extracting teeth. What was it you said about that aspect, Kate?'

'Power. He's taking back the power – or at least he is in his mind. From what we heard – Kat and Bethany, you can tell me if it was the same for you – the abusers were exerting their control over these boys. Pulling their teeth would not only inflict pain, but ensure that the boys did as they were told. Perhaps in the killer's mind, he is taking back that control. I can't explain why he's burning them, though. No one we spoke to mentioned burns. How about you two?'

Bethany shook her head, but Kat was jumping around again. 'One of mine said that they were forced to watch others being burned. A warning. Lighter fluid was splashed about and the abusers would choose, saying *eeny meeny miny mo*, and whoever it landed on had their arm or leg set alight.'

'Fucking hell. So this is definite payback – now all we have to do is narrow down the list. Did anyone with burns come forward?'

'The guy who told me about that was convinced the boys were killed. Once they were burned, they were never seen again. Said the adults told them no one would want to adopt damaged goods.'

'I'm not liking where this is going… Let's hand over what we do know to the Child Abuse Unit. I should go and speak to Nathan.' Maggie looked towards his empty office. 'I'll give him a call, see what he thinks.' When she called him it went straight to voicemail. Maggie left him a brief message and then headed down the hall to DI Rutherford's office. She'd want to be kept in the loop too and wouldn't appreciate having to wait to hear something this significant from Nathan.

When Maggie tapped on the Guv's door and there was no answer, she opened it, and the sight before her threw her off guard.

'Shit. Guv – are you OK?'

Chapter Sixty-Four

Maggie rushed over to DI Rutherford and gently shook her. 'Guv. Guv! Can you hear me?'

Rutherford slowly lifted her head. 'Jesus. What happened?'

'You scared the life out of me. When I knocked and you didn't answer, I peeked in and saw you were slumped over your desk.'

'I must have passed out. I've been here all night.' Rutherford pulled at her blouse. She looked as if she hadn't slept in days.

'Abigail – no job is worth killing yourself over. You're exhausted. Can't Nathan hold the fort for a while, and you go home and catch some sleep?' Maggie always felt odd using the Guv's first name. Although it wasn't uncommon, she'd just been so used to referring to Abigail Rutherford as the Guv.

'I'll be fine. In fact, I'm feeling better already.' She reached into her drawer and took out a small make-up bag. 'Can you do me a favour and grab a blouse from the locker there?'

Maggie did as she was asked and handed DI Rutherford a clean cream blouse.

'Thanks. I'll be ten minutes if you want to wait, then I'll be all ears.'

Maggie nodded and took a seat. At least there was no smell of alcohol. Rutherford probably just collapsed from exhaustion. She wondered whether it was time she raised her concerns with Nathan. If the shoe were on the other foot, the Guv would send her home without hesitation. When DI Rutherford returned, Maggie had to admit she looked refreshed. She felt a little more at ease then.

'That's better.' Rutherford straightened her blouse. 'OK, what can I do for you?'

Maggie went over what they had learned in the interviews, ending with the bombshell that all the men they had spoken to had at least one, if not more, teeth extracted when they were in the boys' homes.

Rutherford rubbed her temples. 'This definitely sheds some light on why our killer is extracting teeth. Any IDs? Was there one who stood out more than another?'

'That's the thing – none of them said anything along those lines. We have the names of those who reported abuse to the police. Bethany is still trying to locate the officer they spoke to – a PC Bram Watson – Scottish fellow, do you know him?'

'Name sounds familiar, but I couldn't say for sure. Might be retired by now. OK, we'll need to locate and speak with him. A case of child abuse, even if nothing goes further, is one that rarely leaves an officer's memories. We'll have to see who we can remove from our lines of enquiry and take it from there, I guess. What about the calls to the newspaper? Anything come from that?'

'Kate has a list and the recordings, so will be going through those and matching against her profile. Some we've already spoken to – they admitted to contacting the *Gazette*. Kate believed the killer would want to set the record straight and call in, but so far it doesn't seem like that is the case.'

'There's still time though. We'll just have to hope he does. Where's Nathan?'

'I don't know. He wasn't in his office, I thought you might know.'

Rutherford cleared her throat. 'Fine. Best we get back to it...'

Maggie stood and headed towards the door.

'Oh, and Maggie?'

She turned to face Rutherford.

'What happened here earlier... Let's keep that between us, please?' Rutherford looked away and started typing something into her computer. That would be all she would say on the subject.

'Sure, Guv.'

On her way back to the main office, Maggie felt uneasy. Was it just pure exhaustion or was something more going on with Rutherford? She'd keep an eye on the Guv, and if anything else caught her attention, she'd speak to Nathan. Rutherford had covered her back on more than one occasion – she'd return the favour for now.

Chapter Sixty-Five

The forensic report on Father Boyle had finally come in from Dr Blake. She had sent her apologies, as her team was overwhelmed with work, so she couldn't make the briefing, but had sent along a video detailing the post-mortem to go along with her report.

Once Nathan had returned to the office, he gathered the team in the incident room and they sat and listened as the pathologist's voice boomed over the speaker system.

'Male identified as Father Francis Boyle. Seventy years old. No underlying health conditions that contributed to the cause of death.' Maggie watched as Dr Blake began her detailed exploration of the cadaver. The pathologist seemed more comfortable and at ease with the dead than she did with the living. There was almost a tenderness in the way she dissected bodies.

'Under Boyle's nails we found some skin which has been sent to the lab for testing. There was also grit, similar to the make-up of the floor where he was found, which would

explain the scratch marks located in the area where I also
believe he suffered a blow to the head. Blood spatter analysts
are writing up a separate report, but from what I have been
told, he was probably kneeling when he was hit on the head
from behind.'

An image flashed on the screen showing a close-up of the
injury to the back of the priest's head.

'Blunt force trauma identified, based on the injury, and the
detail here…' she was pointing to a lacerated area on the back
of Boyle's head, 'is consistent with being hit with an object
such as a hammer or bat. You can see that the skull was
fractured but the injury did not penetrate to the brain.'

They watched as the forensic assistant aided Dr Blake in
returning Boyle to lying flat, face up on the table. 'The bruising
around his neck and ligature marks, as well as petechiae on his
eyeballs, confirm strangulation, and *this* was the cause of
death.' Dr Blake zoomed in on the neck area before she walked
over and lifted his hands. 'The nails driven into his hands and
feet are identified as cut clasp nails. They can be purchased at
any hardware store. These were inserted ante-mortem, and
Father Boyle was deceased when he was covered in lighter
fluid and set on fire, which is different from the last two cases.
Curious, I thought – I'll leave the sleuthing on that one to the
detectives.'

Maggie noted this down and looked over at Kate.
Something had piqued the Doc's interest.

'You'll also see significant bruising on the legs and chest, as
well as two broken ribs. These were caused ante-mortem as
well, so the evidence suggests that Father Boyle sustained
significant torture prior to being strangled.'

Maggie sat back and took in everything they had heard so

far. Dr Blake's findings coincided with everything said by the men they had interviewed. With the priest being one of the main instigators of abuse, and particularly vicious, it was no wonder that the killer had inflicted all the damage they were hearing about. Dr Blake's voice shook her out of her thoughts.

'And you can see here...' Boyle's head had been tilted back and his mouth prised open. 'His left incisor and right canine teeth were torn from his mouth quite crudely. In fact, it was different from the last two victims. This was done post-mortem.' Dr Blake finished off by advising them that more details and test results would be sent over as they came in. Nathan turned off the video and faced the team.

'Thoughts, please.'

Maggie couldn't help herself and jumped straight in. 'Something isn't sitting right with me. Yes – there are enough links to the previous murders to confirm a connection, and those of us who interviewed the men earlier this week know that Father Boyle was a beast in all senses of the word – but...' She shook her head. 'There are significant differences too. If the teeth are part of the control aspect, why did the killer wait until Boyle was dead to remove them? Have we missed something?'

Kat spoke up. 'I'm with you, Maggie. Even with what we know, this one seems even more personal, more vicious, and done over a period of time. The teeth being pulled after death also threw me. Doesn't this scream of someone who is less... uh... experienced?'

Maggie folder her arms. 'Exactly. By now, the killer should have improved upon his method – not the other way around.'

'Dr Moloney?' said Nathan. 'Given what we've seen and what Kat and Maggie have pointed out – do you have anything to add?'

Kate looked up from her notes. 'I think we need to re-examine our theories on the other two victims...'

'Why's that?' Maggie looked at the evidence board, eyes racing over the details, looking for something that might have triggered Kate's sudden turn.

'I know this is something that you may not want to hear, but... after everything we've just heard, we could have more than one killer on our hands...'

The atmosphere in the room had changed – voices rose, officers were mumbling to each other and Nathan was trying to take back some control. Kate had just dropped a bombshell. Even if some of them had thought it at one point or another, they were so close to identifying a killer that this would bring them right back to the beginning, and none of them were prepared to do that.

Nathan held his hands up. 'Can we all just quiet down.' He waited for the murmurs to stop. 'Dr Moloney – you've just thrown a cat amongst the pigeons, but I have to say, we've been all over this evidence and I can't see anything that points to multiple perpetrators in these murders. Don't forget, you're the one who advised a single killer at the start.'

'If I may?' Kate stood and headed towards the investigation board. 'You're absolutely right, and my original profile still stands. We already know that a group of boys made allegations about our victims, which went nowhere. We've spoken to most if not all of them now, and that's when it hit me. I don't think we should rule out the theory that we have someone – a victim of the childhood abuse – who might be manipulating these other men into killing those who harmed them. After the earlier interviews, and learning that some of the men had been burned when they were children, I had to rethink my initial premise about the fires being used as a means to destroy evidence. But as not all of the children had suffered in this particular way, but did have their teeth pulled, I had to wonder whether the fires were actually a ploy to throw you off guard. Boyle also may have the DNA of his killer under his nails. How did he get close enough to scratch his killer? The first three murders were more sophisticated, for lack of a better word.'

'Can I interrupt?' Maggie was looking at the three victims. 'If it is a group of killers, what would they gain? Why wouldn't the one pulling their strings just do it and take the glory?' She closed her eyes and started to visualise the crime scenes. She wanted to see what Kate was seeing. But at the moment, she couldn't.

'If you recall, each murder does have something different from the others. At first I thought this may be because the killer was growing in confidence or displaying anger at those who he felt were more responsible. But after listening to Dr Blake's post-mortem talk on Father Boyle, it all became clear. The men who came to see us and showed us their teeth – different teeth had been removed... What if the pattern lies in the number of teeth removed and with men who haven't come forward yet? Scott Bradshaw had four teeth missing, the Redford fellow had three teeth missing. What if that is the connection we're looking for? Of course, this is all just a theory – we'd need evidence to back up what I am suggesting, but I think it's a line of enquiry worth pursuing.' Kate scratched her head, looking a bit unsure of herself.

Had the Doc returned to work too soon? She was usually spot on in her assessments, but seemed to be second guessing herself. If the team were going to go back to the start, they needed their consultant to be on form. Maggie trusted Kate's instincts, though, and when she saw Nathan nod, she realised he did too.

'Thanks, Dr Moloney. Could we have already spoken to the killers, then?'

'Ahhhh… I wish I was psychic, Nathan. I couldn't say for sure, but I get the feeling that the boys who were abused made some sort of pact in terms of protecting their leader. Each would have their own specific victim, for reasons known only to them, and if the master manipulator hasn't already killed, he may just be the grand finale. Those men who made the child abuse allegations hold the key to all of this.'

'OK, team. If you have any plans for this evening, now is the time to cancel them – we'll need as many eyes and minds as we can get on this. I want you to work closely with Bethany and the analysts. Make sure we have every detail from the child abuse case, liaise with the Child Abuse Unit, speak to any contacts you have at Social Care, trawl through every single story online that you can find. If you come up against any blockages – let me know and I'll make sure we get full access. Kat – go over the interviews you conducted and apply everything from this meeting to the information we have on the victims. Same goes for you, Maggie. And Dr Moloney, although I can't make you stay, it would be great to have your insight and have you available to answer questions as they come up. I'll clear the overtime with DI Rutherford, if you're up for it?'

'Wouldn't dream of missing it. Can I make one final suggestion, which I know may not be popular?' When Dr Moloney looked at Maggie, she hoped Kate wasn't going to suggest what she thought.

'Having Julie Noble involved again would be beneficial. I'd be happy to work with you, Nathan, on a specifically focused press release hinting that we know more, to ruffle some feathers with the killer. I'm convinced they are watching our progress through the press releases. We could hold back any new and significant information we find, to weed out anyone who might be looking for a little bit of fame. I believe you call them the nutters...' Kate raised a disapproving brow.

Maggie groaned. 'Isn't there anyone else we could use? I would consider having Julie sign some form of non-disclosure, as she'll be hearing things that really shouldn't be in the public domain.'

'Not necessarily. She wouldn't have to be present when you hash out the details – plus, as part of the partnership agreement she signed, she'd have to clear anything with the police before she writes about or reports it. I'm not sure what resources or funding are available, but what about considering a toned-down re-enactment? It might prompt some people to come forward. The great thing about the mind is that at times we don't even realise what we do know until something triggers a thought.'

Kate's eyes lit up as she talked and Maggie's earlier worry dissipated slightly.

'Let's not jump ahead of ourselves just yet,' said Nathan.

'We may find something we missed in the evidence, without having to add additional expense.'

'Skinflint,' Maggie scoffed.

'Mind yourself, Jamieson.' One side of Nathan's mouth lifted. He was giving her a bit of leeway while reminding her who was in charge.

'Of course, boss. OK – well, I'm ready to get cracking. Who wants a coffee?' Hands shot up and Maggie counted them. 'I'd like to bring my laptop in here and work, if you don't mind? Having everything in one place will save me time and put me in the zone.'

'Fine by me, and I'm more than happy if anyone else wants to join Maggie – two, or more, heads are better than one. Everyone clear on what they're doing?'

Nods around the room.

'Get those coffees, in Maggie.' Nathan had an authoritative tone to his request. 'Look over every minuscule bit of information and bring me something that will catch us our killer,' he looked at Dr Moloney, 'or killers.'

Chapter Sixty-Seven

Maggie sipped her coffee as she examined each crime scene photo, one by one. She was looking for anything they might have missed, an oddity that they brushed aside, and her frustration grew as nothing stood out to her. She placed her mug back on the table.

'What if we're wrong about all this and it turns out to be a waste of time? He could be out there with the next victim right now, and we're stuck here gawping at photos.' She paced the front of the room.

'We're no further ahead or behind than we were before the Doc piped up about the possibility of multiple killers. So we're not in a position to prevent anything right now, are we? Field officers are out rounding up those you lot spoke to earlier. Take a breath, shake it off and get those cogs moving. I'll be back in a bit...' Nathan headed down the hall towards Rutherford's office.

Maggie watched as Kate began to reorder the evidence photos and jot down names on the whiteboard.

'Have you found something?' Maggie walked towards her.

'I'm matching the teeth extractions. Daniel Firth had two removed – and didn't Kat interview someone who had two teeth removed? Could be they are killing the ones who they believe tormented them the most, and the teeth are what ties them together.'

'I didn't get that impression from the interviews – well, except for Redford – he did set my spidey sense on fire. There is definitely a deep anger, and I suppose I could see him snapping. But even so, taking all the interviews together, are we really saying we have multiple killers?' Maggie just wasn't feeling the same thing as the Doc on this one.

'Hey,' Kat called out, tapping a lighter on the table. 'What if one of us works the single-killer theory and the other works the multiple angle... because looking over your interview transcript and recalling my own interviews, I'm kinda with you, Maggie. I just don't buy this whole lost boys theory...'

'Lost boys?' Maggie wasn't getting the reference.

'Boys-seeking-revenge for each other's shit. I'm just not convinced.'

'Hmmm. Well, it could save some time – you gagging for a fag?' Maggie pointed at the lighter – the tapping was beginning to grate on her.

'Is it that obvious? I'm just going to go for one and will be back in a mo – anyone want anything on my way back?'

'I'm good.' Maggie looked at Kate and she shook her head. 'Would you mind checking what Bethany has found on your way back?'

Bethany's computer system had everything she needed – a laptop just wouldn't cut it for her, so she decided to work in peace in the main office.

Kat had already left and Maggie wasn't sure if she'd heard, but no time to worry about that. She closed her eyes and walked the crime scene of Firth, the first victim. 'He was tied to the chair, no evidence of any sort of assault other than what was needed to secure him to the chair. Hands and wrists bound. Lighter fluid thrown over his trouser legs, the front of his shirt, his face, arms, circled around the chair... What were Sadie Ramsey and Father Boyle bound with?'

'Plastic ties, in the case of Ramsey; Father Boyle was bound with wire... and the nails...'

'Were the ties for Firth and Ramsey the same brand?'

'Dr Blake's report says that it was difficult to ascertain, as the plastic melted, but she noted that when manufactured, each mould bears some identification mark – either a number, a letter or a combination of both, and in some cases together with a company logo – but unfortunately these were part of the unidentifiable bit.' Kate turned the page before continuing. 'Hmmm.'

'What is it?' Maggie sat down.

'Well, Dr Blake goes on to say that the remaining bits of the ties bore some mould details, the most significant of which was considered to be a linear indent, running diagonally across two ridges at the ribbed strap of one of the ties, but it couldn't be found in what little was left of the other tie.'

'So even if we located a bag of ties, we probably wouldn't be able to identify them unless the indent thingy you mention was found... OK, well, it was worth a shot and probably not something we should dismiss altogether... Maybe the killer ran out, could have just bought a different brand, or felt that a stronger tie was needed.' Maggie wasn't convinced of anything at the moment.

'Are the men being brought back in for re-interview having their property searched?' Kate opened her notes.

'If Rutherford can convince the courts, or if the men allow the officers, then yeah. The cable ties would be included in the list of items, as well as copper wiring. Since those synapses of yours are on fire, what else do our persons of interest have in common?'

'You mean other than being at the same care home, being abused, being angry?' Kate was looking at the crime scene photos that were taken when each body was discovered, but Maggie didn't miss the slight sarcasm in her reply. 'Hold on a minute.' Kate rushed out of the room.

What the…? Maggie looked at the evidence board. *What was Kate looking at?* Each crime scene had snaps of the crowds of onlookers that had gathered behind the crime scene tape. Did the Doc recognise someone? A gust of air hit her neck and Kate was back, holding a magnifying glass.

'Very Sherlock Holmes. What did you see?'

Kate held the magnifying glass up against each photo before tapping the last and holding it up for Maggie to see.

'What am I looking at?'

'That guy in the hoodie. He's in all the photos. Most of them, you can't see his face…' She tapped a photo. 'Except this one. I know him.'

'What do you mean, you know him?'

'I don't know why I didn't see it before, but remember when we went out to the homeless shelters looking for that fellow – Music Matty? This guy…' She tapped the picture again. 'He managed one I went to with Kat. He was really helpful, but why is he at all the crime scenes? I think he was here today.'

'Do you remember his name?'

'Not off the top of my head, let me go over my notes and who we interviewed – he should be on your records.'

The pair raced out of the room and back into the main office.

'Bethany, while you have those records open, can you check the name of the shelter manager that Kat and the Doc spoke to when we were looking for the green parka coat.'

'Sure thing. Gimme a sec to open it up.'

Felt like hours before Bethany gave them a name.

'You're a godsend. I'm going to go around and bring him in.'

'Hang on, Maggie,' Bethany called after her. 'The fellow you're after is downstairs. One of the field officers just signed him in.'

Chapter Sixty-Eight

'Can you do me a favour, Bethany, and call downstairs – make sure they don't let him go until I get down there. I need to speak to Kat. Doc, do you want to join me when I'm ready?'

'Sure thing. Just gimme a shout.'

Maggie ran back to the incident room. Kat should be back from her fag break by now. When she entered the room, Kat was looking at the crime scene photos and before Maggie could open her mouth, Kat had turned with a look of confusion on her face. 'I think I know this guy. Have you seen he's actually in a few of these pics? Why didn't I notice that before?'

'That's why I'm here. He's back – downstairs. I don't have time to go through your full notes, so can you give me a rundown? The Doc and I are going to speak with him.'

'Of course. He was really calm at first when the Doc and I spoke to him. Said he had turned his life around, manages a homeless shelter – in fact, he wanted to pay it forward, or some shite like that. According to him, as mad as he was about the abuse, he knew karma would win in the end.'

'So what made his attitude change during the interview?'

'I started asking him why he never pursued charges when he was older, as there was no time limit on cases like this. He lost it then. Had a bit of a rant about how useless the criminal justice system is, and that it would be even harder now to prove a case, because so many people involved were in high positions – so who would believe him? Couldn't really calm him after that. He said he was through talking to the police, and had we done our job in the first place, we wouldn't be sitting there now. I have to say, I kinda agree with him on that one – but I didn't say that out loud.'

'Yeah…' Maggie looked at the floor. When the system didn't work, it could put people off coming forward. 'Did he give you the impression that he could be capable of murder? What was your gut instinct?' Maggie was a big believer in listening to your instincts – many times they had led to her following lines of enquiry outside of the norm and solving cases.

'I'm actually on the fence with this guy. Something didn't sit right, but when I looked over the evidence and his alibi – he was covered. Well, for two of the murders, not the first one.'

'Did he have any teeth missing or comment on that?'

'He had two missing. But he didn't elaborate on what happened.'

'OK, thanks. I'll be downstairs. If you think of anything else we might need to know, text me.'

'Will do.'

Maggie returned to the open-plan office, collected her

notebook and relayed to the Doc the details Kat had shared as they headed downstairs.

'He has some trigger points, then – worth hanging back on those, depending on the answers he gives you. Would you mind if I just observed? If I do have any questions, I'll note them down for you.'

'Sure.' They arrived downstairs. 'He's just through here.' Maggie led the way and tapped on the interview suite door. The field officer came out and Maggie explained the situation. He left them to it.

'Hi, Mr McDade, sorry for all the disruption. My name is DC Jamieson and this is my colleague, Dr Kate Moloney.'

'I don't need a doctor but I think I might need a lawyer if you keep harassing me this way.'

'Harassing you?'

'Yes, first I come in off my own back to help with your enquiries after I saw that news report. Next thing, I'm rustled out of bed and taken into the police station with no explanation, as if I'm a bloody criminal. It's not on!' There was venom in his voice.

Maggie pressed the recorder. 'I'm recording this interview…' Maggie then cautioned him before he exploded.

'Wait a damn minute! Are you charging me with something? Why are you cautioning me?'

'Standard procedure. Would you like a solicitor present? We're not here to trick you, Mr McDade.' Maggie didn't normally offer, as it was always better if they spoke without the solicitor guiding them on what they could/shouldn't say. She found people tended to speak more freely. However, she didn't want him to feel that they were trying to back him into a corner. It was an olive branch and Maggie hoped he took it.

He slumped in his chair and ran his hand through his hair. 'Look, all this is turning out to be really stressful. I'm not trying to be difficult, I just want this over with. Unless you've been in a situation like this, you wouldn't understand. Most people would try and block out things like this with alcohol or drugs. Me? I pushed it down, used it to better myself. I put all that shit with the boys' homes behind me, and it's being thrown back in my face. I told your other colleague that I had nothing to do with any of this – in fact, other than the first murder, when I was tucked up asleep, I wasn't even around for the other two. Surely you can just quickly check and we can be done with all this? I'm tired…'

Maggie needed to tread carefully now. 'I noticed you're missing some teeth. Did that happen at the boys' home?'

'Yes. Fucking savages….' He looked at Kate and Maggie. 'I'm sorry for swearing but… hey, haven't we met?' He was looking at Kate now.

'Yes, we have. We spoke shortly after the first murder. I came by the shelter with DC Everett to ask you about the green duffel coat…'

'Ah yes – see, I don't even own a green duffel coat. Didn't you tell her that?' He jabbed a finger in Maggie's direction. 'Why are you going over the same old things? How many times do I have to say I know nothing about these murders? If you harassed the real offenders like this way back when, you might have stopped all this. Maybe you should be worried about yourselves instead of trying to point fingers at innocent victims.' He stomped his foot beneath the table.

'Mr McDade, please don't threaten me. We're all trying to get to the bottom of this, and believe me when I say that although I can't speak on behalf of my colleagues back then, we're currently trying to find out what's happening now.' Maggie paused to let her comment sink in, but she wasn't going to let him off so easily, despite any sympathy she might feel for him. 'Could you explain why you were at each of the crime scenes?'

His faced paled and then without warning he fainted.

Shit…

'Interview paused.'

Chapter Sixty-Nine

Maggie paced up and down the hallway while Kate stood outside the door, glancing in occasionally, concern etched on her face. They were waiting for the Duty GP to finish checking Sean McDade over, and give them the all clear to carry on interviewing him.

'Do you think he was faking it?' Maggie thought his timing was a little suspicious.

'It looked pretty genuine to me. Your pacing is making me anxious. Can you not stand still for five minutes?' Kate peered through the small window once again. 'Looks like they are wrapping up in there now. Here comes the GP.'

Maggie stood outside the door, opposite Kate. It felt like ages before the GP emerged. He was startled when he finally did come out, bombarded by questions from Maggie before the door had even closed behind him.

'How is he? Can we carry on with our interview? Did he actually faint?'

'DC Jamieson, can you at least wait until the door has

closed?' The GP paused until the door clicked and moved them further down the hall. 'Mr McDade did faint, and although I could find no physical reason for what happened, after hearing a little about why he was there, I believe it was caused by a vasovagal syncope...'

'A what?' Medical terms were worse than police acronyms; Maggie kept the thought in her head.

'He means it was a reaction to an emotional trigger,' explained Kate.

'Yes. Something you asked him triggered a fear or anxiety. He is fit to continue, but if I could offer some advice?'

Maggie nodded.

'If you rephrase your questions so they seem... less accusatory, perhaps... he probably won't faint again.'

Maggie grunted. Pussyfooting around persons of interest to protect their feelings was something Maggie wasn't very good at. 'Fine. I'll do my best. I'm sure Dr Moloney will keep me focused.'

'I will. Thank you, Doctor.' Kate held out her hand and Maggie was sure the doctor was holding it longer than the norm... especially when he touched her own hand for a mere second.

'Think you have a fan there,' Maggie whispered as they returned to the room. She addressed McDade. 'Interview resumed. We hope you're feeling better now, but please let us know if you need to stop at any time. Are you OK if we continue?'

'I'm fine.' He crossed his arms. 'Let's just get this over with.'

'Before you fainted I asked why you were at each of the crime scenes. Do you have an explanation for that?'

'I… uh… I do… but…' McDade fidgeted with a thread that had come loose from his sweater. 'Sorry. I can't do this. I thought I could, but you've forced me to go back to a place I had left behind me. I think it's best if I speak to a solicitor now.'

Before Maggie could respond, there was a knock on the door. 'Interview paused. Will you excuse me for a moment?' Maggie opened the door to find an ashen-faced Nathan looking back at her. He motioned for her to join him in the corridor.

'The wanderer returns. I'm re-interviewing Sean McDade and he's asked for a lawyer. We might have our guy.'

'Don't get too excited. I need you to wrap this up. Another body has been found…'

Maggie was stunned for a moment. 'What?' She took a moment to gather her thoughts. 'OK, I'm going to speak to the custody sergeant – I don't think we should be too keen to cut him loose just yet, and I'll see you back upstairs shortly.' Maggie headed to the custody suite.

In order to hold McDade, she'd need to convince the custody sergeant that the detention without charge was necessary to either secure or preserve evidence relating to an offence, or to obtain such evidence by questioning him. From McDade's reaction to their query about his appearance at the crime scenes, and without knowing the timeline for the murder they were about to attend, Maggie was convinced they had enough reason to not release him on bail. She hoped she was right.

Much to her relief, it didn't take long to convince the custody sergeant – Maggie must have caught him on a good day. She had been gearing up for a bit of an argument, but once he heard which cases she was referring to and that there was a new murder to go out to, he agreed right away. She strode back to the interview room to inform McDade of the situation. She had left him alone with Kate. Not usual protocol, but the Doc was aware of the alarm locations and it wasn't the first time Kate had spoken to people in the police interview rooms on her own.

Maggie entered the room and caught the Doc's attention. 'You might want to head upstairs. I'll see you there, shortly.' She waited as Kate exited the room. 'Mr McDade, I'm taking you to the custody suite where you will be detained for further questioning. I have to remind you that you've the right to legal advice and will be able to contact your solicitor once booked in. If you don't have a solicitor, a duty solicitor will be appointed. If you'd like to follow me now.'

The maximum time that a suspect could be held without charge was twenty-four hours. However, this could be extended by a senior police officer by a further twelve hours if need be, so the sooner this was dealt with, the sooner they could decide whether or not McDade was the suspect they had been looking for all along.

He walked ahead of Maggie in silence. Once they'd reached the custody suite she handed him over and raced back up to the MOCD office. McDade's behaviour niggled her. Could he be responsible for the murder they were about to attend?

Chapter Seventy

Nathan had already left for the crime scene and Kat filled Maggie in on the situation so far.

'The fire was minimal so the killer may have been disturbed before he could finish. The body was discovered by the wife and a FLO is with her now,' Kat explained as they headed to her car.

Driving to the crime scene, Maggie wondered once again if McDade could have been responsible. It would depend on the time of death. Maybe he was disturbed by the police calling him in for interview? But he was home when the police came to collect him and bring him in.

'What are you thinking?'

'Hmmm. What?' Maggie was pulled away from her thoughts.

'Your leg is going a mile a minute. You obviously have something on your mind.'

'I may be putting two and two together and getting five, so

I'll wait until we see what we have first, before I share what's running around this head of mine.'

The crime scene was only twenty minutes away from the police station. A semi-rural property. Kat pulled up behind the forensics van and they signed in and suited up. Maggie saw Nathan talking to someone by the front entrance and proceeded in that direction, leaving Kat to her own devices.

'You in charge, then? What do we have?' Maggie sidled up beside Nathan.

'Yeah, the Guv is stuck in some meeting in Birmingham. We have a Mr Bram Watson – identified by his wife, as the face was not burned, so positive ID was easy in this case. Items inside the home were broken and toppled over. At first the wife thought they might have been burgled, until she walked into her husband's office and found him tied to a chair.' Nathan entered the property with Maggie close behind.

Maggie took in her surroundings and could understand the initial burglary theory. A lamp in the hallway had been knocked over and there were shards of glass glittering on the surface of the tiled floor. The step plates were neatly laid in a path from the hallway, through the living room, where more items were strewn about, and directly into a doorway off on the left.

'He's just through here.' Nathan pointed.

Maggie stepped into the office and spotted Dr Blake. 'A bit different from the last one,' said Maggie. The pathologist didn't take her eyes off their victim.

'I can see why you say that, but there are definitely more similarities than differences…' Dr Blake wasn't offering much with her cryptic responses.

Maggie walked up to the body, making sure not to get in

the way, but close enough to observe. Dr Blake was right – the positioning was similar to the other victims. Mr Watson was strapped by the arms and wrists to a chair, likely taken from the desk it was in front of. Bram Watson was a retired police officer and Maggie was surprised at how he could afford such expensive things. The force would be up in arms at his murder but Maggie was of two minds – if he had been involved in covering up child abuse back in the day, it wouldn't matter to her that he was one of them.

She could smell the lighter fluid, but the killer had only managed to burn his legs – leaving a lot of evidence to be tested against what they already had.

'Were his eyes closed when you arrived?' Maggie found this curious, as the rest of his face seemed contorted, like he was screaming, and but for the makeshift gag in his mouth, he probably would have been heard by the neighbours. Just beyond the wall to their left was the next house – semi-detached. She wondered how thin the walls were and called Kat over.

'Might be worth having a word with next door to see how much they can hear through these walls. Maybe they heard arguing, a scuffle… something before all… *this* occurred.'

Dr Blake snapped her fingers. 'I thought you wanted to know about his eyes?'

Maggie's necked reddened. Her mind was always ten paces ahead of the moment. 'Yes. Sorry – I got distracted by my thoughts.'

'His eyes were shut when we got here. I believe – but can't say for certain – his face was manipulated after death. I think he may have been placed in the chair after he died. Something happened to prevent the killer from following his MO. I'll know more when he's back at the lab.' Dr Blake leaned in and removed the gag from Watson's mouth, passing it to her assistant, who bagged it. Then Dr Blake lifted his top lip. 'Oh, this is unusual.' She signalled for Maggie to come closer. 'Top incisor removed as well as three lower teeth and a wisdom tooth at the back. Of course, any of these could have already been missing, but we'll check it against his dental records.'

'Or we could just ask his wife?' Maggie didn't want to wait that long. If one of the men they had brought back in to speak with had the same pattern, it could further support Kate's theory of multiple killers. Maggie didn't wait for Dr Blake to respond before making her way to the kitchen, where Mrs Watson was with the FLO.

The woman was crying – so quietly that Maggie only realised this when she saw the pool of make-up on the tissue the woman had just put down after wiping her face. 'So sorry to disturb you, and please accept my condolences on your loss. I wondered if you had a moment to answer something for me.'

The woman nodded.

'I'm DC Jamieson, by the way.' She held out her hand and the woman shook it. Cold, clammy hands. Maggie shuddered. 'Could you tell us if your husband had any teeth missing?'

The woman's brows furrowed. 'Why are you asking that?'

Maggie didn't want to upset her further but it seemed she would have no choice. 'The pathologist noticed something and we'd just like to confirm for our enquiries…'

'He had quite a lot of teeth missing. I think one of his wisdom teeth was removed at some point too. The others he lost during his rugby days. He used to play on the weekends, even after he retired from the force.'

Maggie felt deflated. The missing teeth could have

provided a link to one of their persons of interest – but as she thought about it further, it wouldn't make any sense for his teeth to be missing if he was not directly involved in abusing the boys. It was different from the MO but again, if Kate was right, and multiple people were involved in the murders, it could fit.

'I'm sorry, I can't hear what you are saying…'

Maggie realised she must have been mumbling her thoughts out loud. 'Sorry, just thinking aloud. Thank you so much for your time. Once again, I'm really sorry for your loss.'

The woman looked down at the hot mug of tea the FLO had placed in front of her. 'Catch whoever did this to my husband – he didn't deserve to die this way – he didn't deserve to die at all…'

Maggie reached across and rubbed Mrs Watson's arm. 'We'll do our best to make sure that whoever did this to your husband is caught and brought to justice.' Maggie returned to the primary crime scene. 'The wife says he was missing those teeth already.'

'Well, that's curious indeed. Maybe as the teeth were already missing, your killer didn't feel the need to pull any out?' Dr Blake was preparing to leave.

'Yeah, maybe – or maybe he was disturbed before he got the chance.'

'That may well be the case too. I'll leave the detecting to you, detective. I'm done here for now – if you have anything more to ask me, now's the chance, otherwise I'll get my findings to you as soon as possible.' Dr Blake left her assistant and the rest of the forensics team to bag the body and finish collecting the evidence.

Maggie walked around the office, looking at the

bookshelves littered with historical works on World War II, some crime fiction and some forensic books. Maggie selected one of the latter, bulkier than the others. As she began leafing through it, something fell to the floor. A newspaper article – relating to the first and second murders, with sections highlighted. 'Can we bag these forensic books... and his computer, while we're here?' Either Watson was undertaking his own investigation – she knew retired officers sometimes had a hard time letting go of those cases where they thought they had missed an opportunity or failed – or he was more involved than anyone initially thought. Either way, the team would leave no stone unturned to find out.

Chapter Seventy-One

Maggie searched around for Kat and found her outside, chatting to the neighbour in the adjoining property.

The woman in the doorway was animated, arms waving as she spoke. Kat introduced Maggie and the woman gave her an awkward smile before continuing her conversation with Kat as Maggie listened in.

'So then I heard shouting – but I couldn't make out what was being said, and if I'm honest, I wasn't sure it was real or not...' She leaned in closer to the pair. 'I had fallen asleep earlier, so you know when you're in the half-awake, half-asleep state? My mother isn't well and was napping upstairs. I didn't want to disturb her. I listened against the wall with a glass – I'd seen that on TV once, you know – it doesn't really work... I mean, I could hear stuff but no actual conversation.'

Kat was noting down the information as the woman spoke.

'And how long did that go on for?' Maggie was curious as to why people never took further action when they thought something unusual was happening. Often, in the domestic abuse cases she had worked when she had been seconded to the DAHU, neighbours had heard what was happening but felt it wasn't their place to say anything… until it was too late.

'The noise went on until I banged on the wall and shouted I'd call the police if they didn't shut up. Your man next door often had his mates around when his wife was away – she still works, you know. He's retired and his mates and he would be up until ridiculous hours in the morning – card games, I think. I've banged on that wall quite a few times… which is why I didn't think anything of the noise this time around – only that it went on for a bit and I didn't want them to disturb my mother. When they didn't stop, I got a little pissed off, put my shoes on and went banging on his door. You'd think a copper would have more sense… that's what I thought at the time. Obviously, now I realise that something bad was happening… Was it awful?'

'Was what awful?' Kat stopped writing and looked up at the woman.

'In the house. Was he… all fucked up? You know, blood splattered on the walls and shit?' She put a hand to her mouth. 'Oh sorry, that was really disrespectful – poor man is dead and his wife must be traumatised to come home and find him like that… I wish I *had* called the police now.'

Although Maggie wished she had too, she didn't say it. 'You weren't to know. Did you see anyone leaving the property, and can you take a guess at the time when the noise had stopped?'

'It stopped shortly after I banged on the door. Obviously, when I threatened I was calling the police, it must have spooked whoever was in there. Do you think maybe his wife did it? Maybe she was already back… I never thought of that…' She shook her head. 'Sorry – I'm away with the fairies again – of course it wasn't her – watching too much of that *Law & Order* on the TV. No, I didn't see anyone leave. As soon as it quietened down, I checked on my mum and then went to bed myself. I was exhausted.'

The woman was rambling now. Maggie looked at Kat and signalled they probably had everything they needed here.

'Thanks for your time, you've been very helpful. Here's my card, and if you think of anything else, no matter whether you think it's significant or not, you can ring the number and myself or someone will get back to you.' Kat handed over a card and they turned to leave.

'I hope you catch whoever did this. I probably won't sleep until you do. I mean, what if they come back?' she called out after them but neither were going to indulge her. Maggie got the impression she was one of those crime show fanatics. She had been so excitable when relaying what she had witnessed.

'Anything else relevant to the case from her before I joined you?' Maggie suspected there hadn't been, but it was worth asking just in case.

'Just some details on the timings, which may help to form a timeline, but she didn't really see or hear anything. I think she was still in shock… Hence the rambling.' They were at Kat's car now. Maggie leaned against the passenger door and looked back at the house.

'He must have watched the place – he'd know about the neighbours – but how did he get out and away without being seen?'

'Maybe someone did see him. The field officers are still speaking with the others in the neighbourhood. Maybe they'll strike lucky.'

'Hmmm... maybe. Right, let's get back to the station – I need to finish speaking with McDade before they let him go. Even if he wasn't involved in this murder, he knows something, and now that we have one of our own dead, I am determined to make him talk.'

Chapter Seventy-Two

Kat and Maggie compared theories as they drove back to the office, but the more they spoke, the more it felt like a never-ending loop of questions with no answers. Any of their suspects could be credible and cleared if they talked enough. Were they looking for a lone individual seeking revenge, vigilante style, or a group of past abuse victims, taking back their power from those they felt had victimised them the most?

'It's a fucking conundrum, that's for sure. It would be so easy to find suspicion in the behaviour of those we've interviewed – are they covering for the killer? But no matter what happened to them in the past, why would they risk their liberty for one person? Is he Jim fucking Jones and those poor souls are lapping up his Kool-Aid?'

Maggie couldn't help but laugh. 'Have you been watching true crime shows again?'

Kat shrugged. 'Sometimes they help trigger ideas – is that weird?'

'Depends on what type of ideas you mean. You confessing to something, Everett?'

Kat rolled her eyes. 'You know what I mean. The way your own brain pieces things together. Sometimes I see a programme and then a lightbulb moment hits me. Anyway – it's all escalating now and I can't help but feel we're just reacting after the fact.'

'The Doc is working with Bethany, so hopefully we'll have something solid to work from soon. When we get back, I'm going to speak to McDade again, if you fancy sitting in on it? We don't have much time before they have to consider releasing him.'

Kat turned sharply down the side road that led to the back of the police station and waited for the gate to open. 'I'd love to sit in.'

Once parked, they entered the station through the back door. 'Since we're down here, I'll call up and let Nathan know we're back and we'll be interviewing McDade. Do you want to go get him? I'll find you when I'm done.'

'On it.' Kat headed towards the custody suite.

Maggie dialled Nathan's number and gave him a heads up. Time was ticking and once she'd found out where Kat was from the enquiry desk, she joined them. She wasn't surprised to see that McDade now had a solicitor with him.

Maggie took a seat and looked into McDade's eyes as she waited for Kat to turn on the digital recorder, reminding McDade he was still under caution. Introductions were done and they wasted no time in pushing ahead.

'Have you had time to discuss the situation with your solicitor?' Maggie noticed the solicitor was holding a pen tightly. She didn't recognise him as one of the usual solicitors that attended the station.

'I have. I didn't do any of what you think I did…'

'Why don't we pick up where we left off and you tell us why you were identified in crime scene photographs in the crowd of onlookers?'

'No comment.'

Maggie changed tactics. 'Did you know about the crimes beforehand?'

McDade stiffened. His top lip twitched and his voice shook as he whispered, 'No comment.'

Maggie and Kat exchanged glances. They were on to something – his reaction to that question spoke volumes.

'You do realise that we have your computer and our analysts will be going through it with a fine-tooth comb… if you're hiding something, now is the time to get it out in the open. We can't help you otherwise.'

He looked at his solicitor and then back at Maggie. 'No… I can't…'

'Sorry? What was that you said?' Maggie leaned forward.

McDade's eyes glistened. She had him now – there was something on his computer!

'No c-c-comment,' he stuttered.

Maggie clasped her hands tightly together. Her frustration was growing. 'Who are you protecting? You know who's committing these murders, don't you?'

'No comment.' He leaned over and whispered in his solicitor's ear.

'Mr McDade is feeling unwell. You don't seem to have much to go on – everything you've put forth is mere assumptions. So unless you have any evidence to back up your ludicrous questions, other than seeing my client at crime scenes amongst a crowd of other people, who I assume you're not interviewing... I think we're done here.' He stood and tapped McDade on the arm.

'Sit tight.' Maggie glared at the solicitor. 'I think Mr McDade knows more than he is telling us, so I'm going to request that we apply to hold him for a further thirty-six hours. My colleague here will keep you company, unless you need some time to chat with him – perhaps the thought of staying in one of our cells for another night will change his mind.'

A bead of sweat formed on McDade's forehead. He looked at his solicitor – his eyes were pleading for something.

'You have nothing to hold him on, officers. You're bluffing.' The solicitor huffed and gave his client a squeeze on his shoulder.

'Your client doesn't look too comfortable. Do you really want to take that chance? I'm going to ring upstairs and make sure they put a rush on checking his computer – maybe we should also check the one at his job...'

'No!' McDade slammed his hands on the table.

Maggie had hit a nerve.

'Leave my work out of this.' He turned to his solicitor. 'You said I'd be out of here today. I can't stay another night in those pissy cells. They're giving me flashbacks.' He turned back to Maggie and Kat. 'I didn't do this... but I will tell you what I know.'

The solicitor grabbed his arm. 'You don't need to say anything...'

McDade shrugged the man's hand away. 'Get off. I just want this over with now. Where do you want me to start?'

Maggie sat back down. 'How about from the beginning...'

Chapter Seventy-Three

'I would just like it noted that I strongly advise against this,' the solicitor tutted.

'Your client has said that he wishes to disclose some information that could help not only clear him, but stop someone else becoming a victim. Nice to see that saving a life is so insignificant to you, especially when someone in your own field has been murdered.' Maggie couldn't stop herself.

The solicitor's jaw tightened.

'There's something on your computer, isn't there?' Maggie pushed.

'Yes. But I want to make it clear that I wasn't involved in any of it. You have to believe me.'

'We're glad you want to co-operate, Mr McDade. Why don't you tell us what you know?' Maggie softened her tone; but she wanted to tell him that if he knew about the murders and did nothing to stop them, he was complicit.

'It started when I received an email with a link. There was nothing else in the email, and when I clicked the link it took me through to an encrypted site – it was called Angel of Mercy.'

Maggie straightened in her seat. *The dark web...* That would make sense. A Tor browser would anonymise a person's web traffic using the Tor network. It would make it easy to protect a person's identity online. Maggie had seen Bethany use it a few times for cases, but had to admit she didn't know too much about it.

'Did you already have a Tor browser set up?' Kat inclined her head.

'Yes – I don't like the idea of everyone being able to track my movements. I had a hard time in the care system and always feared that those arseholes would track me down to make sure I kept my mouth shut.'

Maggie could follow his logic but wasn't sure if he was being overly paranoid or if he was right to be concerned. The murder victims had kept their secrets well hidden; it wouldn't be of any benefit for them to open a Pandora's box now.

'Who contacted you and *how* did they know how to contact you?' Maggie's mind was running through all the possibilities. They were on to something – her feeling that McDade could be the key to blowing this whole case open was right.

'I don't know...' He gripped the arm of the chair. 'I don't know who it is – I still don't and I've no idea how they found me. Given what they know, it had to be one of the others who were abused like me. I changed my identity on Tor via the onion icon but they still managed to track me. It has to be one of them. How else would they know?' He scratched at his palm, the agitation evident.

Maggie looked at Kat. The little she knew about the dark web did not extend to an understanding of what an onion icon was. It was something she'd ask Bethany about; she didn't want to deflect the interview questions by asking for a tutorial on the dark web now.

'What happened in this Angel of Mercy group, then? Am I right to assume that false names were used in the forum?'

'Yes – I was #TrustNo1.' He let out an awkward laugh. 'There were a few of us in the forum. I couldn't *see* everyone, as people would use various techniques to mask themselves within the group. Someone calling themselves #TheChosenOne ran the forum. At first I wanted nothing to do with it. I have enough nightmares without having to continually rehash the past. But then #TheChosenOne said they could make those nightmares go away and my curiosity got the best of me. They knew exactly what to say, and that's how I knew it had happened to them too...' He ran his fingers through his hair. Maggie could see that the reality of the situation was hitting him hard.

'You're doing great, Mr McDade. Just a few more questions. How was this all supposed to happen?'

'The Chosen One told us where our abusers now lived. Gave detailed accounts of their movements and what they were doing – home, work... even when they went to the shops. They said that we could be involved if we wanted to, but they would be happy to be the *sole angel*, delivering justice and making our abusers beg for mercy before he sent them to hell.' McDade's breaths quickened. 'I didn't want to be involved at all, but I'm not going to lie – knowing that those bastards would get what was coming to them lifted a huge weight off my shoulders. I could finally put it all behind me... I would be free.'

'Why is it that you were seen at all the crime scenes, in the crowd, then?' Maggie suspected she knew the answer but needed to hear him say it.

'I don't know.' He shrugged. 'I wanted to see for myself that this person was doing what they said they would. I didn't have the courage to do it myself because I would...' McDade's solicitor touched his arm and shook his head.

'I'm not here to hide anything. I want the police to know everything, it's caused me just as many sleepless nights as remembering my past has.' The room was silent. 'If I was strong enough, I would have done it myself... or at least helped. Instead, I watched from the sidelines.' His eyes glistened.

'Were you given specific details about the crimes?' Maggie didn't want to push too hard, but they were so close now. McDade was opening up and she needed him to trust them.

'We were given the details afterwards... minutes after each... erm... murder happened... We were told who was killed, where and what time. I guess that was so they could get away in case one of us broke the trust and felt the need to contact the police? But we had other options...'

'When were you initially contacted?' Maggie was curious how long this 'Chosen One' had been planning this.

'Eighteen months ago...' He looked down at the table.

'What the hell? You've known for eighteen months that this was going to happen, and never once did you think of contacting the police?' Kat's eyes widened.

'I know... I didn't believe anything would come of it. It was like private therapy sessions at first – we all talked about our experiences, our abusers and what we would like to do to them, and then... it started to happen and...' His body shook.

'Can we take a moment please? I'd like to speak to my client,' the solicitor interjected.

Maggie was reluctant to stop at this juncture. 'Why don't we see if Mr McDade wants to stop?'

He looked at his solicitor and then back at Maggie and Kat.

'I think I want to take a break now. Would I be able to get some water or a coffee or something?' He smacked his lips together. 'My mouth is dry.'

Maggie sighed louder than she had meant to. 'Off course, we'll get that sorted for you. Would fifteen minutes be enough?' The solicitor nodded, Kat stopped the recording and they both left the room.

Kat and Maggie walked to the kitchenette located at the end of the corridor.

'I can't believe he knows all this shit and didn't once think of coming forward.'

'I know. But I kind of feel sorry for him.' Maggie grabbed a jug and filled it with water.

Kat moved back in surprise. 'You do? What happened to the ice queen?'

'Maybe I'm softening as I get older?' Maggie laughed. 'He and the others went through a horrendous experience, are possibly suffering from some form of PTSD or other mental health issues, so even though he may now be feeling guilty – part of him... and the others... would want to see justice served on those people who let them down – their abusers. Not saying he's right, but I can understand it.'

'You definitely are getting soft. Should I give Bethany a

heads up about the Tor group? We still have a few people waiting to be interviewed – might help the officers to have those details.'

'Good thinking. I'll head back and carry on with the interview – bring him some water.' Maggie noted the clock on the wall. Their time was running out and she needed to wrap this up, as no one wanted another body in the morgue.

Chapter Seventy-Four

Maggie returned to the interview room, placing the jug of water and plastic cups on the table. She resumed the interview once the recording device was on, and explained Kat's temporary absence. Now it was time to pull out all the stops and go for the jugular.

'You've had time again to discuss things with your solicitor. I think we've shown that although we empathise with the situation, you really need to start giving us names. We need something solid, as I'm sure no one in this room wants another death to happen. You wouldn't want another killing on your conscience.' She clasped her hands together and placed them on the table in front of her.

'I don't know real names, not from the forum, it's all handles. It doesn't take a genius, though, to guess that those in the forum were probably involved in the original complaint to the police. You know – the allegations when your lot did nothing.'

He was getting cocky now and this irked Maggie. 'We've

been over that before, Mr McDade, and I understand why you're angry, but I'm dealing with the here and now. Who is next on the list?'

A look between him and his solicitor passed. 'Joanne Mole. That's the last on the list that I know of. I was surprised that the details were shared in advance, but then, there were no rules. I don't know when it's going to happen.'

Maggie stood and paused the recording. 'Gimme two minutes, please.' She stepped outside the door and rang upstairs. Nathan could then locate Joanne Mole and get her to safety. They'd need to plan it so that it wasn't obvious; they'd want the killer to think the person was still around.

She had an idea.

Maggie returned to the room, turned on the recorder and came straight out with her thoughts. 'Would you be willing to make contact with this "Chosen One"… maybe suggest that you'd like to be involved?'

His solicitor jumped on that immediately. 'Absolutely not. You're not using my client as your bait, DC Jamieson. I suggest you come up with another idea.'

Maggie glared at him before looking McDade in the eyes. 'You wouldn't be in any danger. You wouldn't even be leaving the police station. He'll know your writing style, so it's best it comes from you. You'd just need to go into the forum and say that you want to be involved… that you don't want to be on the sidelines anymore – ask him where it's going to take place and how to meet. I presume there's a private message box – if it came from there, it might make it look more authentic.'

'I'll do it.' McDade's shoulders relaxed. Maggie was relieved he agreed.

'I strongly advise against this,' his solicitor blurted out in a huff.

'I'm already screwed. I'm going to prison for my part in this, for sure…' He reached across the table towards Maggie. 'I need to be kept safe – he'll kill me when he finds out. Can you do that?'

'We'll make sure all that's covered and we'll inform the CPS that you were very co-operative – who knows what will happen then? You could end up with a suspended sentence…' Maggie wasn't convinced that was true, but didn't want him backing out under pressure from his solicitor.

Could it be over now? A killer in the cells before the week ended? Maggie looked at her watch. They needed to act now.

'I'm going to take you back to the custody suite where you'll be charged with conspiracy to murder. I'm sure your solicitor will look at getting you bail, but that won't even be considered until tomorrow, so if you make yourself comfortable, we'll get you something to eat. Someone will get your laptop set up and get the ball rolling.' Maggie stood and held the door open. McDade looked like a broken man – the seriousness of the situation was setting in. As he brushed past her, Maggie touched his arm and tried to reassure him. 'You're doing the right thing, Mr McDade, and I meant what I said. I'll be sure to let them know how much you co-operated with us.'

He gave her a weak smile. He was like a dead man walking towards the custody suite, and no matter how she felt about the horror he had endured as a child, she was more concerned with preventing any further murders.

An arrest was imminent – she could feel it in her bones.

Chapter Seventy-Five

After leaving McDade with the custody sergeant, Maggie raced back upstairs, finding the Doc, Nathan and Kat huddled around Bethany's desk. There was a lot of chatter.

'Sorry to break up the party here, but McDade has agreed to make contact with the killer via the Angel of Mercy forum. Looking at the time, we probably need to strike while the iron is hot… before he has time to sit in his cell and rethink his position.'

'Stand by, Maggie. I'd have to clear this with Rutherford first. We'd also have to work out a strategy of how we're going to respond to this.'

Although Maggie heard Nathan, her focus turned to Bethany, as another idea invaded her head. 'Bethany, can you stand up for a minute?'

Bethany frowned but did as she was asked. Maggie circled around her like a buzzard hovering over its next meal. 'You're perfect.'

'Erm… perfect for what? Can I get back to my computer now?'

'Of course. I was just thinking that if Nathan could clear it with the Guv…' Her mind was working in double time. 'What if we set up a meet? If Bethany dressed like a guy and went in place of McDade once the contact has been made via the forum? McDade told us that this "Chosen One",' Maggie rolled her eyes as she said the name, 'tells them what's going to happen and to whom – he gives them the chance to be involved, but no one has taken up his offer so far. The details are usually shared just before or after a murder. We'll have plans in place for the intended victim – Joanne Mole – so the risk there is minimal. We could have our killer behind bars and end this once and for all.' Maggie felt a rush of adrenaline through her veins. After feeling like they had been two steps behind the killer, she now felt that they finally had taken the lead.

'Whoa. I appreciate what you're saying, but you've been around long enough to know that something of this scale takes time to plan. We can't risk rushing in and putting Bethany or anyone else in harm's way.' Nathan placed his hands on his hips – a sure sign that he wouldn't be persuaded to go against the procedures, even just a little bit.

'But Nathan…' Maggie understood his reluctance, even if she didn't agree with it.

He held up a hand. 'But nothing. Measures are already being actioned to ensure that Joanne Mole is given a Threats to Life warning and offered some help so that she is safely away from her home over the next few days. My suggestion to you… to you all… is that you go home, get some rest and be back here at seven a.m. sharp. We can then look at what we have, co-ordinate a plan and take this arsehole down.' As far as Nathan was concerned, the conversation had ended. He walked back to his office and shut the door.

Maggie looked at the rest of the team. 'Anyone up for a quick drink down the road?'

'You don't have to ask me twice.' Kat ran over to her desk and grabbed her coat.

Both Bethany and the Doc nodded and replied simultaneously, 'I just have a few things to finish up, I'll meet you there.'

Maggie laughed. 'OK, Kat and I will get the drinks in and see you at The Black Swan.' Maggie grabbed her coat and packed up her bag. 'See you soon.' She tapped on Nathan's door and gave him a wave.

———————

'Do you think he was being honest with us then?' Kat rummaged through her bag and pulled out her cigarettes.

'Who, McDade?'

Kat nodded.

'Yeah, I do. When I left him at the custody suite he seemed resigned to his fate, wanting to put a stop to all of this.'

'I hope for his sake you're right.' Kat picked up the pace. 'Tell you what, I'm gagging for a cuppa.'

Maggie noticed the grin on Kat's face and couldn't help but laugh. 'I forgot, you don't drink, do you?'

'Nope, fags are my only real vice... oh, and swearing, I guess, but I've tried to curb that too... you know, to be professional and all that shit.'

'Well, don't hide yourself because you think you have to –

there's a time and place for everything, and when you're with your team, you can just be as sweary as you want... I bloody am!'

Kat took a long drag of her cigarette. 'You're not wrong there.'

The pair approached the pub and Maggie waited while Kat finished her cigarette. 'Just a tea then? What about crisps or nuts?' Maggie was feeling peckish; she couldn't remember if she had eaten lunch or not. This was becoming a regular occurrence and she'd have to be more mindful.

'Salt and vinegar, if they have them.' Maggie watched as Kat headed to a booth in the corner. The pub wasn't busy, which was why Maggie chose it, and it would allow them some privacy. A lot of their colleagues came here, which was another reason Maggie had chosen it.

Maggie placed her order and paid. The barmaid said she would bring it over when it was ready. Maggie sat opposite Kat and before the drinks had arrived, the Doc marched in the door and joined them.

Kat played with a napkin while the Doc took in the atmosphere, and the silence was beginning to make Maggie anxious. *Did they think she was off her rocker for her earlier suggestions on the case?*

'How comfortable do you think Bethany would be to go undercover, pending Rutherford's approval?'

'When I left her at the office, she didn't seem too keen on the idea. I have to admit, I'm not sure she'd be the right person – she prefers to stay behind the scenes, and as confident as I am in her abilities, any doubt could lead to huge mistakes.' Hearing what the Doc said, Maggie could see she might be on to something.

'She could easily pass for McDade though, Maggie is right there,' Kat added.

'Let's look at it logically though – from an objective point of view. Your "Chosen One" – and I really hate that name, but if you look at the profile, it totally fits, so I shouldn't be surprised – he'll have done his homework and he'll know exactly how McDade walks, talks, any quirks... You'd have to be one hundred per cent confident that Bethany could pull that off before placing her in that position.'

Trust Kate to say out loud what Maggie had been thinking – it had been niggling in her mind. But just when she was about to concede, Bethany burst through the door.

Chapter Seventy-Six

'Are you going to tell us what you've found out or are you going to keep hopping about until you tire yourself out?' Maggie instantly regretted the terseness of her question when Bethany's face dropped. She had meant it to sound light-hearted but obviously had failed.

'Sorry, of course.' Bethany squeezed into the booth beside Kat. 'We finally managed to tighten the list of complainants against the Chatham House care workers, rather than across the care homes that the initial findings pulled up. There were seven boys, but when I cross-referenced our information, we have only managed to locate and interview five with that group we just finished. The sixth and seventh boys seem to have disappeared off the face of the earth after leaving the home at sixteen. But they could have changed their names or used aliases – so that would make it difficult to track them down.'

'Shit. So we could have already interviewed the killer? Have we managed to locate the other two? I don't mean to doubt your skills…' Maggie felt a chill at the back of her neck. *Could they have already spoken to the Staffordshire Scorcher?*

Bethany grinned. 'Of course I did. Well, one of them anyway – still working on the last one. Turns out the guy I found was homeless for a significant period of time, got into a little bother, but uses an number of different aliases – he's on probation and Sarah Hardy is his officer.'

'What the hell? What's he on probation for?' Maggie shifted in her seat. Sarah was not going to appreciate the extra attention.

'Causing Death by Careless Driving. He's flagged as a MAPPA Level 1 offender.'

As all of them knew, MAPPA was a system of sharing information and combining resources to maximise the risk management in place for each individual offender, with Level 1 being ordinary management.

'Shitballs. Only senior officers sit in attendance, so we'll have to wait around for any news.' Kat wasn't wrong. It could take all day to learn any updates, depending on how long the meeting went on for.

If Bethany was right, they wouldn't need to use McDade to make contact – all Sarah would have to do would be to recall him, and the police could arrest him as soon as the paperwork went through.

'If my memory of Probation practice is right, it meets the criteria for an emergency recall, as the risk to the public is very high and unpredictable. We could have him in custody in a matter of hours.' Maggie wasn't convinced Probation would act without a risk management meeting first.

'He does appear to meet a lot of what I identified in my profile, too – but so could a lot of people with a similar background.' Kate took a sip of wine and her lips pursed. Maggie had to order something different to what Kate usually got as the bar didn't stock it, and it seemed it wasn't the best choice.

'I don't want to get too excited, it may not even be our guy. Other than the name change, why didn't we pick this up sooner?' Maggie turned to Bethany.

'Because we didn't search aliases. He has a list as long as my arm, and each one has a different date of birth. I mean, eventually we got there, but we don't even know if his address or anything is correct.'

'While we wait for recall, can't we have someone pick him up for questioning like the others?' Kat looked at Maggie.

'Nathan was actioning that as I left, but there were three different addresses listed. They'll obviously check the one he provided to Probation. But we know how easy it is to provide details and then just move about,' Bethany informed them.

Maggie tapped the table. At that very moment she was desperate to go back into work and learn as much as she could before the morning, but she'd only end up tired and possibly unfocused, missing crucial bits if she acted on impulse.

'Right, I think I'm going to shoot off now. Anyone need a lift?' Maggie looked around the table.

'I can drop Bethany off,' Kat offered.

'I just live around the corner, so I'll walk out with you.' Kate stood and put her jacket on. Although the days were warmish, there was a definite chill in the evenings.

'See you all tomorrow.' Maggie grabbed her bag, slid out of the booth and followed Kate out.

'I can see you're itching to get this guy in – just remember, he could be another victim who isn't even involved in this online forum. I'd hate to see you get your hopes up.'

'You sound more and more like Nathan, the longer you're at the MOCD. That will be the first thing he says to me tomorrow morning,' Maggie said with a laugh.

'He's right. Anyway, this is where I need to turn off. 'Night.'

'You sure you don't want me to walk you back?' After Kate's stalker experience, Maggie could sometimes come across as an over-protective friend, but she couldn't help it.

The Doc rolled her eyes. 'I'm grand. I can see my door from here. You're more than welcome to stand there and watch me go in.'

'OK, OK.' Maggie held her hands up. 'I'll see you in the morning.' She walked around the corner towards the police station's car park.

The drive home had her running through everything they had on the case so far. She wanted to call Sarah and forewarn her, but that wouldn't go down well if a recall was actioned. It could be used as part of an appeal. Maggie wasn't even sure Sarah was at work. With everything that had happened, someone else might be managing her cases.

Outside her house, she sat in her car for a moment and closed her eyes. She needed to shut down before going inside. She took a deep breath and compartmentalised everything she had learned this evening, and suddenly she felt tired.

A tap on the window startled her and she gasped when she saw her brother. There was blood all down his face.

Chapter Seventy-Seven

Maggie jumped out of her car and raced around to her brother. 'What the hell happened?' Blood dripped down his arm.

Andy was attempting to stem the flow of blood with a tea towel. 'I'm fine. Looks worse than it is. I was debating whether to drive to the hospital or call an ambulance – might need stiches. Then I saw you pull up.'

Maggie moved closer and pulled his hand away. 'Let me see.' There was a gash just above his eyebrow. 'Looks like you probably do need a stitch or two. What the heck did you do? Get in… I'll drive you to the A&E.' It wasn't the evening Maggie had planned, but it would stop her from obsessing about the case for a little while.

Andy got into the passenger seat and lay back, holding the towel to his head.

'Keep pressure on it. What were you doing?'

'I was changing a bulb in the kitchen when there was a

knock on the door. I must have lost my footing on the stepladder and hit my head on the corner of the counter.' He pulled an envelope out of his pocket. 'Here. This was at the door when I got there.'

Maggie took the envelope and shoved it in her pocket. 'Did you lose consciousness or anything?'

'No, nothing like that.'

They arrived at the A&E and after waiting an hour, Andy was stitched up and given the all clear. On the drive home, Maggie went into protective sister mode, giving him a lecture, and even though his eyes were closed, she knew he was awake. Things were still strained after their argument about money, with unanswered questions hanging over them. Now was not the time to explore them though. Maggie wasn't even sure she wanted to, in case she learned something she didn't want to deal with.

'Sit down and I'll make you a cuppa.' Maggie's stomach turned when she walked into the kitchen and saw all the blood. It was like a crime scene... with cat prints. 'Fucksake, Scrappy,' she tutted. Once the kettle had boiled and she had made sure Andy was comfortable, she returned to the kitchen and started cleaning up the mess. All the blood pulled her back into thoughts about the murder investigation, no matter how hard she tried to ignore them.

Other than keeping Joanne Mole safe, she wondered if the man calling himself the Chosen One was the person they had identified. *Did he know how close the police were to stopping him?*

A shout from the other room nearly caused her to bang her own head on the counter.

'Hey! Come here and check this out.'

'Nearly finished.' She gathered up the ruined towels and threw them in the bin. The TV was on and Andy was focused on the news.

'It's raging – there'll be nothing left of that place once they put it out.'

Maggie sat down beside her brother and listened as Julie Noble reported on the fire that was burning a house in the background.

'Did she say where that was?'

'Yeah, some house in Farley Stone…'

She had the answer to the question she had been asking herself earlier. *He knew.* It didn't take long to guess the house belonged to Joanne Mole – she pulled out her phone and dialled Nathan's number.

'*I can guess why you're calling.*'

'You've seen the news then?'

'*Yeah – he knows we're on to him. So there goes any of the plans we spent hours putting together…*'

'Just when I thought we had the advantage. Have you contacted the Duty SPO in Probation? I think you'd have enough to convince them to do an emergency recall now. Once he's been picked up, we can question him.'

'*DI Rutherford is doing just that. But Probation may not play ball, as all we have now is circumstantial – we don't even know if it is him.*'

In the past there had been some conflict between Police and Probation on the information they required to action a recall. There had also been a lot of criticism towards Probation for missing opportunities to recall based on evidence that an individual's risk of serious harm may be raised, like in this case. But at the moment Nathan was right – all they had was that Ryan Kent was one of the men who had been abused and he had not come forward. The fact he used aliases and had previous convictions for arson was probably not enough.

'Surely we can search his home, like we did the others. He has a motive and form. The others have pretty much been cleared of the murders, and nothing other than their involvement in this secret forum links them to the offences.' Maggie recalled reading about Operation Notarise, where the National Crime Agency (NCA) had made hundreds of arrests after announcing they could find anyone, even if they were using the dark net. She shared these thoughts with Nathan.

'Hang on a minute. I have a call coming through.'

Maggie paced the hallway as she waited for Nathan to return. Minutes felt like hours and then she heard the words she had been hoping for.

'We got him. He was caught on CCTV dumping something in an industrial bin behind the Sainsbury's in the town centre.'

That was where Music Matty said he found the duffel coat. Must be close to where the killer lived. 'OK, I'm coming in.' Maggie had grabbed her coat.

'It's late. We have the MAPPA meeting in the morning and enough now to ensure the emergency recall goes through. The fire is being dealt with and no bodies were found – so nothing for you to do. I need to get back to Probation. Do me a favour and get some sleep, as the next forty-eight hours are going to be critical…'

Nathan's tone told her that protesting would be futile. 'Fine. But if anything develops, call me.'

'Of course. See you tomorrow.'

Maggie ended the call and returned to the living room.

'What the hell was that all about?' Andy had changed the channel and was now watching some show on fishing.

'A development on the case I'm working.' She sat down. 'Finally got the fucker.' She couldn't help herself. This was huge. 'Was there anything else on that fire?'

'Nah. Julie wrapped it up pretty much after you left. What's happening between you two, by the way? I haven't seen her around here lately... I had hoped that you'd finally met someone.'

'Julie and I are just friends... It's way too complicated to get into. Anyway, I don't have time to think about that. How are you feeling now?' Maggie leaned over and looked at the cut on his head.

'I'm fine. No dizziness, nausea, confusion or an inability to process or retain information, no sensitivity to light, or vision distortion,' said Andy, rolling off all the signs the emergency nurse had told them to look out for, as if he was trying to prove a point. 'She said that only a small percentage of people who hit their heads actually end up concussed. I'm fine.' He pushed her hand away.

'Hmmm. OK.' As his big sister, she would always worry, no matter how much he protested. She lay back and closed her eyes for a moment. 'I have a big day tomorrow, so I'm going to just curl up here and keep an eye on you for a bit.'

'You'll be wasting your time.' He stood and turned off the TV. 'I'm going to bed.'

'Well, make sure your phone is by your bed – do you have that pamphlet?' She scrabbled to sit up.

He pulled the leaflet out of his pocket and waved it in her face.

'OK. Message received. I'll see you in the morning.' Maggie headed up to bed and set her alarm for a few hours later. She'd check on him then. He needn't know. No matter how much he pissed her off, she would always protect him.

Chapter Seventy-Eight

Maggie wasted little time getting ready that morning. Once she'd checked in on Andy and he'd assured her he was fine, she felt better about leaving him. After a quick shower she got dressed, fed Scrappy and let him out, before grabbing her things and jumping into her car. She'd call Andy later.

Maggie couldn't believe that they might have their suspect in custody before the end of the day. The normal forty-minute drive to work flew by as she raced up the dual carriageway. The police station car park was relatively quiet, as shifts were changing before the sun rose. She parked and ran through the back door, taking the steps two by two up to the MOCD offices. She arrived at the open-plan office breathless, and bent over as a stitch in her side reminded her that despite her new yoga routine, she was still relatively unfit. The thought of doing additional exercise made her cringe, but it might have to be done before the next police exam. A failure on the exam could mean a desk job until she could pass, and there was no way she would let that happen.

Maggie threw her coat over her chair, dropped her bag on the floor beside her desk and logged in. She wanted to see if they had Ryan Kent in the cells – though it wouldn't make any difference, as she wouldn't be able to speak to him before the MAPPA meeting. That's if the meeting still went ahead. They would have to take a joined-up approach to addressing his risk and make it clear to Probation that they didn't believe he could be safely managed within the community, despite whatever a sleazy lawyer tried to say after recall.

Someone tapped her on the shoulder and she nearly fell out of her chair.

'Fucksake, Nathan. You nearly gave me a heart attack.'

'Sorry – I thought you heard me come in.'

'I was thinking about the MAPPA meeting. How many are coming?'

'Police, Probation, Social Care are the main agencies. Representatives from Housing and the Drug and Alcohol services will also be present. Looks like there were previous alcohol issues – though he seemed to clean up his act and secured work at the homeless shelter down the road, doing outreach. That obviously allowed him to blend in during the night. He was literally under our noses this whole time.'

Maggie hadn't looked at the full case record before Nathan had interrupted her, so hadn't reached any information about his work. 'Which homeless shelter? McDade also worked at a homeless shelter.'

'The one just off Station Street – you spoke to the manager there, from what I read last night.'

'You're bloody kidding me! How come everything has come together so neatly now? Don't you find that odd?' Something had been bothering her ever since she learned that Mr Kent was known to Probation and the Tor ISP was traced so easily.

'Don't look a gift horse in the mouth. It may seem like it came together easily, but that's because everyone has been working stupid hours to get this sorted. When you have a minute, come through to my office and let's go over everything. Kent was picked up in the early hours, stinking of petrol. He's not said a word but forensics are going through his flat with a fine-tooth comb. He has a solicitor.'

'Who is it?'

'Same firm as McDade, I believe.'

'Isn't that a conflict of interest?'

'Different solicitor. He's just here acting as support, apparently. From what I heard, the firm denies a conflict of interest, given that they are defending both men against what they are calling a "gross miscarriage of justice" in the first place. It will be up to the judge to decide, given that the clients have no apparent issue.'

Maggie tapped her pen on the desk. 'Guess as long as we get what we need, they can battle that out amongst themselves, as you say. Do you want a coffee? I'm going to grab one and then I'll be in to see you.'

'Gagging for one. See you in five.' Nathan headed to his office and Maggie went to the kitchenette to make the drinks. She made herself a large coffee in her travel flask and used one of the communal mugs for Nathan. In his office, she passed him his coffee and sat, waiting to hear what information they had learned so far.

'Prints on Kent match those we have on record. The

emergency recall went through as we had hoped it would – though the Duty SPO was grilling me for all the details before he would action it.'

'They have to – when I worked in the DAHU, I saw how difficult their position is. They argue that if the person is such a risk, why aren't we arresting them? And in a way I can see their point, even if I don't agree with it.'

'I guess. I just remember a few cases where we had shared information and they refused to action recall – then the shit hit the fan when said person went on to commit heinous crimes. But that's not why we're here.' Nathan booted up his computer.

Maggie listened as Nathan explained her role in the upcoming MAPPA meeting and shared the details of what was known so far. Her earlier thoughts about how everything had just seemed to come together so quickly niggled at her mind. Were they being played by the man who dubbed himself 'the Chosen One'?

Chapter Seventy-Nine

Maggie couldn't sit in on the MAPPA meeting and had to wait to be called. She positioned herself in the main office at a spare desk so she could see down the hall and watch the various partnerships go in and out as they shared their information with the panel. As soon as she saw Sarah Hardy come out, she ran down the hall towards her.

'Hey! How did it go in there?' Maggie nodded towards the main office, hoping Sarah would want to talk. She might even be able to add some insight before they interviewed Ryan Kent.

'How do you think? I've another Serious Further Offence to contend with now. I'd be surprised if I didn't get a warning on my record. What gets me is that I didn't see this coming at all.' Sarah followed Maggie to the office and waved at the team. Maggie pushed out a chair and offered it to her. Her faced seemed to have aged by ten years and Maggie wondered if she needed to offload.

'I just can't see how this is even possible. I knew a little about his background but he had been attending counselling. Well, I thought he had, but it turns out the signed appointment cards were forged. I was due to talk to his therapist next week. Nothing flagged from the alcohol services – he definitely was attending those, as we had regular joint meetings. Plus there were no complaints from the shelter where he worked…' Sarah shook her head. 'I never would have placed him at such a high risk of harm – not at this stage. I mean, even when he committed the original offence, he held his hands up, took the punishment and worked really hard to address his offending and reduce his risk on release.'

'Sorry – I couldn't help but overhear what you were saying…' The Doc pulled up a chair. 'That does seem unusual. Although on paper he does fit the profile we've discussed, any one of those people we spoke to would as well – except I'm not sure they would have worked so hard to address their past.' Kate tugged at her ear.

'What are you saying, Doc?' Maggie had a bad feeling in the pit of her stomach – something just didn't fit.

'Based on what I heard in the MAPPA meeting earlier and from what Sarah is saying now – is Ryan Kent intelligent and manipulative enough to pull off such a carefully executed plan?' Kate didn't look convinced.

'Exactly what I was thinking. I wish they'd hurry up and finish so that we can go down and interview him. I think we'll get a better understanding of the situation. I've heard he's being really co-operative – I wouldn't have expected that at all.' Maggie stretched her arms. She was beginning to feel restless and needed to do something to stop her driving herself and her colleagues crazy. She hated feeling useless and that's exactly how she felt at the moment.

Sarah looked between Kate and Maggie. 'Do you think you got it wrong?' A look of relief washed over Sarah's face momentarily.

'I don't think that's what we're saying. Like the others, Kent was definitely involved somehow – he was caught red-handed getting rid of evidence and stinking of petrol – there's no getting away from that fact… but…' A thought hit Maggie like she had just run into a brick wall. 'Shit – gimme a minute.' She stood. 'Where's Joanne Mole?' she called out to Bethany.

'She and her family are staying in Hockton – sister's place, until they can sort something else out more permanent. There's a patrol car outside their home. Why?'

'Can you just make contact – check that everything's OK?' She turned to Sarah and Kate. 'Excuse me for a second.' Maggie ran down the hall towards the conference room. When she looked in, everyone was standing – it looked like the meeting was about to wrap up. She pushed open the door.

'Guv… Nathan – can I have a quick word?'

The pair waved her over.

'What is it, Maggie? We're just about to brief the team.' DI Rutherford picked up her notebook.

'I think we have a problem.'

The pair looked at each other and back at Maggie. 'Well?' They replied in unison.

'I've just been speaking with Kate and Sarah. I don't think Ryan Kent is our guy.'

'He was pretty much caught red-handed, Maggie. How did you come to that conclusion?' DI Rutherford wasn't impressed.

Maggie relayed everything that she, Sarah and Kate had discussed, while Nathan and DI Rutherford listened. From the look on their faces, they seemed to believe that Maggie could be on to something.

'Has anyone contacted the officers stationed outside the house?' Rutherford paced the room.

'Bethany is doing that now.'

'We need to question Kent now – he may know something. He was co-operative before. If we can break him – it could save us a lot of time.'

'My thoughts exactly.' Maggie had worried that she would have to fight her case more, but for once, it appeared that everyone was on the same page.

DI Rutherford instructed Nathan and Maggie to conduct the interview while she went and updated the team.

Downstairs Maggie and Nathan learned that Ryan Kent was in an interview suite with his solicitor. *Perfect.* After knocking on the door, the pair entered and Nathan did the introductions. Kent's solicitor invited them to sit. Maggie explained what would be happening and Nathan began the questioning.

'Mr Kent, we have some new information that may please you and your solicitor – perhaps even clear you of murder. You've already confessed to your part in the arson attack, so we're giving you one chance to come clean. This offer will not be on the table for long. If you don't co-operate, I can assure you that we'll make sure the CPS use every means possible to see that you spend the rest of your days behind bars.'

Maggie's eyes widened. Witnessing Nathan's assertive side, she was reminded of the partner she had before he took on the role of DS, and she liked it. It was usually her who played the bad cop role. Kent slumped in his chair. Maggie saw his eyes glisten and a tear roll down his face.

Time to play good cop.

'This must be a big burden to carry, Mr Kent. As my colleague has said – if you get it off your chest now, we can help you.'

The clock on the wall was ticking so loudly in the silent room, Maggie was on the edge of her seat. When Kent finally did speak, he said something that no one in the room was expecting.

'It wasn't me... but I know who you're looking for.'

Chapter Eighty

'Well, spit it out then!' Maggie was losing patience.

'What DC Jamieson means is that if you do know who is responsible for this, it would go very much in your favour to share that information with us,' Nathan said, leaning forward.

'He goes by "the Chosen One" in the forum. He messaged me privately and said he needed a favour. It was for the greater good and would end all this... I was conflicted and the more I thought about it, the more I realised it could only be Brendan O'Donnell. After this all started, I spoke to some of the others. You see, we kept in touch – what we went through... well, you form a bond and we'd meet sometimes – talk about everything, share our experiences and even joke about what we'd like to do to the arseholes who ruined our lives. We were just *joking* though.' The words caught in his throat. 'I'm so sorry. I didn't think... I don't think any of us thought about the implications for their families – we just wanted them to pay.'

'Brendan? What's his full name?' Maggie had recognised the name from the list but they couldn't locate him when Bethany did her checks.

'Yeah, sorry. Brendan Hugh O'Donnell. Uses his middle name now, though – Hugh. A big man in Social Care – in the building around the corner.'

Maggie felt a pain in the pit of her stomach. No wonder he hadn't wanted them to look into the child abuse cases with Claire. Maggie turned to Nathan. 'Can I have a word outside?'

He nodded and they stopped the recorder. 'We'll just be a moment.'

Maggie walked down the hall and found an empty room, Nathan followed behind her. 'I feel sick, boss. That's Claire's supervisor. We've already spoken to him at the start of the investigation. He knew exactly what we were looking for, so no wonder he was always a step ahead, but we had no reason to be suspicious of him. I mean yes, he tried to halt what we were doing, but that's not uncommon between agencies. How can we be sure that Mr Kent is telling us the truth?'

'We can't. But we have nothing else to go on. I spoke to him myself a few times but…'

Before Nathan could speak, Kat burst through the doors. 'Thank fuck. I panicked when I couldn't find you. Joanne Mole has gone missing. When Bethany called the officer, he checked the house and learned she went out the back way. She told her family she'd be back shortly after receiving a call – something to do with work. When her family warned her to let the officers outside know, she said it would be quicker to just deal with the matter. They said she was stubborn like that. Bethany is working on triangulating her location now. What do you want me to do?'

'Shit. Go back upstairs and see what Bethany has found out. I'll speak to Rutherford now – we'll get as many field officers on the ground as we can to look for her. Maggie – go back in there and see if Mr Kent knows anything else. He was clearly used as a distraction and we bloody fell for it.'

Maggie didn't need to be told twice. She returned to the interview room, turned on the recorder and began interrogating him for more details. 'No more games. You'd better hope my colleagues don't get into your private Tor messages before you share the information with us, or else everything DS Wright promised you will be thrown out the window.' Maggie leaned forward. 'And I promise you – we'll make sure that the CPS nail you to the floor.'

Kent's body shook. This wasn't the reaction she was expecting – no defiance, no sly look – he was afraid.

'I told you everything, I swear. He threatened my sister and her kids if I went to the police – but I'm here, aren't I?'

'That wasn't by choice though – was it? He must have told you something.' Maggie glared at Kent, hoping to play on his fear.

'I… I… don't know any more than I told you.' He turned to his solicitor. 'Please. Tell her – I don't know anything more. I just want it all to stop.' He pulled at his hair.

'C'mon, Kent. Think! Think hard. Your so-called Angel of Mercy forum must have told you something more. Maybe you didn't realise it at the time…'

'What did you just say?' His eyes widened and his lip twitched.

'I said you must know something…'

'Not that – the Angel of Mercy. There was an old graveyard about a mile away from the last children's home we were all at.' He snapped his fingers. 'Just off Rifton Road. We used to meet there... by the Angel of Mercy statue, outside of this old mausoleum we would sneak into when it was cold outside. At least amongst the dead we knew we were safe...'

'Are you sure about this?' Maggie pushed her chair out.

He nodded his head. 'Yes... Why didn't I realise it when he spoke about being our Angel of Mercy? Of course that would be where he took the final one... like an offering. I hope it's not too late.'

'For your sake, I hope so too. Come on. I'm taking you back to the cells. You'll be formally charged with conspiracy to murder...'

Maggie took Kent back to the cells and left him with the custody sergeant to deal with. She raced back to the MOCD office. 'Guys! Kent told me about a graveyard just off Rifton Road where they all used to meet. How far away from Joanne Mole's property is the address?'

Kat was on her phone, punching in the information. 'Less than half a mile. Fuckshits!'

'Fuckshits indeed. Right, is Nathan with the Guv?'

Bethany turned, her mouth opened and then closed, then she pointed behind her.

'I'm right here. What is it?'

Maggie explained what Kent had told her and although it was nothing definite, it was more than what they had before. 'Kat and I can head out now, but you might want to check if any other officers are closer to the cemetery. We can meet them.'

'I'm on it... But Maggie – no heroics. If you arrive there first, wait for back-up. This guy literally plays with fire. I'll get there as soon as I hear something…' With that, he was in his office and on the phone, immediately organising all available officers to the potential crime scene.

'Let's go!' Maggie grabbed her jacket off her chair and ran after Kat.

Chapter Eighty-One

He paced around his living room, a bead of sweat forming on his brow. *Something is going on.* His eyes dropped to the laptop. Black screen. He didn't want to check again. No one had logged into the forum for over twenty-four hours and when the alert popped up, he knew the clock was ticking.

'Clever coppers…'

He watched her approach the cemetery and his jaw tightened. He didn't think it would be so easy to lure her to meet him. He had told her over the phone that he had a video from her time at Chatham House and he would release it. Her response had shocked him.

'Who do you think you are? You're messing with the wrong person.'

'Still as arrogant as ever – even after all this time. I know exactly who you are and if you want to keep that sweet granny image of yours, I suggest you do as I say.'

He gave her the details and despite the venom in her voice, she'd meet him. Adrenaline raced through his veins, the closer she got.

'Where are you then? Cowering in a corner somewhere? Show yourself!' Joanne Mole screamed into the distance.

If she wasn't such a bitch he might admire her confidence. He stepped out of the mausoleum and once she had spotted him she began to run in his direction.

'Are you the one who called me then, or is the coward in there?' She poked him in the chest as she stretched to look over his shoulder. 'I can't wait to see what you think you have on me,' she challenged.

'In there.' He stepped out of her way. 'Have a look.'

She hesitated initially but curiosity got the better of her. You know what they say – curiosity killed the cat. She stepped inside and he followed close behind. 'There's nothing here – what the hell?' She turned sharply and faced him. 'What are you playing at?' Her eyes formed into slits.

'You really have no idea who I am, do you?'

'Should I?' She eyed him up and down, hands placed firmly on her hips.

'My name is Hugh O'Donnell.'

'And? Am I supposed to know you?'

'My full name is *Brendan* Hugh O'Donnell. That ring any bells, you spineless, arrogant bitch?' His blood boiled.

Recognition sparkled in her eyes, and then a booming, deep laughter. 'Well, if it isn't little Brendan. Changed your name around a bit, haven't you? I can see your leg is shaking – still scared of me? I never would have guessed it was you behind all those murders. Didn't think you had it in you.' She took a step closer and Hugh raised a fist.

'Hit women now, do you? Just like your daddy… you filthy piece of shit.' She was inching towards the door but there was no way he was going to let her get away.

He grabbed her by the upper arms and head-butted her. Blood gushed from her nose as he heard the cartilage crunch. She slumped in his arms and he dragged her out to the Angel of Mercy. 'Your time has come to pay for what you've done.'

Chapter Eighty-Two

K at punched the details of the cemetery into the sat nav, but her attempts to race out of the police station car park were scuppered by the automatic gate being so slow to open.

Maggie belted up and grabbed hold of the handle above her window – she had no doubt she would need to brace herself.

'Why didn't any of the others mention the cemetery?' wondered Kat. 'By the sound of it, it was a pretty significant place for them all.'

'PTSD? Denial? Or maybe they had just buried those thoughts – I'd like to think they weren't intentionally complicit in hiding Hugh O'Donnell's identity. From the interviews, I got the impression that they didn't want to be involved but felt they had no choice, and perhaps a little part of them was probably pleased that O'Donnell was able to do what the criminal justice system never was...' Maggie stared out the window. Part of her could completely understand their need for revenge, but what they allowed to happen, especially after the first murder, was just not something she could swallow down easily.

When they arrived at the graveyard a chill ran down Maggie's spine. 'Fuck, I hate graveyards. At least the fucker choose daylight to make his move,' she said.

Kat shrugged on her jacket and exited the vehicle. Maggie checked her police duty belt and Kat did the same. They needed to be prepared, as Maggie had no doubt that their killer would be expecting them.

Maggie sniffed the air. 'Do you smell smoke?'

Kat raised her hand and showed Maggie her cigarette. 'Sorry, I thought I'd have a quick one before the rest of them arrive.'

Maggie didn't know whether she should laugh or shout at Kat. 'Just hurry up. I think I hear them coming.'

Kat took a final drag before opening the door and stubbing her fag out in the ashtray.

The cavalry had arrived. Maggie met up with the group of officers as they exited their vehicles. Before she could speak, her phone buzzed.

'Hey, boss. You close?'

'*About five mins away. Have you spotted anything?*'

'Nothing yet. Just here with some of the field team. We'll wait for you before we decide the next steps.'

'*Oh, that's very kind of you, Maggie – since I am your boss.*' She could hear the smile in his voice and ended the call.

Within a minute or two, Nathan had pulled up and joined Kat, Maggie and the team of officers huddled around one of the cop cars.

'We'll split up – the cemetery is closed off with that

wrought-iron fencing. In this weather it will be slippery enough that any escape attempt would be more difficult.' Nathan pulled out an enlarged map of the cemetery that Bethany had provided and spread it on the bonnet of the police car. 'Three of you go via the left. Three via the right. The remainder of us will go down the middle. There is a lot of overgrowth, so keep hidden as much as you can – that way we'll keep the element of surprise. But I don't want any of you trying to be a hero…'

Maggie could feel Nathan's eyes on her but continued to stare at the map.

'OK. We're all clear?' asked Nathan.

Nods.

'Let's go catch ourselves a killer…'

Maggie, Kat, Nathan and two field officers headed straight for the cemetery gates. Once they were opened they went through, and everyone took their positions.

Maggie and Kat crept along the gravestones, looking ahead but trying to keep out of sight. The mausoleum and the Angel of Mercy statue could be seen in the distance, but the women weren't close enough to make out any significant movement.

Her heart rate accelerated. Maggie could hear the *thump, thump, thump* banging in her ears as she tried to keep her breathing in check. A movement up ahead, and she stopped. Nathan came over and joined her and Kat, while the other two officers waited.

'Did you see that?' Nathan asked.

Maggie nodded. 'Someone is coming out of the mausoleum.'

'Approach with caution. I'll alert the others.' Nathan

returned to his original position and Maggie watched his lips move before he signalled for them to move forward.

Maggie's knees were sore from how she was walking – crouched down low, her knees cracking with each step – but she didn't want to risk being seen.

Ahead she saw Joanne Mole. She was shaking her head but no sound was coming out of her mouth. It must be taped over. She was secured to the statue by rope and Maggie could see the shape of a man beside Joanne. She recalled her meeting with the Social Care manager – this man was a similar size. It had to be Hugh O'Donnell. He wore a black baseball cap, pulled low, and a black bomber jacket and jeans. It was hard to make out his features. He was shouting at the woman but Maggie couldn't make out what he was saying. He was reaching down for something. More muffled sounds from the woman, and she continued to struggle against the bindings.

They were inching closer. To her left, Maggie could see the other team approaching – they dropped to the ground and crept forward like soldiers in war. Maggie and Kat positioned themselves behind gravestones. A shiver went down her spine, as she wasn't keen on standing on someone's grave. She did her best to avoid any flowers or items that the families had put there.

The killer was still shouting at Joanne – her head shook furiously as he shoved her hard against the statue. Maggie looked over at Nathan. He held a hand up – wanted them to wait for his signal.

'He's going to set her alight if we don't make a move soon,' Kat whispered.

'Nathan knows what he's doing. He won't let it get that far.' Maggie watched as O'Donnell became more animated, arms flailing, circling Mole like she was his prey. He was shouting something about Joanne being a disgrace. How she shouldn't have ever been allowed to have children, but now they would see her for the monster she was. Maggie couldn't make out all the words, as they faded once they lost sight of him.

Kat began to inch forward and Maggie grabbed her arm. 'Stay back, or you'll be spotted.' When they saw him pull the lighter fluid from his bag and spurt it generously over Joanne and the ground before her, Nathan shouted, 'Go! Go! Go!'

Chapter Eighty-Three

Mayhem ensued. Hugh O'Donnell turned towards them and pulled out a lighter.

'You think you'll have time to save her? Stay the fuck back or I will set her on fire right now, starting with her face!'

The team had him surrounded on all sides in a circle formation. He spun around slowly, fingers firmly wrapped around the lighter, and watched them. Maggie looked at Nathan. He shook his head and mouthed, 'Not yet.'

Fucksake!

The man started squirting the lighter fluid towards them. 'I said, stay back! How many lives are you prepared to risk?'

'I think I can take him, Maggie.' Kat was moving slowly ahead. Every time the man turned to look at the other officers, she took a step forward and was ignoring Nathan's signals.

A branch snapped beneath Kat's foot and their killer looked up with hatred in his eyes.

'I bloody warned you!'

Kat lunged forward and everything after that seemed to happen in slow motion.

Leaping up and jumping in front of Kat, Maggie yelled, 'Noooooooo!' She felt something wet hit her forehead and her back, before she fell forward and landed on top of Kat. More fluid hit her arm and hand.

Kat coughed beneath her, winded. Maggie looked up and saw the lighter shaking in Hugh O'Donnell's hand. Before the officers could grab him, he bent over and lit the ground. A stream of fire came towards her, and there was a WHOOSH as her arm and back caught on fire.

The officers wrestled O'Donnell to the ground but Maggie couldn't hear anything after that. She rolled off Kat and felt her arm burning. She tried to stand but stumbled and then began rolling in the grass. Next thing she knew, Nathan was standing over her, using his coat to douse the flames. Her skin tingled, and when she saw that it was burned, everything went black.

Chapter Eighty-Four

Maggie had no idea how long she had been unconscious. She heard voices but none of the words were clear. It was like they were talking to her under water. Someone touched her cheek and she flinched.

'Hey... Maggie. Can you hear me? It's Nathan. The paramedics are here. Can you sit up?' His voice quivered and she found it unnerving.

What happened?

Maggie's eyes fluttered open. Nathan was looking at her with concern and then relief. 'I'm fine.' Then it all came back to her and she tried to push herself upright.

'Hey. Just sit there. Everything is under control here. O'Donnell is on his way to the police station and Joanne is safe. She's in the ambulance over there with Kat. Some officers from the Child Abuse Unit are on their way and will be dealing with her once she gets the all clear from the medics.'

'Oh my god. How's Kat? Was she burned?' Maggie tried to look past Nathan but he held her back.

'Kat's fine. Some singed hair and a slight burn on her neck, but you took the brunt of it. Just sit still while the paramedics look you over. Now is not the time for that bloody stubborn streak of yours to emerge.' His voice was stern but he smiled.

Maggie sat still as the jacket sleeve on her injured arm was cut off. She looked at her arm. It was red and the slight breeze blowing felt like a thousand little knives prodding her. 'Ooooh, that hurts like a bitch and doesn't look good.' Her voice was calm but inside she wanted to cry. The pain was unbearable and she realised she'd probably be left with a scar. She feared she might pass out again.

The paramedic took immediate action. Maggie watched as he treated the burn with cool water. 'We need to reduce the skin temperature, stop the burning process, numb the pain and reduce any swelling,' he explained to Maggie as he took action. After cooling the burn, he covered the area with a clean dressing. 'We'd like to get you in the ambulance and over to the hospital to look at the burns on your back.'

'My back is fine.' Maggie tried to turn her head but the pain took over. 'Shit.' She held out her good arm and Nathan pulled her up and walked with her to the ambulance.

'Go to the hospital. Get checked out. There'll be plenty of time to join the interview once you get the all clear.'

'But I'm…'

'I'm not asking you. You need to have those burns seen to.'

Maggie sighed. She knew Nathan was right but she wanted to be there when they started questioning O'Donnell. 'OK.' She crossed her heart. 'I promise. I'll get checked out, but if I get the all clear, I really want to be part of the interrogation.'

'Of course.' He tapped her leg. 'See you soon.'

Maggie watched as Nathan whispered something to the paramedics before looking back and giving her a wave.

In the ambulance, Maggie was asked to lie on her stomach while they cooled the burn on her back. 'How does it look?' It was sore but her arm felt worse.

'Your boss warned me you'd be fishing for some answers. Well, it's not as bad as your arm. Your jacket and shirt took most of the damage and the accelerant didn't reach this far. You were lucky.'

Maggie didn't feel lucky, but nodded anyway.

———

At the hospital, Maggie was checked over and was disappointed to hear that she wouldn't be leaving the hospital today. The doctor advised that she shouldn't underestimate the severity of her injuries, as it took approximately twenty hours for a burn to fully 'declare' itself.

She only half listened as the hospital staff told her that second-degree burns were more difficult to diagnose because they presented with a wider range of characteristics. Because of the thickness of the skin involved and the increased damage, the burns would have immediate blistering and would also have a moist appearance. She remembered looking at her arm before they had bandaged it up, noting that the blistering had started almost immediately.

The doctor was looking at her chart as he waffled on about second-degree burns being very painful, and she had to stop herself from rolling her eyes – *No shit, Sherlock.* He was quite confident that they were not third-degree burns; if they had been, the nerve endings would have been destroyed and she wouldn't be feeling the pain she was now. He also mentioned possible scarring – but Maggie didn't even care about that. What she really wanted to know was how soon she would be out so she could go back to work.

'Thanks for taking the time to explain all this to me – but how long will I have to stay in the hospital?' Maggie bit her lip, preparing for the worst outcome.

'Well, overnight at least. We need to make sure the burning process has completely stopped. The fact that you're feeling pain, although you may not think it now, is a good sign. A burn is a devastating injury, so you may want to talk about it with someone. I can't force you to stay here, but I'd prefer it if you did. We're notified your brother and he's on his way.'

Maggie was too tired to argue. 'I'll stay tonight but I have to get back to work tomorrow, so if someone can be around so that I can find out what sort of treatment I'll need to look after this myself, and get me signed out…'

'I had a feeling you might say that. A nurse will be around in the morning. Try to sleep on your side. Although that burn on your back is minor, if you move about too much you'll probably be very uncomfortable.'

'Thank you.' Maggie yawned. She fought her tiredness long enough to text Nathan, and then she gave in to the exhaustion.

Chapter Eighty-Five

The moment she woke up she was harassing the nurses, and after being given some painkillers and other items to look after her injuries, as well as a few warning signs to look out for, Maggie called a taxi and headed straight to Stafford Police Station. Andy had popped in the night before and dropped off some things for her, and the police had collected her burned clothing for evidence.

When she walked into the office the room went quiet. Kate, Bethany, Nathan all spoke at once.

'What are you doing here?'

'Are you OK?'

'You should be at home resting.'

And finally… 'I'm so sorry, Maggie. It should have been me and not you. I don't know what I can say to… It should have been me…' Kat could barely look at her.

Maggie held up her hand.

'I'm OK, guys. Yes, a little sore but the consultant said I'm fine to be back at work.' The consultant had said no such thing, but a little white lie wouldn't do any harm. 'And as for you, Kat – you would have done the exact same for me – for any one of us – so none of that guilt bullshit, OK?' She smiled. 'What's been happening here, then?'

'O'Donnell refused to talk about anything when he was brought in. Then he said he was too tired to talk, so we returned him to the cells, came back to the office, and we were just discussing our strategy when you arrived... Impeccable timing, as always...' Nathan went to touch her arm but Maggie moved away.

'Sore arm... and back... no offence...' Nathan meant well and she probably would have smacked the injury accidentally if the shoe was on the other foot, so she wasn't angry. 'Can I be a part of the interview?'

'DC Jamieson.' The sternness in the voice was not lost on Maggie.

Maggie turned to see DI Rutherford behind her. 'Tell me you have astral-projected yourself here, because really you are lying comfortably in a hospital bed...'

'Hi Guv. Hospital released me...'

Rutherford brushed by her and grunted before stopping in the centre of the room. 'Well, that's good for us then. OK – let's get this case wrapped up as quickly as possible. We've a killer in the cells and enough information from the others in the online forum, the past history and the connections to all the victims. This should now be an open-and-shut matter. Nathan – you and Maggie go out to his flat – I want you to keep an eye on her...' Rutherford pointed at Maggie. 'Forensics have been there most of the night, so see what you can find out. Bethany – make sure all the online evidence can be tied to our suspect. Dr Moloney – I'd appreciate an updated final profile and risk assessment based on what we know now. And Kat – go through the statements of the others involved. Pick out everything we can use to nail this bastard. Everyone clear?' Without waiting for a reply, DI Rutherford left them to it.

'You OK to sit down?' Nathan's brow furrowed.

'My arse didn't get burned,' Maggie said with a laugh, and then couldn't stop once Nathan had joined in. 'Yes, I took a taxi here – just don't be a speed demon.' She wasn't sure she should be going with Nathan, but if she wanted to stay a part of the process she'd have to keep that thought to herself.

'Well, I see your attitude hasn't been affected. OK – I don't think the flat is too far anyway. Let's go.'

Maggie followed Nathan to his car and within ten minutes they were outside Hugh O'Donnell's flat. Maggie hid her surprise at the location. She recalled Kate's geographical profile suggesting that the perpetrator's home would be the anchor point, given that the murders took place depending on where the victim lived. They had all been so spread out, it was harder to track the connection. 'Christ, he was practically on our doorstep.'

Nathan unbuckled his seat belt and nodded in agreement. The pair walked towards the detached house that had been divided into flats. The entrance was around the side and Maggie stayed close to Nathan as they signed in and suited up. She looked around while Nathan chatted with the crime scene manager. The back garden led onto a large field that ramblers, walkers and hikers probably used on a regular basis. If her sense of direction was correct, the paths behind the flats led in various directions and would be a good way for him to come to and fro, relatively unnoticed.

Nathan was snapping his fingers. 'Earth to Maggie. You with me?'

'Sorry – just checking out the back there – I bet that's how he got around. He doesn't own a vehicle, does he?'

'Nope. Though from what I saw from his days in the boys' homes, he was adept at stealing cars,' Nathan offered. 'You coming?' He pointed at the doorway and Maggie followed him in.

Maggie caught a mixture of scents as she stepped inside. The air was musty but there was something else. Mould, cleaning products and… *coconut*. Some of the windows were covered with newspaper and the others with a yellowing netting. The room was sparsely furnished with a two-seater couch and a small table in the corner with a television set on it. Behind the couch, another small table with two chairs and a bookshelf next to it. A kitchen at the back. 'I'm going to have a look around.'

She turned and walked towards the bathroom at her right. She popped her head in and greeted the forensics officer. 'Anything of interest?'

'Just collecting DNA samples. Nothing obvious here.'

Maggie spotted coconut shampoo in the shower. She didn't believe that O'Donnell had used his home for anything other than a base. He might even have another property, but so far they hadn't found anything to confirm that. The murders were planned but also had an opportunistic element to them.

She walked into the bedroom and was immediately struck with a feeling of sadness. There was a heaviness in the room – like when you go to a funeral, the sorrow seeps into your soul. Maggie had to take a moment. The forensic guy was tagging and bagging items and laying them on the bed, ready to be taken to the lab. She scanned the items and her eyes immediately were drawn to the jar full of teeth… far more than those that had been taken from the victims. She made a mental note to ask O'Donnell about this.

The forensic guy was just about to remove some items from the wall when Maggie stopped him. 'Sorry. Do you mind if I just have a look before you dismantle it all? I won't be long.' Maggie took out her phone and took some pictures for her own use. She cast her eyes over yellowed newspaper clippings, photographs with faces scratched out, pictures of young boys with no smiles on their faces, a cross with a charm hanging over it – an angel…

Maggie had seen everything she needed to and left the room to find Nathan. He was standing by the bookshelf and holding what looked like a piece of paper in an evidence bag.

'What've you got there?' She squinted her eyes to try and read inside the plastic bag.

'It's his list. It's a lot longer than we thought it was.' Nathan pointed to another list on the table. 'Those are all names of, I assume, the abused boys. I recognise some of them from those we've interviewed. A few are circled. I think they are the ones who are in the forum.' He flicked his head towards the kitchen. Maggie looked on the counter to see a laptop being bagged up. 'Hopefully the cyber guys can get some stuff off there. Identify anyone else who was involved.'

'I'm not going to lie. I feel pretty shitty about this whole case.'

Nathan nodded.

She said, 'I absolutely believe that O'Donnell did the wrong thing – that if he had come to the police now, the Child Abuse Unit could have worked on historical convictions of his abusers – of all of their abusers. And then he and the others could have found some help to work towards healing their trauma… As a social worker, he would have known all this…' Her emotions got the best of her but she didn't want Nathan to see and instead winced. 'Bloody arm… Think I need my meds. I can walk back to the station or catch a lift with someone, if you need to stay longer.'

Nathan took one more look around. 'I'm good to go. Let's find out what he has to say for himself.'

Chapter Eighty-Six

When they arrived back at the station, Maggie stopped in the kitchen for a glass of water to wash down a painkiller. She knew it would be a little while before it kicked in, but just the thought of pain relief brought a sense of calm over her.

She threw her jacket over her chair and grabbed her notebook. 'Any updates we need to be aware of?' she called out.

'I'm still finalising my profile – what was the flat like?' Kate turned her chair to face Maggie.

'Fucking miserable. You can almost feel the pain when you're in there. Dark, damp and despondent. His bedroom was covered with pictures, and an angel charm was strung on top of a wooden cross that had been nailed onto the wall. The forensic guys were collecting it all as we left, so you could hit up Dr Blake and see if she could send the pictures over to you.'

'Thanks – good idea. Though everything you said was what

I had thought would be the case. Were there any tokens collected?'

'A jar full of teeth… a lot more than those we know have been extracted.'

'My guess is that mixed in with the murder victims' teeth we'll find his own, and perhaps the teeth of some of the other abused boys. He's probably been collecting them from his time in the boys' homes – they could have fuelled his desire to seek revenge.'

'It's something I'll definitely be asking him about.' Maggie took a mental note as the Doc returned to whatever she was working on.

'Nothing more from me either – the guys we interviewed have all coughed up to their involvement through the forum,' said Kat. 'Only Kent was directly involved – a distraction ploy, as we suspected. The CPS think it might be difficult to get a conspiracy charge, but the men will be charged with perverting the course of justice, or obstruction for not coming forward. They weren't clear whether they will proceed with prosecution yet. Might be that we just caution them.' Kat shrugged.

Bethany hadn't responded but Maggie could see she was still focused on the video and CCTV evidence. If she had had something noteworthy she would have joined in. Maggie turned and headed towards Nathan's office. She tapped on the doorframe. 'You ready to interview him now?'

Nathan held a finger up as he finished typing whatever it was he was entering into his computer. Once done, he stood and grabbed his blazer. He looked much better than she did, and she looked down at herself, all of a sudden remembering that she hadn't showered and was wearing an oversized sweatshirt which she had in her bag when she went to the hospital. Even though her brother brought her a change of clothes when he had visited, he had forgot a clean shirt and she was too out of it to remind him at the time. But the loose top was the best thing for the burns, as it didn't rub up against her wounds.

'Right. Before you came in I was told he's with his solicitor in Interview Room 3. I advised the enquiry desk to let them know we'd be with them shortly.'

Maggie waited as Nathan walked past her, and the pair of them headed down to the interview suites. Inside the room, she hit record and sat as Nathan did the introductions.

Would he try and claim he didn't know what he was doing? Would he blame the system? Or would he accept the consequences and make this easy for them? She waited with bated breath.

Chapter Eighty-Seven

The tension in the room was palpable. One side challenging the justice system, the other side working for it.

'I'm not a monster, you know. I can see how you are looking at me, assessing me, trying to see which box I fit in. I did exactly what I needed to do – well, nearly. You let Joanne Mole get away. Her screeching laugh is ringing around in my head as I sit here and look at you.'

'Joanne Mole will be dealt with if she needs to be – the matter is being handled by the Child Abuse Unit. But we're not here to talk about those allegations, we're here to deal with your crimes.' Maggie paused. 'What we don't understand is why now? You have a highly respected role in Social Care, a position of trust. You worked with children who went through experiences similar to yours. How is that setting a good example?'

'Don't you think I thought about that?' His face reddened. 'But it was for me and those boys I let down when we were growing up. I had put it all behind me until I saw them all living normal, happy lives, while the rest of us went through hell to come out the other side. Karma.'

Maggie shifted in her seat. Her arm was aching and sweat beaded across her forehead.

'I'm sorry you were injured...' Hugh O'Donnell looked at Maggie's arm. She hadn't been expecting an apology, but she nodded. He was like Jekyll and Hyde – the man in front of her was smart, helpful and well-meaning, but he had a darker side seeking revenge and stopping at nothing to get what he wanted.

'I didn't intend to hurt you – I just had to finish what I started. For all of the boys... and for me. It's why I had to stop you pushing further when you were speaking to Mrs Knight at the office. You understand, don't you?'

Nathan looked at Maggie and raised his eyebrows. He could see what Maggie saw – Hugh O'Donnell was trying to connect with her. Maggie took her cue. 'Apology accepted. Unfortunately none of that matters, you'll still be charged – though I'm sure we could get it down from attempting to kill a police officer in the line of duty to common assault.'

'Doesn't much matter now, does it? I've got four murders hanging over my head, plus an attempted murder, kidnap and whatever other charges I'm sure are waiting for me.'

Maggie bit her lip. 'Do you want to tell us a bit more about how this all started?' She didn't get the impression that O'Donnell was going to contest anything at this stage.

'Sure – but before I do, there's a list in my house – naming all the abusers, along with a list of everyone that I know they abused. I just need to know whether there will be any charges brought against them. I will tell you everything then – no point in lying. You got me bang to rights.'

'We saw the list. All that information will be forwarded to the Child Abuse Unit. We can't and don't want to make any false promises at this stage, but what I can say is that we will do our best to make sure that the old case is reopened, and those who are still alive will be questioned about their role in what happened to you all,' Nathan advised.

'Fair enough. Shall I just start from the beginning?'

Chapter Eighty-Eight

O'Donnell's solicitor jumped in before anything else was said. 'I just want it noted for the record that despite my advice,' he looked at his client, 'Mr O'Donnell has decided to disclose everything in relation to his involvement, and this should therefore be taken into account as mitigating circumstances by the CPS.'

'As DC Jamieson has said, we'll make sure to pass on how co-operative your client was in interview, but we're only responsible for interviewing and charging Mr O'Donnell – anything that follows is the CPS's decision.' Nathan's voice was soft in tone. It was obvious to all in the room that this was a difficult interview, given the background and circumstances that led to the murders in the first place.

'It's not me who should be sitting here – *they* created me.' The disclosure was spat out not in malice but in a *why-did-I-end-up-here?* kind of way. 'If I had been believed, if we all had been believed all those years ago, none of this – *none* of this would have happened.' He said this through gritted teeth. Hyde was back.

Maggie empathised with him. He was right in one sense: the murder victims should have faced the full force of the law years ago for the crimes they committed against children – children like Hugh O'Donnell.

'What happened to you as a child was tragic and despicable. But surely, a man in your position knew that there were other ways to deal with it – pursuing a case of historical child abuse against them when you were older, for one. You had the connections and a respected position in the criminal justice system. What is even sadder is the fact that you re-victimised those who had been abused by making them complicit in your crimes. Now they will have to pay the price of their decisions too...' Maggie let that last bit sink in.

Hugh O'Donnell sat back and stared at Maggie. She could see she had got to him. His eyes glistened, but the anger still simmered beneath the surface.

'No one forced them... They wanted to see our abusers suffer just as much as I did.' They were just words and Maggie wasn't convinced he believed them, but it was probably what he had told himself each time he went into that forum to justify his actions and give himself permission, even if it was against his usual moral code.

'You're right, but you did threaten them. You said you'd come after their families. You coerced them into co-operating. You were no better than your abusers.'

'No. Don't say that!' He slammed his fists on the table. 'I wouldn't have harmed them.'

'But how were they to know that?' Maggie didn't want to press the matter, but the Doc had pointed out that he was actually manipulating the men in the forum, the same way they had all been manipulated by their abusers, and he'd need to hear it to understand the implications of his actions. They needed him to talk about the murders – leaving no doubt to the CPS when the time came to charge him. 'Can we talk about the murders now in more detail, for the record?'

Another glance from O'Donnell's solicitor and a nod told Maggie that he had every intention of disclosing the crimes. They wouldn't have to use any tactics to get a confession this time.

'You seem to have everything figured out already. What more do you want to know?'

'Let's start from why you chose the specific victims, as your list shows the number of abusers was much larger.'

'You're right, the list was long. But the arseholes I... *took care of...* were all directly involved in abusing me and not allowing justice to be served. Daniel, Father Boyle and Joanne Mole actively played a role in the mental torture and physical abuse that I and the other lads were forced to endure during our time in the care homes. What made it worse was that when we were moved to another home, they seemed to follow us, reminding us that there was no escape. No one to tell. Then when we finally managed to run away or escape and go to the police, Officer Watson didn't even believe us. If you look deep enough, you'll find that Father Boyle was a distant relative of the copper – fucking cover-up or what? Whatever Watson told the CPS at the time, Sadie Ramsey ate it up and decided that there wasn't enough evidence to prosecute. They left me no choice... If the law wasn't going to do anything about it, I was going to make sure those bastards burned in hell and were exposed for what they did.' He stopped and took a large gulp of water.

'From what we've read, these people removed teeth as a form of punishment after pinning you and the others down. Is that why you removed the teeth before setting them on fire?'

He fiddled with something in his mouth before removing the false teeth and throwing them on the table. 'Does that answer your question?'

Maggie's eyes widened. 'Were all your top teeth removed?'

He replaced the plate back in his mouth. 'Yes. Some were pulled out, others were kicked out. Some I had to have removed when I was older, as they were broken and became infected. Fucking animals.'

'There were more teeth in the jar we found than the ones removed from the… victims.' Maggie notice him flinch when she called his abusers 'victims' and she felt apologetic, but they *were* victims, as were their surviving family members.

'I collected any of the teeth I could find after the abuse took place. I thought if I could collect enough, they could be used as evidence – but as you know, it didn't make a blind bit of difference. So I held onto them as a reminder, and then later I added those fuckers' teeth to my collection. And since I wouldn't have the pleasure of actually seeing them in hell, I burned them alive. I wanted – I needed – to see them suffer. It brought me relief. They showed us no mercy and I reciprocated. Do you know what I mean?' His eyes glazed over. 'I'm sorry that their families will now learn the truth about their loved ones – but they deserved every last ounce of pain inflicted on them. Can you just charge me and get this over with? I'm guilty. I just want to rest now. I'm done.'

As you wish, Dr Jekyll…

Maggie looked at Nathan and he nodded before reading Hugh O'Donnell his rights. He was formally charged with the murders of his abusers, amongst a slew of other, related charges. Hugh O'Donnell slumped in his chair, seemingly satisfied – he held out his wrists to be cuffed and taken to the custody suite.

Chapter Eighty-Nine

Two Weeks Later

Nathan briefed the team after he and DI Rutherford had spoken to the CPS. There had never been any doubt that Hugh O'Donnell would be charged with the murders. However, the CPS had agreed that his mental health had played a role in his decision making, and although he knew his actions were wrong, they were looking for a report from Probation to support the mitigating circumstances surrounding the offences.

Lucy Sherwood had been in touch to say that she would be writing the pre-sentence report and would recommend a psychiatric assessment. She advised that after a discussion with the CPS, O'Donnell agreed to plead guilty to manslaughter on the grounds of diminished responsibility pre-trial, and would in all likelihood be sentenced to life with a minimum recommendation of twenty-five years in custody. They would push for a hospital direction under s45A of the Mental Health Act with a limitation direction. That meant the judge could issue a criminal sentence and a hybrid order. O'Donnell would be removed to a secure mental health unit for treatment, but if the need for that treatment should conclude, the Secretary of State could then decide whether he would be taken to prison to serve the remainder of his sentence or released on licence. It allowed the future decision to be taken at the time, not predicted from this point, when the duration and outcome of treatment were not known.

The explanation offered Maggie some comfort, as she really felt for O'Donnell and wondered what kind of person he would have grown up to be, had he not suffered such trauma in his younger years. She knew that the abuse was not an excuse, as she had come across many people who had suffered similar if not worse forms of childhood trauma and didn't grow up to be killers – but it saddened her to know that he felt he had no choice and had lost faith in the system to mete out the appropriate justice. She only hoped that once he had received psychiatric help, he would be able to move forward. He would still be a good age when he was likely to be released, and there would still be time for him to live a fulfilling life in the community, with any support he might need.

Maggie had heard that the Child Abuse Unit would be charging Joanne Mole with her part in the abuse of young boys under her care. A case had been opened to look deeper into the past abuse and question those whom they could find in terms of their roles in it. All the boys, now grown men and including Hugh O'Donnell, would get their day in court to testify against Joanne Mole and anyone else charged. That was a small comfort to all the team, as it didn't sit right that justice had been only on the side of the abusers in the past.

'I don't know about you lot, but I could sure use a drink...' said Maggie.

'I'll get the first round in.' Nathan's offer was met with cheers. Maggie was looking forward to a much-needed break.

Chapter Ninety

Chapter Ninety

The pub was filling up by the time Maggie arrived. Not one for socialising with the team except for the occasional night, she eased onto a bar stool at a small table closest to the door.

Her arm ached slightly and the skin on her back felt a little tight, but she expected that. She had been told that it could be three to four weeks before the burns healed. She would have a constant reminder of this case, as if the child abuse wasn't enough.

'There's our hero!' Nathan placed a drink in front of her. 'Gin and tonic. You do still drink that, right? Feels like ages since we've done anything remotely fun outside of work.' He looked out the window. 'Kind of miss our partner days…'

Maggie smiled. 'Me too, but for what it's worth, you're a great boss and you weren't much of a partner anyway.' She kicked him gently under the table.

'Very funny. How's the healing going?' He pointed at the

bandage loosely wrapped around her arm. 'You comfortable there? We can move to another seat if that's better for you?'

'The stool is fine... That's why I chose it.' Maggie hadn't realised she had been shielding her arm like a mother bear protecting her cubs. She moved her arm away. 'It's really fucking sore, if I'm honest, but Dr Blake said that's normal and it looks to be on track in terms of the healing. Might be some scarring, but...' She shrugged.

'You went to a pathologist to check your arm?' Nathan shook his head and laughed. 'Why am I not surprised? Where's the rest of the gang?'

'The Doc was going by her place to change and feed Salem. Kat's gone to buy fags and Bethany headed home. You need to make that woman go on holiday, or she's heading for burnout. Where's the Guv?' Maggie strained her neck, looking around the room.

'Erm...'

Maggie noticed him squirm on the stool and avoid eye contact.

'Spill it, Wright. What do you know that I don't?'

He looked at the table beside them and then leaned forward and whispered, 'This needs to stay between us.'

'OK.' Maggie crossed her heart. 'Tell me.'

'She's pregnant.'

'Pregnant? Whoa.' Suddenly everything began to make sense to Maggie. The moodiness. The exhaustion. 'Wait a minute – how?'

Nathan tilted his head to the side. 'Didn't your parents teach you about the birds and the bees?'

'Don't make me kick you again. I mean, not how did she get

pregnant, but how did it happen? I didn't think she was seeing anyone while all the divorce shit was going on… not that I would know anyway, but… Do you know who the father is?'

'No, she didn't say, but I do wonder if it might be DCI Meechan…'

Maggie slapped the table. 'Her ex-husband? No way. I thought he was remarried or engaged or something? Also, she didn't really like him much, did she?'

'Yeah, but they worked closely on the Living Doll case. Maybe there was a flicker of flame there. Who knows? If she wants to tell us, she will. Anyway, I think she's struggling with what she's going to do. She only told me the basics, as she said she may need me to cover some things. I heard a rumour, though, that Meechan might be back while they look for a permanent replacement.'

'Well, that should be fun.' Maggie's mouth twisted.

Kat and the Doc arrived, which signalled the end of that conversation, and Nathan went to buy the drinks he had promised them. Just in time, too, as Maggie gulped down the last of her G&T.

'How's your brother? I thought I saw him the other day in town, but I was too far away to catch his eye.'

'He's fine now, Doc. A little scar on his head. Still plans on moving out.' Maggie still had concerns about where he was getting all the money from but didn't want to ruin the night. She had been tempted to rummage through his room and look at his bank statements, but she needed to trust that if he had started gambling again, he would tell her.

Nathan returned with the drinks and Kat thanked him before she got up and walked over to some of the field team at the opposite end of the pub.

'Was it something I said?' Nathan looked over his shoulder.

'Probably,' Maggie joked. 'I think she wants to get to know the other officers a bit better. Still feels a little on the outside at Stafford, but she'll be fine.'

'So have you given any more thought to taking a break yourself? You know, as your boss, I can make you if need be. Maybe go see…'

Maggie held up her hand. 'Listen closely as this will be the first and only time you hear this from me.'

Nathan leaned in. 'I'm listening.'

'You're right. I do need to get away, let my burns heal and sort a few things out with my parents. I'll drop into the station and book the leave on the system. Three weeks OK with you?'

'More than OK and deserved. It will be quiet without you, but I'm sure we'll cope.' Nathan smiled.

'Room for one more?'

Maggie turned and was surprised to see Julie Noble plonking herself down on the stool that Kat had just left.

'What are you doing here?'

'I invited her – I hope you don't mind. Julie played a part in closing this investigation, so I thought it only fair.' Nathan nudged the Doc. 'Kate, there's a few people I'd like to introduce you to. They're very interested in hearing about the work you're doing with the MOCD.'

'Of course. Nice to see you, Julie.' The Doc picked up her drink and bag, and followed Nathan.

'Do you think they wanted to leave us alone?' Julie smiled.

'Not very subtle, are they?'

'Would you like another drink? You seem to be enjoying them.' Julie pointed at the half-empty glass in front of Maggie.

She had gulped down most of the drink Nathan had just bought her.

'One more couldn't hurt, I guess. But I really shouldn't drink any more alcohol on this medication, so a sparkling water and lemon would be perfect.'

Julie left to get the drinks in and Maggie watched her. She admired the journalist's ability to just walk into a pub full of coppers and fit right in, like she was one of them, even though most of the time she clashed with them. When Julie looked over her shoulder and gave her a wave, Maggie felt the heat in her cheeks and wondered if she had made a mistake putting her personal life on hold. She might have to rethink that. She wondered if Julie had any interest in visiting Scotland. It could be just what the doctor ordered.

THE END

Acknowledgments

I'd like to thank everyone who has cheered me on and supported me so far on my writing journey. I'm so grateful to be able to share my stories and I can't do that without any of you.

I'd like to thank my family and friends both near and far, for the tremendous support they have given me – you all mean the world to me.

A massive thanks to my editor Bethan Morgan for her patience, understanding, guidance and belief in me as a writer and to the whole One More Chapter team – you strengthen the series and make me want to be a better writer!

Special thanks to my beta readers and everyone who has allowed me to use their names! And for the *most* part, their characters are nothing like them in real life... ha ha!

A heart-felt *thank you* to all the authors, crime writing/reading community and festival peeps who have been so incredibly supportive, inspirational and kind – you have no idea how much it means to me – you know who you are – a thousand #thankyous would never be enough. So many to name, but I love each one of you!

To the blogging community and my blogger friends, I want to name you all, but I can't – so if you are reading this and thinking "is she talking about me?" the answer, as always, is – *Hell yeah, I am*! Love you all. Special mention to Sarah Hardy for organising the most EPIC blog tours via Book on the Bright Side Publicity. She is a legend!

A massive thanks to the Bookouture team (both the authors and my colleagues) for all the amazing advice and cheers!

Of course, I will always mention Tamworth Probation/Tamworth IOM; Stafford IOM; and all my remarkable ex-colleagues within the Police and Probation Service. Your dedication and professionalism continue to astound me – you will never be forgotten.

Finally, a massive thanks to all the readers. There are just no words to convey how much your support and reviews have meant to me. You make me believe I can keep on doing this and give me a reason to write.

A Note from Noelle

The books are set in Staffordshire; however, I have used some literary licence by making up names of towns/places to fit with the story.

Having been a Senior/Probation Officer for 18 years, I left in 2017. There are some references to the changes that were implemented in 2015, but I went all nostalgic and some of the work/terms refer to a time when Probation was all one service – though the service is coming together under the public banner once again, which will make any future books easier. Any errors to police procedure/probation or any other agency mentioned within the story are purely my own or intentional to move the story forward. And if you think something sounds unbelievable – don't be so sure – fact is often stranger than fiction!

ONE MORE CHAPTER

YOUR NUMBER ONE STOP

FOR PAGETURNING BOOKS

One More Chapter is an
award-winning global
division of HarperCollins.

Sign up to our newsletter to get our
latest eBook deals and stay up to date
with our weekly Book Club!
<u>Subscribe here.</u>

Meet the team at
<u>www.onemorechapter.com</u>

Follow us!

🐦 <u>@OneMoreChapter_</u>
ƒ <u>@OneMoreChapter</u>
📷 <u>@onemorechapterhc</u>

Do you write unputdownable fiction?
We love to hear from new voices.
Find out how to submit your novel at
<u>www.onemorechapter.com/submissions</u>